# *The* Safest Place *in* London

Also by Maggie Joel

*Half the World in Winter*
*The Second-last Woman in England*
*The Past and Other Lies*

# The
# Safest Place
## in London

## MAGGIE
## JOEL

ALLEN&UNWIN
SYDNEY·MELBOURNE·AUCKLAND·LONDON

First published in 2016

Allen & Unwin
83 Alexander Street
Crows Nest NSW 2065
Australia
Phone:    (61 2) 8425 0100
Email:    info@allenandunwin.com
Web:      www.allenandunwin.com

Cataloguing-in-Publication details are available
from the National Library of Australia
www.trove.nla.gov.au

ISBN 978 1 74331 060 1

Set in 12/17 pt Minion Pro by Midland Typesetters, Australia
Printed and bound in Australia by Griffin Press

10 9 8 7 6 5 4 3 2 1

**MIX**
Paper from
responsible sources
**FSC**
www.fsc.org    **FSC® C009448**

The paper in this book is FSC® certified.
FSC® promotes environmentally responsible,
socially beneficial and economically viable
management of the world's forests.

For my aunt, Anne Benson

# PART ONE

# UNDERGROUND

# CHAPTER ONE

Odessa Street was situated just north of Bethnal Green Road in London's East End, part of the sprawling warren of terraces put up in a great hurry during the late Victorian period when the easternmost reaches of the city were full to bursting and needed somewhere to overflow. It was bordered at one end by the red-brick arches of the bridge that had once carried a branch line of the Great Eastern Railway, long since decommissioned and fallen into disrepair, and at its other by the Hero of Trafalgar public house, which had had no beer to serve since 1942 and had closed its doors, seemingly for good, a year later and now stood abandoned and boarded up, a magnet for looters, deserters and local children. The north side of the street was overshadowed by warehouses, repositories in a previous century for the bolts of woven cloth and French-polished cabinets bound for the West End, but more recently used as a temporary mortuary when the hospital was unable to cope.

The occupants of Odessa Street came and went, sometimes in the dead of night when rent was owing, their numbers varying as births and deaths, new arrivals and hasty departures dictated. Number 42, located halfway along its length, was connected to the identical row of houses on the other side of the street by the lines of washing that permanently crisscrossed the slender space between and from which grey and never-quite-dry washing hung. It was, like its neighbours, a simply constructed dwelling consisting of two rooms up and down, with a privy in a tiny bricked yard outside and at some point a scullery had been added at the rear. Two families currently resided at number 42: the Rosenthals, who lived upstairs, and the Levins, who lived downstairs. There had been menfolk in Odessa Street at one time but at this present moment—January of 1944—the men were, for the most part, absent, Lenny Rosenthal being in Burma fighting the Japanese and Joe Levin having recently returned to convoy duty in the North Atlantic courtesy of His Majesty's Royal Navy. And so the women and children were left to cope as best they could.

On this particular day—a Saturday evening at a little after six o'clock—the wireless set at number 42 erupted with static, the electric light bulbs flickered and, a moment later, the air-raid siren began. Nancy Levin, serving tea in the kitchen, a pan of spitting chips clasped in both hands, her lips clamped around her cigarette, said, 'Bugger,' under her breath.

She was a tall woman with a slimness that was only partly a result of wartime privation, deep-set green eyes and a heavy brow that hinted at Middle-European ancestry. One or two loose strands of long yellow hair were visible beneath a care-lessly wound headscarf above very high, dramatically shaped eyebrows, a small nose and a mouth set hard.

The fat in the chip pan had begun to congeal.

Nancy Levin had recently turned twenty-four. A wife. A mother. She had, for a time, worked in a hat shop on Bethnal Green Road. She had dreamed of working in Bond Street. She had grown up in a boarding house less than a mile away and had twice seen the ocean, though on neither occasion had she bathed in it. She had never met her father and her husband had left that morning to return to the war.

'Bugger,' she said again. She turned off the gas and put down the pan.

A small child, three years of age, was seated at the kitchen table watching in anticipation.

'Don't you touch them chips,' warned Nancy, and she went out into the passageway to listen for the single long note of the all-clear. Out of sight of the child she closed her eyes and offered up a silent prayer:

*Not tonight; any night but tonight.*

The siren continued to wail. The all-clear did not sound and the chips, quietly sizzling in the pan, were destined never to be served. Nancy experienced the small wave of despair and anger that followed every failed prayer.

'Right, that's it, Em,' she announced as the kitchen, the small child, the chips slid back into focus. 'We're going down the shelter.'

Emily Levin watched the still-sizzling chips that were just out of reach and her mouth opened in mute protest then closed again in the way of one whose life has been lived entirely in wartime and for whom hope, inevitably, was crushed before it could properly flourish.

Her mother left the kitchen and wrenched open the door to the cupboard under the stairs fumbling in the blackout in her haste to turn off the gas.

Outside the siren continued to wail.

When the raids had first started the sirens would go off when the German bombers were flying over the English coast. Now, and for reasons best known to themselves, Fighter Command waited until the bombers were approaching your district before alerting you. This meant that the time from hearing the siren to actually hearing the first low drone of the approaching German squadrons was no time at all. For eight months they had lived like that—September '40 to May '41—when every night there had been a raid and it seemed like the world had ended. Then, quite suddenly, the raids had ended and everyone had emerged, dazed and stupefied, into the world—which, it turned out, had not ended after all. And now the tide had turned. Now the BBC daily reported Allied victories in North Africa and elsewhere, Hitler had been pushed back to Italy, Hitler was on the back foot, and yet out of the blue there had been a raid last night and it looked likely there was to be another one tonight. Somehow, the second time around, it was worse.

Nancy emerged from the space under the stairs pulling on a man's overcoat over her dressing-gown, as though she were someone for whom night and day held no distinction. She paused to glance at the ceiling. The Rosenthals occupied the two rooms on the upper floor but the top half of the house was silent and she had not seen or heard any of the numerous Rosenthal children nor Mrs Rosenthal herself all day. Nancy snatched up her own child, ramming a particularly ugly red woollen hat on Emily's unwilling head, and with her free hand retrieved the bundles of blankets and bedding that had been put away months ago and hurriedly dug out again yesterday. Her final act was to whip out a compact from the pocket of the coat and a lipstick from the other pocket and, with a deftness born of practice, she applied the vivid red to her lips, peering with a critical eye at the result in the tiny mirror. (A man had once stopped her in Shoreditch High Street to take her photograph. She should be in films, he had said, she should be on the page of a magazine. He had handed her his card, though his intentions had turned out to be carnal rather than artistic.) Nancy snapped shut the lid of the compact and they left the house, locking the front door behind them as though there was every expectation that the house would still be there waiting for them in the morning.

The siren had cranked itself up to a shrill scream and for the second night in a row Odessa Street braced itself for death to fall from the sky.

The feeble winter day had long ago sidled into a protracted evening and Nancy shivered. Outside was as dark as only a British winter combined with a wartime blackout could be. Odessa Street was all but abandoned. Many people had left for good—bombed out and rehoused elsewhere, families who had lived in the area for three, four generations vanished with no forwarding address as though they had never existed, and whether they intended to return if the war ever ended, who knew? In most cases there was nothing for them to return to.

A bucket of sand resided permanently on the doorstep of number 42 for use in case of a fire, though nowadays it was so full of cigarette ends its use as a fire retardant was questionable. Nancy sidestepped it, fumbling in the darkness to locate the mains tap to turn off the water just as the anti-aircraft gun in Victoria Park started up, abruptly drowning out the siren.

Behind her, Emily let out a horrified gasp and turned to push her way back inside the house, ramming her tiny body against the locked door.

'Em! What you playing at?'

Nancy shot out a hand to grab her and Emily struggled to free herself, twisting and squirming and lashing out a foot that struck her mother in the shin. For the briefest moment Nancy imagined herself patient, sympathetic, loving. That was the kind of mother she wanted to be, the kind of mother she imagined her own mother had been. But the reality of it, motherhood during an air raid, was somehow quite different.

'We ain't got time for this!' And she smartly slapped the back of Emily's legs.

'*My blanket!*' Emily wailed, and in the moonlight her face was white and stricken.

Cursing, Nancy unlocked the door and ran back into the house. After a brief but frantic search she located the filthy scrap of scratchy brown blanket that Emily had not slept with since she was a baby but that now, inexplicably, she would not be parted with, and returned with it to her distraught child.

'Next time we go without it. Next time I go without *you!*'

Emily rammed the piece of blanket to her cheek, a fierce look on her face, and made no reply.

But at last they were ready and Nancy grabbed her child's hand. 'Come on,' she said, swinging their arms as though as they were going down the shops because she felt guilty about the slap. 'Herr Hitler wants to bomb us but he won't catch us, will he?'

'Mum, he might,' Emily replied, for she was a realistic sort of child. And she was still smarting about the slap and the near disaster with the blanket.

And in this vein they set off at a grim pace down Odessa Street in the blackout, trying to remember where the worst of the debris and craters and potholes were. Nancy had a torch but the blackout shield she was obliged to cover it with meant she could see almost to the end of her toes but no further. The few remaining residents of Odessa Street could occasionally be seen, shadowy figures overladen with belongings and children, dodging the craters and the debris of a house that had been bombed the night before. The Auxiliary Fire Service and the salvage crews and decontamination squads still worked to contain the damage and the air was thick with smoke that rose in vast plumes hundreds of feet into the night sky. Earlier in the day they had been ankle deep in water from all the fire hoses and a family of ducks had sailed down the street, oblivious to the chaos all around.

Their pace quickened as they reached the destroyed house but once past they slowed.

'Mummy, what about our tea?' said Emily, who had been preoccupied and silent for a time.

'It'll get cold.'

'Will somebody steal it?'

'They might. And if they don't, well then we'll have it for our breakfast.'

Emily considered this. 'I hope no one steals it.'

'So do I,' said her mother, and thus finding something they could agree on they hurried on their way in silence.

The anti-aircraft gun had stopped and around them the street itself now fell silent as though the last building in London had collapsed. A single searchlight silently swept across the night sky and mother and daughter paused to gaze about them. As the searchlight moved to another part of the sky and the street fell into darkness once more, Nancy took a firmer hold of her child's hand and set off again, not wishing to linger. There were other sorts of people out after blackout as well as air-raid wardens and salvage crews. As she thought this she saw a solitary figure on the other side of the street—unmistakably a man—standing perfectly still as though there was no raid, as though he was watching them. Nancy swung her torch so that it was pointing directly at him and the figure merged into the shadows, as silently and swiftly as a rat, and was gone. Yet the sense that he had been watching them—watching her—persisted. The distant droning of enemy aircraft sounded on the wind and a moment later the AA gun burst into life again. Their pace quickened as they hurried beneath the arches of the disused railway and turned the corner, and soon they could see the entrance to the tube station ahead. The shriek of a falling explosive sounded in another street and was followed by a muffled thud. This was the signal to abandon any pretence of not running. Nancy felt her heart crashing against her ribs. She could be quite calm, she had discovered, scrambling over bomb debris in her own street, but when the station was in sight, when she could see the flight of steps disappearing underground and they had begun to think about being safe but they were not quite safe yet, that was when it was hard to breathe, that was when her heart crashed painfully. It only lasted a minute, maybe two, and no one else needed to know. Emily did not need to know—or perhaps Emily did know; perhaps Emily always knew when her mother was frightened.

They passed the Salmon and Ball public house, closed and shuttered up in the darkness, and there was a stream of people all around now, pushing and slipping in icy sludge that was already turning to frost. No one spoke. A large woman wrapped in a dirty grey blanket blocked their way and to stop the panic that was bubbling up inside her Nancy squeezed Emily's hand. 'Not far now,' she said. 'Nearly there.' But her words were lost in the drone of aircraft above and the ack-ack-ack of the AA gun followed by another explosion somewhere off to the west, Shoreditch perhaps, or the City.

Emily pulled urgently on her hand, impatient with the shuffling old woman, but there was nothing to be done about it. The station entrance was a bottleneck, made worse because Bethnal Green had never been an operational station, was still under construction at the start of the war, unfinished and never opened, the tracks not laid yet, the escalators not functioning. The crowd surged forward and they plunged down the short flight of steps. Nancy propelled Emily through the turnstiles and onto the escalator.

The escalator was very long and very steep, reaching down into the depths of the station, offering safety if you concentrated and kept your footing, a horrible death by suffocation in a crush if you did not. Nancy reached out, feeling with the toe of her foot in the dimly lit cavern for the edge of the next step.

Once they were down and inside the station they would be safe.

# CHAPTER TWO

A short distance away another mother and daughter were hurrying towards the same shelter.

Mrs Diana Meadows of The Larches, Milton Crescent, Chalfont St Giles in Buckinghamshire had got on the wrong bus. She had thought they were heading west. Instead their bus, in the blackout and displaying no route number, had carried them east, and by the time they had realised it they were halfway to Shoreditch. They had swept up their belongings and leaped from the bus and now found themselves on an unknown street in the disorientating confusion of the blackout with no possibility of getting home that night.

Then the air-raid siren had gone off.

Diana Meadows let out a little gasp of dismay. The eerie wail of the siren—a sound utterly unknown in the pleasant and leafy environs of Buckinghamshire—shattered the darkness and filled her with terror. She could not move. Let it be a false alarm, she prayed. All around her people had begun to emerge out of the dark. Faceless and fleeting, they passed and were gone, like ghosts, but she could not move. She could not join them.

She was thirty-nine years old and she wore a tweed coat from Liberty that had beaver at the collar and cuffs. It was prewar, of course, but everything was—everything of quality anyhow. She had had her hair set at the hairdresser in Amersham only the day before and the stiff new curls sat unwillingly beneath the smart little hat she had placed on her head on leaving the house. She had powdered her nose. She had studied her profile in the hallway mirror, and had registered with a disappointment that had become habit a small, almost snub nose and a chin a little too long, lips a little too thin, eyes a colour that could never quite be pinned down. An English face, plain and serviceable, but never beautiful. But her hair was set. And her hat was smart. Her gloves too—slender and fawn-coloured and fastened with little buttons at the wrist. But no one who passed her on this dark street wore gloves. No one wore smart little hats. Her coat—a tweed coat from Liberty—had become invisible. Or she had become invisible inside it.

Why could she not move?

'*Mummy!*'

Beside her, three-and-a-half-year-old Abigail stared up at her wide-eyed, clutching Teddy tightly in both hands and in her distress—though only dimly comprehending their predicament—holding him upside down. The child was a facsimile of her mother (the flat little nose, the funny little chin, the thin little lips, the pale features and the dark hair), though when Diana looked at her child she saw only Gerald—the sticking-out ears, the thick dark brows, the unshakable belief in right over wrong— and saw nothing of herself, and was glad.

'*MUMMY!*'

Let it be a false alarm. Frozen, Diana clutched Abigail's hand, clutched Teddy's paw. No one paused to help them. No one seemed to notice them. One woman swore at them when they did not move out of her way. And the darkness, it seethed and thickened about them, its tentacles slithering deep inside Diana's clothes and she remembered as a child being so afraid of the dark that she had screamed in terror night after night.

The all-clear did not sound.

But she was not helpless. She may be alone and a long way from home and a little frightened but she was at least as good as these shapeless and faceless figures who pushed past her without a thought. And she had her daughter to protect. Diana grabbed the arm of a passing man and demanded in a voice that served her well at the tennis matches she had adjudicated at her local club: 'Please tell me where the nearest shelter is. We are lost. We went to a pantomime and we got on the wrong bus and—'

She made herself stop. The man did not need to know they had been to a pantomime yet the urge to explain their presence in what was, one must assume, London's East End was para-mount. She knew she could not possibly blend in and nor, quite frankly, would she wish to.

'The station—go to the tube station!' the man shouted as he pulled his arm free.

Of course: the tube station. That was where people in London sheltered.

'Thank you so much—' But he was gone. 'We shall go and shelter in the tube station,' Diana said to Abigail. 'You'll like that, won't you, darling? It will be a grand adventure.'

14

They set off at once and it was a relief to be moving swiftly, if not at a run—no one else was running—then certainly at a brisk pace. Abigail, who was flagging even before the adventure had begun, made heavy weather of it, and Diana had to half drag, half carry her.

But now Abigail stopped, jerking her mother to a halt too.

'Mummy, we *didn't* go to a pantomime.'

Diana could only dimly make out her child's form in the blackout, her face was quite invisible, but her voice was full of indignant consternation and it seemed extraordinary to Diana that this was what Abigail was pondering as they hurried together through the strange and frightening darkness.

'Don't be silly, Abigail. We must hurry. Oh, do come *on!*'

And though she clearly did not think this a satisfactory reply to her observation, Abigail allowed herself to be led onwards. They passed shops, boarded up or derelict, and row after row of bombed-out terraces, gaping black holes in the black night. But ahead the busy street on which they found themselves reached a junction with a much larger thoroughfare. They passed beneath an archway beside a pub that was shuttered and dark, and on the corner was, unmistakably, the entrance to a tube station. They saw the comforting red and blue and white of the Underground sign and the stream of people disappearing into its depths. Which tube station it was hardly seemed to matter: Whitechapel, Shoreditch (*was* there a station at Shoreditch?) . . . Stepney, perhaps?

'Here we are—almost safe now!' Diana shouted above the rising noise of the siren, for they had made it, the two of them; in this hostile environment, they had triumphed!

But Abigail promptly sat down and refused to move. At this display of defeatism when they were so close to their salvation, Diana felt a moment of despair. She kneeled down, and pleaded with her child to get up, but Abigail closed her eyes and shook her head resolutely. 'Teddy doesn't want to go down there!'

From where Diana was standing Teddy looked extremely keen indeed to get down into the safety of the tube station, but sadly he was in no position to say so. 'Very well, then. I'm going to leave you both here on your own to fend for yourselves.'

At this, Abigail scrambled to her feet and flung herself at her mother's legs. This hampered their progress, especially as Diana was carrying her best handbag and a small travelling case containing sundry other items she had thought it necessary to bring with them on this day trip into London, along with some that she had procured during the course of the day, but they were at least moving in the right direction and, once they joined the flow, the sheer mass of urgent and frightened people behind swept them along so that really all one had to do was to keep on one's feet and not trip.

In this manner they were carried down a short flight of steps and across a concourse, they squeezed through the open turn-stiles (one did feel a little conspicuous not purchasing a ticket, even under such unusual circumstances) and found themselves at the top of the escalator.

The crush of people was suddenly much denser as they were funnelled onto the stationary escalator and Diana grasped the handrail with one hand and her child's hand in a fierce grip with the other, not caring at this moment if she hurt her, concerned only with keeping both eyes on the lip of the stairwell just ahead.

An old woman wrapped in a grubby blanket blocked their way. Another woman, much younger with a determined expression and a small child in tow, grabbed the old woman's arm and practically pushed her down the escalator. But now the crush of bodies behind them intensified and almost at once Diana lost her grip on the handrail and was swept away down the escalator, her feet barely touching the ground, and she scooped Abigail into her arms in the nick of time.

*Phee-oow! Phee-oow!*

Unseen enemy bombers flew overhead dropping incendiaries, or perhaps landmines—it was hard to tell, especially if you were more used to reading about the raids in *The Times* than experiencing them firsthand. But there was no need to look up for they were safely inside the station and all Diana could see above them was the enormous curvature of the enamel-tiled ceiling that led down to the platforms and the streams of people on all sides. The bottom of the escalator was in sight and with one final leap into the unknown they were at the bottom, carried by the sea of people onto the eastbound platform.

They had made it, they were safe, and she held Abigail tightly to her. All they had to do now was find a spot where they could sit tight and wait it out.

But there was no spot.

Every inch of space was taken. Diana stood in the entranceway in silent dismay as around her the platform dissolved into a sea of bodies all trying to find a place on the hard concrete with whatever blankets and bedding they had brought with them, seething and wriggling like the glistening black cockroaches that had frequented the cellar of her dad's old shop in Pinner before the First War and that scuttled away to the corners when you opened the door and turned on the gaslight on a summer's evening.

Where were they to go? They could not stand here, and already people behind them were jostling. For a moment Diana resisted, standing her ground—for where was she to go?—but the crash of bodies behind was too great and she was propelled forward, right to the platform's edge where, beyond, lay the electrified tracks.

*'Wait! Stop! Please stop!'* she cried, but they did not wait, they did not stop, and she gasped and flung out a hand to stop herself falling. For an agonising moment she teetered on the brink of the platform, closed her eyes, and Abigail, in her arms, stared over her shoulder into the abyss and screamed. Then Diana opened her eyes and saw that the tracks could not be seen for all the people sheltering down there.

But the electrified tracks? Even as she thought this she saw that there were no tracks, that this stretch of line was not yet completed, that the people sheltering down on the lines, and further into the tunnel, were perfectly safe. There was even a crate placed just here so that one could step down. Diana availed herself of the crate, she stepped down, and as she did so saw the Underground sign on the tunnel wall: they were at Bethnal Green, and though sudden tears threatened to overcome her she did not give in to them.

They had made it. They were safe.

# CHAPTER THREE

The station swirled in a thickening cloud of cheap Woodbine and Craven A cigarette smoke mingled with the cloying odour of damp bedding and too many unwashed bodies in close proximity. Diana, holding her dismay tightly in check, wondered: How long are we to remain here? One of her gloves had lost its button during their headlong flight and both stockings were now laddered. For a moment she did not quite believe this double catastrophe, laying a finger on the laddered stocking, gazing dumbly at the spoiled glove.

The raid could not last all night.

But they did last all night, she knew that. And even if a miracle should happen and they got the all-clear before midnight they could not possibly make it home; the last train would have long gone. They would be stranded. They would have to find a hotel at Liverpool Street. Yes, she resolved, if they could make it as far as Liverpool Street they would get a hotel. It helped, making this decision, gave one a sense of having some control over events. In the morning they would return home, they would tell Mrs Probart about their adventure, they would write a letter to Gerald, and in a month or so Abigail would forget.

In the meantime, it was simply a question of sitting it out.

She had found a position not far from the entrance to the tunnel. It was strange to see the tunnel, the Underground station, from the angle at which a train driver must see it, or a mouse down on the tracks scurrying away into the darkness. She closed her eyes, pushing down thoughts of mice. Of rats. And yet people were sheltering there, right inside the tunnel, almost swallowed up in its blackness. For it stretched away into oblivion, into East London, and when she tried to think what station would be next heading eastwards she could not. There was nothing: her knowledge of London stopped dead at Liverpool Street.

The place she had found for herself and Abigail allowed just enough space for her to sit on the hard compacted earth (the tweed Liberty coat!) her legs beneath her, her handbag clutched tightly in her hand, the little travelling case at her side and Abigail on her lap. Abigail stared about, wide-eyed and silent, at the sprawling, shifting spread of humanity, at the gaping mouth of the tunnel.

'Mummy, Teddy doesn't like it!'

Diana stroked her hair. She had brushed Abigail's hair this morning and placed a hairband on it and Abigail had sat squirming, waiting for the ordeal to be over, impatient to return to her dolls, to her bricks, to her world. She had not wanted to come out for the day. She had not wanted to come up to London.

'Teddy wants to go *home*!'

'Sssh, sweetheart. We'll go home as soon as it's safe. Until then we shall just have to make the best of it, shan't we?'

'It *smells* funny!'

Abigail was determined not to make the best of it. And there was no denying it did smell funny. Worse than funny. Diana pulled her handkerchief from her handbag and held it to her nose. She would not look at the people all around them; their presence was vivid and compelling without one actually needing to view them. For they seethed, spreading like some virulent Victorian disease that began less than three inches from her feet and stretched without end in every direction. A family of half-starved children shuffled past, their eyes huge and too large for their faces. Their mother was barely out of adolescence herself. She walked dully and without expression, as though she had awoken to find herself in the middle of a war with five runny-nosed children to provide for and no husband in sight. Diana dropped her gaze lest the woman see her staring but the woman seemed to see and hear nothing. And perhaps that was the trick.

Up on the platform tarpaulins formed a closed-off area where, one presumed, the lavatories were. But what horror lay beyond the tarpaulins? Buckets? Were they expected to use buckets? She would not go there, no matter the discomfort. She pulled Abigail closer to her, wondering about her child's bladder capacity, knowing it was really only a matter of time. To see and hear nothing, yes, that was the trick. She imagined herself relating this to Mrs Probart, putting it in her letter to Gerald. But why had she gone up to London at all, he would ask in his reply, and why bring Abigail?

The air seemed to be thinning as more and more people sucked it in and coughed it out again and Diana felt her chest constrict. It was just her imagination. She knew the air could not really be thinning.

She would not mention it to Gerald. There would be no letter. And in a month or so Abigail would forget.

The piece of ground that, in their panicked flight, Diana had found and claimed was right beside a woman and child with a pile of belongings and bedding that the woman had rather ungraciously moved aside in order to make space. The woman was in her early twenties with a scarf tied over her head from which strands of fair hair had escaped. She wore vivid scarlet lipstick and had high, shaped eyebrows over eyes narrowed either in annoyance or to ward off the trail of smoke from her cigarette, all of which gave her a severe, rather hard face—but what should have been cheap, vulgar even, somehow was neither, somehow was striking. It was a beauty—vivid, compelling, and yet, somehow one knew, that would fade, if not this year then the next. The woman wore, oddly, an old apricot dressing-gown with a man's overcoat slung over her shoulders and the cigarette was wedged in the corner of her mouth as though she had placed it there some hours earlier then forgotten about it. She was deftly laying out bedding, provisions and her child on the ground as if she had done it all fifty times before, which no doubt she had. There was something rather splendid about this woman who would not have looked out of place in the pages of a magazine but whom fate had put here, in the East End, in a tube station with a cigarette in her mouth and a small child. It set her apart from the wretched mother and her five starving children. The child, like its mother, was fair-haired and bundled up in mismatching clothes with a ghastly little red knitted hat on its head. She had the same neat little nose and deep-set eyes as her mother, with that same severity, almost hardness about her that was a little disturbing in a child so young. It was the child who saw Diana, her mother oblivious it seemed, absorbed, unconcerned. It was the child who stared back at Diana with black eyes that glared with a measured look that was somehow furious and patient both at once.

Diana felt herself shrivel under the gaze and she looked away and hugged Abigail to her, feeling her own child's sleek good health, her plump little arms, her rosy cheeks—streaked at the moment with dusty tears—her shiny chestnut hair pushed neatly off her face by the gay little hairband. But oddly this felt, now, like something to be ashamed of, something, instinctively, to hide. For the other woman's child was wretched, her hair lank and unwashed and undoubtedly nit-infested, her features were grey, her arms and legs pitifully thin, and it was easy to blame the war, to blame rationing for the little girl's miserable state, but what sort of existence would she live normally in a place like this?

One ought to feel compassion, thought Diana, yet she felt nothing. Worse, she felt revulsion. It was the war: it focused one's priorities. Her priority was her own and her child's safety. And Gerald, of course. Nothing else mattered. And if they did not look after themselves, who else was there to turn to? Both her parents were dead. John was dead—more than twenty years dead, though it was extraordinary to realise it. Gerald, thank God, was *not* dead—or if he was, the Ministry of Defence had not yet informed her of it.

The child had a scrap of blanket clutched to her cheek but now its eyes had settled, disturbingly, on Abigail. No, not on Abigail— on Teddy. Diana felt tiny creatures crawl up over her flesh and she pulled Abigail closer to her. She closed Abigail's little fingers tighter about Teddy's round, furry tummy.

Gerald was somewhere in North Africa, or perhaps the Med, or even the Near East; it was difficult to know with any certainty because all he could say in his occasional letters and hurriedly scribbled postcards was that it was hot, that the flies were a jolly nuisance and that he had acquired a marvellous winter tan—he could just as well have been writing to her from the terrace of a hotel on the French Riviera. Wherever he was, it was safe to assume he was not on board a ship in the North Atlantic being bombed by U-boats and that was a comfort, for Diana had a horror of him drowning in rough seas. But Gerald was in a tank regiment so the chances of his dying at sea were, thankfully, remote.

Abigail, clearly having waited what she considered a long enough time, stirred restlessly. 'Mummy, when can we *go home*?'

'Darling, I know it's not very nice, but however horrid it is, however much we dislike it, we must always remember that it's far, far worse for Daddy than it is for us.'

She had used this line before and Abigail had accepted it, for the most part, though what she understood by the term 'Daddy' Diana could hardly imagine, for Abigail had met him just the once and as this was the day after she was born it hardly counted. Her daddy was a figure as mythical as Father Christmas, which was wretched for Abigail (though she appeared unconcerned by it), wretched for herself, who had had no husband for the past three years, and of course dreadfully wretched for poor Gerald.

Diana spat on her handkerchief and wiped away the dust and grime from Abigail's shoes, giving the little silver buckles a polish. The futility of this was clear in Abigail's silent observation but she could not stop herself. She wiped harder.

Gerald had been thirty-eight already at the outbreak of war with quite a senior position at the merchant bank of Goldberg Staedtler in the City, which, though not exactly essential war work, still it had seemed that this, coupled with his age, would keep him out of active service. And so it had proved, with Gerald drafted to the newly created Ministry of Supply in the early weeks of the war. There had followed a strange but not entirely unpleasant period, with Gerald travelling into Whitehall each day rather than to the City, and, apart from the rare occasions when he was obliged, by weight of work or civil defence drills, to sleep in the office, their lives in those first months of the war had not changed noticeably. They had still played tennis on the weekends and, when rationing allowed, had a roast on Sunday. True, they had listened gravely to the Home Service news each evening on the wireless, and in a burst of patriotic duty Diana had ordered Mr Baines to dig up the garden and plant vegetables—she had drawn the line at keeping chickens—but, on the whole, the war had barely touched them.

After Dunkirk everything had changed. Gerald had got his call-up papers.

'I'm jolly good at figures, but Lord knows what use they'll make of me in a uniform,' he had observed as she had kissed him goodbye at the station. She had wondered the same thing.

He was fit enough—the tennis saw to that—but in a battle? She hoped, she trusted, the military would have the good sense to keep him behind the front lines.

He had been attached to a tank regiment.

And she had been proud but uncertain—what did joining a tank regiment *mean*? She could not picture what it might entail, what exactly he might be doing. At least he would not drown in rough seas, and for that she was grateful, though she supposed he could suffocate or be burned alive inside a tank. It had seemed important for his sake to minutely consider these things, but she found it hard to imagine either of these two scenarios with any clarity. She had put it out of her mind because she found she could not live in this state of muted panic (though other wives seemed able to) and, though it seemed disloyal, she had resumed her life, or tried to. There was one complication: she was seven months pregnant.

They had been married ten years by then and though there had been two other pregnancies both had miscarried in the first few months, the last one four years ago. This one, coming as it had out of the blue, had appeared—seemingly against all expectations—to be heading towards full term. They had been realistic about its chances from the first, not speaking of the child's future, making no preparations in their home for a new arrival—not even a cot—taking nothing for granted. Yet as each month had progressed and nothing had gone wrong, they had taken to sitting side by side of an evening, holding hands, not speaking, looks exchanged every now and again.

And then, with two months to go, the army had swooped in— cruelly, sadistically it had seemed—and taken him from her right when she had needed him most. She was utterly alone but she *would* make the baby survive, if only by sheer force of will. And she was not alone in one sense: wives all over England were in the same position, though other wives had mothers and sisters and in-laws. She had none of these, and Gerald's parents had died out in Ceylon when he was at boarding school. He had an elderly aunt somewhere near Inverness, but what use was that? Diana had been alone. And yet when the time had come there had been a team of nurses and a wonderful midwife who had said she was doing splendidly. She *did* do splendidly: she had produced a perfect, a beautiful baby girl. She had named her Abigail, after Gerald's mother. Gerald had just completed his initial training and had been allowed forty-eight hours leave to visit her and the new baby. When he had arrived, so strange in his army uniform, leaning over the cot to stare at the tiny thing they had produced together, he had been unable to speak. At the end of his leave he had said, 'Well, whatever happens, now I shall just have to make sure I return in one piece.'

But with the war now in its fifth year there appeared to be no end in sight. Abigail had celebrated her third birthday last September much as she had celebrated her first and her second and looked destined to celebrate her fourth—which was to say, fatherless. Diana made an annual visit to Timms Photographic Studio in Amersham, where the elderly Mr Timms sat the protesting Abigail on a settee and tied a handsome bow around her hair or handed her a toy monkey or placed a puppet on his hand to distract her while he took her photograph: a photograph that would find its way, via the British Forces Post Office, to Gerald, wherever he might be—in his tank in the desert, or back at company headquarters or in an officers' mess in Cairo . . . she had not the least idea. But he always got it eventually and in his reply he marvelled at how she had grown—no longer a baby but a little girl!—and that was perhaps the hardest part to bear, for Abigail had grown, was growing, almost daily and Gerald was missing it. The last time she had visited Timms it was to find that old Mr Timms had died and his boy had taken over the business although, as the boy had just received his call-up papers, it seemed likely there would be no more photographs for the duration.

Beside her, cross-legged on the ground, Abigail sat absorbed, smoothing the fur out of Teddy's two small round amber-coloured glass eyes—for he had become a little ruffled in their headlong flight—but now she looked up and said in a loud voice, 'Mummy, you *lied*! You said we went to the pantomime but we *didn't*!'

'Abigail, it hardly matters—'

'I *want* to go to the pantomime! *Why* can't we go to the pantomime?'

It had been a mistake, Diana realised, to bring Abigail with her.

And the little girl in the red woollen hat watched them, her gaze never wavering. Diana felt something cold pass through her body. She wished the little girl would stop staring.

# CHAPTER FOUR

'Stop gawping, Em! And hold still.'

Nancy spat on her handkerchief and wiped it vigorously over her child's squirming, resistant face. She could remember how it felt having your face scrubbed. It was something her own mother had done.

It was the only thing she did remember. Everything else about her mother, the exact circumstances of her own existence, she had heard second-hand and had woven together into a sort of whole. There was a town, remote and coal-blackened, on the Northumberland coast, where a quarter of the menfolk had been killed in pit disasters and where her mother, a girl called Jessie Keys, had been born in the final weeks of the old century. Perhaps wishing more for herself than early widowhood, the young Jessie Keys had departed the mining town in the early years of the Great War and headed south, arriving in the sprawling and squalidly over-flowing streets of the capital, where she had taken up the post of scullery maid in a Mayfair household. There she had remained until it was discovered she was carrying excess baggage beneath her suddenly snug-fitting maid's uniform, and she was hastily turned out.

The excess baggage came courtesy of Charlie Blyth, a youthful employee of the Royal Mail whose job it was to deliver telegrams to the Mayfair household. Perhaps Jessie had thought it an omen that Charlie shared his surname with the remote and coal-blackened town she had spent her first fifteen years trying to escape and the last four yearning for, but he had proved to be a disappointing suitor. As the unfortunate Jessie had squeezed the baby out of her tired body in the upstairs room of a Shoreditch boarding house under the watchful eye of a sympathetic landlady, Charlie Blyth was crossing the Irish Sea en route to Dublin, or perhaps America, and was never heard of again.

With the war over and the flu epidemic sweeping across an already-ravaged Europe, Jessie, unwed and unemployed, had turned her hand briefly to seamstressing before discovering more profitable employment that could be conducted in the comfort of her own bed. On a bitterly cold November night, following a day on which the sun had failed to rise above the rooftops, she had died, painfully and wretchedly, of consumption, leaving four-year-old Nancy in the care of the sympathetic landlady.

This was the sum of Nancy's knowledge of the woman who had, however fleetingly, been her mother, and much of that was supposition, blank spaces filled in by her own imagination.

'Mu-um! Stop!'

Emily had put up with the vigorous rubbing of her face as long as any child could be expected to do so and she threw up her hands to fend off her mother's ministrations. Giving up, Nancy picked her up and planted her on top of a sandbag, straightening the red woollen hat which had almost come off during their headlong flight, sweeping the hair out of Emily's face. If there was anything of Jessie Keys in her grandchild's face, Nancy could not tell, as she had no photographs of her long-dead mother and she could not remember her face.

Emily, seated atop the sandbag, was too young to remember the first weeks of the Blitz, the terror, the panic, the utter unrelenting chaos. Now bunks lined the walls of the platform, though you had to get down here at four in the afternoon to grab one, and there were latrines, though you tried your best to avoid using them, and there were shelter wardens ticking off names on clipboards. There were trestle tables already piled high with tin mugs and three huge urns waiting to be lit by the women from the Women's Voluntary Services. Now it was a way of life and they had got used to it, Nancy supposed.

She watched two very elderly sisters in matching hats and woollen mittens spread a picnic rug on the ground and settle down to knit. You might have thought they were enjoying a day out on Clacton seafront were it not that they paused in their knitting every so often to swig something fortifying from a shared thermos flask. An elderly Jewish man passed by carrying a small, battered case as though he was embarking on a voyage, muttering in agitated Yiddish, searching for someone, searching for a place to sit, but there was no place to sit and no one called out to him.

Poor old sod, thought Nancy, but she didn't make room for him. She had just spotted a man in a raincoat standing motionless some distance away at the platform entrance, his hands thrust deep in his pockets, hat pulled down low so that a shadow fell across his face. The man's eyes slid from left to right, his head unmoving as though he was searching for someone he didn't wish to find. Nancy thought of the figure she had seen in Odessa Street earlier, the figure that had melted into the shadows when she had looked at him. It seemed unlikely it was the same man. Even so, she looked away.

The drone of enemy bombers was suddenly directly overhead and down on the platform the hum of conversation ceased. A whine, louder this time, was followed by the familiar *whooo-osh* then *caroomph* as the first wave dropped.

*Phee-oow!*

*Car-oomph!*

The first bombs hit their targets. They hit something, at any rate, and Nancy closed her eyes and felt the breath pump in and out of her mouth very quickly and her head start to ache as though there was something inside her that needed to burst out. Tonight everything seemed heightened, sharpened, and it was only partly due to the raid.

She opened her eyes to see the two sisters on the picnic rug engaged in a bizarre tug-of-war over the thermos flask. She could smell their terror. It did not get any less frightening, just because you were old and at the end of your life. She had found it heart-breaking in the first months of the Blitz seeing elderly men and women who, having endured a lifetime of drudgery and hardship, must now spend their final years being bombed in a tube station. But she no longer thought this. She no longer noticed.

'Mum, I'm *hungry!*' Emily said, moving restlessly, rubbing her tummy, pulling a dismayed and pitiful face.

'We're all hungry, darling,' Nancy sighed for they had neither of them had their tea and it would be hours yet before the ladies from the WVS came round with their sausage rolls and cups of tea. And in the meantime the chips were on the kitchen table, already cold. If the two of them survived the night, if the house survived, they would be having cold chips for their breakfast—it would not be the first time. Last winter things had got so bad they had existed on dripping and lemon rind, sucking it till just a piece of yellow skin remained to be chewed then swallowed and, when they had run out of fuel for the stove, on raw potatoes, standing at the kitchen table because they had used the chairs for firewood, surrounded by rows of empty tins and jars that claimed to contain flour and sugar and butter and lard but almost never did (a cruel echo of a more plentiful time), with an unreliable gas ring that had finally failed when an incendiary had hit the nearby gasworks. Eventually the kitchen table too had been chopped up and Nancy had had to stand at the sink to squeeze the last out of a pile of watery grey tea-leaves. Emily had had a half-starved, animal look about her—but all the children looked that way. Nancy had lain awake wondering how they would manage.

Then Joe had come home on leave and everything had changed.

An explosion caused the air to reverberate and again all conversation ceased, eyes raised upwards. Dust and earth dribbled from a crack in the ceiling. A moment later a long low rumble signalled the collapse of a building above. After a moment the rumble faded and everyone took a deep breath and got on with what they were doing.

Nancy lit a fresh cigarette. She could sit it out: the bombs and Emily's hunger. She had done it before. The cigarette would calm her. She watched out of the corner of her eye the smartly dressed woman who had arrived late, flustered and panicked, with her child, and who was now seated awkwardly on the floor, her legs curled beneath her and looking as out of place, Joe would have said, as the King and Queen walking into the pawnbroker on Hackney Road.

The little girl was perched on her mother's lap clutching a teddy bear and at the mother's side was a small blue case, the handle of which the woman clasped as though it contained her jewels—and perhaps it did. She had no blankets or pillows or bedding or warm clothing with her, or indeed anything that might be of the least use for a night in a shelter. Clearly she had not expected to get caught in an air raid. The tweed coat she wore, the smart little hat and silk stockings, the polished black court shoes and long elegant gloves over long elegant fingers suggested she was on her way to a cocktail party or shopping in Bond Street. The fur at her collar was smooth and sleek and moth-free, even if it was prewar.

Posh, but not wealthy, Nancy decided. And not pretty, either, despite her posh outfit. In fact, she looked a bit like Mrs Wallis Simpson and there was living proof, if you needed it, that you could have all the money and all the best clothes in the world and still not look very pretty. Though there was something—what was it? dignified, perhaps?—about this woman that somehow compensated. And her neck was as beautifully slender as a swan's. She was well past thirty, perhaps nearer forty, which was odd for the mother of such a little girl. But the plainness accounted for that: clearly she had been overlooked by every man she had met until, late in life, some man had come along, had taken pity perhaps—or that was how it seemed to Nancy, who had married at nineteen. The woman's gaze seemed very far away but the look of controlled panic on her face was unmistakable.

The woman chose that moment to look around and, caught staring, Nancy nodded at her, softening her eyes into a smile she did not feel.

~

The cigarette was finished. Emily had fallen into a restless sleep, her eyelids flickering from side to side as though tracking the aircraft high above, and Nancy reached down and brushed a strand of hair from her face. Emily was easier to love when she was asleep; perhaps all children were. Her face was still streaked with dirt and Nancy stifled the urge to spit on her handkerchief a second time and try to wipe the remaining dirt off, for she was oddly aware of the smartly dressed woman sitting a few feet away whose child was plump and spotless, her chestnut hair sleek and shiny and held in place by a natty little hairband. The coat she wore was a tiny perfect copy of her mother's coat, and on her feet were the kind of shoes Princess Elizabeth might have worn—smart and shiny with little silver buckles on top. Nancy looked at her own child, who was dressed in clothes salvaged from bomb-sites. But Emily was asleep, dead to the world as the world tore itself apart above her, and what did it matter if her face was dirty?

Nancy leaned her head back against the wall of the tunnel, feeling some small part of her unwind, and wondered if Joe's ship had sailed yet. She closed her eyes as an immense weariness overcame her and somewhere in the space between dreaming

35

and not dreaming she saw a vast gunmetal-grey warship slip silently away from the dockside and out to sea. The ocean was gunmetal grey too and the sky—indeed, her very dreams were gunmetal grey. She saw the ocean, smooth and calm and safe, a haven, and the horizon, towards which the ship sailed, was a place of calm serenity.

A baby began to scream and she sat up. She would not sleep, it was too early yet and, besides, she did not even know if Joe's ship had sailed. Not that it made any difference—Joe had gone and she would not see him again perhaps until the end of the war, if he made it that far.

The fact of his departure was a sharp ball of pain inside her that came and went, sometimes no more than a dull ache and other times catching at her throat and taking her breath away. At this moment it filled her up, squeezing the life out of her, but after a moment or two it lessened.

Joe had left that morning, three months' rest and recuperation ending abruptly with the arrival of his recall papers for his new ship just when she had got used to having him around. His ship was due to depart on the evening tide and where it was headed she had no idea and she doubted Joe did either. His last ship had been torpedoed somewhere between Iceland and Greenland and he had spent three days adrift in a lifeboat. The entire ship's company had died, he had said, dozens of men, though neither the papers nor the wireless had reported it. He had been picked up by a passing merchant ship and spent a fortnight in a hospital at Liverpool, then they had sent him home to recuperate. That had been October. Joe had been at sea three years. She had worried that they wouldn't know each other, or worse, wouldn't like each other. They had been married so short a time before his call-up that they were still getting used to each other when he left. She worried that what he had gone through—three days adrift in a lifeboat, the ship's company lost—would affect him. But hadn't she witnessed dreadful things herself? Limbs blasted across a street, burnt torsos belonging to people she had once known, a baby burned black in a fire . . . So then, they were neither of them the same people they had been when they had met and married. But it worried her all the same.

Joe had come barrelling along the street one afternoon in October in his sailor's uniform with his kitbag over his shoulder and a big grin on his face hiding whatever uncertainty hid beneath, and Nancy had imagined a hundred times what that moment would be like, what they would say to each other, but it turned out there was nothing to say for she had burst into tears and run at him. That had surprised her, that surge of emotion. Where had it come from? There had been no warning of it. She had not cried when he'd left nor at any time since, even when she'd heard he'd been torpedoed but was safe. It had not seemed real. She had felt—nothing really, only a sort of dull amazement.

Yet there she was in the street, holding on to him and sobbing.

But later, after she had run out to him in tears, he had stood in the kitchen not knowing what to do with himself, taking up so much space and neither of them finding the right words. The distance between them seemed too great. He was not hurt in any way that she could see, other than the sunburn and blisters, but he spent the first week at home trying to count all the men who had died, counting fretfully on his fingers, remembering each name. But never when she was in the room, never when he thought she was watching him. He sat in the armchair with his sleeves rolled up and read the paper, he went to the pub and drank watery wartime beer, he rolled his cigarettes and in the evenings he listened to the wireless and, when the news came on, he railed against the politicians and the government and the navy and the Admiralty and anyone, really, who sat in an office and made decisions while he was out there getting his arse shot off. She liked that: his fury, his energy. But apart from that first moment when she had burst into tears and run at him, they had forgotten how to be close.

And Emily, born seven months after Joe had left and now more than three years old, was a stranger to him as much as he was to her. Her demands, her constant presence, seemed to surprise him, and sometimes it was funny and other times it made him furious. At night, when Joe wanted what any man wanted after three years at sea, Emily's sleeping there in the same room with them infuriated him, but he had grown up in a small house with many people, they all had, and her presence quickly became familiar to him.

Emily greeted the sudden appearance of a dad with a mixture of disdain and open hostility that lasted up until the first tins had arrived. For Joe had got himself signed on at the dockyard, unloading the few convoys that made it past the German U-boats. He was supposed to be on sick leave and there he was putting in shifts at the dockyard. Nancy was furious. But it was hard to be angry with the extra money—and that wasn't all. After his first shift Joe came home with two tins of peaches and a tin of Carnation milk wrapped in a sack. How he'd done it without being caught she didn't know and she didn't ask. They ate the peaches and drank the Carnation and sent him back for more.

But that would stop now Joe had gone.

This morning she had scrubbed the front step and Emily had played in the bomb wreckage in the street outside as Joe had flung his things into his kitbag. It was all new, his kit; he had lost everything in the ship that had been torpedoed so the navy had given him new stuff. It didn't look new—it looked like a hundred sailors had used it before him—but she made sure it was clean at least. Joe placed his new sailor's hat on Emily's head and laughed at her. He didn't tell them the name of his new ship and Nancy had not wanted to know because his last ship had been torpedoed and it seemed like bad luck. Seeing him in his uniform for the first time, Emily went suddenly shy. She understood he was departing—that huge, heavy kitbag was hard to ignore—but what did it mean when you were three? By the end of the day she would have forgotten him.

'Right then.' Joe placed his kit on the floor. He had shaved, making a better job of it than usual, as though he wanted to make a good impression on his new ship. 'Em, you mind you look after your mum,' he said, tweaking her nose, and instead of looking outraged Emily regarded him wordlessly, silenced by the uniform and the kitbag and an awareness of something terrible but unspoken.

'You got everything?' Nancy said.

'Think so. You'll be alright, then, will you?'

''Course we will. We're used to it, ain't we, Em?'

Emily nodded uncertainly.

'Don't do anything daft,' Nancy added.

"Course I won't. Right then ..." And he had picked up his kitbag, slung it over his shoulder, and kissed them both goodbye.

Nancy had stood at the door with Emily and together they watched him till he had turned the corner.

Nancy scanned the sea of faces on the platform above. The man in the raincoat whom she had noticed earlier had gone from his spot in the entranceway. Perhaps he had crossed to the West-bound platform or gone back up to the street. Perhaps he had found the person he was searching for. She shivered, knowing with a sudden and certain conviction that the man was a police-man and for the first time she was glad Joe had left. She placed a hand softly against her stomach. She was pregnant again but she had not told Joe before he had gone.

# CHAPTER FIVE

Another bomb exploded somewhere up on the surface and Diana ducked—it was impossible not to, though no one else did. She studied the dial of her watch but was unable to calculate how many hours they had been down here—one hour, two? Nor could she work out how many hours more they were likely to remain. The explosions overhead and the space between the explosions prevented her brain from undertaking even the most rudimentary calculations. She gave it up. And meanwhile more and more people and their children, their bedding, their belongings, their elderly parents surged onto the narrow platform above that was designed only to take workers to the docks and weekend shoppers up West.

If they took a direct hit it would be carnage.

The woman in the headscarf and her child were so close Diana could see the brand of cigarette the woman smoked, the stitches on the red woollen hat worn by the little girl, could smell on their clothes the chip fat from their last meal. Their very proximity alarmed her. The woman had smiled at her but the smile was cold. Unfriendly. Diana had looked away. This was a public shelter and the bombs made no distinction between one person and another but her presence, she could feel, was not welcome. If it came to calamity it would not be herself and Abigail they would rush to help. So many people seated very close by. She kept her gaze dully neutral but even so she felt eyes on her, crawling over her inch by inch, noticing.

Abigail was dozing. Her head lolled against Diana's lap, eyes half closed, safe in the twilight place between sleep and waking. If Diana had come alone she might not have got on the wrong bus, she might have made it home and be opening her front door at this very moment, taking off her hat, pulling off her shoes. But she had brought Abigail, putting them both in danger. And it was not merely that she had exhausted the babysitting goodwill of Mrs Probart. It was to provide herself with a cover, an excuse to come up to town, because a mother and child were, somehow, less conspicuous than a woman on her own.

Perhaps it was not too late to leave? She imagined herself gathering up their things and simply walking out. She presumed no one would stop them.

Another explosion sounded high above and her arms closed tightly around the little case and around Abigail and she waited, her eyes closed. The explosion rumbled away finally into nothing and with it any hope that they might leave before dawn. She would not think about it. She would think, instead, about Gerald, who was surely having a worse time of it than they were. She would think of their suffering, hers and Abigail's, as something that must be borne for his sake. She tried to imagine where Gerald was, what he might be doing at this very minute—standing atop a sand dune with a pair of field glasses or at an officers' club drinking pink gins or inside a tank barking out orders to a subordinate—but it never seemed quite real. She never quite believed in it, in Gerald as a soldier. Even after three years it still seemed so improbable, so unlikely. In her mind he was dressed as he had been the first day she had met him: forever in tennis whites in the summer of 1928.

They had met at a tennis party in Ruislip in the expansive gardens of an Edwardian villa on the edge of the golf course. Marian Fairfax had invited her. Marian, who moved in somewhat higher circles than Diana (her father being a specialist at a London hospital and her mother being distantly related to an air marshal), was an old school friend whom Diana had not seen a great deal of in the seven years since they had both left school. Diana, under no illusions about her social worth, had been invited that day on the strength of her backhand, which was unrivalled among her particular set and had won her as many admirers as it had lost her friends. Even so, she had only received the invitation when another friend of Marian's, a girl called Bunny, had dropped out at the last minute.

They were a party of eight, four teams of mixed doubles, and strawberries and gin and tonics were served on a silver tray by a man in a spotless white coat. For Diana—who had left a rather average school in Pinner with a handful of minor exam passes and enrolled in a local secretarial college, where she had done moderately well, and now worked in the front office of a local solicitor's firm—the strawberries and the gin and tonics and the man in the spotless white coat with a silver tray were like a glimpse of some exotic coastline seen from the deck of a ship far out to sea. And yet she was acutely aware of her social worth so that the strawberries, which were better than any strawberries she had ever tasted before, stuck in her throat and turned to ash in her stomach; the gin and tonics, though intoxicating, burned like acid; the man in the white coat looked down his nose at her even as he served her with polished deference. She hated it, she wanted to leave as soon as she had arrived, and yet the thought of returning to the dreary little flat above her parents' shop seemed like a slow death.

She was paired that day with a man called Ed whose wife, Phyllis, had been paired with some other man. Whether this deliberate splitting up of couples was strategic or merely a part of the fun Diana was uncertain. Her partner, Ed, a vigorous-looking fellow with very black hair, inspected her through narrowed eyes and remarked, 'I understand you possess a sound backhand,' and though his words suggested a compliment they were delivered in such a way that he might have been comment-ing on an alleged and rather shameful misdemeanour rather than her sporting prowess. A little bewildered by her partner's tone and rather wishing the man had been paired with his wife, who in turn had been paired with a tall and nice-looking young man with wavy dark hair and very definite eyebrows and a ready smile, she nevertheless acquitted herself admirably and they easily enough won all three of their matches and were set to play another couple in the 'final'. The wife and her tall, nice-looking partner had proved a fairly hopeless combination and were now sitting out as vocal onlookers, so that Diana wished she was seated next to the nice-looking man, whose ears stuck out, but in an endearing way, she decided. But she was in the final and he was an onlooker—though he appeared more taken up by his gin and tonic and by the wife of the man called Ed than by a girl with a sound backhand who lived above a shop in Pinner. She would try extra hard, Diana resolved. And then she resolved that she would not try at all because she suspected a man found it unattractive if a young lady tried too hard, particularly at physical activity.

She was aware of the sweat stains under her arms.

It was not her finest set of tennis. The man called Ed becoming increasingly cross, the wife who made sarcastic calls from the sidelines, the man in the white coat with the silver tray whom she could see always in her peripheral vision walking back and forth across the lawn, the nice-looking man with the eyebrows who clapped and said, 'Oh bad luck,' when she sent an easy forehand thundering into the net—all of it put her off.

She would never be asked back. She had a sound backhand but when the time had come, when the pressure was on, she had buckled. She had been found wanting.

Their opponents—a couple named Cecily and Johnny who seemed to know Ed and were unconcerned by his increasing irritation and who, by comparison, appeared to be having a marvellous time—played brilliantly. As Ed and Diana moved swiftly towards an inevitable defeat, Diana's sound backhand finally deserted her and Ed's patience deserted him. He snatched at a volley that by rights was hers and sent the ball straight at the girl, Cecily, who was crouched on the far side of the net ready to pounce. The ball caught her squarely in the face and she keeled over backwards.

'Good *God*—Cee, are you alright?' cried her partner, running over, and there followed a lengthy delay while icepacks were produced and sympathetic words spoken. Eventually, Cecily's wellbeing assured and nothing more life-threatening than a black eye and colourful bruise being the upshot, the match was declared over and, as the other couple had forfeited, Diana and Ed were declared winners. Diana felt this a little unjust and said so but Ed didn't hear her.

Standing in the conservatory dabbing sun-reddened and perspiring faces with towels and quaffing great quantities of chilled lemonade, the acerbic wife, Phyllis, walked up to her husband, Ed, and said, in a voice that hushed the room: 'You hit that ball at poor Cee on purpose.'

'What a ridiculous thing to say!' he countered, barely looking at her, but a hush fell over the room.

'It's not ridiculous. We all saw it. You did it deliberately.' Phyllis somehow managed to sound both bored and spiteful, and if her objective had been to provoke her husband she succeeded, for he rounded on her now, taking her by her arm.

'*How dare you accuse me?*' he demanded, his fingers closing tightly around her upper arm so that she gasped in sudden pain. He let her go at once, throwing his towel to the floor and walked off.

A horrible silence ensued. The wife rubbed her arm and gave a high-pitched, frightened little laugh that only made things worse, then she too left, making some excuse to their host.

Afterwards, everyone was a little stiff and formal and the fun had gone out of the day, and Diana began to wonder if she too might offer some excuse and depart.

'That was rather beastly, wasn't it?'

'Oh!' she said, because the tall, nice-looking man with the ears and the eyebrows and the ready smile had sought her out to offer her a fresh lemonade and to make a comment on what had happened and he had the most marvellous voice, sort of solid and comforting, just like the man on the BBC. 'Yes. Yes, it was, rather.'

'Look here, I'm thinking of pushing off. Party seems to have ended somewhat abruptly. Can I give you a lift? I'm Gerald, by the way.'

∽

It must be nearing midnight. A hurricane lamp hung from the ceiling swinging crazily and Diana attempted once more to read the time on her watch by its light but gave up.

An elderly woman with swollen ankles sporting a volunteers' armband appeared on the platform's edge bearing a tray of sausage rolls and hot cocoa in mugs, and the way she loudly and coarsely spruiked her wares suggested she spent her daylight hours out on a market stall. When the woman saw Abigail she fell silent. She gently stroked Abigail's pinched face, then she reached over and patted Diana's hand before moving on. As though she could sense their fear. Their isolation.

They ate ravenously, wolfing down the rolls and licking their fingers for every last crumb. With food in her stomach, Abigail dozed, but Diana could not sleep.

She thought about her old school friend Marian whom she not seen again since that afternoon in 1928, and Marian's friend, the girl called Bunny, whose decision to drop out of the tennis party at the last minute had changed the course of Diana's life. It was a little humbling and a little frightening to realise how one's destiny might be shaped by something so small, by someone else's decision.

She thought of her vegetable garden, which had failed.

After the first year of the war the wonderful Mr Baines had gone to live with his elderly sister in Cirencester, they'd had a series of early winter frosts and the soil had proved too chalky. The failure of the garden would have been inconsequential enough under ordinary circumstances, but in wartime it had assumed catastrophic proportions.

It was the reason she had come up to London.

The chalk was the main source of the problem, for the Chilterns was, essentially, one very long chalk escarpment that ringed the outer rim of London from Watford to Uxbridge. And yet they had brought it upon themselves, she and Gerald, choosing to live in a place that was not merely built on chalk but positively boasted about its chalkiness; 'Chalfont', they discovered, meant a chalk spring. This had seemed perfectly delightful in 1930 when they toured the pretty little village preparatory to buying a house here. Now, when the beautiful begonia beds had been dug up to make way for marrows and carrots and running beans, the chalk was the stuff of nightmares. Other women tossed and turned at night haunted by ration books and clothing coupons. Diana lay awake fretting about her vegetable garden.

And yet other people's gardens did not seem to suffer the way hers did. When one peered into the neighbours' gardens one saw broad beans as tall as golf clubs, tomatoes as shiny as jewels, carrots as abundant as—well, as carrots had been before the war. Everywhere she saw gardens brimming with bounty. But at The Larches nothing seemed to grow. And yet that first autumn when they had dug up the flower beds and sowed vegetables, there had been a decent enough crop. The second year the results had been disappointing. This last autumn the crops had failed altogether. Baines had left instructions. It had seemed straightforward enough. Diana had sowed when he had told her to sow, she had planted, she had fertilised, she had watered. She had watched as the shoots wizened and died, as no shoots appeared at all, as the chalky earth coughed up a tomato the size of a marble, a solitary dwarf carrot, a runner bean fit only for a doll's tea party.

The vegetables had failed. *She* had failed.

She had wondered then, What *am* I good for? She had passed a handful of exams and done moderately well at a secretarial college; she had learned shorthand, though she doubted she could remember much of it now, and could type at a speed of thirty words a minute (a good typist could do forty-five). She still had a sound backhand, though she had not played tennis in four years and could not find a way, in her present circumstances, to put this particular skill to any practical use. She was a wife and a mother and she supposed that she had made a fair job of both these things—and were these not, when all was said and done, the two most important roles a woman could have? But she had not seen her husband in more than three years and she had failed to put fresh food on the table for her child. She had lived with her failure for many months and told no one because defeatism was now a crime in wartime.

In the weeks leading up to Christmas, she had decided to go up to town to do her Christmas shopping, even though Christmas in wartime (and this was their fifth) was a pitiful affair. Abigail, however, was excited, though having only experienced wartime Christmases Abigail's expectations were set rather low.

She had taken the nine o'clock train, arriving at Baker Street a little after ten o'clock. She had made her way by bus to Bond Street and there ran into Lance Beckwith.

'Diana Pettigrew! Is that really you?'

He came out of nowhere (in fact, he came out of Boots, the chemist, but she wasn't to learn this until later) and the use of her maiden name disorientated her for a moment. It was another moment before she realised who he was, this tall middle-aged man, incongruous in a light grey suit and a paisley-pattern silk scarf on this drearily overcast December day, a soft felt hat pushed to the back of his head and a smile in his eyes.

'Lance!' And at once the drearily overcast December day and the few hurrying Christmas shoppers and the stream of red buses and black cabs on Bond Street, the sandbags, the bombsites, the uniforms faded away. She thought of sunshine and birds singing and trees thick with summer foliage from a summer that had ended more than twenty years ago. It was Lance.

'Diana Pettigrew. Well I never.' He stood back to regard her, his eyes narrowing as though he viewed her from that distant place, that summer twenty years ago, but the smile never wavered, so that she felt a little flustered. Of course he was older, there were lines at the corners of his mouth and eyes, and the flesh at his cheeks had sunk a little, but still she felt a little flustered. 'You haven't changed a bit!' he said.

Diana laughed. 'That's what people say when someone has deteriorated beyond all recognition.'

'That's not what I say! And anyway, it's not true as I recognised you instantly.'

She laughed again, conceding this. 'I, on the other hand, would probably have passed you on the street without another glance if you hadn't stopped me.'

That was untrue. He looked so different to every other person in Bond Street that morning she would have noticed him regardless.

'Oh dear. Have I gone so badly to seed?'

'Not at all. You look the picture of health and vitality—as I am sure you well know. Where have you just sprung from? The Riviera?' Lance had an unseasonal tan on his face and hands.

'Boots!' he replied, holding up a small brown bottle as proof then banging his chest. 'I may look the picture of health and vitality but this climate is doing its best to bring me low.'

'I wouldn't have guessed it—you look marvellous!'

'What an outrageous flatterer you've become, Diana. I would not have believed it of you. Come on—let's find a cup of tea somewhere. What do you say?' And he held out his arm to her.

She had not even begun her shopping, had planned to complete everything by lunchtime so that she could lunch at Debenhams in Oxford Street and catch the two o'clock train home. Having tea with Lance Beckwith was not on the agenda but she took his arm and went with him anyway, because of John.

He found a little cafe on Conduit Street, a dreary enough sort of place into which one would not dream of going but for the war. As it was, they were grateful for the tiny three-legged table they were allocated in the window, and the mismatching folding chairs they sat down on, and the menu which was a single sheet of typed paper with the words . . .

*Tea*
*Bread and butter*
*Bread no butter*

. . . printed on it, and Lance remarked that it would be quite amusing in a music hall comedy sketch and Diana agreed and suggested they order the tea. His hair, now that he had removed his hat, was very black, too black to be entirely real. She steered her gaze away from it. It did not quite fit the sense she had of his otherworldliness, the whisper of tropical skies and exotic locations that hung around him, eclipsing, for a blissful moment, the drabness of wartime London. She forgave him the too-black hair.

Once they had ordered, Lance offered her a cigarette and when she refused leaned back in his chair to light one for himself with a long and thoughtful gaze.

'You're married,' he said, noticing this fact with the sharpness of a man who made it his business to notice such details.

'Yes. Gerald. 1930. He's a stockbroker. *Was* a stockbroker. Currently he's with the tank regiment. One child, Abigail, aged three and a half, at home in Bucks and under the watchful supervision of a helpful neighbour.' She smiled. And thus could her life be summed up. 'I'm Christmas shopping. You?'

'Ah, nothing so conventional, I'm afraid.' It seemed he was going to leave it at that, but after exhaling a stream of smoke he went on, ticking each item off on his fingers: 'Not married, no kids, certainly *not* a stockbroker, definitely not a home in Bucks or Herts or Middlesex or Berkshire or indeed anywhere within striking distance of a golf course—and, as you can see, no tank regiment,' he finished with a flourish. 'Not that I've anything against golf courses, you understand, it's just I've no wish to live near one.'

'I don't think we *do* live near a gold course,' Diana protested. 'Or if we do, I've never come across it.'

'Impossible. Nowhere in Bucks is more than a mile from the nearest golf course.'

'Well, I shall have to take your word for it. How did you avoid the tank regiment?' she asked, deciding to be direct.

'Easy. Out of the country. South America. Argentina mostly. Spent most of the last ten years down there following one business opportunity or another. Interesting place. Usual rules don't apply. It can make a chap or break him.'

All of which told her precisely nothing, though it did explain the unseasonal tan. 'And which was it? Did it make you or break you?'

'Both. And neither—for here I am, as you see!' He laughed and was saved from further explanation by the girl arriving with their tea, which she slopped onto the table with all the ceremony of a pig farmer at swill time before promptly demanding payment.

'Beautifully done, my dear,' Lance said to the girl as he handed over sixpence. 'One could be at the Ritz.'

She ignored this and left.

Diana laughed, and it was wonderful to laugh when it had begun to seem that laughter played no part in one's world.

'Lance, it's so very good to see you,' she said, surprising herself by reaching across the table and squeezing his arm. And then she ruined it by saying, 'You're the only person left who knew John. The only person I can talk to about him,' and there they were, the old tears that she had not shed for a decade or longer, but she smiled because she really was happy to see him. And Lance, bless him, just smiled and patted her hand and let her pour the tea, which gave her the space to compose herself.

When she had, and the first mouthfuls of tea had been drunk, they talked about John, for Lance had been her brother's school friend and knew stories about him that his family did not know, and there were other stories that they both knew and that they remembered together and laughed over, and she talked finally of that dreadful day, of John's motorcycle running at speed into a wall a mile outside Cambridge on a summer afternoon in May in the final weeks of term, a brilliant young man's life ended in a senseless motor accident, and Lance listened in silence. He knew the details already, but everyone's experience of death is different, and when she had last seen Lance, at the funeral, it had still been too raw to talk of such things. They had shaken hands at the church door and agreed to keep in touch.

She had not seen him in twenty-two years. And now he and she were the only ones left who remembered.

'Your parents are both . . .?'

'Dead, yes. Mum within the year. I don't think she ever really got over John, you know. And Dad six years later.'

A horrid six years, with Dad waiting to die.

Diana spoke simply because it was the only way to express the sheer horror of that time. They had folded up and died, her family, in that single moment when John's motorcycle had crashed. But no, they had *not* all died, for here she was, the sole survivor. She thought of herself seated in a lifeboat adrift in an ocean as the rest of her family sank beneath the waves.

Then Gerald had rescued her.

She did not tell Lance this; rather, she smiled at him and let a comfortable silence fall between them. She wondered what he thought of her, a middle-aged wife and mother. She had been a girl still at their last meeting at the door of the church. Seventeen, gauche and unformed, just out of school, and he had been a friend of her brother, in a formal suit, shaking hands with her dad like a man who had been out in the world, though he must have been barely twenty-one himself. So tall and strong, as her family had crumbled around her. She had wanted to stand before him and feel his arms holding her up, holding them all up. Instead, Lance had gone and twenty-two years had passed. And now they sat together in a cafe in Conduit Street.

Their table was bumped by another couple brushing past as they weaved their way towards the door, a GI and his girl, unspeaking and grave, intent only on themselves. Do we look like that? she wondered. Grave, intent only on ourselves? Do we look like a couple? The thought came unbidden and she pushed it aside uneasily even as she thought of the hat she had chosen that morning, the slim black gloves she had selected and that lay now on the table beside her, her fur coat from the final summer before the war but still in good condition; she thought of the lipstick she had applied hastily in the hallway mirror before she left home and not reapplied since. She had no sense of how she looked now to Lance. To any man.

'You must find it lonely,' he said. 'With your husband away.'

She reached for her gloves and smoothed the seam of one of them with her finger. Why had she taken them off? It was cold and normally one would not remove one's gloves in a small and rather seedy cafe in Conduit Street. She looked up, smiled. 'But I have Abigail. She is a comfort. Though one does feel such a failure as a mother, trying to provide for her.' She stopped, ashamed at the triteness of her reply. She slid her fingers into her gloves, snapped the little buttons at her wrist, and looked up again. 'Yes, I find it lonely. Dreadfully.'

'It's a difficult time,' he said, and whether he meant John's death or the war or both or neither did not seem to matter.

'Yes,' she agreed; it was a difficult time, but she felt a calmness she had not felt in a long while.

'Come and see me.' He slid a card over the table. 'I think I can help.'

Diana thought of Gerald, who had rescued her and who was in North Africa or perhaps elsewhere, and as Lance poured her a second cup his card lay on the table between them.

Lance could help her.

## CHAPTER SIX

The sympathetic landlady at whose Shoreditch boarding house Nancy Levin had been born and where, four years later, her mother had died, had proved to be a good friend to the Keys, initially to the deserted and friendless Jessie and later to her orphaned daughter.

Mrs Silver, for this was the landlady's name, took a certain satisfaction in rescuing the destitute. 'A person don't need to be a Christian to have Christian morals and virtues,' she had often said, which was to say Mrs Silver had been born into the Orthodox Jewish faith and had no more time for the Christian faith than she had for Judaism, which she had abandoned at the age of seventeen when she had fallen pregnant to a rabbi and had set out into the world on her own terms.

It was in this world, then, that the four-year-old Nancy had found herself and in which she soon thrived. Mrs Silver's own children being long since grown up, and there being no Mr Silver (the title 'Mrs' being one that Mrs Silver had conferred on herself without feeling the need of a minister to confer it on her), and being over fifty and feeling a lack in herself that a sweet-natured, four-year-old child might fill, Mrs Silver had offered the child a home. True, Nancy was expected to fetch and carry for Mrs Silver's boarders, run errands and generally pay her own way, but this was the natural way of things, and it still left time for her to attend the overcrowded school down the street to learn her letters and numbers and scripture.

At thirteen, Nancy finished her schooling, intending to expand her role in the boarding house run by Mrs Silver with a view to someday taking over the business. At this point, fate, as it had done before, stepped in, striking the sixty-year-old Mrs Silver down stone dead, of a stroke, over breakfast one bright morning in May. Nancy, finding herself alone and abandoned for the second time in her short life, her modest ambitions thwarted, wasted little time in self-pity (for her predicament was not unusual, she saw thwarted ambition and families lost every-where she looked) and soon found herself a position in a hat shop in Bethnal Green Road.

The hat shop was owned by a Madame Vivant who spoke with a heavy French accent though she came originally from Hoxton and was no more French than the hats she sold which were labelled Made in Paris and Made in Milan though they heralded from a large factory in Birmingham. Nancy found herself on five shillings a week in a dingy back room packing and unpacking stock. It was a far cry from the Shoreditch boarding house, but the wages were better and the other shop girls were fun—Miriam, a giggling dark-haired Jewish girl from Aldgate, and Lily, a willowy, delicate-looking girl who walked with a stoop to hide her almost-six-foot height. There was also Mme Vivant's assistant, a girl called Milly Fenwick, who was a little older than the others, and who only spoke in sharp tones to remind you of something you'd failed to do, but on the whole Nancy considered she had landed on her feet.

Six years passed rapidly. Nancy now knew about hats; she peered at the hats in the windows of the Bond Street shops and dreamed one day of working there. She had, in short, a new ambition. Mrs Silver and the days in the boarding house in Shoreditch already seemed very distant. Perhaps it would have happened, too. At the time Nancy had believed it: her own hat shop, her own girls. There was nothing wrong with ambition. But there was fate, too, and she had not reckoned on that.

They had taken the train to Clacton for the Whitsun bank holiday, herself and Miriam and Lily, a few short weeks before the start of the war but far enough away that war had not even seemed a possibility. On that day—a pleasingly warm and cloudless day, the sort of day that you hoped for on a bank holiday but rarely got—the three girls had ridden the rollercoaster (twice), bathed in the pool, seen the Punch and Judy show and finally, having exhausted the pier, linked arms and run laughing along the esplanade.

And this was there they had run into Milly Fenwick and Milly's young man, to whom she had recently become engaged.

'There's Milly!' Miriam exclaimed, flapping a hand, her words indistinct as she tackled a wad of fluffy pink candy floss.

There was Milly, frozen on the esplanade with her young man beside her, in her Sunday-best coat and shoes and one of Mme Vivant's newest and most expensive creations perched on her head and an expression on her face like she had bitten into a toffee apple and chipped a tooth. But Miriam marched over and demanded, 'Is this your young man, then, Milly? Why dontcha introduce us?' And Milly, cornered, said 'This is my fiancé. This is Joseph.'

'Joe,' he corrected her.

Nancy said nothing, offered only a polite smile. Milly's young man was like any number of young men you might see striding along Bethnal Green Road on a Saturday night: an ordinary face, smooth-shaven, a chin with a dimple in it, and unblinking grey eyes, thick dark brown hair slicked down with Brylcreem beneath a grey felt hat pushed to the back of his head, jacket slung over his shoulder, a collarless shirt unbuttoned at the neck, the sleeves rolled up over thickly muscular arms, hands in pockets and a girl on his arm. And Nancy wondered why *him*, and why *Milly*, for they did not look like a match at all. She had imagined Milly with a clerk or a policeman, someone dull but polite. Not this. This man had a swagger. You wouldn't trust this man at all.

A seagull swooped down and hovered above his head letting out a shrill cry, as though it was calling to him or marking him out in some way, and he shot it a curious look. Then the grey eyes turned to her, looking at her, and she saw his eyebrows go up in slow, dawning surprise as though he knew her and had run into her unexpectedly, which was strange as they had never met before. He stared at her with an odd, dazed expression.

'I'm Joe,' he said, even though they had done all that already, the introductions. But he wasn't introducing himself to them all, he was saying it to her. And the way he said it, it was as though he had said, *It's me, here I am*, though why he would say that or why she would think it, Nancy couldn't say.

She made no reply. Instead, she turned and walked away.

Afterwards, she thought, why had she walked away like that? She didn't know then and she didn't know now. She only knew that she had looked at him and something had lurched within her.

Milly made some excuse; there was some prior engagement, some pressing reason why she and her fiancé must depart at once. No one tried to prevent them leaving and in another moment Milly and her fiancé had gone.

The day ended right then and there, though it was still mid-afternoon. The sun slid behind a cloud and the laughing, shouting, excited voices around her sounded muffled in Nancy's ears. Her head felt clouded and choked and confused and she hardly attended to the words of her two friends. The trek back to the station took an eternity, and when they arrived the London train had just left and it was an hour till the next one, so they sat on a bench and Miriam chattered and Lily ate a bun and Nancy could not speak.

That was all. Nothing had happened, yet everything had happened.

That night, Nancy sat up late filled with a thrilling despair. He was Milly's fiancé.

She went to work the next day and it was like any other day, but it was not like any other day. She could not look at Milly. At the end of the day she came out of the shop and there he was, Milly's young man—Joe—standing outside, and Nancy was not surprised. She knew he was not there to see Milly.

'I had to see you,' was all he said. And Nancy understood because she had to see him too.

A few weeks later Milly's engagement was called off. Milly did not say why and no one asked. She moved about the shop with a pinched look, her movements rigid, jerky, her fingers fidgeting constantly. She looked at no one. She spent most of her time in the room at the back of the shop and some days she did not come in at all. Then one morning the pinched look had gone. Milly emerged from the back of the shop. A month later she married a policeman named Wainwright and left Mme Vivant's employ to take up residence in Old Ford Road in a house that overlooked the park. And when, a short time later, Nancy married Milly's young man, Joe, no one questioned it.

They were married the final weekend in August, just a week before war was declared and the same day Joe had been scheduled to marry Milly—the registry office had already been booked and Joe said, Well, they held the Coronation on the same day, didn't they, even though it was a different king who was crowned? And Nancy, who had stood in the crowd at Westminster and watched the new king pass in his gold state coach on the way to the Abbey, agreed.

༄

Nancy sat up with a start. Her neck and legs were stiff and numb. She had been dreaming of Joe, of their wedding at the registry office at the town hall. Joe's two older brothers and his mother had come and, even though they lived only the other side of Whitechapel Road, the way they carried on Nancy had got the feeling none of them had ever set foot in Bethnal Green before. Joe's older brother had worn a flashy suit to the wedding like some American film star and had a girl on his arm who looked like a tart. His other brother had looked bad-tempered and clearly hadn't wanted to be there at all. As for his ancient mum, she looked like she hadn't left her own house since Queen Victoria died. All the girls from the hat shop had come—except for Milly, of course. And it had rained. That was all she remembered, really. After the wedding Joe said there wasn't room for him and her to live at his mum's house and Nancy had been glad, but Joe knew of a family who had done a midnight bolt from a place in Odessa Street. Two rooms all to themselves, he'd said, if they acted sharpish. So they had acted sharpish and had moved in on the Tuesday. And on the Friday war had been declared.

Ah well, Joe said, we had a nice three days, didn't we?

And so they had, and longer really, for the navy had taken their time sending Joe his call-up papers. But they had, eventually, and a week after he'd gone she'd found out she was carrying a child. She'd been angry with Joe then, angry with the navy and the government and Hitler, because Joe had left just when she needed him. But there was nothing to be done about it. She had the baby on her own, she looked after her little girl on her own. And they had done alright on their own for three years, she and Emily, aside from last winter when they had nearly starved and she had had to beg some shifts down the market and at a pub and had even, on occasion, gone out at dawn scavenging in bins and in the gutters for whatever she might find. Aside from that then, and even then, they had survived. It was surprising that you did survive. People were starving but mostly they did not actually starve. Still, there was no denying things had improved after Joe's return. She had put on a little weight—she was about to put on a whole lot more.

Her hand went to her lower stomach and rested there till she felt calm and still. She wanted this baby. Joe's baby.

'Mum!'

Emily was tugging at her arm.

Billy Rosenthal from upstairs was making his way across the mass of sleeping bodies towards them and he was carrying the baby. There were seven Rosenthal kids, Billy the eldest and the baby just three months old; at least with Len Rosenthal now in Burma Mrs Rosenthal was guaranteed a respite for a time. Len had got a twenty-four-hour pass just over a year ago and the baby was three months old. Please God, his wife had said, that Len get no more leave at least until the war was ended. Mrs Rosenthal, so paper-thin and yellow-tinged, hardly a tooth left in her head, her hair already grey with a permanent cough that racked her body, did not look like she would cope. Sometimes she didn't cope and on those occasions Nancy, who only had the one to look after and who was just downstairs, helped out. This looked like being one of those times.

'Mum says can you take him,' Billy said when he reached them. He was a half-starved waif of a lad with eyes too large for a face gaunt with hunger, in a threadbare pullover and men's trousers that hung off him and looked like they had been lifted from a corpse.

''Course we can, luv,' Nancy said, and she gave Billy a smile as she took the baby. Billy disappeared back into the chaos of bodies. Emily, who had been oddly quiet all night, now perked up. She patted the baby's head in a proprietorial way and launched into a complicated rendition of a nursery rhyme that involved three mice and a clock. Nancy rocked the baby gently on her knee. Her own baby would come in July, which was no time at all away, and perhaps the war would be ended by then. She doubted she could even have got pregnant this time last year, the way things were, the two of them starving—and considering what had happened that was just as well . . .

She had got some shifts working at the Black Bull in Silk-weavers Row, one of the few public houses still open, still with an occasional supply of beer. On one particular night, the coldest night of the winter so far, a GI wandered into the bar. What the Americans were doing in Bethnal Green, Nancy didn't ask. She presumed he was lost. She didn't ask his name; if she had, he would have given her a false one. At closing time, they left the pub together and did it right there in the open in some dingy back alley, fumbling with clothes and stockings and underwear, wildly, like two people out of time without a past or a future. She never saw the GI again and the Black Bull was bombed not long after so there were no more shifts. Afterwards, she thought very little of it. She had been lonely. It was not an excuse but she felt no need of an excuse, it was simply what happened in wartime.

There had been no reason for Joe to find out. No reason at all. But Joe had found out, for she had told him. The fact of this baffled her, even now, two months later. They had gone out, she and Joe, a fortnight or so after Joe's return, when his sunburn had begun to fade and the blisters to heal, leaving Emily asleep in her bed. They had gone to the Oxford Arms, a pub that, so far, had survived the bombing, and on the way home a tart accosted him. The tart—a girl so thin you imagined a bus going past at high speed might drag her into its slipstream and mangle her beneath its wheels like a leaf—tottered on high heels with painted-on stockings, her face a pale moon with a slash of scarlet at the mouth, ghoulish in the blackout, and a dress hitched high up her leg so that you got a flash of her underwear. And if that doesn't turn you off I don't know what will, thought Nancy, unamused, as the girl leered at her husband and draped an arm around his neck as though she, his wife, were not even there. Bloody nerve!

'Wotcha say, darlin'? Fancy a bit of it, do ya?' was the girl's sales pitch and Joe laughed, basking in her lurid advances, and he laughed even louder when Nancy had flung the girl's arm off him and pushed her so hard the girl had staggered backwards.

'Bloody nerve!' Nancy said and Joe said the girl hadn't meant no harm, she was starving, probably hadn't eaten in days, poor kid.

But Nancy was furious.

'We're all bloody starving! We've all gone days on end without eating—d'you think I went out selling my body to the first sailor what come along? That would be alright, would it?'

And he had replied that, if it was a question of survival, well, you did whatever you had to do, he knew that now.

His answer, calm and reasonable as it was, and coloured inevitably by the events he had just undergone, only infuriated her further. 'Well, I'm glad you think that way. So it don't bother you none if I let some other man—a *GI*—have his way with me a while back, while you was out there bobbing about in the sea?'

Why had she said it? Joe would never have known. But out

it had come, just like that, and she had been as surprised as he. Almost.

She regretted it at once. Joe's face changed, the laughter gone, the reasoning, the calm, vanished. Instead a sort of cold hardness replaced it and she felt a flicker of fear. A heartbeat passed, then another, before he exploded, launching into a pile of wooden crates by the kerbside, kicking them into smithereens, and she watched, frozen, unable to stop him and unable to leave, aware that she had been a second away from feeling the force of those kicks herself, that many men would not have aimed their fury at a defenceless pile of wooden crates by the kerbside. When the crates were destroyed he turned away and left her, walked off into the night in the direction from which they had just come.

She had never seen such fury in him. That he had it inside him, that she could be the cause of it, frightened her. She went home quickly. Arriving at the house she somehow expected him to be there ahead of her, though it was impossible. She sat for a time at the place where the kitchen table had once stood. Then she set out the breakfast things for the morning, put their air-raid provisions by the front door in case they were needed and got herself ready for bed. She lay awake, listening for his return.

What if he did not return?

When she heard him finally come through the door many hours had passed, or she imagined they had, and her relief was matched by her fear. He hesitated outside their door and she reasoned that surely he would not hesitate like that if he was still angry, if he was still violent. Perhaps he would sleep in the kitchen, perhaps he would pack his things and leave and she would find him gone in the morning—

He came into their room, got into their bed and lay there, breathing loudly and quickly as though he had been running. The minutes stretched out between them interminably, a kind of torture, the two of them lying side by side in the bed, and she could not think what to say and she could not touch him. Eventually he turned to her, still angry, still wishing to hurt her, she could sense it in him, but instead he flung aside the bedclothes and her nightgown and they did it, right then and there, as loud and angry and frenzied as two animals.

And that—that was the moment! She knew it now, nearly three months later. Another baby, made in war, but this one was a baby created in a moment of utter, complete and angry harmony.

She wanted this baby.

⤫

It was quiet now, surely long after midnight. The Rosenthals' baby had fallen into an exhausted sleep, his tiny fist curled tightly around Emily's thumb, and Emily, having concluded her nursery rhyme, sat quite still though her eyes blinked sleepily and her head lolled, aware that the slightest movement would wake him, as though there wasn't an air raid going on above them.

Eventually Billy returned, his face stern with concentration as he stepped carefully, stern with the seriousness of the task he had been set, though his life was one such task after another.

Nancy handed back the baby. 'He was good as gold,' she whispered, as though whispering in an air raid made any sense.

'Mum says fanks.' And Billy was gone.

Beside her Emily stirred restlessly, a hunger in her eyes that was only partly due to lack of food. 'Mummy, we could *keep* the baby.'

'It ain't our baby.'

'But if we *took* him then we could *keep* him.'

She had not told Emily about the new baby. She knew she should, should prepare her, but she had not. Some part of her wanted to keep the secret all to herself.

A yard or two away sat the posh woman, still awake, clutching her child and her belongings and rocking back and forth, murmuring to herself or to her child, a curious, terrified expression on her face. Everyone else slept. Someone should sit and talk with her, thought Nancy, for the woman was clearly frightened, clearly alone. But Joe had left that morning and the pain of his departure was too fresh. She did not think she could talk to a stranger when the memory of his leaving was so new, so keen. She preferred to keep it to herself, to nurse it until it dulled.

As she thought this her eye was caught by a man up on the platform, a stocky figure, dishevelled and hatless and wearing civilian clothes, who was making his way across the sleeping bodies, picking his way, searching each face, and a shadow crept over her when she ought to have cried with joy, for Nancy had seen that it was Joe.

# CHAPTER SEVEN

The world had gone mad. And it was her own government, it was red tape and regulations that had brought Diana to her knees.

The increasingly stringent, increasingly petty regulations issued by the Board of Trade, the Ministry of Food, the Home Office in relentless and successive waves were every bit as terrifying, in their way, as the waves of Messerschmitts that nightly flew over London. It was simply not possible to keep up with them. Something that had been perfectly legal in peacetime, that had been perfectly legal *last week*, was now illegal, was punishable by fine or imprisonment, was reported in the newspaper to the open-mouthed glee of family members and neighbours and to the utter, undying shame of the poor, horrified, often unwitting defendant. Why, in Chalfont St Giles, no less (!), a young mother had been had up in front of the magistrate for turning on a light in a room before closing the blackout curtains! That was it—that was her crime. Her defence—that her baby had been crying—had been thrown out. She had been fined sixty-five pounds. A week later a woman in Cedars Road had been fined for throwing away a used bus ticket instead of recycling it. She had been fined one hundred pounds—it was that or three months prison. The incident had been reported in the local paper. The woman, a Mrs Purcell, who was fifty-seven and prominent in the local Women's Institute, had not set foot outside her house since.

Diana had begun to open the weekly local paper with a growing dread of who she might find there, waiting in a state of almost permanent anxiety for a constable to knock on her own front door. She had done nothing wrong—her windows were covered and her lights were off, she wasted nothing and she reused every-thing, she bathed in two inches of water and she spoke to no one about anything more confidential than the weather—yet still the idea that one might, however inadvertently, have broken some regulation, kept her awake at night.

But that had all changed in an instant the day she had run into Lance Beckwith in Bond Street two weeks before Christmas.

Diana clutched Abigail and her handbag and the little blue travelling case. Her fingers ached, her arms were numb. She could no longer feel her feet. She felt desperately tired but she would not let herself sleep, not for a minute. Besides which, she needed the lav, though there was no question of going, no question at all.

'Mummy, will we live here now?'

Diana sat up with a start. Abigail was crouched on the hard ground beside her, no longer clutching her mother, no longer panic-stricken, but a worried frown shadowed her face.

'No, darling, of course not! We're just sheltering for the night because it's not safe outside. In the morning we shall go home. Tomorrow night you'll sleep in your own bed.'

'Teddy too?'

'Yes, Teddy too.'

'And Uncle Lance?'

For a moment Diana thought she must have misheard.

She had waited a week after the Bond Street meeting to telephone him. A day or so later she had received a postcard from him saying his telephone was out so she had replied in similar vein, sending a postcard and signing her name '*D*', as though she were a spy in a novel. She had wished she *were* a spy in a novel; she might not feel so unclean. She might feel patriotic. She would make a poor spy, she realised, as she felt things too much, she could not switch off her conscience and she had an idea that a spy—a good spy—would need the ability to operate guilt-free. That would be a blessing, to be guilt-free, but also a small death. One's conscience was, after all, what made one human.

As a result of the postcard she made another trip into London, a few days before Christmas. She would not be taking Abigail with her and pretended, as she dressed her child over breakfast, as they listened together to the Light Programme on the wireless, that it was just a normal day. Which it was until Mrs Probart from next door arrived to babysit. Abigail, at last understanding her mother was planning a trip without her, flung herself at her mother, wrapped her arms around her leg and refused to let go. Mrs Probart, who had four grandchildren in Leicestershire whom she only saw once a year, picked her up and swung her into her lap. 'There now, sweetheart, don't take on so! Your mummy will be back in no time at all. Poor little mite. Hitler himself might be at the front door the way you're carrying on.'

'Oh, Abi, darling!' said Diana, dismayed. 'Mummy has to go out for a while. It won't be for very long.'

But Abigail would not be placated and Diana felt despair. She sank down into the armchair and pulled her hat off. Abigail was hungry, that was all. She just needed enough to eat. But there wasn't enough to eat, there was never enough to eat, and it seemed to Diana that her daughter's cries were a vocal embodiment of her own failure.

'Now, Mrs Meadows, don't be silly. Off you go. We'll be just fine, won't we? We'll have such fun together while Mummy's away, won't we, poppet?'

Abigail screamed.

Diana hesitated, then she stood up, her hat in her hand.

'Go on, dear. Off you go, now, and don't worry about a thing,' said Mrs Probart, and Diana felt her dismay grow. She had told Mrs Probart she had a medical appointment in Town. She had said she was to have some tests. She had been unspecific. She had intimated something was amiss. Mrs Probart had closed her down at once before she could say more. Of course she would babysit, there was no question of it. She was only too happy to help. You *poor* dear.

'Bless you,' Diana said, leaving at once because she could no longer be in the room with this dear old woman who just wanted to help.

She paused at the hallway mirror to reaffix her hat. Then she reapplied her lipstick, though it would be a two-hour journey till she got there. She smoothed her gloves over her fingers and pulled the fox fur stole around her shoulders. Up to this point she had not raised her eyes to her face in the mirror other than to apply the lipstick. Now she looked at herself and saw a woman she did not know, a woman who was about to do something she would have thought unimaginable a few short months ago.

A final farewell to Mrs Probart stuck in her throat and remained unspoken and, under cover of her daughter's cries, she slipped out of the front door and away.

A bus came through the village every hour on the hour but by a quarter past it had still not arrived and twice Diana made to leave and twice she turned back. At last the tiny local bus trundled around the corner and drew up at the bus stop with no explanation of its tardiness over and above a general sense that this was wartime and any bus turning up at all should be a cause for celebration not complaint. Diana boarded and took a window seat. The other passengers were all Home Counties wives like herself, in smart little hats and black gloves and fur-collared winter coats and stout black court shoes, hoping to catch the ten o'clock London train, but it was wartime and no one spoke as the train may or may not arrive and no one had any expectation of getting to Town or of finding any of the things they wanted there even if they did.

Her journey had begun inauspiciously and Diana braced herself for every sort of delay that the war and the bus company and the Metropolitan Railway might throw her way, so she was unprepared for the bus driver putting his foot down and swinging around the country lanes as though he were at Le Mans, getting them to the station with time to spare. She was unprepared for the ten o'clock train arriving to the minute and the guard blowing his whistle fifteen seconds later. She was unprepared for the winding country lanes and the bleak winter fields and the endless rows of hedges flashing past in a rush so that they reached Rickmans-worth in such good time the guard paused for a cuppa as the steam engine was replaced with an electric. In no time they were off, this time on the electrified lines, and they sailed through Pinner and Harrow and Wembley like the *Flying Scotsman*.

Outside Neasden they stopped. There was no warning, there was no station in sight. The train simply stopped; its engines throbbed, softly and distantly, then fell silent. They sat and did not move. Diana sat and did not move. Beyond the window the ravaged suburbs of north-west London lay before her. A sprink-ling of overnight frost still covered the mounds of earth and rubble. Outside no one stirred. The street below her window had an abandoned feel to it. She wondered where everyone had gone. She thought about the train in which she sat perched high on its embankment, sealed and silent with its cargo of wives in their fur coats and their Liberty gloves coming up to Town to shop.

After fifteen minutes the guard could be heard outside down on the tracks, picking his way carefully because the rails were live, announcing that a bomb had landed on the line ahead and they would be stuck until it was defused or went off.

'How thrilling!' announced the portly woman in a fur coat who had got on at Chalfont & Latimer and was seated opposite her, the only other occupant of the compartment.

It was not thrilling. It was infuriating, it was inconvenient, it was a little frightening and it was, potentially, deadly. No single part of it was thrilling. Diana gave her a tight smile. The woman was wearing a very ugly hat that she was almost certainly very pleased with and a great deal of powder on her face that gave the impression she had been caught in a bomb blast and was coated in dust. Diana slid further into the corner, her face close to the window, putting a barrier around herself intended to discourage conversation. It was now entirely possible, perhaps even likely, that she would be prevented from continuing her journey. She studied the sprinkling of frost that lay on the mounds of earth and rubble below.

'My grandchildren will be very excited when I tell them about this!' the portly woman said. It did not quite ring true. It was an act. Her eyes were very wide and blinking rapidly and her gloved fingers moved fretfully over her handbag. The woman was frightened.

Diana gave her another quick smile. She stood up, pulled the window down and stuck her head out. Up and down the length of the train other people were doing the same thing, heads bobbing in and out, looking up and down, looking for the bomb as though there would be something to see. There was nothing to see.

'What can you see, my dear?' said the woman.

'Lots of people sticking their heads out the window,' Diana replied. She sat down and closed the window. 'I expect they'll offload us and send us back on another train and we'll all be home in time for lunch,' she said, because the woman was anxious and it cost her nothing to be friendly, to offer reassurance. She gave an encouraging smile and as she was already pretending to be something she wasn't—a woman going up to Town to undergo medical tests—she found she could also pretend to be something else she was not, which was a young woman who was perfectly calm in a crisis. And it was easier to pretend with a stranger.

She realised it was increasingly likely she would not be able to keep her appointment.

Lance had told her he was not married. No, that was not quite true—he had merely said he was not married, which did not preclude the possibility he *had* been married. Lovers then. Yes, there would have been many, in South America. What sort of women did he like? Not the sort who travelled up to Town on the Metropolitan Line train in prewar fur coats and prim hats and fussy black shoes and their last-but-one pair of silk stockings. No, something altogether more exotic. Or was that simply the impression he wished to give? Perhaps it was all a front and he was as conventional as the next man? He had seemed conventional enough, she supposed, as her brother's school friend twenty or more years ago. She realised she could not read him at all while she knew herself to be an open book. He had guessed at once at her loneliness and her attempt to deny it had made her ridiculous. Of course she was lonely, every wife in England was lonely. She had her child, yes, but he had exposed a longing that was like a physical presence. He had made that longing worse. She was a book that was not merely open, it was underlined and annotated with student notes provided. And yet she had exchanged furtive postcards with Lance, signing her name with a single initial, avoiding any reference to the reason for her visit, merely agreeing a time—did it not suggest that some part of her, at least, welcomed the clandestine?

The train did not move. She pulled out her compact and re-applied her lipstick. They were stuck, all up, for three hours.

At the end of that time the engine started up, the train slid cautiously forward and a round of restrained cheers rang up and down the carriages. All thoughts of shopping in Town had gone and all anyone wanted was to get home so that, when they slunk finally into Finchley Road, the train emptied. The portly woman in the fur coat was the first to leap off. She had not stopped talking from the moment the train had sprung back into life till the moment it had arrived at Finchley Road and her departure left more than a merely physical absence. Diana took a slow, steady breath and stood up, preparing to leave too. But she had invented a medical appointment. If she gave up now her deceit would be for nothing and it had cost her a great deal already. She sat down again and when the train headed into the tunnel towards Baker Street she was the only passenger.

Now that she was in London, the city and the people and tunnels and the trains and the buildings swept over her so that she became tiny and her lie became unimportant. She changed onto the Circle Line, eastbound. The wives and grandmothers from Buckinghamshire and Hertfordshire were gone. Now her fellow passengers were dock workers, civil servants from the various wartime ministries, servicemen and women. At Liverpool Street the train swung southwards and Diana got out. She followed a stream of people up onto the street and along Bishopsgate, turning left and becoming at once lost in the warren of tiny lanes and passages, eventually turning back and retracing her steps and asking for directions. When she finally found Botolph Passage she was so late it was beyond late. But the war turned notions of time on its head and, finally deciding she was at the right place, she walked up to a seedy little door and, after a moment's hesitation, opened it and entered.

The building was an old Victorian warehouse. A hatch and

a little platform far above her head indicated where, in another age, goods had been delivered; the faded letters of a long-gone merchant were just visible on the brickwork. She climbed a narrow stairway that turned in on itself once, twice, a third time before she reached the top floor. She met no one. The place appeared to be deserted. Paint and wallpaper peeled from the walls in great strips with brownish damp stains visible beneath, and at various points someone at some time had placed mouse-traps that contained nothing but a thick layer of dust which suggested that even the mice had departed. At the top of the final twist of the stairs she was met by a passageway and a single unmarked doorway. She stood before the doorway, but only for a moment. She had come this far. She was not about to change her mind.

She straightened the seams of her stockings, raised her hand and knocked twice.

# CHAPTER EIGHT

It was Joe. He was still some distance off, making his way across the sleeping bodies, stopping and searching each face, searching—Nancy presumed—for her.

But how could it be Joe? He was meant to be on his ship, he was meant to be sailing on the evening tide. And he was not in his sailor's uniform. They had seen him off that morning in his new uniform; now, inexplicably, he was back, wearing a battered old duffle coat that did not belong to him and without a hat.

He saw her at that moment and at once started to make his away over, his face set hard, something controlled and awful in his eyes. The shadow that had come over her lengthened until Nancy felt her skin recoil at each new place that it touched. But she sat quite still. She did not want Emily to wake and she reached out blindly and laid a hand on her sleeping child's head.

'They was waiting for me!'

Joe crashed down at her side, crouching low and breathing in short gasps. He had brought with him the cold night air and the damp and the acrid stink of smoke from outside, and something else: an edge that had not been there before, a danger that had a different taste to it than the usual danger of air raids and bombers overhead, of unexploded bombs and landmines.

'What do you mean? Who was waiting for you?' She tried to read the answer in his eyes. They had frightened her a little that first day on the seafront at Clacton, but today they were the eyes of a boy. He was so young, the man in him seemed to have been stripped away.

'The *cops*,' he said.

For a time neither of them spoke. Joe crouched low by her side, his eyes flicking from side to side, watching every movement on the platform around them, and Nancy stared at her hands clenched tightly together in her lap. His words did not sink in and she did not want him to explain them to her. She just knew Joe was back when she had thought he was gone and she wanted to touch him but she felt as though her touch would be unwelcome, that he was locked inside some place without her.

'*Christ!*' he said eventually, and he turned and peered into her face.

And Nancy, dazed by his look, thought: *You were meant to be the strong one*. But now she was not sure.

'Joe, there was a man outside the house. I saw him this evening when the siren went off, standing outside in the shadows. I didn't think nothing of it at the time but he was watching us, I'm sure of it. I think—I'm sure he was a policeman.'

Joe's face fell. He ran his hand over his chin; it had been clean-shaven that morning, but now she heard the bristles scratching against the palm of his hand. 'I almost went to the house—but then I thought you'd be down here so I come here instead.'

But she had not yet told him the worst part: 'Joe, I think he was *here*! The same man—I swear it was him, up on the platform. A few hours ago.'

'Bloody hell,' he whispered.

And she had been certain the man had been looking for someone, that he was looking for Joe—though of course that was just plain daft and she had pushed the thought down but now—

'Joe, what's happened? I don't understand.'

'I told you. They was there. I seen them soon as I arrived at the dockside. Two Docks police and a plainclothes.'

It still seemed bewildering and, perhaps because she did not understand, Nancy felt a flicker of hope. 'But they could have been waiting for anyone, not just you!'

Joe shook his head. 'They takes one look at me and that was it. They was off—blowing whistles and shouting and all sorts. I only just legged it out of there before they could nab me. I hid out in some warehouse.' He paused to lick his lips, then he shook his head. 'Christ, that was hairy! Bombs dropping left and right, and me a bloody sitting duck in a tinderbox. Hours I waited. Then I made a break for it and made me way here.'

Nancy saw him running through the darkness, hiding out in a warehouse, bombs dropping, and suddenly she felt angry. This was his home! They had *no right* to chase him! Not after all had been through, all that time in the ocean, all those men dead . . .

'But how did they know? I mean, why was they waiting for you?'

Joe shook his head. 'No idea. P'raps they been watching me for a while. I don't know.'

Perhaps they had been watching him. She let this sink in. Perhaps they had watched him since October. In early November a convoy had made it through, miraculously dodging every U-boat, arriving at the docks loaded with supplies for a nation with only a few weeks of food reserves left. Armed guards had been stationed at the docks, the government had issued new laws with the severest penalties, and the men unloading the ships were searched routinely going in and out of the wharves. But there was always a way: a guard who could be persuaded to look the other way, a clerk who deliberately miscounted, a hole in the fence that even the dogs hadn't located. And so it was that a steady stream of goods had found their way onto the streets and into back rooms and onto market stalls and beneath the counters of local shopkeepers, and some of it had found its way into the pantry at 42 Odessa Street.

The Levins had eaten well at Christmas. Nancy wore a new pair of silk stockings. Emily tasted her first piece of chocolate, her first banana, her first tinned peach. Joe toasted the navy with a bottle of Canadian scotch. It had all ended abruptly with Joe's recall to duty; the Levins would go back to rations and dried eggs and bread and dripping and five-day-old tea-leaves. These things had seemed appalling a few hours earlier as she had stood on the doorstep and watched him leave.

'But Joe, it was only a few odds and ends. It was just stuff you could carry, stuff we could eat 'cause we was starving. That was all. It weren't enough to hurt no one.'

Joe frowned. He said nothing.

83

'Joe? I mean, if you turned yourself in . . .?'

'If I get caught it's fourteen years. Fourteen years penal servitude.'

Nancy reeled. 'But what about your new ship?'

Joe said nothing. On top of it all he was now a deserter.

～

Neither of them had spoken for some time. Joe seemed quite calm. He sat on the hard ground sharing her blanket, his knees drawn up to his chin and his arms wrapped around them, observing the people sleeping around them as though he and they were separated by something impassable. The people slept or they got up and shuffled over to the stinking latrines. They coughed and snored and their babies cried, sleeping on as the raid continued far above, sleeping on as Joe silently observed them, as Nancy silently observed Joe.

Whoever had once owned the buff-coloured duffle coat was at least two sizes smaller than Joe and it was stretched tightly across his shoulders and ended above his wrists, showing an expanse of black-haired forearm. Where had he ditched his sailor's uniform? Nancy wondered. The thought of him tearing it off and stuffing it into a ditch or into the river appalled her. There seemed no way back from it. No way to undo what had happened. The world around them had changed, shifted on its axis so that everything looked the same but nothing was the same. A hope that had glowed inside her when she had thought the war must surely end soon and perhaps Joe would survive and make it home had withered and was now finally extinguished.

Emily slept on, lying between them, and this was a good thing.

84

Joe did not touch her, even when she murmured and fidgeted in her sleep under the blanket to find a warmer spot, a more comfortable position. Instead he hugged his knees more tightly, not looking at her, so that it seemed to Nancy that now he was on the run, a fugitive, he was tainted. He *was* tainted, they both were, and she felt them separate and cut off from everyone else, just as though they were both of them adrift on an ocean. She would have preferred that, she told herself, to this terrifying and silent waiting to be arrested.

And if he was arrested . . .

She could not bear it. All that had seemed unbearable before dissolved now into nothing and she wondered at herself for all the worrying and fretting over trifles that no longer mattered. She could not feel her feet, her hands, her lips, the tips of her fingers. She was numb with cold but it was a coldness that came from within and had nothing to do with the blasts of chilled air that blew out of the tube tunnel or the frozen January night far above. She was too cold even to reach out and touch him. They were separate and cut off from everyone but they could not touch each other.

'What if you explained it to them?' she found herself saying. 'If you told them we was starving, that you took one or two things. Maybe it wouldn't be that bad. Maybe it would be only a short stretch.'

'I can't go to prison.'

And that was that. Besides, he was a deserter, too, now. There was no explaining it, there was no good outcome. She nodded, accepting what he said, allowing the hopelessness to swallow them up.

'Joe, what we gonna do?'

But instead of answering her question he shook his head in wonder. 'You wouldn't believe what it's like up there in the street. Lucky for me, I s'pose, hardly any folk about up there, but you wouldn't believe it. It's like the world's ended.'

Nancy made no reply. The world *had* ended and she didn't need to go up to the street to see it. They fell into another silence, which Joe finally broke. 'I'll go to Ireland,' he said, turning to her. 'If I can.'

Nancy looked away. She had had him to herself for such a short time, three months, which was longer than most women got with their husbands in wartime—longer than her own mother had got with her father—but still the unfairness of it took her breath away. She had got used to him lying beside her in the bed; she had got used to them curled up against each other on those dark winter mornings with the ice on the windows and their breath hanging in the air like a moment in time caught forever. She remembered how, on Christmas Day, he had sat cutting shapes out of a folded newspaper and turned them, magically, into hats, and how Emily had shrieked with laughter and how, later that evening, the electricity had gone out and the look on his face when she had immediately grabbed the torch and gone off to check the mains switchboard—as though she hadn't learned how to cope while he was away, learned how to be the man! And some men might have resented that but when she returned, knocking the dirt from her shoes and the dust from her hair, it was to find him and Emily playing tiddlywinks together on the floor by candlelight. She couldn't think of a time when she had loved him more than at that moment.

Except perhaps than at this moment.

'Ireland?' repeated Nancy bleakly. 'But—how?'

Joe shook his head. 'Don't know. I can get to Liverpool at least. Harry will help me. He'll know a bloke who'll get me some papers. Once I get to Liverpool I'll be alright. I'll get on a boat, I'll be safe.'

Nancy listened but his words seemed without meaning, insubstantial, like raindrops on glass. Harry was the elder brother who had been bad-tempered at the wedding and Joe saw him infrequently. She had never known him turn to Harry for help.

'But Ireland . . .?'

Joe reached out, not looking at her, his hand covering hers, his fingers curling tightly around her fingers. They stayed like that for a time and Nancy thought, Ireland–Ireland–Ireland.

'When will you go?'

'Soon. Before dawn anyway. While the raid's still on. Safer then.'

'Don't go back to the house, Joe, promise me you won't!'

'I won't go near the place, don't worry about that.' He turned to look at her again. 'But you have to get rid of anything that's left over—the scotch, the shoes, stockings, all of it. Toss it—toss the lot, or you'll be done for receiving. Promise me you'll do it soon as you get home tomorrow morning!'

'I promise, Joe.'

He nodded slowly, taking a long, deep breath, and they fell silent again. They had made the best plans they could for the time being. There was nothing left to arrange.

He would be safe in Ireland, thought Nancy, if he made it there. But what then? He could never return. The war might end but Joe could never return. If he did, he would be arrested.

'I'll send word,' he said. 'You can come over later, when it's safe. You can join me.'

Nancy tried to imagine the two of them, her and Emily, on the boat with a small suitcase, arriving in Dublin (did the boat go to Dublin or somewhere else? She did not know) and him standing at the quayside in an Irish suit and an Irish hat, smiling and waving. She did not know what an Irish suit or hat looked like, or if Irish men wore suits at all. And meanwhile, it was after two in the morning and soon he would be leaving. She smiled and thought, *But I cannot bear it.*

The night wore on and the air raid that did not let up outside seemed less real to her than ever before. She wanted it to go on forever.

'Soon as I get there,' Joe said, as though they had been speaking all this time and not sitting in a dreadful silence, 'I'll send word. I'll get work and you and Em will come over.' He smiled and she knew he was picturing it, right now, in his head.

But it was no good.

'Joe, we live *here*. This is our home. What we gonna do in Ireland?' She hated that she had said it out loud when she had wanted so much to keep the thought to herself, and she saw the determination slip for a moment from his face. He squeezed her hand though he made no attempt to answer her question.

But what *would* they do in Ireland? This was her home and it made no difference that her mother was from a Northum-berland coalmining town that Nancy had never set foot in, that her father had deserted her before her birth. What mattered was that she had been born in the upstairs room of a boarding house in Shoreditch and London was in her blood: Stepney and Shoreditch, Mile End and Poplar, Spitalfields, Aldgate and Bethnal Green, Whitechapel Road and Commercial Road and Brick Lane and Cable Street and Vallance Road, Victoria Park in the east and Bishopsgate in the west—these places were the perimeter of her world.

'Once we're there, we can go anywhere,' Joe said, turning to her, looking into her eyes, pleading with her to see what he saw, for he had seen the world from the deck of a ship and it held no fears for him. 'We could go to America.'

And it was a measure of the love she felt for him at this moment that she returned his look and said, 'Alright.'

So that was it: they would go to America.

After that they spoke no more. The bombing did not let up and it was like the early days of the Blitz, back in '40 and '41, but Nancy found it no longer mattered what happened to the city above for she had already left it.

'It's time,' Joe said.

Nancy watched in a sort of fog as Joe scanned the sea of bodies, scanned the entrance to the platform, scanned every face. Then he turned back to her and held her tightly for a minute, he touched his hand to Emily's cheek, and he was gone. She did not watch him go, she would not look. It was worse than seeing him go off to the war, worse than seeing him return to his ship, worse than knowing he might end up dead at the bottom of the sea, blown up, captured, drowned; it was worse than all this.

I cannot bear it, she thought, but I *will* bear it and Joe will send for us and we will go to America.

# CHAPTER NINE

'I'd almost given you up,' Lance said, ushering Diana inside.

'I know. There was a bomb on the line at Neasden.'

'Oh, bad luck,' he said, as though she had lost a button from her coat or left her umbrella on the train. 'Well, you're here now. I was just about to go out, actually, so you timed it well.'

Only in wartime could almost four hours late be described as timing it well.

Lance was in the same light grey, wide-lapelled suit as before, a crisp white shirt, open at the neck. But the tan had faded and there was no sign of the silk scarf. His hair, as black as before, was swept back from his face and ruffled as though he had run his fingers through it. It needed a cut, was too long, somehow, for England in the winter, though Diana had a sense he was unaware of this. The soft felt hat lay before him on the desk of the small office. For it was a small office. She had not known what to expect—his flat, perhaps, or a room in a lodging house. But this was an office-cum-storeroom with boxes of all shapes and sizes lining three of the four walls from floor to ceiling. A small gas heater and a battered filing cabinet, two folding chairs and a packet of sandwiches, half eaten, on the desk completed the picture. Lance swept the hat and the sandwiches to one side and pulled out one of the chairs for her, removing yesterday's newspaper which lay open on it.

'Sit, sit,' he said, indicating she should take the seat. 'Cuppa?'

He located a kettle and two cracked white porcelain cups minus their saucers and disappeared through a doorway at the rear of the office into a second room from where, a moment later, she heard the sound of a tap being turned on and a match being struck. He returned a moment later and pulled out the other chair and sat down, regarding her exactly as he had in the cafe. But now the tension between them was of a different nature— they were no longer strangers linked by a young man's death. Now they were co-conspirators. The rules had changed subtly. Not subtly, for Diana felt like someone standing on a precipice about to jump.

The kettle began to whistle softly.

Would Lance expect more from her than just payment in money? If he did, would she oblige? She did not know. The rules were unclear to her. He had guessed so easily at the loneliness inside her. The room was horribly cramped and sordid and his hat and sandwiches were on the desk. He had swept them aside and, if he did expect more than just money, perhaps it was here on the desk that they would do it.

'Milk? No sugar, I'm afraid. Come to think of it, no milk either. Black tea okay?'

'Fine. Thanks.'

He handed her a cup, took a mouthful of his own tea, placed it on the desk and leaned forward.

'So, Diana, tell me. What do you want? I have pretty much anything you can name: tinned sardines, tinned pears, tinned peaches, condensed milk, powdered milk, cigarettes, spirits, soap, American chocolate, Brazilian coffee and as much Spam as you can carry. Nothing perishable, of course, but other than that, sky's the limit. What's it to be? I've even got a couple of US Air Force parachutes back there—' he indicated the back room with a jerk of his head '—don't ask how! So if you feel like running up your own pair of under-things on the Singer, be my guest.'

Diana's head was spinning. The cornucopia of goods he had just reeled off was making her feel a little faint. Were they here, in this room? She could smell them, surely; yes, she could smell each item. Her mouth went dry. The room, Lance, faded from her vision and she saw, with frightening clarity, herself pushing a bowl of tinned peaches towards Abigail, pouring the condensed milk over, Abigail's eyes wide and bright as searchlights, her delighted, astonished squeal as she tasted the peaches, the condensed milk for the very first time.

'Doesn't the US Air Force need its parachutes?' she replied faintly.

'Not these ones!' He laughed. 'Bloody great tear in them.' Then he became serious. 'Diana, if you're worried about where this lot came from, you should be. It's contraband. Black market. Don't delude yourself. Everything I have here is purloined and someone, somewhere is going to go without so that you and your little girl can have it.' He paused and gave an expressive shrug. 'If you don't want it, well, that's okay. I won't think less of you.

I might even think more of you. But if you *do* want it, don't kid yourself.' He took another sip of his tea. 'And so we're clear, if you get caught with this lot on you, you're on your own. This office shuts down and disappears on a regular basis. It has to. I wouldn't have survived this long otherwise. You get caught, you're on your own, and we're not talking a minor motoring offence. This is serious. You understand?'

'Of course. I am not a child. I understand the risks.' She spoke quickly because his words terrified her. And her reply terrified her more. 'How much does it cost?'

'Tell me what you want and I'll tot it up.'

So she wrote down her order and he did some arithmetic and she pulled out her purse and handed over a large number of notes then waited as he packed the various articles into a bag for her and handed them over. At the last minute he silently placed an extra tin of condensed milk into her package with a wink and she remembered that he was her dead brother's school friend, that Lance had waited outside the church at John's funeral to shake her parents' hands, and the dismay that she had been keeping in check swelled inside her. She left as soon as she could, not meeting his eyes, and vowing that, should she make it home, she would never, never return.

But she had returned—of course she had—on four separate occasions, each time lying to Mrs Probart about further hospital tests, the hint of a minor surgery that might be required, and Mrs Probart, in her kindness, her concern, had popped over every few days to see how she was faring, patting her hand, bringing vegetables from her own garden because the vegetables grew in Mrs Probart's garden where none grew at The Larches and

Diana, dismayed by her neighbour's generosity, tried in vain to refuse them.

And Abigail grew sleek and plump and her cheeks were rosy and her appetite grew and she became used to the sweet and sugary things that now routinely came her way. And she whined and sulked and threw her bowl and took off her shoes and threw them at her mother when the sweet and sugary things ran out and the cupboard became bare again. And so Diana returned, making the journey into London and persuading herself it was just a social call, that she was visiting an old friend of the family. And Lance played along. They talked and drank tea and the transaction at the conclusion of the call was handled swiftly and discreetly. His office remained at Liverpool Street and she told herself this was a good sign, for it suggested the danger was minimal, but his words to her that first time haunted her: *If you get caught with this lot on you, you're on your own.*

Her dreams were filled with policemen. When she saw one for real in the course of her day—the local bobby on his bicycle, the constable standing on the village green taking down notes following some motoring accident or talking to the landlord of the pub about some licensing issue—the blood drained from her face and she turned and walked in the other direction, even on the days she walked with Abigail to watch the ducks carrying nothing more incriminating than an umbrella and a raincoat.

Christmas had come and gone and so too the worst of January before Diana had returned for one final visit, and this time she had brought Abigail with her. She had done this because she could no longer bring herself to lie to Mrs Probart, and because she now understood that payment for the goods was purely monetary, that nothing else was expected of her. Besides, somehow it did not seem quite so furtive, so underhand, going in to London, going to visit Lance, when she had her child with her.

'Where are we going?' Abigail had demanded that morning, unconvinced by a journey that did not involve the park or food or toys.

'We're going to pay a visit to your Uncle Lance. He can't wait to meet you. If you're very, very good, he might give you something.'

'What? What will he give me?' Abigail wanted to know, accepting the fact of a hitherto-unknown Uncle Lance without a second thought.

It was Diana's fifth trip. This will be the last, she told herself.

The day was bitterly cold. A raid in London the previous night, the first in months, had disrupted the trains and consequently they had arrived at Lance's office much later than usual and she had said nothing to him about bringing her child. She had hesitated outside the old warehouse, suddenly uncertain, with Abigail pulling impatiently on her hand and grizzling with exhaustion after the long, long journey. But Lance had been charming, had taken to Abigail at once, the way some men do with small children, finding things for her to play with, dandling her on his knee and teasing her, laughing indulgently when she showed off and not minding too much when she got overly tired and became petulant and bad-tempered. But when Diana had taken Abigail to the lavatory in preparation for the long homeward journey, waiting outside the tiny cubicle to check she was managing alright, Lance had come in and taken her arm and pulled her outside.

'That was a mistake, Diana, bringing your little girl. How exactly are you going to ensure she says nothing? What is she going to say when the nice policeman sits her down and asks her where all this lovely food comes from?'

He spoke in a low tone, quite pleasantly, but she could see the fury in his eyes and she was shocked by it, feeling her face grow hot.

'I'm sorry, I—I didn't think.'

'No, you didn't. You shouldn't have brought her here. You shouldn't have told her my name. It was stupid.'

Abigail had emerged then, pulling at her dress, her shoes damp where she had stepped in a puddle or had a little accident, and Diana busied herself helping Abigail to wash her hands at the cracked and stained basin in the corner.

When they returned to his office Lance was sweeping piles of papers into a box. She saw other boxes hastily sealed and stacked haphazardly on top of each other. *This office shuts down and disappears on a regular basis*, Lance had said. He offered to see them out but it was perfunctory—he clearly wanted them gone—and Diana said no, thank you, they could manage. They had left in a hurry down the long, winding staircase, the small travelling case, heavy now with its illicit cargo, banging against Diana's legs and Abigail trying valiantly to keep up.

It *was* stupid, Diana realised, fighting back sudden, ridiculous tears as they reached the ground floor at last. We won't come back, she resolved. We won't return here and I shan't see Lance again, or not for a long time. And Abigail would say nothing. Abigail would forget quickly where they had been and why. She would forget there had ever been a man called Uncle Lance.

Children did forget things very quickly—she knew that even if Lance, who had no children of his own, did not.

They had arrived at Lance's office much later than usual because of the train disruption and they emerged now into the evening blackout, and in her anxiety to get home Diana had boarded the wrong bus. And now here they were, in the East End of London, caught in their first ever real air raid. If she was asked, she would say they had gone to a pantomime up west and got on the wrong bus. It was half true. But no one had asked, and in the meantime her fingers ached where she was clutching the handle of her case so tightly.

ᶜᵛᵔ

The bombing had let up for the time being, or had moved away, and into the silence a child cried.

Diana clutched the handle of the case and her fingers ached. It was a small overnight case, very lightweight, in pale blue vinyl with a metal handle and gold clasps burnished with age and use. Inside it was lined with imitation pale blue silk with a deep pocket sewed into the lid in the same material and two canvas straps with buckles with which one could secure the contents tightly. It was Gerald's case, though Diana had never seen him use it and she wondered if he had inherited it, perhaps, at some time. It was rather cheap and battered, and next to her Florida alligator handbag with the morocco leather purse nestling inside it looked cheap, out of place, but it was lightweight and that was the thing.

The little girl was awake. Her mother, the woman with the fair hair and the shaped eyebrows, had been minding a baby earlier, brought by a small, grubby child who had emerged out of the chaos to hand it to her, and though the baby clearly was not her own she had walked up and down with it, unconcerned by its screaming. A bomb had fallen and another and the woman had not flinched. A near miss, the rumble and shaking of the station, the horror of their crowded circumstances, none of it touched her. The woman was fearless and splendid, and Diana imagined her the heroine of a government propaganda poster captioned *Hitler Beware! Mothers of Britain Stand Firm!*—or something nonsensical like that.

Of course it was absurd and Diana had looked away before the woman noticed her watching.

After a time the baby had been reclaimed by the same small, grubby child, its place taken by a man in a duffle coat with an unsettling intensity in his eyes who had sat with the woman for a time and they had whispered together, touched once, then sat in silence. Eventually the man had got up and gone. Now the woman sat and did not move. Did not smoke, even. During the man's visit her little girl had slept, her head on her mother's lap, but now the child was wake and she watched Diana with a face that showed no expression, with eyes that saw through the cheap pale blue vinyl of her case to the bounty within.

Diana clutched the handle of the case and her fingers ached. She uncurled them to flex each one. She could not sleep and she would not sleep, there was no question of it.

'Need the lav!' said Abigail, pulling at her mother's hand.

Diana had no feeling in her legs and wondered if she could stand even if she wanted to, but there was nothing for it. She got stiffly to her feet. Ought she to take the case? She took her handbag and left the case—they could hardly take it with them—casting a doubtful glance around her to see who was watching. The little girl was watching. Everyone else slept. The little girl did not move but her eyes saw everything.

Diana took Abigail's hand and they picked their way over the people towards the large tarpaulins up on the platform proper. The smell grew more intense as they approached and they held their handkerchiefs over their faces. Naturally there was a queue and Abigail cried, 'Mum, need to go!' because now it was urgent. Abigail hopped and crossed her legs and eventually it was their turn. They braced themselves and found a latrine and it was best not to look where they were stepping or look at anything at all really, and when it was done and they realised there was nowhere to wash their hands, they came out.

And Diana saw Lance Beckwith leap off the escalator and emerge onto the platform, breathless and dishevelled and clearly terrified.

# CHAPTER TEN

Joe had gone. He had appeared out of thin air and their lives together here in London had ended. Now they must wait. On some unnamed date in the future, Nancy would pack up what remained of their lives and she and Emily would leave London forever for some unknown and undreamed-of place across the sea.

And each second that passed took Joe further away from them.

The blood pumped in her ears. She was one heartbeat away from leaping to her feet, scooping up Emily and running with her up the escalators and into the fire-stricken night, running after Joe, calling out his name, searching place after place for him and finding him or not finding him—either way, each possibility seemed a catastrophe.

But Nancy did not leap up. She did not run after Joe. The blood pumped in her ears. And meanwhile Emily slept on, unaware of the cataclysmic events that had transpired, that would change her life. The war would end and other dads would come home but Emily's dad would not. There would be no medals and his name would not appear on any war memorial.

But Emily was not asleep. She lay unmoving beneath the blanket, her head on her mother's lap, staring at the blue travelling case that the smart woman had brought with her down to the shelter and that clearly contained nothing of use in an air raid as the woman had not opened it once but had sat stiffly clutching the handle. Now the woman had gone, taking her little girl with her, and the case was left behind.

The distant boom of an explosion caused the floor to vibrate and Nancy looked up. Small cracks appeared in the ceiling, dust trickling down, and Emily's hand darted out and made a grab, not for the blue travelling case, but for the little girl's teddy bear that lay beside it, almost hidden and similarly abandoned.

A second explosion echoed distantly and all around heads bobbed up, bodies shifting, pulling blankets closer about them as though a blanket could protect you from a bomb blast. The bombing had picked up again and a murmur of voices accompanied it. People were frightened when no one had seemed very frightened before. It was being woken from their sleep that did it.

The teddy bear was gone, as though it had never existed, and Emily pulled the blanket tightly around herself. Of the mother and her child there was no sign. Presumably they had gone to the latrines and when they returned the little girl would discover her teddy was missing. Her mother would be angry with her, would conduct a search, would tell the child off and the child would cry.

The teddy would not be found. The mother would not confront the people seated around her, she was not the type. She would tell the child to be quiet. She would tell the child she would buy her another teddy bear.

Nancy searched for her cigarettes, pulled one from the packet and stuck it in her mouth, striking the match and observing the flame flare, tasting the dry little flakes of tobacco on her lips. The tip of the cigarette glowed redly.

She could hear a baby crying, screaming furiously, and she realised she needed to be up and moving about, that something might snap if she did not get up at once. She located the Rosenthals easily enough. In the heaviest months of the Blitz the railway company had installed bunks up on the platform proper and this was where the Rosenthals had positioned themselves, looking very settled with a bunk of their own, with their bundle of blankets and pillows and a foul-smelling potty covered with a cloth for the youngest ones to use as the trip to the latrines was not always safe. Billy Rosenthal saw her and waved. He was squatting beside his younger brother, Stanley, and had one of the littlest girls—Pamela or Barbara, she didn't know which, always had trouble distinguishing the younger ones—bouncing on his knee. Mrs Rosenthal was nursing the baby, or trying to. His face was red and scrunched up and he was bawling fit to burst. Mrs Rosenthal saw Nancy and gave a wan smile which turned to relief as Nancy took the baby off her. Nancy had brought half a sausage roll with her which she divided into pieces. The baby was too young for solids really, but she put some on her finger and let him suck it. The rest she shared among the youngest kids.

Nancy saw them then, the mother and daughter, emerging from the latrines a little distance away, faces white and shocked, as well they might be—a visit to the latrines at this stage of the night was not for the faint-hearted. The little girl was adjusting her skirt, holding out her hands to her mother as though she did not know what to do with them. The mother spoke to her, offered a handkerchief, then looked up, and perhaps she saw Nancy and recognised her and perhaps she did not. Either way, the child spotted something at that moment and darted off and they were gone.

'He's enough to frighten off Adolf all on his very own,' said Mrs Rosenthal of the baby, pushing the hair out of her exhausted face. Her thin fingers seemed to be just bone and her dress was soaked through with sweat as though it was summer and not the middle of winter.

'He's got a set of lungs on him, alright,' Nancy agreed, but she didn't mind it, didn't mind it at all. There was something special about this one. She had been there at his birth, holding Mrs Rosenthal's hand in the squalid upstairs room in Odessa Street on a wet Sunday afternoon the day after Halloween. A midwife had come, finally, when they had all but given her up, and the baby had stuck fast so that Mrs Rosenthal had screamed like a dying animal and there had been a moment when they'd thought the baby was lost. Perhaps that would have been for the best—the midwife had certainly seemed to think so, for when the baby was at last ejected from poor Mrs Rosenthal's broken and spent body, she had held it up by its ankles, all bloodied and crumpled and purple, like a dead thing already, and she had looked at Mrs Rosenthal and at the squalor of the room they lived in and at the six other kids sitting outside waiting, wretched and unfed, in the stairwell and she had said, 'Do you want this one?' The baby was almost dead anyway; it was a small matter to help it on its way. ''Course I want it!' Mrs Rosenthal had declared, loud as you like. 'He's my little boy. 'Course I want him!' And now the baby was three months old and thriving, as much as any baby thrived down here, with a horde of brothers and sisters to look out for it.

'You alright, luv?'

Nancy looked down and saw Mrs Rosenthal studying her, a little frown on her face. Was she alright? The question took Nancy by surprise. Their lives, hers and the Rosenthals' (a shared toilet out the back, paper-thin walls, a meter for the electricity that broke down without warning, an intermittent water supply, uncarpeted stairs and a ceiling that shook every time someone slammed a door), were as intimately entwined as that of husband and wife. She had held Mrs Rosenthal's hand while her baby was stuck fast inside her yet Nancy had never once used Mrs Rosenthal's first name (which was Sylvia) and she had never once gone to her with a problem of her own that was not connected to the outside toilet or the electricity meter or the intermittent water supply. They were intimately entwined but utterly private from one another.

And so Mrs Rosenthal's question took her by surprise.

''Course,' she said, patting the baby's back. I'll tell Emily she must give it back, she decided, for the little girl and her teddy bear had been on her mind, though she had only now realised it.

'Your Joe got off alright to his new ship, did he?'

Nancy buried her face in the baby's blanket and made no reply.

When she and Emily were gone would the Rosenthals move into their rooms? They would leave at night, just before dawn, for that was the way it was done in Odessa Street, and she did not know if they would say goodbye to the Rosenthals before they left or not. The war might be over by then. Len Rosenthal might have returned—or he might be dead.

'Yes, Joe got off alright.'

'It's a bloody miracle,' said Mrs Rosenthal, indicating the baby, who had stopped crying and was now sleeping, good as gold.

And Nancy agreed that yes, it was a miracle. She handed the baby back—the urge that had made her leap up and abandon Emily was fading. She made some excuse and left. She would see them in a few hours when they returned at dawn, worn out and bedraggled, to the house—if the house had survived—and they would all get on with their lives just as though nothing had happened, just as though Joe was back on a ship and at sea.

The bombing continued, if anything had worsened, and people were moving restlessly about so that her path was blocked and she was forced to take a circuitous route back. The rows of bunks continued on down the length of the platform, two, three, four people wedged into each one, and as she passed they watched her, every one of them, as men in a cellblock might watch a new inmate.

She felt again the urgency to be moving, active, but now it drove her back to Emily, drove her to think about her own baby growing inside her, hers and Joe's. Let it be alright, let this baby be alright. And she wondered then where the baby would be born.

As she reached the final row of bunks right at the end of the platform a hand shot out and grabbed her. Fingers closed around her arm, gripping it, pulling her in, pulling her down, and she found herself seated on one of the bunks facing Milly Fenwick and two staring little boys.

'Hello, Nancy,' said Milly. 'We thought it was you.'

# CHAPTER ELEVEN

'Mummy, look—it's Uncle Lance!' said Abigail, and she tugged at Diana's hand.

But Diana did not move. For he stood with his coat flapping open and shirt collar awry, his hair unkempt and fallen forward over his eyes, out of breath and glancing behind him at the escalator down which he had just come, snatching at his hat and mopping his brow with it. This was not the urbane Lance in a silk scarf recently returned from South America who had sat across from her at the Conduit Street cafe, nor was it the hard-nosed Lance conducting dubious transactions from behind his desk eight, nine hours earlier. And this was not Lance caught in an air raid—she had an idea he would not be concerned by a raid. No, this was something quite different.

*You shouldn't have brought her here*, Lance had said. *You shouldn't have told her my name. It was stupid*, as though simply by bringing her child with her Diana had somehow compromised his safety, as though his very existence was so precarious. At the time she had been furious, embarrassed. Now, in the dimly lit concourse, she saw the whites of his eyes, wild and staring.

'Mummy—want more chocolate!'

And in a second Abigail was gone, letting go of her mother's hand and darting off into the crowd after him.

'Abigail, *stop!*'

Diana lunged after her. She could see Abigail's tiny figure just ahead of her, just out of reach, weaving between the people, and just beyond her was Lance, who had turned to the left and then to the right and now seemed almost to retrace his steps. Perhaps he saw Abigail or had heard her cry, a small child in a tweed coat with little mittens sewn to the cuffs and smart little shoes with silver buckles running towards him, and for a moment he seemed to regard her in bemusement.

Abigail, who had run full tilt at a man she had met only once in her life and in a place that was utterly unfamiliar and alien to her, suddenly lost her nerve and pulled up short. This gave her mother precious seconds to swoop down and whisk the girl into her arms. Whether she would, at this point, have raised her hand to wave to Lance or opened her mouth to call out to him afterwards Diana did not know, but before she had time to wave or call out, before she had time to wonder why, when Lance's office was at Liverpool Street, he would choose to take shelter in Bethnal Green, three men appeared out of nowhere and surrounded him.

At first Diana could make no sense of it. The men seemed to have followed him into the station, pursuing him down the escalator, and what flashed into her head was the boxes hastily sealed and haphazardly stacked in Lance's office and the frown on his face that she had assumed was for herself but that she now realised had been for this.

She did not move, though Abigail squirmed furiously in her arms. The three men surrounded him and Diana thought of children in a playground surrounding their victim. But these were not schoolboys. She smelled the cheap cigarettes they smoked and she saw the brims of their hats, stained dark and steaming slightly from the rain, though it had not been raining earlier; she saw a rash of dark stubble on a chin, the callouses and blackened fingernails of another, the fresh mud caked on the heel of a boot—impressions, fleeting but profound. If words were exchanged she could not hear them, and in a moment, no longer, they separated, the three men melting away into the crowd, gone.

Lance remained where he stood, alone now and dazed it seemed, then he reeled away. His felt hat had come off and rolled away and Diana found it at her feet. She could see the cream silk lining inside the hat which ordinarily would display the mark of a good tailor but the lettering, she saw, was in Spanish.

She stepped forward, her heart thudding, but still she did not call out.

He made for the latrines, though he stumbled almost at once and put out a hand to the wall to steady himself. His hand slid, leaving a dark mark on the painted brickwork, like soot, thought Diana, as though Lance had been out there in the air raid calmly lighting a fire. Or oil, perhaps it was oil. He sank to the ground and did not move and his hand slid from the wall creating an arc as he fell. And it wasn't soot or oil.

# CHAPTER TWELVE

'Nancy Keys. Who would have thought?'

For a moment Nancy could not reply. It was Milly Fenwick, who had left Madame Vivant's hat shop to marry a police constable and live in a house near the park. Milly Fenwick, whose wedding Nancy had not been invited to, whom she had never—in five years of air raids and bombing—seen sheltering here in this Underground station; and whom, if she thought about it—which she had not—she would have assumed had her own cosy little Anderson shelter in her own little back garden overlooking Vic Park. Yet here she was, Milly, just the wrong side of thirty and looking it, too, the long shadows failing to hide the lines at her neck and mouth, the puckering of lips that perhaps no longer held any of her own teeth, the small eyes that had swept over Nancy unseeingly all the years they had worked side by side but that now fixed on her and would not let go.

Here was Milly, whose fiancé Nancy had stolen.

'Milly.'

She wore a clever little hat that might have come from Bond Street but might, equally, have come from a stall down Petticoat Lane, in a prewar winter coat with fur trim (but rabbit not beaver) and lace-up Oxfords in patent leather with a Continental heel that would have cost half her pay packet in 1939 but that five years later she was wearing in an air raid, her hair—no sign of grey yet—held neatly in place underneath her hat by a hairnet (no headscarf for her), her lips carefully outlined and coloured in lipstick an unflattering shade of mauve, her face thinner (though everyone's face was thinner), and you might describe her as slim if you were being generous, gaunt if you were not. And seated on the bunk beside her were two identical little boys in short trousers and matching pullovers, hair neatly parted and combed, observing Nancy unblinkingly from behind the lenses of large wire-framed spectacles.

'Fancy us seeing you here,' Milly said, as though they had met somewhere quite improbable, like a West End show or a posh teashop in Piccadilly, and not in the only shelter for miles in the suburb they had both worked in and both, presumably, still lived in. The remarkable bit was that they had never run into each other before tonight. Or perhaps they had, Nancy realised. Perhaps Milly had seen her many times but had never before stopped her.

In which case, why now, why tonight?

Milly's eyes were very bright and they did not blink, not once, nor did they leave Nancy's face.

'These are my two boys. Nigel and Adrian. Boys, say hello, please.'

The two small boys regarded Nancy with a curious intensity. 'Hello, please,' they responded in unison and their mother gave an indulgent, slightly irritated smile.

'How d'you do?' Nancy replied, unnerved by their unblinking gaze, unnerved by Milly's unblinking gaze. The bunk they were seated on was very low—they were stacked three high and this was the lowest bunk and the space between the thin little mattress and the slats of the bunk above was about the distance from hip to shoulder. The two little boys could sit quite happily cross-legged on the bunk with no inconvenience. Milly, and now Nancy, had to hunch down so that their heads were almost below their shoulders. It was restrictive. It was oppressive.

'They're both bright as buttons,' Milly said, leaning forward a little and speaking slowly, carefully, as though she had said something not commonplace at all, but quite profound. 'Their dad says he can't understand where they get it from but you only have to look at Reg to see it.'

The boys, who were bright as buttons, continued their silent scrutiny.

Reg was Milly's husband. Nancy had met him once when he had come by the shop after work to see Milly and had found him dull and unimaginative. If his boys were bright as buttons they certainly didn't get it from their dad. But if Milly believed in her husband, who was she to mock? They had never been friends— Milly had not encouraged it, but was not some guilt attached to herself, to the other girls, Miriam and Lily? Had they, perhaps, excluded Milly? Was it not their fault that Milly had remained outside, alone? And now here they were, she and Milly, both married, both mothers, both sheltering in a raid, and really what was there to set them apart?

'My Emily's just turned three,' Nancy said.

But there *was* something to set them apart, something awful and earth-shattering that could not be undone, that even a war could not soften.

Milly leaned forward so that her face was inches from Nancy's and quite suddenly the very air around them turned chilly.

'*Do you think I care?*'

Nancy sat perfectly still. She had wondered in the weeks after she and Joe had begun courting what it would be like if they ran into Milly one evening at the pictures or dancing at the Palais, but they never had run into her, not once in all that time, and gradually the likelihood of it had diminished and the likelihood of Milly finding out, or caring, had diminished with it. Now it was certain and immediate. For Nancy Keys was Nancy Keys no more. She was Nancy Levin and the woman seated before her, an inch from her face, was the girl Joe would have married, and never mind the house overlooking the park or the two neatly dressed little boys, this was the real Milly Fenwick.

'*Do you think I care?*'

Nancy pulled back sharply, unable to reply, unable to get up and leave, and the hand that had shot out and grabbed her wrist and had not let go since suddenly tightened painfully and she stifled a gasp. Milly's face had been in shadow but now it was an inch from own face and was enormous, bloated, and Nancy could not move. The fingers tightened around her wrist. The unblinking eyes narrowed a fraction and there was something triumphant in them.

'*I saw him*. He was *here*, not an hour gone. I saw *him*! *Joe.*'

There, she had done it, said his name out loud at last, and perhaps it was the first time she had said it in all these years. How odd it must sound to her, how familiar yet unfamiliar the word must feel on her lips.

'He's a *deserter.*'

And now Nancy could not move; though she recoiled from those lips, from those words, she could not move.

'You got a bloody nerve! Sitting there, telling me my man's a deserter! He did his bit, went off to serve his country. Not like some—'

'I know what I saw!'

There was a strange light in Milly's face, her eyes gleamed like a child on Christmas morning. Like a child who has murdered both its parents on Christmas morning because it did not get the presents it was expecting.

'You saw *nothing*! Joe's home on leave.'

'I saw him.' Milly's breath was warm in her ear. 'Creeping about in civvies, an old duffle coat, no hat, black trousers. I saw him looking over his shoulder like he knew the coppers were after him.'

Throughout this the little boys had sat unmoving, dispassionately observing every detail. Now Milly cocked her head a fraction towards them.

'My Reg rounds up men like that every day. Don't he, boys?'

'Our daddy's a policeman,' they said in unison.

'And what he does he do with deserters, boys?'

'He arrests them and throws them in prison where they belong.'

It was grotesque. Did they even know what they were saying? There was something inhuman about them.

'Where has he run to, Nancy? His brothers' house? Does he think he'll be safe there?'

'You know *nothing*—'

The fingers pressed into Nancy's wrist. She felt her tendons protesting, the bones crunched together. And Milly leaned closer, Milly said what she had waited five years to say: 'You think you can steal my man and get away with it? You're nothing but a cheap tart.'

The two little boys sitting unmoving behind her, their eyes wide, slowly licked their lips.

'He deserved what he got and you deserve what you got: a cowardly deserter.'

'Say what you like! It don't change nothing.' And now, finally, Nancy could say what she had waited five years to say: '*He chose me over you!*'

She wrenched herself free—and for a moment she *was* free— but Milly's words pursued her: 'We're going to the police station, Nancy Keys, just the minute we get out of here!'

Nancy fled, tripping and falling in her haste to escape, throwing out her hands to break her fall; a woman tried to help her up but Nancy pushed her away. She needed to run but she could not, the ocean of bodies in every direction was too great. She scrambled down off the platform's edge, falling again onto her hands and knees, pulling herself up and finding herself at the tunnel entrance. She paused to catch her breath. She had come too far down the platform, was at the wrong end of the station from where Emily waited for her. She looked down at her hands, which were dirt-encrusted and cut and beginning to sting. Her stockings were torn. She needed to catch her breath.

Milly's hatred swam around her, it cut into her as the tiny pieces of grit cut into her hands. You loved him once, thought Nancy. You loved Joe. But the journey from love to hate, it turned out, was a short one, and one that was rarely, if ever, made in reverse.

She could not catch her breath. People were watching her, curious, wondering. For there were families sheltering here, right inside the tunnel. She made herself stop, straighten up, stand quite still, at the mouth of the tunnel. It drew her gaze, pulled her in. It emitted a strange musty, damp, electrical smell. A wind whistling distantly blew the scarf about her head, whipped the strands of hair into her eyes. The very last family sheltering the deepest inside the tunnel were wrapped up like Arctic explorers, only their eyes showing, huddling like people on a mountain top or on the edge of a precipice. And beyond the last family was darkness. If you went inside, if you walked far enough, you would reach Liverpool Street. It was perhaps a mile, which was no distance at all on the surface but underground in the darkness would be an eternity. She had never been afraid of the dark—for why be scared of something you could not see?—but this darkness, it leaped like a flame, touching something quite primeval within her, and she shivered. When she peered into the darkness after just a few yards there was nothing. A void. Probably sound itself was obliterated, though she heard the wind again. Anything might go on inside there and no one would know. A girl had been raped a few months back, down here during a raid, and no one had heard a thing. You could bring someone down here and finish them off, do away with them, and no one would ever know. You could put your hands around someone's neck and strangle them or slip a knife between their ribs—if you had a knife—and no one would know.

She thought of Milly Fenwick and her two little boys who would go to the police station just the minute they got out of here.

# CHAPTER THIRTEEN

If she had not had Abigail with her perhaps Diana would have gone to help him. As it was, she fled, her child clutched tightly in her arms.

She ran and she did not stop, pushing past everyone who got in her way, jumping over bodies and stumbling and almost falling and getting up again and setting off once more. She did not look back. She did not look into any of the faces that appeared before her, rearing into view and vanishing again. She did not think about the face she had just seen on the floor of the latrines, crumpled and hovering on the very edge of existence; she did not think of the blank, empty faces of the three men who had surrounded Lance and who may or may not have noticed her and her child. She leaped from the platform and fell, plunging to the ground and landing on the blue travelling case, which was untouched and unharmed exactly where she had left it and which broke her fall though it badly bruised her knee.

'Mummy, you're hurting me!'

Aghast, Diana righted herself and carefully placed Abigail on the ground, smoothing down her hair, trying with shaking fingers to locate the hairband which had come off in their mad dash and was now around Abigail's neck. 'There, that's better, isn't it? I'm sorry, darling. Mummy's sorry.' Her voice sounded high, unnatural. Her fingers would not stop shaking.

'Mummy, why did we run away from Uncle Lance?'

Lance staring with empty eyes, staring into the face of death. She had done nothing to help him. She had not lifted a finger.

'Sshh, darling.' She stroked her child's hair. Forced herself to stop. Made herself clench her fingers tightly to make them stop shaking. But what could she have done? Her own safety, hers and Abigail's, was paramount. He would not have expected her to do anything, any more than he would have gone to her assistance. He had said it himself: he knew the risks. He had brought it on himself.

'But *why*, Mummy? Why did we run away?'

All the same, she had not tried to find a policeman. She had not alerted any of the wardens. She did not even know for certain he was dead.

'It's a game. We're just playing a silly game. Now, sit still. Mummy's . . . a little out of breath, that's all.'

Someone would call the police. But perhaps, by then, they would all be out of here; perhaps the raid would be over? It would be best, she realised, if they had left by the time the police were called. It would be best if Lance—

'Everything is going to be just fine, you'll see. We'll be going home soon and then we can have a lovely breakfast together, can't we?'

For the night could not last much longer and the little blue travelling case was still here, safe and sound and stuffed full of Carnation milk and tinned peaches and American coffee and bars of chocolate and pilchards and sugar and dried milk and tea. Diana pulled it to her and held on to it. She closed her eyes. She no longer thought about Lance Beckwith, who had once been John's friend. That part of her life was over.

Diana had not tried to find a policeman. But a policeman was trying to find her.

He made no sound, or none that she could hear above the now-constant rumble and distant booms above and the ebb and flow of voices all around, but still something made her look up. At first all she saw was a solitary figure picking a path through the chaos and her eyes went to him and passed on, not stopping, barely registering. Then they slid back for no other reason than that this was a man not in a uniform but in a worn mackintosh, hands deep in pockets, a hat pulled low and a shadow at his chin that suggested he had not shaved in many hours. Dressed like a gangster but not a gangster. Somehow she knew instantly—horribly—that he was a policeman, a fact that was confirmed by the presence of a uniformed constable a step behind him.

They were making their way steadfastly, unwaveringly, towards her, and her body went cold with terror.

She did not run—there was no question of that. Instead, Diana closed her eyes, buried her head in Abigail's hair, tried to catch her breath. They had found him then. And he was dead. But if he was not dead? For an injured man could speak, a dead man could not.

'My, don't you look pretty?' she said to Abigail, holding on to her child because her whole body was shaking and if she looked into her daughter's face nothing bad could happen. But she could not see Abigail's face. She saw through a very long tunnel herself, a tiny figure, from the moment that she had first run into Lance outside Boots that morning before Christmas and she saw every moment since, herself hurtling, unstoppably, towards this point.

'Madam? Is this case yours?'

Slowly she turned to look at him. The policeman was standing before her and she saw an exhausted face caught in the moment where youth slides uneasily and perhaps prematurely into middle age, his voice dull, eyes circled by dark smudges but still searching her, still taking in every part of her, everything that was Diana Meadows, all that she had done and not done, from her smallest lapse in judgement to her involvement in wholescale organised criminal activity. Behind him an ageing constable with watery eyes and broken veins on his nose waited patiently, shifting his weight from one foot to another.

'Madam?' A note of impatience now. A man used to asking questions of strangers, used to interfering in other people's business, and Diana's stomach plummeted down, down, so far down it seemed to pin her to the floor. Her hand, the one that was holding on so tightly to the small blue travelling case was burning. If she released her grip she knew the palm would be branded with its mark forever.

Forever. She had destroyed forever. Her future was now a police station, an interview room, charges, a formal arrest, the shameful telephone call to their family solicitor (a man who had come to their wedding and whose shocked gaze she would not be able to bear), a court appearance, newspapermen and smug reports in the local paper pored over gleefully by everyone she had ever known. And prison. For there was every possibility the magistrate—sickened and outraged by the constant stream of petty and not-so-petty thefts coming before him—would decide to make an example of a well-to-do middle-class housewife who ought to have known better and hand down not a hefty fine but a prison sentence.

And there was Gerald. She would kill herself, she realised, before she let it come to that.

But . . .

Diana peered at the policeman, her heart thumping, the blood surging in her ears. 'I'm sorry. What did you ask me?'

The policeman sighed. 'I said, is this child yours?' And he pointed not at the little blue travelling case with its damning cargo of contraband, but at a child, that woman's child, the thin little lank-haired thing with the ugly red woollen hat who had been abandoned a while ago by its mother and was lying wrapped tightly in a blanket mutely watching them.

'Oh!' Diana gasped and the policeman and the ageing sore-footed constable and the people all around them and the platform itself wavered in and out of focus, in and out of existence for a moment as everything shifted once more.

She started laughing. Could not help herself. It was a dreadful sound and there was no humour in it. The policeman and the constable and even Abigail all watched her. She made herself stop. 'No!' she gasped, and another little laugh escaped. 'Not mine. Certainly not.'

'Do you know where its mother is?' He did not ask the child itself, who was awake and was regarding him, regarding them all, malevolently, some inbuilt reflex telling it to distrust any police-man, to distrust anyone.

('Mummy, I can't find Teddy,' said Abigail, but no one seemed to hear her.)

'Yes, yes, I saw her. She is up there, with a family,' said Diana, for she had seen the woman, just for a moment, as she and Abigail had emerged from the latrines, and she pointed now to the spot where she had seen the woman, getting to her feet in her eagerness to show the policeman where, to describe the people, the place, in detail.

The policeman and the constable left and for a long time—it felt like a long time but perhaps was not so very long at all—she was elated, her elation gradually softening to a sort of light-headed calmness. A near miss, she told herself, she told Abigail, who did not appear to really understand nor fully appreciate their narrow escape.

And when the station rumbled and shook and dust began to stream from the ceiling and cracks to appear in the walls, and as all around them heads lifted and muffled screams and shouts rippled the length of the platform, Diana did not gaze up, Diana did not scream. Far away bells could be heard and sirens, though they were surely too far underground to hear such things so perhaps she imagined that. This thought—of being safe so far underground and at the same time of being trapped beneath the ground—had worried her a few hours ago, had induced a paralysing and breathless sense of vertigo and claustrophobia all at the same time. But not now. Not now they had survived the near miss.

She did not think of Lance Beckwith at all.

# CHAPTER FOURTEEN

Nancy had believed, absolutely, in Joe's escape, in his nocturnal flight across the city, his clandestine meeting with a man who could get him the right papers, his flight across the country and finally across the sea. She had believed, unquestioningly, in Joe's eventual and ultimate success. But Milly Fenwick had vowed to denounce him—the man she had once agreed to marry—and all at once Joe's escape seemed perilous, his eventual success no longer assured, his capture and incarceration a distinct possibility.

She must think. For she wasn't helpless, she could help Joe. There were things she could do, actions she could take. She must think.

But in the meantime it was foolish to be blundering about the station on her own, leaving Emily alone and unprotected. This thought struck her horribly and Nancy began to make her way back, hurrying, though her way was blocked at every turn and she slipped and stumbled and her panic rose again just when she had got it under control. She had left Emily on her own. She often left Emily on her own and nothing bad ever happened, of course it didn't, she was always good as gold, but now all the certainties, all the risks she took daily and without a thought, seemed breathtakingly foolish and a thousand horrific consequences crowded into her head.

She craned her neck to locate Emily through the sea of bodies, but identifying one small child amid so many proved impossible when surely a mum ought to be able to pick out her own kid in a crowd at once. But she was too far away, her line of sight was blocked by a dozen, two dozen people.

The bombers were back. She was aware of an increase in her heart rate, a flutter against her ribs that made her breathless, and the need to reach Emily became urgent, for a terrible, almost unthinkable dismay had descended on her: *what if Emily had been taken?* There was no logical reason to think this, yet you heard about such things: kids being snatched, babies taken from their prams right outside their own front doors and never heard of again. A girl had been raped in the tunnels just a few months ago. If something happened to Emily she would never forgive herself. And she would never be able to face Joe, who had done everything, risked everything, for them both. She would kill herself if anything happened to their little girl.

But nothing had happened, for there she was! Safe and sound and sitting up with the blanket wrapped about her skinny shoulders, looking for her mother with a frightened, anxious face, and Nancy laughed aloud in her relief, and the need to hurl herself beneath the wheels of a train rather than face her husband's grief and recriminations vanished. She had allowed her fears to get the better of her. She was in control: she would protect Emily and she would protect Joe, too, if she had to.

Before she had gone even a few steps she saw the two men coming towards her. One was the man she had seen in the shadows standing outside her house so many hours ago when the air-raid siren had first gone off and had seen again much later in the entranceway to the platform and had convinced herself was a policeman: a tallish, slender young man in a long, shabby raincoat and a soft felt hat, damp from the rain and pulled low over his brow, a face shadowy with stubble. She had convinced herself he was a policeman and now her guess appeared to be spot on, for right behind him was a police constable with an ugly enlarged nose, red-faced and out of breath in a uniform that was stretched tightly over a swollen belly. Two policemen coming towards her. A long way off but they spotted her in the same instant that she saw them.

They had arrested Joe. For a moment she could not breathe. Some spark of life died away.

But the two policeman started forward and so she ran. There was nowhere to run. She was on a platform packed with sleeping people, there was only one way in or out, aside from the tunnels at each end. She could hide down there in the tunnel, but could she could make it along the tracks, in the darkness, to the next station, to Liverpool Street? And there was Emily, she could not abandon Emily. Each possibility for escape was dashed the instant it presented itself. She needed some luck, on this night when it had all come crashing down about her; she deserved something, surely?

∽

When it came, salvation was delivered by the Luftwaffe. Not a direct hit—not that, God forbid—but a near miss, a strike so close it caused the whole structure of the station to rumble and shake, for dust to stream from the ceiling and cracks to appear in the walls. It caused heads to lift and muffled screams and shouts to ripple the length of the platform. It caused all eyes—just for that moment—to gaze upwards. How could it not? You were not human if you did not, in that instant, gaze upwards. It lasted a few seconds, no longer, but in that time Nancy stopped running and threw herself to the ground, not to avoid the bombs but because some ingenious, quite unknown part of herself had worked out that there were hundreds of people lying on the ground and that, lying on the ground with their coats over them and their faces covered, it was all but impossible to tell one person from another. In the moment that all eyes were gazing upwards she threw herself to the ground, pulling her coat over her head, and was gone.

She hoped she was gone. If she had got it wrong, if the two policemen had not been distracted like everyone else by the explosion, if she were not in fact invisible, then she was trapped. They would find her and arrest her and there was precious little she could do to prevent it.

Until that happened she would wait, when already her heart was bursting and her breathing so rapid she couldn't quite think. She would wait. How long? She could not risk lifting her head. She would count. She would make herself wait a full ten minutes. So she counted, one to sixty slowly and steadily, ten times. As she counted and one part of her brain maintained a steady and calming rhythm, the other part imagined the bodies all around her dissolving away to leave her lying alone and naked and horribly exposed. Every instinct told her to leap up and run but she made herself lie perfectly still.

Ten minutes, or thereabouts. The bombing had gone quiet again, but everyone was talking, moving about, frightened. She lifted her head an inch, two inches, from the ground. The back and shoulders of an elderly man were almost touching her. The old man smelled of stale beer and stale piss, of unwashed clothes. She could see the worn, loose threads of his coat, a darned patch already undoing, a collar half torn off. She could hear his ragged, phlegmy breathing. Every sensation seemed heightened and extreme and terrible. She raised her head to look over the old man and saw another old man, a sea of old men, the same and different and endless.

Of the policemen there was no sign. No sign at all. She had evaded them! For a moment she revelled in her good fortune, in her ingenuity. She sat up, and now that she could afford the luxury of thinking things through and not simply reacting in a blind panic it occurred to her that perhaps, after all, Joe had not been arrested. For if he had, surely the policemen would be interrogating him, would be charging him right now. They would not be wasting their time chasing Joe's wife in an over-crowded tube station during a raid. No, it was far more likely Joe had evaded them too, was even now making his way, stealthily in the blackout, to the man who would provide the right papers, to the railway station to catch the first train north in the morning, to the ship that would take him across the sea to freedom.

Cautiously she got to her feet and her limbs felt curiously light and difficult to control and her head spun dizzyingly. It was all for Joe, she realised; if she believed in him she could go on, and she did believe in him now. She crouched low and stayed low as she began to make her way back, keeping to the shadowy overhang just below the platform's edge. She would leave at once, go with Joe this very night, all her hesitations and fears, all her doubts had gone.

But there was Emily and the fact of Emily made it impossible.

There was still no sign of the two policemen who seemed to have vanished into thin air. Dawn was still an hour or two away but all around folk were awake and restless after the near miss. A steady stream of elderly people and small children got up and stretched and shuffled off to the latrines, rearranged themselves on the ground, squabbled in angry whispers with their families and with the strangers around them, and all of this gave her cover. This time she saw Emily at once, picking her out instantly in the crowd of people, and though only a short time ago Emily had been anxious and frightened, now she appeared to have accepted her abandonment and the near miss and was sitting patiently with the blanket wrapped around her, waiting. A child born during a war in the downstairs room of a house in Odessa Street had realistic expectations about her life and the options that were available. This evidence of her child's stoicism—or perhaps it was merely Emily's acceptance of her lot in life—brought tears to her mother's eyes. She would not abandon her again, no matter what happened. This was her pledge to her waiting child.

Nancy was still too far off to pick her up, to hold her, still she could see Emily's patiently waiting form and she could make her pledge. It was a moment of joyful reunion with her child even if it was only in her mind.

In the next instant the policeman in the raincoat (who had not, in fact, vanished into thin air but had instead worked his way methodically along the platform, shaking and waking one sleeping figure after another in his quest to find her) did now find her—indeed, she walked straight into him—and for a second, two seconds, they faced each other. Nancy saw a much younger man than she had expected, his narrow face and hollow cheeks not so very different from those of the hungry and exhausted people around them, his dark eyes blurred by the dark shadows beneath them, the ghost of a beard along his jawline proof of the many hours that had passed since he had shaved that morning. She did not see triumph in his dark eyes, merely a sort of tired inevitability.

It made no difference. Another bomb landed and this one was not a near miss, it was not a miss at all, and Nancy saw the policeman who had pursued her and then she saw nothing.

# CHAPTER FIFTEEN

Diana heard a loud bang that sent a wave ripping through her body with a force that seemed to blast apart every molecule and simultaneously suck the air out of her and she screamed, though her scream was heard by no one, not even herself. Then came a terrifying whoosh as a cloud of smoke and dust and debris plummeted from the ceiling in such a rush the world must surely have ended.

And then nothing. Silence.

Diana lay face down on the ground. She waited to die and the shaking of the ground and the roar of the world ending made her wonder if she had, in fact, already died, if this was death. In that instant she could not be sure. The difference between life and death seemed arbitrary.

And then it stopped, for the most part. The roaring in her ears continued but the world was no longer ending. There was a stillness, there was a silence—aside from the roaring in her ears; an eerie silence of many people listening, waiting, or many people dead. Diana became aware of herself lying face down on the ground, could taste dust in her mouth. She could not be dead, she reasoned, if she could taste dust in her mouth, and she lifted her head. Others lifted their heads. For they were still here, the station was still here. The world had not ended. And those who had done it all before and knew how these things were stood up on wobbly legs and brushed themselves off and said it was not a direct hit, for had it been a direct hit they would none of them be here, or not in one piece at any rate, and the station itself would be a large crater filled with molten, smoking rubble and body parts. But it had seemed, at the time, to be a direct hit.

All that had happened was that the roof had partially fallen in.

Diana Meadows had seen it fall in as it had fallen directly onto the woman with the headscarf who had been returning to her child and the tired policeman who had at just that moment approached her. Diana had had a perfect view of the two of them standing only a few yards away from one another and in another moment they had vanished in the whoosh of smoke and dust and debris that had plummeted from the ceiling. Afterwards, Diana lifted her head, others lifted their heads, but these two did not. The woman and the young policeman had gone and Diana, in the moments that she realised she had not died, that she tasted dust in her mouth, knew with a strange clarity that they were both dead.

She had survived when others had died. And her child was still cradled in her arms. She hugged her, she talked to her, she reassured her, though her words made no sound and Abigail offered no reply.

Ghostly figures began to move about in the choking dust,

making no sound at all, their faces covered by handkerchiefs, but moving silently, talking to each other silently, and that was odd, before it occurred to her she could hear nothing but the roaring in her ears. But I am not frightened, thought Diana. She did not know why she was not frightened. It was inexplicable. She had survived when others had died. And her child was still cradled in her arms. She sat on the ground and held Abigail tightly to her breast and rocked her back and forth, talking to her as all around them the ghostly figures moved silently and futilely. A short distance away was Teddy, whom they had thought lost, turned quite white by a coating of the thick, choking dust and just out of reach. But Teddy had survived too.

The woman and the policeman were dead. But the woman's child was alive, she saw. The child had not died. The little girl stood a little distance away, her mouth open. She was clearly screaming but she made no sound, or none that Diana could hear. And no one came to her. Diana closed her eyes and stroked Abigail's hair and for once Abigail did not object.

Time passed. She didn't know how much time. And sometimes she saw herself from very high up, which was odd, and she had a sensation almost of vertigo as she gazed down at herself, very small and insignificant a long way below. And other times she felt a great crushing weight pressing against her chest so that she could not get enough breath, though there was no weight that she could see. But still it pressed. And the people around her emerged then melted away though they did not move, it was simply her ability to sense them that came and went.

The station was to be evacuated. It was no longer safe. She wondered how she knew this when no one spoke. She could see rescue workers and firemen newly arrived from the surface appearing out of the cloud of thick dust in their uniforms and helmets, their faces covered, clambering over the debris. She could see an ambulance crew with stretchers. They were up above her on the platform. No one had made it down here below the platform yet. She studied the people all around her, the people she had shared this night with, and saw that many were trapped, and others were milling about dazedly, bleeding from cuts and abrasions, nursing injured limbs. But she herself was not trapped, Diana saw, her legs were perfectly free, she had no cuts or abrasions, or none that she could see, none that she could feel. There was just this pressing weight. She could not see her own face so she put up a hand and touched her cheek, her nose. It felt quite as it should. She had survived when others had died. She studied Abigail's face which was perfect, flawless, untouched.

And meanwhile the poor wretched child, motherless now, had made its way to the place her mother had last been and began to pick at the pile of rubble and debris. It was pitiful. Someone would help her, surely, sooner or later. They would not leave the child, someone would come and claim it. The man in the seaman's duffle coat would come for her.

But the man did not come.

Instead two firemen reached them and jumped down, faceless and anonymous men who gently moved the little girl aside and set about removing what debris they could. They moved methodically, expertly, gloved hands pulling piece by piece until a body emerged. They stopped at one point and waved then started moving the debris with more haste and a stretcher was called for. There was a long moment of frenzied activity when Diana became aware that one of them was alive, or might be alive. A body was pulled out and put on the stretcher and wrapped in a blanket and taken away, a body with a pulse, alive, or not yet dead at any rate. The firemen continued their work and a second body was found and this one too was placed on a stretcher and covered with a blanket but this time the head was covered and there was less haste and no one came to take the second stretcher away in the ambulance; instead it was laid out on a clear space on the platform, a human form covered with a grey blanket, and the two firemen were called away to search for other bodies elsewhere.

One dead, one not quite dead. Diana had seen the shadowy stubble and the short brown hair of the policeman on the first stretcher. And from beneath the blanket on the second stretcher a single foot protruded, a foot bare of stocking or shoe but still recognisably a woman's foot, perfect and unblemished and very white, very still. Diana stared at the foot.

No one had remembered about the little girl. She had crept over to the lifeless form on the stretcher and now she lay down beside it, beside her dead mother. The horror of this image struck Diana but at some remote level. She pulled Abigail closer to her as though this might shield her from the appalling sight.

A rescue crew began pulling people up onto the platform and leading them away. But still Diana did not move. Really, they were quite safe, she and Abigail, right here in their little spot near the tunnel entrance. They would stay here. The debris had fallen all around them but had not touched them. They had survived.

'Come on, luv.'

Diana looked up into the blackened face of a fireman, his eyes red-rimmed and very white in his smoke-blackened face, his helmet and boots and waterproof suit massive beside her. 'Time to go,' he said, and it was odd that she knew that this was what he had said when she couldn't hear his voice. Perhaps he had in fact said something completely different; perhaps he had said, 'Sorry, missus, you're sitting on a mine and if you get up it will go off.' But that didn't seem likely for his face was gentle, his eyes were gentle, odd for such a hulking brute of a man in boots and a fireman's helmet. Water coursed in rivers off his shoulders and dripped from the rim of his helmet. He held out a grimy hand to help her. He seemed to want to take Abigail from her.

'WE ARE QUITE ALRIGHT,' Diana assured him, and she wondered if she had shouted this because the fireman started slightly. She had heard the words quite clearly inside her own head but not in her ears, which was an odd sensation.

The fireman made some reply. He held out both arms as though he would take Abigail from her but Diana clasped her child tighter to her and after a moment the man appeared to be called away to help elsewhere as he stood up and left. But they were quite alright, she and Abigail, and after a time Diana got unsteadily to her feet, for they could not remain here. And why had the fireman ignored the poor, stricken little girl? she wondered. Perhaps he had not seen her, for she lay quietly beside the stretcher. She was oddly still. Surely the poor child could not believe her mother was alive?

It was time. Awkwardly, stiffly, Diana got to her knees. Her legs quivered beneath her, as feeble as cardboard, but did not give way. She took a tentative step then another before turning back and reaching down to scoop up Teddy: he had survived; she would not abandon him now. Abigail would never forgive her. They made their way, scrambling and uncertain, up onto the platform. From here they made their way to the stretcher and Diana kneeled down beside the lifeless form covered by the grey blanket where the single bare foot protruded. She wanted to say a prayer—it would be a prayer not just for the dead woman but for them all, the dead woman's child and herself and her own child—but in the end she said nothing as she didn't know what such a prayer might sound like.

It was time. She lowered her gaze to Abigail's face, which was perfect, flawless, untouched, just as though the explosion had sucked the breath out of her, had sucked the life from her body. So still. She could be sleeping. No sign of an injury, nothing to show that she was gone, just an absence of life. Diana kneeled. Another Diana, watching from very far above, saw her take the lifeless form that was at her breast and lay it beside the dead woman. Saw her bend over and for the final time kiss her child's smooth, white face. Saw her get calmly to her feet. Her child was dead.

She turned to the little girl who had lost her mother and who was crouching, senseless in her grief, beside her mother's body, and she picked the child up in both arms and walked out of the station with her.

Outside the dawn had come. Brilliant sunlight blinded them. A dozen, two dozen people milled about. Rescued shelterers sat on the floor with blankets wrapped around them. First-aid crews handed out steaming mugs, men from a fire crew stood silently sipping drinks. Hoses and buckets and shovels and axes lay in piles at their feet. Stretchers were being loaded into waiting ambulances, a young woman with a limp was being led away. A man was having his head bandaged, his face and hands bloodied. The entrance to the station was blackened and smouldering, many of the bricks charred where a fire had broken out. It had rained in the night so that everything was shiny with that damp after-rain smell, and after the shouts and cries and screams and the crash of falling rubble there was now the silence of a sky free of bombers and searchlights and flak, the silence of an English winter morning.

Diana saw all this and saw none of it. The roaring continued in her ears but she could make out other sounds now, too, though they were muffled and that was fine. The great pressing weight had gone, right at the very moment that it had overwhelmed her. A woman in a maroon apron reared into her line of vision to thrust a mug of tea into her hands, to place a blanket around her, but Diana veered away from the woman. She tasted dust and ash on her lips. She swallowed and ash coated her tongue and her throat. She picked her way over the debris, passing piles of rubble and the twisted girders of smouldering metal and the skeletons of houses that had been hit during the night. Hoses were strewn across the streets and huge puddles of water were everywhere. A column of thick black smoke rose hundreds of feet into the air, covering everything with a choking, seared smell that grabbed at the windpipe and sucked the air out of her lungs. Many of the buildings had been cordoned off. On the ground were strewn pieces of furniture, items of clothing, a doll's head. Odd shoes. A hat. On the corner of Bethnal Green Road someone had hung a Union Jack and it fluttered limply in the chill winter air.

Diana picked her way carefully, maintaining her balance with difficulty as she held the little girl in both arms, though unhampered by the little blue travelling case, which she had not brought with her nor even given a thought to. They made their way to a bus stop. Surprisingly they did not have to wait long. London had been bombed and people had died but this morning the birds were singing and the buses were running. A number 8 bus came along and they got on and the bus pulled away and left.

PART TWO

OVERGROUND

# CHAPTER SIXTEEN

## *North Africa*

Gerald Meadows kneeled down beside a dead German officer and saw that the man's eyes had been picked out by vultures. Two gaping black holes stared blankly back at him and a swarm of flies shot into the air and swirled angrily about him. Otherwise the man's face was untouched, the flesh puckered a little and peeling from the sun, but the forage cap still on his head, his unit insignia glinting in the sun, his uniform, that of a captain in the Afrika Korps, intact. His holster was empty. Someone had been here before them. The man was lying on his back and Gerald could see no obvious sign of how he had died. If he turned the fellow over he would see some gaping wound in the back of his skull or a scorched, bloodied hole in his back.

Gerald stood up. They were not here to investigate anyone's death.

A short distance away a burnt-out armoured vehicle lay on its side as though it had struck a mine or been hit by an anti-tank missile. Perhaps the dead officer had been thrown from the car.

It was a distance of thirty, forty yards but it was possible. Anything was possible, it seemed, in war. The limits of what one assumed was possible, in terms of human endeavour, human survival, human depravity, just kept expanding. Perhaps there was no limit. Perhaps the very notion of a limit was pointless.

Gerald walked away from the dead officer, ostensibly to look over the burnt-out vehicle but really just for form's sake. The vehicle had been destroyed, there was nothing salvageable. The upholstery was gone, the radio melted, even its markings had been burned off. It had clearly been here a long time, months perhaps. And yet the corpse was fresh. In the desert a two-day-old corpse was bloated and blackened and riddled with maggots. If you pulled, even gently, at a limb while searching for documents or identity discs it would come off in your hand.

But this corpse was fresh. Where had he come from, then?

The war here in the desert had ended six months ago with the capture of Tunis. Most of Rommel's troops and what remained of the Italian forces had been rounded up. Most, but not all. Some had escaped, made their way along the coast hoping for some sort of Dunkirk-esque evacuation by the German Navy that had never eventuated, or fled south into the Blue—like this chap, presumably. Had he been trying to get back to his own lines all this time? He would have been better off surrendering to the Allied forces rather than dying out here alone, in a desert, his eyes plucked out by vultures.

I would have surrendered, thought Gerald.

He studied the ground. Clearly the poor bastard had not come here on foot, yet there were no tracks, or none discernible in the rough scrubby terrain. Desert stretched in all directions, rocky and impassable in this part, unscaleable soft sand dunes elsewhere, and it was odd, he reflected, referring to it as 'the Blue', for there was every colour in the desert except blue. But that was what the men called it. And it was beautiful at dawn and at dusk when the myriad colours, the sudden change in temperature, made you stand in awe to see it. The rest of the time it was a hellish cauldron.

And the flies. They were enough to send a sane man crazy. He brushed them away from his face and readjusted the scarf that he wore wrapped Arab-style around his head. It was not official military headgear but the usual rules did not seem to apply in the desert. He had arrived fresh off a troopship three years earlier, laden down with all manner of kit, none of which seemed to have been designed with desert warfare in mind. Now all he wore—all any of the men wore—were his boots, a single pair of khaki drill shorts, a shirt so caked in dried sweat it was stiff as a board, and the headscarf. Aside from a change of underwear and a ground-sheet and his mess tin and canteen, this was all the kit he had. It was all he needed.

Enderby and Crouch stood a little distance away, not together, smoking their foul cigarettes. Enderby, their gunner, stood in the shade provided by their stationary tank, squinting at some papers he had pulled from his pocket. Crouch, their driver, stood a little further away on a slight rise, surveying the horizon, a hand shielding his eyes, the other hand swatting the unceasing flies. They both waited silently, patiently, unquestioningly, for Gerald to decide what they would do next.

What *would* they do next? He wasn't entirely sure.

It had bothered him at first, that constant need to give orders, to make decisions. It had seemed wearying, burdensome, potentially catastrophic, but they had survived thus far. Indeed, it had turned out that his decisions made very little difference. They would stay the night or move on; they would head south or bear east, they would stop and investigate, they would continue on their way. None of it actually seemed to matter. The war in the desert was over, the rest of the division had landed in Italy in September and were now back in England for rest, refitting and retraining. A handful of skeleton units had been left behind on a mopping-up operation: salvage and rescue, though there was nothing to salvage and no one to rescue.

Gerald pulled a battered chart and his sun compass from his shirt pocket and studied both carefully, hoping to find something that would help him. There was nothing on the chart. It was a chart of the desert. They were some sixty or seventy miles south of Khoms, between Misrata on the Mediterranean coast and the desert settlement of Bani Walid, which was, one presumed—one hoped—somewhere to the west, though it had thus far eluded them. They weren't lost, there was no question of that, it was just that their exact position at this moment was tricky to pinpoint. Their tank had a hundred-and-thirty-mile range and they had enough petrol for one more refuelling, assuming the petrol had not evaporated in the can.

The rest of the division had landed in Italy and they had been left behind. Gerald hadn't questioned it, one didn't, though the assumption among one's fellow officers was that one was chomping at the bit to follow the action, to get across to Italy. In truth, it had been a relief to be left to trundle around the desert in a light tank. But now the division was back in England, and he and Enderby and Crouch were stuck in the desert unable to find the only settlement for hundreds of miles. It was no longer a relief. Gerald stuffed the chart and the compass back in his pocket and looked over at his men.

Enderby and Crouch. They sounded like a small but long-established firm of solicitors whose business was made up entirely of wills, entails and probate. Gerald rather liked the firm of Enderby and Crouch. He sometimes imagined their offices, housed in a Georgian building on one side of a square in a small market town in Suffolk perhaps, or Lincolnshire.

The reality of Enderby and Crouch was somewhat different. Enderby, a short, taciturn dairy farmer from Northallerton, had reddish-blond hair, ears that protruded like jug handles and a fair complexion well suited to the low skies, short days and endless winters of North Yorkshire and utterly unsuited to the crippling heat and relentless sun of the Western Desert, so that his skin was permanently burnt, blistered and peeling.

Crouch, who was equally diminutive, heralded from Waltham-stow in north-east London and had worked at Smithfield meat market before the war. He had something of the disreputable bookie about him, and where Enderby had a thin, almost malnourished frame, Crouch was lean and wiry, packed with all the pugnacious energy of a bantamweight boxer. He viewed the world through suspicious eyes and sharp features and a mass of very dark, brylcreemed hair, and there was Jewish blood, Gerald presumed, a generation or so back.

The fact that both men were below average height perhaps went some way to explaining their presence in the tank regiment. It certainly wasn't their skill as soldiers. You didn't want a six-foot chap in a tiny, cramped vehicle with no windows save for a flap through which the driver could see out and a turret to climb in through. Gerald knew this because he was a shade under six foot himself and could attest to how extremely inconvenient it was.

Enderby and Crouch did not like each other. They tolerated each other when the confines of the tank dictated it, but once the turret hatch was open and they were both outside smoking their foul cigarettes or striking up a brew they squabbled like a married couple, and Gerald, for the most part, let them—so long as it didn't come to blows, which occasionally it did. He had been presented with the pair of them in November and the three of them had been making short, and sometimes longer, incursions into the Blue ever since.

In the new year their field of operations had expanded south and west, and they had encountered only unresponsive smoking Arab men on camels, the occasional opportunistic civilian Europeans driving big old thirties cars who had resurfaced now that the war in the desert was ended, and one or two other straggling Allied units like themselves. They had found no sign of the enemy, other than corpses and burnt-out equipment and vehicles. Anyone who had made it this far had either died or turned back. It had been five days since they had left GHQ and they were running low on provisions as well as fuel. Their means of transport on this seemingly unending and purposeless mission was a Light Mk VI, a tank that had once been the mainstay of Britain's overseas territories but was now largely redundant. Vickers had ended production four years ago when the division had switched to the heavier Matilda and Cruiser tanks and later the American Grants and Shermans. The Mk VI had an off-road top speed of twenty-five miles per hour, which meant it could be outstripped by all but the most sluggish Panzer. It had space for just three crew: the gunner, a driver and the commander, who doubled as radio operator. The radio, their only link back to GHQ and the outside world, did not operate at this range, though every so often Gerald placed the headphones over his ears and listened to the unvarying and eerie storm of static that seemed, to him, to be the sound of the desert. As well as a short-range radio the Mk VI was fitted with one .303-inch gun, which had jammed the only time they had tried to use it, and one .50-inch Vickers machine gun. The Mk VI's half-inch of armour stopped rifle fire and machine-gun bullets sure enough, but against the German 88mm anti-tank guns it afforded as much protection as, say, a tennis net might.

'What's the score, then, guv'nor?' said Crouch, coming down from his position on the ridge, scratching his backside furiously and shaking his head disgustedly as he spat out a fly. The muscles in his sinewy arms rippled beneath the leathery-brown skin and it was an easy stretch to see him right back at Smithfield after the war, a carcass slung over his shoulder, in bloodied white overalls caked in sawdust. He would survive, Crouch would, when others who had shone more brightly, who had made a difference, had died.

Gerald thought of Ashby, just briefly, and then he stopped.

'Your guess is as good as mine, Crouch,' he replied mildly, fishing for a cigarette. Crouch's guess was not as good as his, they both knew that, and it didn't need to be, Crouch being the trooper and Gerald being his commanding officer, but it served them both to relax the formalities a bit. It made being stuck in a small tank with two other men just bearable. For they all slept together under the same tarpaulin at night and they all shared the same rations. They all knew when Crouch's dysentery had returned and that Enderby had not been able to shit in five days. And they all knew why they were really here. If they had been a crack team they would have been on that troopship heading towards the Italian coast, they would be with the Americans fighting their way towards Rome. As it was they were lumbering about the desert in a clapped-out Mk VI mopping up. None of them had any illusions about this nor any complaints, and as such Gerald could see no reason why they needed to be forever saluting and jumping to attention and all that nonsense, not in the desert.

And they had done their bit, had taken part in the skirmishes around Mersa Matruh and Sidi Barrani in late '40 and early '41, arriving in Tobruk to see the Italians surrendering in their thousands. They had retreated with the rest of the division to Cairo in '42 after Rommel and the Afrika Korps had landed, they had played their part in both the El Alamein battles. They had followed the division into Tripoli a year ago and six months later had finally linked up with the Americans and swept triumphantly into Tunis. They had seen the King himself thanking the troops. In three years they had come under fire, they had experienced mechanical failures in the middle of minefields, their guns had jammed, they had had their tank shot from under them and had leaped for their lives under enemy fire, they had become bogged and stranded and lost, they had rounded up prisoners, they had shot at their own troops in the madness and the confusion and been shot at from above by the RAF. They had seen men die and had seen other men scream with pain and cry out for their mothers. They had each of them played his part and the war, this part of the war at least, had been won.

If it had been left to him, Gerald accepted, they would probably have lost. But they had not lost. The war in the desert was over and better men than he had won it. And perhaps that was how it was—a handful of really good men made the decisions and performed heroically and everyone else just did what they were told.

He thought of Ashby, whose Sherman had been hit by a shell on the first day of the advance at El Alamein. He had watched it happen and there had been no question of survivors. The earlier Shermans ran on high-powered and highly inflammable aircraft fuel. Ashby's tank had exploded into a firebomb that had lit up the pre-dawn desert. That was how wars were won. And El Alamein had been a spectacular victory.

It was best not to think. War was something one took part in but did not understand. He suspected it was so for most of the men, in this war and in previous ones.

༄

Gerald had grown up in the shadow of war. An uncle, his father's only brother, had died in the second South African War in the first days of the new century, a few weeks before his own birth. He was fourteen at the outbreak of the Great War and spent his years at a minor public school in Dorset watching as the senior boys left in a blaze of glory, went off to France and were cut down a few weeks later, and he fully expected to join them. But the armistice came in his final year of school and he was spared.

He was not spared for long. A telegram arrived at the school just a week later announcing the death of his parents in a road accident.

They were out in Ceylon, his father a railway engineer who had accepted a position in the colonies in the first year of the war and took his wife with him, leaving Gerald at the minor public school. The war came and he and they were separated, and he felt it keenly, but most people were separated in war. His father, Percy Meadows, a kindly man with an anxious nature and a tendency towards melancholia, wrote him letters full of technical details and fascinating statistics about the railway. His mother, Abigail, a stout, hearty clergyman's daughter who laughed a lot at life but whose laughter turned to tears sometimes when she thought no one was looking, wrote him endearing letters that described in colourful detail colonial life and the other wives and the endless tennis and polo parties and the trouble with the servants and, once, how an elephant had come crashing through a wall and into the house.

None of it seemed entirely real. His parents' sudden death, caused when the car they were travelling in had gone off the road and over a precipice in some mountainous region, did not seem real either. His form master took him aside and that was real. The headmaster called Gerald to his office and offered awkward condolences, he attended a memorial service in the village of his father's family. And his parents' letters ceased, all but one letter from his mother, sent the week before her death and arriving, disconcertingly, four weeks after it.

They were gone. In an instant everything had been swept aside. He experienced something akin to vertigo, as though he, too, were plunging over a precipice, but after so much death it seemed churlish to make too much of it. The world had seen an orgy of death, it was tired of death, tired of mourning. Gerald kept his mourning to himself. He stayed on to the end of the school year, for the fees were paid in advance and his only relative now was an elderly great-aunt in Inverness. After his final exams he had little idea of what he might do, so his form master found him a position in a brokerage firm in the City. It felt an arbitrary decision, going directly into a position rather than trying for Oxford or Cambridge, going into a business about which he knew nothing, but his parents had not left him well provided for so in the end the decision was one of necessity as much as choice.

He joined Goldberg Staedtler. This distinguished firm, located at Ludgate Hill, had established its offices in the dying years of the eighteenth century when the war against America was raging on the other side of the Atlantic and, unimpeded by the blockades and restrictions of that time, had made fortunes on the back of the tobacco, cotton and sugar trade. For a young man of limited funds and no family, and therefore no distractions, it provided a place and a reason to work hard. By the age of twenty-eight, Gerald made senior broker.

Then he met Rosamund and it all came crashing down.

She was the sister of Maurice Lambton, a fellow broker, and had recently returned from New York from where she had, enticingly, retained a trace of an American accent. For some reason never adequately explained, Rosamund was known to everyone, even her own parents, as Bunny. It was a name she somehow lived up to while not appearing to, affording Gerald fleeting glimpses of herself then vanishing with a flick of her hair out of a room and seemingly into thin air. They met at a dance in Mayfair a week into the new year. She wore a knee-length chiffon dress of bottle green hemmed with silken tassels that shimmered when she moved, a mink stole, a string of pearls at her throat and long black gloves, and she smoked her cigarette through an ivory holder. Her hair was bobbed and gleamed with a silky jet shine over a shapely nose and a pointed aristocratic chin and brooding green eyes that made one think of a Siamese kitten lapping a saucer of cream. She danced with everyone that night and appeared to adore everyone equally.

It was bewildering and Gerald was smitten.

He spent a wretched time in the days and weeks that followed, eventually engineering an invitation to a weekend party at a house in Berkshire. Bunny would be there. Bunny *was* there. He was smitten afresh. His every thought was of her, his only desire to see her, she filled his head and his heart, she coursed through his veins. She opened a door and showed him a part of himself he had been unaware existed and he galloped through that door like a horse over a fence. Certainly there were other young men at that weekend party, but Gerald bided his time. He picked his moment. He got up before dawn and presented her with a crocus at breakfast. She laughed, but afterwards she looked at him differently.

She invited him to a dance in Belgravia the following week. In an agony of joy he danced with her until dawn and walked with her along the Chelsea Embankment, which was nowhere near the dance or her house but seemed a romantic thing to do. When they reached Albert Bridge and were too far from anywhere to walk back home he put her in a cab and kissed her through the window. She laughed and his heart lurched.

At Easter he arrived at her house with his dead mother's engagement ring in his pocket, but she had gone out for the evening. He paced up and down her street until midnight, at which time she arrived home in a cab in the arms of another man.

After that was a bad time. He plunged back to that place he had inhabited ten years previously, when his form master had taken him aside to announce the death of his parents. He had thought it a place he would never return to yet here he was. On that occasion ten years before he had steeled himself against the pain because everyone was in pain, his pain had been filtered through a prism of four years of cataclysmic war. But this time, ten years later, there was no prism. This time the pain was his alone, raw and terrible, and he reeled. The door that had opened, that *she* had opened, taunted him, and when he looked through it now he saw a no-man's-land of crushed hope and despair.

He closed and bolted the door forever. And perhaps, during this time, he looked no different, for he was young enough that pain did not outwardly leave its mark, but his heart had turned black.

A few months later, as a favour to a friend, and only when he had been assured Bunny would not be there, he attended a tennis party in Ruislip.

༄

'Guv! Looks like smoke over there!'

Enderby jogged over, stumbling over the rocky terrain, kicking up sand and dust with his boots. He was short enough in the leg that the hem of his khaki shorts almost reached his shins.

His shirt sleeves were rolled up—all their shirt sleeves were rolled up—but Enderby's rolled-up sleeves came down over his elbows. A deep permanent red sunburned V showed at his neck where his shirt was undone, a flash of almost translucent white skin visible where his headscarf had come loose.

'Over there!' he said, pointing.

Crouch, a short distance away, scoffed. 'What smoke? Out 'ere?' You're 'avin' a laugh.'

Enderby ignored him and indicated the western horizon. 'Over there.'

Gerald looked. He could see nothing. He lifted his field glasses to his eyes. Was there perhaps something, a dark shadow, shimmering in the heat? It could be smoke but it could just be low cloud or a mirage. Or a town, it could be a town. He knew it probably wasn't.

'We're heading that way anyway,' he said, making a decision. 'Let's move out.'

But they finished their cigarettes first.

⤴

There was no smoke. And there was no town either. There was nothing.

After some hours they stopped on a crest and refuelled, Enderby cursing when Crouch spilled a few precious drops of petrol on the ground then shouting at him when he lit a cigarette too close to the engine. Gerald left them squabbling and went off to relieve himself.

The feud between the two stemmed from a night out and a girl in Tunis six months earlier. In the week following the city's liberation a sort of madness had taken over the liberating troops and the newly liberated people that had seen soldiers running wildly down the streets, singing and dancing and drinking and feasting, firing guns and flares and rockets in the air and blasting the horns of purloined vehicles, scaling buildings to hang flags and kiss girls. The French residents had opened up what was left of their cellars and the liberating army, British and American, had been drunk for a week. And some of it had been spiked with petrol and anti-freeze by the Arabs who hated the liberators as much as they hated the Germans occupiers and a number of officers had died horrid deaths. Amid this insanity, Enderby— who had a girl called Elspeth back home in Northallerton—had danced with the widow of a dead French government official, but it was Crouch who had boasted the following morning that he had spent the night with the woman. Whether Crouch had in fact made this conquest Gerald doubted, but Enderby had gone for it, had gone for Crouch's throat, and the two had ended up in a cell and on report. But rather than put them on a charge, the army had, in its infinite wisdom, decided to send them off into the desert together in a tiny Mk VI with Gerald as their commanding officer.

Or that was how it felt. It was entirely possible no one had made any such decision, that the fact of Enderby and Crouch ending up together in the desert on this pointless mission was just an accident of fate. Gerald had been in the army long enough not to question its wisdom or to read too much into its decisions. In the first weeks of his arrival and attachment to a tank regiment he had let himself think, with a sort of surreal bemusement, *But I am a stockbroker*. What am I doing here in a tank in the desert? It was a lazy thought, it was cheap, for everyone was a stockbroker or a meat-carrier or a dairy farmer or a butcher or a miner or a teacher. Ashby had been a barrister.

A barrister, for God's sake!

He was the first person Gerald met as he staggered down the gangway of the troopship in Cairo in late November '40 with a full kit and a gas mask banging against his lily-white knees. Ashby, already brown and lean as a native, having been there a month, an unlit pipe dangling from the side of his mouth and eyes permanently narrowed against the searing heat and the blistering white light, took one look at him and, with a sardonic laugh, tossed his gas mask into the Nile and led him to the mess.

They left Cairo almost at once, with the division, and hurtled on that extraordinary five-hundred-mile advance across the desert to overrun the fleeing Italians, taking a hundred and thirty thousand prisoners, capturing four hundred tanks. Ashby was there with him the whole time, his pipe in his mouth, a wry laugh always on his lips. Ashby, who had been a barrister in civvy street, helped him. They helped each other. Like Gerald, Ashby had a wife and small child in a middle-class suburb of London. They talked about 'after the war'. They went through Sidi Rezegh, the retreat from Tobruk, Gazala, Mersa Matruh, Alam Halfa, the first El Alamein. They would both survive or they would both die.

It had not occurred to Gerald that one of them might die and the other survive.

He thought of the burning Sherman in the pre-dawn desert. Fourteen months had passed and it was looking increasingly likely that he, Gerald, would survive but Ashby was dead, fourteen months dead. Gerald would make it home and he had assumed that, on his return, he would seek out Ashby's widow and child, but now he was no longer sure. The reason for seeking them out was no longer clear.

༄

The place he had found to relieve himself was a ridge a little beyond the spot they had chosen to stop the tank and as he crested the ridge he found himself at the top of a vast escarpment with a steep drop beyond. At the bottom of this escarpment was a large flat area in the middle of which was an abandoned Scorpion, its arms stuck out before it.

A minefield. And they had almost missed it. Missing a minefield was actually better than driving into one, but still it was a bit slack to have simply driven blithely past utterly unaware. Not that there was much one could do with it except chart its position. If one knew one's positon . . . Still, they could record it.

'Crouch! Enderby! Over here.'

'Bloody 'ell! How'd we miss that?' Crouch said, joining him on the crest of the ridge, and when Gerald offered no reply, 'How long d'you think it's been there?'

Gerald shrugged. 'Since '41 at least, I should say.'

Most of the warfare in the last two years had been concentrated along the coastline far to the north, but this Scorpion looked in good condition and completely undamaged. It was a flail tank, a vehicle with two extending arms designed to be sent into a minefield ahead of the men, the arms beating the ground and making a pathway though the mined area. In reality the Scorpions overheated rapidly in the North African climate and the petrol evaporated after only a couple of hundred yards or so. If they didn't overheat their air filters got so clogged with dust they simply broke down, at which point they either had to be repaired on the field of battle under enemy fire or they were abandoned—as this one evidently had been. At Alamein the sappers had ended up going in on foot with bayonets, prodding the earth and locating the mines that way.

'Looks in good nick,' said Crouch, making no move to go down to it.

'How long's that thing been down there, then?' said Enderby, joining them, his flat Yorkshire vowels even more pronounced than usual.

'Dunno. Why don't you go down there and take a shufty, Endy?' suggested Crouch with a sneer.

'I ain't going nowhere near no bloody minefield. Is it one of ours?'

Gerald cast his field glasses over the terrain and something glinted in the sunlight at ground level. No, the mines weren't theirs. They were German anti-personnel 'S' mines, about the size of a tin can buried just beneath the ground with three prongs sticking up out of the sand. That was what he could see, the tip of one prong. He lifted his gaze to take in the entire plateau. How many were there? How far did it stretch? No way to tell. If you stepped on one of these the initial explosion flung the mine upwards. A secondary explosion sent hundreds of steel ball bearings into the air. He had seen it happen, he had no desire to experience it for himself.

'I think we chart its position from a safe distance and move on,' he announced, giving his final order of the day, and Crouch and Enderby almost fell over themselves in their haste to comply.

They were soon underway again, steering well clear of the minefield, which meant moving over rough rocky terrain. This was not good news for the Mk VI, which was a very short vehicle in relation to its width, meaning it lurched alarmingly and if they weren't careful Crouch, in the driver's seat up beside the engine, would throw up. They were already driving with the hatch open from the last time he had spewed.

They were headed in a vaguely westerly direction and sooner or later they were bound to run into someone and hopefully it would be someone from their own side. That was about as much as one did hope for. The bigger picture—battles, strategy, theatres of war—there was no point worrying about, for one could do nothing about them. Gerald had no illusions about his own, or his men's, heroic capabilities. Mostly what had been required of him over the last four years was to know when to take cover and when to run and when to sit tight, which he had done, often, sealed into the tank providing support for the infantry and under heavy enemy fire hour after hour and not being able to return fire or to turn and run or do anything really except take it and hope it would be alright.

And sometimes it wasn't alright.

༄

Gerald had gone to a tennis party in Ruislip in the summer of '28.

He went with bad grace, determined to hate everyone and everything. Finally Marian Fairfax, at whose house the tennis party was held and at whose behest he had sacrificed his Saturday to motor into darkest Middlesex, took him aside and roundly scolded him. Chastened, smarting but still aggrieved (for what did Marian Fairfax know of his black heart?) he changed into his tennis whites. Bunny hadn't come and in her place was a girl he didn't know. She was a curious little thing, not pretty, her snub nose almost like a child's and her chin a little too prominent and lips too narrow around a too-large mouth that badly applied lipstick had only accentuated. But she was poised, somehow, with an elegant neck and very fierce, very frightening little eyes that told him she was out of her depth socially and that she minded this very much. The girl—her name was Diana—had been part-nered with Eddie Devlin, which was bad luck for her as Eddie always took the whole thing very seriously and made his partner pay if they fluffed a shot. But miraculously the girl was up to it, more than up to it; she matched him shot for shot, whipping out stunning backhands one after another. It was marvellous to see and the most marvellous part was that the girl's fear utterly vanished and she glowed, positively glowed—until Ed sent a ball right at poor Cecily Porter's face in the deciding set and that was the end of that. They had won, Eddie and the girl, but Gerald could see her dismay at the manner of their victory and when Phyllis Devlin caused a nasty little scene afterwards her dismay turned to horror. An outraged horror, he saw; the outraged horror of a very upright, moral person when faced with a bully. And, damn it, Ed *was* a bully. And, as much to his own surprise as hers, Gerald presented himself to the girl shortly afterwards and suggested he drive her home.

It was all a long time ago. A tennis party in Ruislip in 1928.

Where the *hell* was Bani Walid?

Gerald stuck his head out through the Mk VI's turret and scanned the western horizon. What if they should get this far, survive three years of war, only to die like this, blundering about in the desert? He was the commanding officer, it was incumbent on him to keep his men safe, to get them home. He imagined, with unsettling clarity, an ageing and weathered Mrs Enderby many miles away in Northallerton, a woman with broken veins in her legs and bunions on her feet, waiting for her boy to come home. He imagined Endersby's Elspeth working silently and solemnly in the dairy, day after interminable day, waiting for the boy who would never come home. He had a little more trouble picturing Crouch's family, imagining a violent, angry father and a terrified meek woman, Crouch's mother, living in nightly fear of her husband's fists. He imagined the telegram coming to the house and the terrified, meek Mrs Crouch falling into a faint from which she would never recover. He could see it all quite clearly. The longer he spent in the company of Enderby and Crouch the more vivid these images of their families became, and always he pictured them at the moment at which news of their sons' deaths were received.

He would not picture the same scene in his own house, with his own family.

There was something up ahead. Gerald snatched up the field glasses. Yes, a dark, square shape, not a building, too small for that, but definitely manmade.

'Crouch, north thirty degrees!'

It was a Panzer, unmistakable by its grey colouring. A big old Panzer III just sitting there, alone and abandoned, in a flat and utterly barren area of scree and gravel. Nothing else for miles in any direction. It was the first intact Panzer they had come across. What was it doing all the way out here? It had a range of only about ninety miles at most, and a top speed off-road of twelve miles per hour. She made the British Mk VI seem like a sports car by comparison. She was larger than their own Mk VI, a five-man vehicle with a three-man turret. At her hull was almost an inch of armour which made her invincible against the Allies' anti-tank guns—if you took her face on. From the sides and the rear she was useless and a well-aimed machine gun could pierce her like a piece of cheese. She was an obsolete model, superseded by the Panzer IV years back, and perhaps that explained her presence out here, for she would not have been risked in battle, would in all likelihood have been abandoned during the final Axis retreat, or taken by those wishing to avoid the advancing Allies.

He gave the order and they trundled warily towards it, pulling up fifty yards short. Crouch switched off the engine and inside the Mk VI no one spoke. After a moment Gerald jumped down and cautiously circled the immobile Panzer on foot. It was caked in a thick crust of sand and the caterpillar tracks were worn almost to shreds, but just below the turret the insignia of the Afrika Korps, a black cross and palm tree, was intact. The turret hatch was closed. Gerald walked over, aware that Crouch and Enderby were watching. The tank was abandoned; he was certain of this. The dust had settled all around it. No tracks were visible before or behind, though the terrain was so scrubby, the winds so quick and intense, that any tracks it might have made—even an hour ago—would long have vanished. He climbed up onto the body and stood for a moment beside the hatch. He was close enough to read the manufacturer's details on the rim: DAIMLER-BENZ ·

STUTTGART · 1938. His heart was thudding in his chest, which was odd because the war in the desert was over and he had survived. But his heart was thudding.

He eased open the latch and swung the lid back, brandishing his unloaded pistol as he did so and ducking lest a shot was fired. But no shot was fired. After a long moment he peered inside then jerked back at once as the smell of decaying flesh struck him. He turned away, gagging and choking. Bloody hell, he thought furiously. It had not even occurred to him someone might be dead in there. He stuck his head back inside, this time seeing the driver's seat, the gunner's perch, a damaged radio set.

And a body.

It was slumped over the fuel chamber at the rear of the tank, a gunner in fatigues, arms flung out before him, his cap on the floor at his feet, the side of his head dark red with matted hair and blood. A second wound, on his leg below the knee, was festering, the flesh black and putrid. Gerald pulled his scarf up over his mouth and nose.

'Crouch! Enderby! Get over here. Let's get this poor bugger out.'

If they were going to salvage the Panzer, and it was not clear to him if they would or would not—it might simply depend on how much fuel it had—they were not going to drive the thing away with a corpse inside.

They came running, Crouch first, Enderby a few yards behind, both with that odd reluctant run of men commanded to do something they really had no wish to do.

'Looks like a gunshot wound,' said Gerald, climbing down inside the Panzer. His foot kicked a Luger that had been lying on

165

the floor near the man's cap, sending it skidding away beneath the driver's foot pedals. As it began to cross his mind that the man had pulled the trigger himself, that the gaping wound in the side of his head was self-inflicted, the body let out a groan.

Gerald jumped back, banging his head painfully on the roof. Crouch, who was climbing after him, lost his footing and fell with a sickening thud onto the metal floor. Enderby, still standing outside on the top of the tank, fell back with a shout and disappeared.

'Bloody *hell*!' cried Crouch, scrambling to his feet and backing away. 'Bugger's not dead,' he added unnecessarily.

'Well, he's not exactly going anywhere, is he?' said Gerald, prodding the man with the end of his pistol, which merely elicited another groan. The man was alive, but barely so. 'Come on, let's get him out, for God's sake!' And they manhandled the fellow feet first out of the turret hatch and then over the side of the tank, where, horribly, they dropped him and he rolled off the tank and onto the ground and lay, face down, letting out a dreadful wheezing whine that was barely human.

*Dear God*, thought Gerald. He scrambled down and they turned the man over and lay him on his back. The side of his skull was gone, blown away by the Luger, and there was nothing they could do for him. The other side of his face was quite untouched, and it was the face of a young man badly malnourished and unshaven for many weeks, his skin blistered and destroyed by the desert sun and deprivation. His eyes were wide open though they seemed not to see anything, thank God. Enderby fetched a canteen and they wet his lips, which were cracked and swollen and bloodied, but he was too far gone to notice.

Dusk had come and they were going nowhere, now, till dawn. They broke out their meagre rations and, as the temperature began to drop, huddled on the groundsheet beside the tank and listened as the man made horrid gurgling, drowning sounds in the back of his throat.

'*Die*, you bastard, *die!*' muttered Crouch in a low voice.

But it was almost dawn before the man took his final breath.

# CHAPTER SEVENTEEN

A man had no control over his life. It was daft to think otherwise.

Five months ago the navy had placed Stoker 2nd Class Joe Levin on the corvette, HMS *Polyanthus*, on North Atlantic convoy duty. The *Polyanthus* had already survived a number of transatlantic crossings, cheating death, avoiding—somehow— the U-boats that roamed the northern oceans. The odds were against you. But a stoker spent his life in the ship's engine room shovelling coal. He did not calculate probabilities, he did not plot positions on a chart. That was for other men.

In September of '43 the *Polyanthus* set off from Liverpool, part of a convoy of sixty-five merchant vessels escorted by nineteen warships bound for New York and Halifax.

At the end of his first shift the sun emerged over the stern and Joe smoked a cigarette, gazing at the line of ships that stretched as far as the horizon, and he wondered how the U-boats, patrolling a line south of Greenland and directly in their path, could possibly miss them. The Germans had a new type of torpedo, one that homed in on the sound of a ship's engine and its propeller. What could you do? Turn off your engine and drift? Or plough on and trust to luck? The stoker was the first to die when a torpedo struck, the last to make it to a lifeboat. And yet some convoys did make it through. He himself had crossed the Atlantic and he had returned. A line of sixty-five ships in an ocean this big was like trying to locate a single star in a galaxy full of stars.

And so it was. Day after day there was no landfall and no sign of anyone or anything. The lashing grey waves merged with the low grey skies so that the war might have ended, the land might have been swallowed up by the ocean, and you would not know it.

Some convoys did make it through.

But not this one. On the sixth day, at a point somewhere between Greenland and Iceland, the U-boats found them. A Canadian ship, the *St. Croix*, was the first to be sunk. The *Poly-anthus*, turning back to pick up survivors, was struck next. She broke up and sank so quickly barely a handful of men survived. Clinging to the scorched remnants of their ship through the night, some of the survivors froze to death. The remaining few were picked up at dawn by HMS *Itchen*.

All but two. Two men in a lifeboat were missed. In the darkness and the rough seas, in all the chaos, and as their shipmates were pulled aboard the rescue ship, a stoker and a petty officer watched helplessly as the current took them further and further away. The petty officer, mortally wounded in the explosion, died quite soon after. The stoker, who had been blown clean out of the vessel when the torpedo had struck and who remembered nothing at all of the explosion, now salvaged the dead man's clothes in an effort to keep warm and pushed the man's corpse overboard.

Then he waited to die.

A day later the *Itchen* was hit and sank, along with most of its crew and the few survivors from the *Polyanthus* who had been plucked from the ocean the day before. Stocker 2nd Class Joe Levin, after three days adrift, was picked up by a passing Polish merchant vessel and a week later was recuperating in a Liverpool hospital suffering nothing worse than hypothermia, dehydration and frostbite.

He spent a fortnight in the Liverpool hospital, and while he lay in his bed on the ward with his fingers and toes in bandages, watching the nurses pad softly back and forth and listening to the seaman in the bed opposite scream for his mother, he found himself thinking about the lack of control a man had over his life and the futility of thinking otherwise. He thought about the red-haired nurse with the lilting Highlands accent who worked the night shifts and who smelled of carbolic soap and whose uniform rustled with starch so that he knew she was coming seconds before she entered the ward. At night he dreamed about the dead petty officer whom he had stripped and tipped overboard. He saw the man's bloated corpse lying on the seabed in utter darkness many fathoms beneath the sea, then he saw the corpse picked clean by all the various creatures of the ocean until only a skeleton remained, but the skull still had eyes that watched him, accusingly.

On his last night, as the rest of the ward slept and the seaman in the bed opposite wept quietly, the red-haired nurse with the lilting Highlands accent came to him in the still of the night. She crept into his bed and gave him what he had waited a fortnight for. It did not surprise him that she did so. He was a man who had cheated death and he had done so not with any great skill or prowess, but simply by dumb good fortune and the nurse recognised this. She gave herself to him, in part, as a reward but in some other, almost indefinable way, in the hope that his good fortune would rub off on her, would permeate her. She said nothing whatsoever to suggest this but Joe felt it and he did not question it.

After two weeks in the hospital the navy had sent Joe home to recuperate and after more than three years at sea, after nearly four years away, he had had to learn how to live in a house with a wife and a small child. And they had had to learn how to live with him.

⌒

An explosion somewhere to the south-east—the docks maybe—caused a low rumble and the air lit up a brilliant yellow and Joe dived for cover. The last thing he needed was a sky lit up like Guy Fawkes Night. He had found a narrow passageway between two buildings, barely wider than the breadth of a man's shoulders, and he crouched there, swallowed by the shadows, until the sky turned black once more.

It was the first time he had stopped running since he had left Nancy in the Underground station and he leaned his head back against the brickwork and closed his eyes, drawing in slow, deep breaths. He still wore the buff-coloured seaman's duffle coat he had purloined from the warehouse he had taken refuge in and now he stuffed his hands into its pockets for warmth, feeling the coat stretch across his shoulders and ride up at his wrists, feeling his own stocky frame fit uneasily inside another man's clothes.

He pulled up the hood of the coat, wishing he had taken a hat. He was making his way south. He was, he believed, though it was difficult to be sure, in Three Colts Lane.

He didn't pause for long. Even in the air raid people were out and about. He eased himself to his feet and set off once more, moving in a low crouching run with both hands thrust out, partly for balance, because the ground was uneven at best, partly in case he ran slap bang into something or someone, because he could see no more than a yard or so in front of his face. The clouds that had blanketed this part of the city for some hours shifted and a pale moonlight now illuminated his way. Joe stopped dead. This wasn't Three Colts Lane. He had missed his way in the blackout.

Where, then, was he? He stood quite still, his heart hammering under his ribs, the boom of distant explosions rippling through the air and making the earth beneath his feet vibrate. There were buildings on both sides, warehouses perhaps, and a large structure a little way ahead that stretched up and over the road. A railway bridge. He listened for footsteps ahead or behind him but could make out nothing. You'd have to be crazy to be out in this—crazy or desperate.

What was to be done? Go back and try to retrace his steps or press on and trust he'd find himself somewhere familiar soon enough?

A train rattled over the bridge in the darkness, making a terrific sound in the deserted lane, and Joe realised the bombing had stopped, for a time at least. The train showed no lights but it was going east. This was the overground line that took you north-east through Walthamstow and Wood Green as far as Chingford, or north to Seven Sisters and Edmonton and Enfield.

Only a goods train would be travelling at this hour. Carrying munitions, perhaps, or armaments. He stood quite still, waiting for it to pass, wincing every time the wheels sent sparks spraying into the darkness. It would make a good target for any stray passing bomber.

The last railway truck rattled nosily overhead and was gone and the laneway shuddered into silence. Not silence: a rat scurried over his foot, distant sirens, shouts, the bells of emergency vehicles testified to the continuing chaos of the raid. But it was to the south, over towards the docks, wasn't it? There had been no bombs behind him, from the direction in which he had just fled, had there?

Joe turned, his fingers clenched tightly in his coat pocket, feeling every muscle, every nerve tense and ready to spring forward. He wanted to go back, to run full pelt back to the Underground station to find Nancy and Emily. In his head he was already running and his heart was racing and he was gulping down breath after breath to fill his aching lungs. But he had not moved.

He mustn't go back.

He bent over, his hands on his knees, breathing deeply. He searched for a cigarette then stopped himself—the flare of the match would advertise his presence as accurately as a searchlight or the blast from a police whistle.

After a moment he straightened up, feeling his alarm slowly dissipate.

Behind him was the unmistakable crunch of a man's footsteps on broken glass, a heavy step in boots, perhaps a fireman, policeman, serviceman. He didn't wait to find out but set off once more, moving swiftly, under the railway bridge, keeping close to the side of the street, a shadow among shadows, finding his way not by memory or starlight but by instinct. This way was south and now this way and now this. When at last he swung into Whitechapel Road he stopped as though as he had walked into a wall. It was dark, of course, but his eyes had adjusted by now. He could sense the broad east–west thoroughfare before him and a little to his left the giant edifice of the London Hospital, black against a black sky.

Thank God. Here was a place he had left behind when he had met Nancy, but here was a place he fled to now when he needed help. Something welled inside him. It was the same feeling he had had adrift in the lifeboat when the Polish ship had appeared out of the mist and his life had been saved.

He waited a few minutes in the shadow before venturing to cross the wide road. Even in a blackout, with a raid going on half a mile away, Whitechapel Road was never entirely deserted. And there were plenty of men out tonight simply because there was a raid on, and each one of them was every bit as desperate as he was and would not hesitate to cut his throat and rob him if it advanced their own position. It wasn't just men. Out of the darkness a girl emerged, shivering in a summer dress, her thin arms wrapped around herself, pacing the roadside. She turned to stare at him, her face was as white as the whites of her eyes. You'd have to be desperate to ply your wares in a raid, in the blackout, on a night this cold. But there was always someone more desperate than yourself, that was what war taught you.

The girl saw him, called out to him, but her words were lost in another explosion. This time it was to the west, towards the City, and under its cover Joe darted over the road and plunged down the first side street he came to, and then another. He heard the drone of an enemy aircraft right overhead and he dived into a doorway, crouching, his hands covering his head.

❦

After his three days adrift in the North Atlantic he had spent three months at home recuperating. One month for each day— that had seemed the least the navy could do; three months for the entire ship's company lost, eighty-five men, roughly one day for each man. Two or three days each, he reckoned, for the few who had survived and been picked up by the *Itchen* only to be torpedoed a day or so later, and a day or two for the petty officer whose body he had tipped out of the lifeboat and who lay now at the bottom of the ocean. And with each day of his leave some part of him had thought, *The navy has forgotten about me, they have forgotten I am here. If I just keep my head down they will let me be.* For, by then, he had learned how to be at home with his family, and they had learned how to be with him.

It had not been easy. He had been married so short a time before his call-up that all he wanted on his return was to be alone with his wife, to remember who she was, to learn what it meant to be a husband. But they were not alone. There was Emily, who had grown up in a house with only her mum and the Rosenthals upstairs, who had no place in her world for a dad, had no use for one. She had screamed when he had arrived home in his uniform with his sun-blistered skin and his bristly chin and smelling of the sea. Nancy knew how to handle her and he did not. He learned, quickly, to resent how much of his wife's time, his wife's energy, the kid gobbled up.

It was not a happy house that first week or two.

Then Harry turned up.

He appeared one evening at Joe's local when Joe had not even told his brother he was home with an offer of work down the docks. It was extra money, Harry said, and Joe welcomed the idea, though Nancy, when she found out, was furious.

But a convoy had come in and after his first shift Joe arrived home with two tins of peaches in syrup and a tin of Carnation milk and his wife and child fell on him like he had won the Victoria Cross. The kid ran to him, screaming with delirious excitement. After this they had got along just fine, he and the kid. He took her to the park, though it was all dug up for the war effort. He carried her on his shoulders through the stalls on market day and sat with her on his lap at his local letting her lick the froth from his beer. He marvelled at all the things she could do and say, this tiny perfect creature that was a part of him and a part of his wife, at times almost a miniature of Nancy the way she became cross in a moment just as his wife did, the way she would shrug her tiny shoulders with contrary stubbornness.

She tripped one Sunday evening after tea on the hard kitchen tiles and split her lip and he felt his insides turn over. He scooped her up and felt the world a hostile place closing in around them.

It had not been easy with Nancy either, and her love had required more to coax it than a tin of peaches and a can of Carnation milk. In a world of rationing and bombs and blackouts his wife had learned to survive on her own. And then he wondered, had she already been that person when he had met her, orphaned and alone, brought up in a Shoreditch boarding house? He did not know. The person he had written frantic, bored, yearning letters to from his bunk on board his ship seemed not to exist except in his own head. His wife was strong. She hardly seemed to need him. Her beauty and her strength overwhelmed him, it frightened him. The two of them, she and the kid, had grown to fill the space he had left and he felt clumsy in her presence, a grotesque giant of a thing, too large for the furniture, too tall for the room, always crashing into things. He blamed his sea legs for this; he had been at sea three years, it took a while to learn how to be on dry land.

At night he thought about the red-haired nurse with the lilting Highlands accent who had crept into his bed on the ward and made love to him as a stranger would. His wife made love to him in the same way, like a stranger, and that disturbed him. And it bewitched and transfixed him. The evening she had told him she had gone with another man he thought he would go mad. But he did not go mad. Instead he crossed the space that had separated them and woke the next morning beside her in their bed. It turned out his wife knew him better than he knew himself.

He had not let her out of his sight or out of his heart since that morning.

∽

The enemy aircraft had flown right overhead and a searchlight tracked it across the sky, followed a second or two later by a burst of fire from an AA gun. He looked up, watching the tracer bullets from the gun create a flickering red trail before fading away. The first greyish tinge of dawn glowed faintly in the east.

177

The night was ending and he needed to be further away than this by daybreak.

He had taken a stupid risk going to the tube station to find Nancy, but she needed to be warned, for there was every chance the police would go to the house, might even arrest her. And he had needed to tell her his plan, which had appeared to him, laid out like a map, as he had sat with her: they would go to Dublin, and from there to America. He had been to America, to New York. A man could get lost there. They could start a new life. He had sat with Nancy and remembered the coves and inlets and endless beaches of Long Island and the wharves on the dockside at Brooklyn, the ferries hopping to and from Staten Island, the statue that overlooked the city at the point where the East River met the Hudson. If he could just have explained it to her he knew that Nancy would understand, would feel the excitement, the hope that he had felt when he had seen these things. But he had been unable to explain it and she had been filled with dismay, not hope, at leaving London. He was unsure if he had convinced her or not. But she would come, he knew, because it was better to be far from home in a strange place with your man than it was to be safe at home without him.

But so far his journey had got him only as far as Whitechapel, and America was as far off to him now as it must have seemed to Nancy a few hours earlier.

He left the doorway in which he had taken refuge, moving silently, and there was silence now, the AA gun had fallen still, the enemy aircraft gone. It was quiet enough that he heard the bells of an ambulance suddenly loud dead ahead and he realised he had become disorientated and was much closer to the hospital than he had supposed. He followed the sound when he ought to have gone in the other direction, away from it, and he saw the ambulance pulling up at the front of the hospital, a second one close behind. And then two more—four ambulances, one after another, their bells ringing, and into the emerging dawn nurses, porters, a doctor streamed from the hospital and moved from one to the other opening doors, pointing, shouting, directing.

Something had happened, something had taken a direct hit.

And now a fifth ambulance appeared but this one had no bells ringing and it drew up not at the main entrance but at a side door where the mortuary was. No one ran to open its doors.

This was the moment to leave. The darkness was fast disappearing and all around him people in uniforms were shouting and running. It was not a time to be standing around waiting to be observed, waiting to be questioned, although in the chaos no one did observe him, no one did ask questions. All the same, it was time to leave. A young woman stood at the bottom of the steps in a volunteer nurse's uniform madly checking a clipboard, flipping over one page after another as though she could save a life simply by finding a name on a list. Joe went over to her.

'Miss, what's happened?'

She looked up, peering at him through round spectacles with the bewildered expression of someone who had worked through the night. 'A bomb went off. At the Underground station where people were sheltering. I'm sorry, but you'll have to move. We've got a lot of injured.'

'Which underground station? Whitechapel?'

But Joe could see Whitechapel Station. It was just the other side of the main road. He could see it had not taken a direct hit. Shoreditch then. Aldgate. Stepney—

'Bethnal Green,' said the woman. And she hurried away.

The seams of her stockings were crooked and little spots of mud were caked on the back of her legs as though she had been splashed though it had not rained for days. Joe turned away. In the cab of the first ambulance a woman driver sat with the door open, smoking a cigarette with nicotine-stained fingers and watching her ambulance being unloaded in her rear mirror and he approached her.

'I say, don't stand there,' she called out, waving him away. 'We're about to take off. You'll be mown down.' She had a clipped voice, like the voice of the woman program announcer on the BBC.

'How many hurt?' he asked, ignoring this.

'About a dozen I should say, but really you must—'

'Any dead?'

Before she could answer her colleague jumped in beside her and she tossed away her cigarette and started up the engine.

'Please, miss—*any dead*?'

'Two,' she called out. 'Mother and child, I think.' And they moved off and he leaped out of the way.

He was quite calm. There had been a hundred, two hundred mothers and children in that shelter. There was no reason to think it was them. He watched the stretchers being unloaded and followed behind, moving from one to another, peering at each face. When they had all been unloaded and the last ambulance had gone he walked around to the side entrance and it was still there, the fifth ambulance. No one had bothered with it. But at that moment the mortuary door swung open and a porter emerged, followed by a second man, and they walked over and cranked open the rear doors of the ambulance. They disappeared inside, re-emerging a moment later with two lifeless forms on stretchers, one an adult—he could see a single uncovered foot sticking out of the end of the blanket, no shoe, no stocking, clearly a woman's foot, and the porter twitched the blanket to cover it. The other form was much smaller, a child. Joe watched. He was calm. Somewhere in the distance he heard a low drone, becoming louder. An aircraft.

'Move aside, please,' said the porter as they manhandled the first stretcher up a short ramp and through the door. The man paused then, glancing up and scanning the dawn sky, seeking out the source of the sound.

'Are they from the tube station?' asked Joe, pointing. 'A mother and child? Please, mate, let us take a look, I need to know if—'

'Just let us do our job,' the man interrupted tersely. He seemed anxious about the droning, which was louder now.

'Blimey, let the man look if he wants to,' cut in his colleague, who was fat and wheezing and pink in the face and seemed glad of an excuse to stop. 'These two ain't going anywhere, are they? Here.' And he pulled back the blanket from the remaining body, the child.

Joe stood and looked down. He saw a dark-haired little girl with a red hairband and a very white, still face. It wasn't Emily. It was some other child. He looked at her and felt his heart would break because a little girl had died. He had thought he would be relieved, that the relief would make him faint, sick, but there was no relief. Though he did feel faint and sick.

'Let me see the other one,' he pleaded, turning away from the lifeless form before him. 'Let me see the mother.'

But the AA gun started up then with a sudden, short burst, and the gun emplacement must be right here on the hospital roof, for the noise made him reel and clap his hands to his ears. It made sense to put the AA gun on the roof of the hospital, which was the highest building for miles around, though it was crazy too, a gun on the roof of a hospital—you would think it made the hospital a target for enemy bombers. As he thought this, the enemy bomber flew right overhead, filling the whole sky, turning dawn back to night-time, and Joe flung himself to the ground, covering his head because the aircraft was surely going to fly right into the hospital, and the AA gun burst into life again. He curled into a ball and his fingers dug into the concrete.

# CHAPTER EIGHTEEN

## *Cairo*

The Light Mk VI was done for. They had limped into GHQ late
in the afternoon and the engine had blown up. They had rescued
their kit, saluted the old girl, given her an affectionate pat on the
turret and abandoned her to her fate. No one had seemed to mind
or to question it. The roads leading into Cairo were littered with
abandoned military hardware that no one had the inclination or
the time to salvage. Gerald had made his report to Cathcart, his
CO, and Cathcart had seemed supremely uninterested and given
him no further orders. That was fine by Gerald. He had had a
long bath, dug out a change of clothes and presented himself at
the officers' mess, where he proceeded to drink large quantities
of pink gin in the company of an adjutant from the Royal Rifle
Corps and a captain from the Argylls.

The mess swirled about him disconcertingly in a pungent fug
of Turkish cigarettes and Turkish coffee. Before the war the place
had been the bar of a lavish turn-of-the-century European hotel
that in daylight hours afforded magnificent views over a sweeping

MAGGIE JOEL

terrace, a polo field and a croquet lawn down to the banks of the Nile. Now the blackout blinds and stuttering hurricane lamps threw the interior, crowded with wicker chairs and tables and potted palms, into flickering relief. A radio tuned to Egyptian State Broadcasting idly played light music in the background and a copy of a week-old *Egyptian Gazette* lay discarded on the table before them. Six months ago, a year ago, the whole place had been teeming with South Africans, Greeks, Maltese, Cypriots, Czechs, Poles, Australians, New Zealanders—officers from all over the Empire, with sappers and engineers and infantry, with signalmen and airmen and naval commanders, even the top brass, and one had had to fight for a seat and elbow one's way to the bar. Now the war had moved elsewhere and the place had a neglected, somewhat depressing air to it and the only men left were the wounded, the pen-pushers and the salvage and clean-up boys. The single barman, a bald Egyptian with a drooping moustache and a resigned air, polished glasses and looked bored.

There had been no letters waiting for Gerald upon his return and that had surprised him. So instead he addressed the adjutant who had a letter open before him and who was marginally less drunk than the captain from the Argylls.

'What's the news from home?'

'My wife's left me,' said the adjutant, a large man with a clipped moustache and rapidly blinking eyes. He reached unsteadily for a cigarette and swore when it dropped to the floor.

'I say, I'm most dreadfully sorry, old boy,' said Gerald, who had only met the fellow an hour before and had already forgotten his name. He gave the man one of his own cigarettes and lit it for him. 'Jolly nasty for you.'

'Ran off with a Yank!' the man said, sitting up and becoming bellicose. 'Bloody little tart! He's welcome to her.'

'Aye. You're well shot of her, mon,' said the captain, a Glaswegian with an almost impenetrable accent and a florid complexion, his eyes half closed by alcohol. It was not clear to Gerald if these two already knew each other and if the captain in the Argylls was therefore in a positon to make an informed observation about the adjutant's wife or was merely drunk. 'They're all bloody tarts!' the man added, addressing his tumbler of gin morosely.

'Not all, surely,' said Gerald. 'My wife—'

He paused, not quite certain what he had been going to say. He wished them to understand that his wife was not a tart, but he could not quite bring himself to utter the word in the same sentence. It felt wrong, thinking of Diana in the same breath as a tart. It defiled her, somehow. It defiled him.

'My wife is a good woman,' he said finally, and because it was the truth.

'You're a lucky man,' said the Scot darkly, as though he found something sinister in Gerald's assertion.

'Bloody little tart,' said the adjutant and, to their horror, he began to weep silently.

They got the poor chap back to his quarters and the Scot wandered off to the brothels in Clot Bey to find a tart of his own, leaving Gerald to kill the remainder of his evening alone. Having no wish to spend it in the company of other morose or belligerent fellow officers, he wandered past the commandeered Semiramis Hotel and the closed and blacked-out palaces and government offices in Midan Ismail and down towards the riverside.

The air had a different quality here away from the desert, having an almost tangible viscosity that made one's flesh clammy to the touch. The flies were gone but in their place angry mosquitos buzzed, and crickets, frogs—or at any rate some unidentifiable form of wildlife—croaked and sang and chirped loudly and relentlessly the closer one got to the river. Wide, graceful steps led down to the water at this point, framed by a regal line of palm trees, and he imagined that, in another era, white-suited colonial officials and their wives would have paraded, liveried man servants scurrying a step behind wielding elegant white parasols. Now the few people one met were government officials in battered panama hats or the girls sitting smoking outside the brothels or locals in their long white tunics peddling, for a few piasters, whatever came to hand and who regarded one with suspicion if not open hostility. The European hotels along the water's edge that had all been requisitioned during the desert war had, for the most part, been decommissioned but were sadly knocked about, an echo of their former selves showing keenly the effects of four years of military occupation and enemy air strikes. Still, it was safer here in the European part of the city. He had an idea if he strayed too far he'd end up as a corpse floating in the river. He had been here in '42 when Rommel had been a mere two hours away and the local traders, in anticipation of his arrival, had displayed *Rommel Wilkommen* signs in their shop windows.

He had reached the river's edge and he paused. Small naval craft were moored to a pontoon along with a scattering of merchant vessels and the smaller, rickety craft favoured by the locals. The water lapped gently, a crust of detritus washing against the bulwark. Moonlight shimmered on the water's surface, illu-minating what the blackout tried to obscure, and he could make out the shadows of the bridges that crossed to Gezira, the island that sat squarely in the middle of the river, and on its northern tip Zamalek, where the ex-pats had lived in those far-off days before the war.

There had been no letters waiting for him. He did not fear that his wife would run off with a Yank, for he trusted implicitly in her fidelity and in their marriage. It concerned him that her letters to him had not got through, had perhaps been sunk by enemy action, or that his letters to her had somehow failed to arrive. In his last letter he had taken some time to describe the desert at dawn to her because it had struck him at the time as something beautiful and he had sat on the roof of the Mk VI and tried to put down in words how it had seemed to him. Of course, it was entirely likely the censors had struck the whole lot out as it gave away his location—though what use the enemy would make of it he could not imagine. But the rest of the letter, where he had asked after her and Abigail, about the rationing and the bombing, where he had recalled in vivid detail a tennis match they had attended together before the war, she would have been able to read that part. In that dawn sitting on the roof of the tank he had wanted to write, *I am alive! Ashby is dead but I have made it!* but he did not write that. Instead he asked about the rationing and recalled a tennis match.

He had taken Diana to Wimbledon once because she had never been. It had been the year the Americans had made a clean sweep of it and they had watched Helen Wills Moody easily account for Elizabeth Ryan in straight sets and Diana had applauded wildly and enthusiastically and he had felt his heart lift. Afterwards they had eaten strawberries and clotted cream out of a bowl with their fingers and he had asked her to marry him. He had had no engagement ring with him, for he had not expected to ask her. It had struck him at the time what a very different thing this was to the thing with Bunny. That had been a voyage, exhilarating and terrifying but tainted by wretchedness and despair and, ultimately, hopelessness. With Diana it was a steady but satisfying climb on a warm August afternoon in the Peak District. Later, when he had located his mother's engagement ring and presented it to her, she had said, 'What was your mother's name?' And when he had told her she had said, 'How beautiful, I wish I had met her', and, 'If we are to have a little girl that must be her name.'

They had married at Marylebone Registry Office after a downpour on a cool October morning and when they had emerged as man and wife the pavements had gleamed wetly in the sunlight.

But there had been no little girl, and no little boy. There had been two babies in the early years of their marriage that Diana had lost in the first months of her pregnancy and then nothing. He had been unconcerned at their childlessness, for that appeared to be their fate. Diana had been twenty-five when they had married then, somehow, suddenly, she was thirty-five and he forty and he had felt keenly her growing misery, had assured her it did not matter. But it did matter, dreadfully, to her. It was a sort of craving in her, as if without a child she was unfinished, incomplete. He could not feel the same way but he saw how she suffered and it grieved him.

War had been declared and it seemed to Gerald that his wife had declared her own war, that she had begun rationing, had hidden herself in the deepest shelter, already. The war would make very little difference.

He had been seconded to the Ministry of Supply. It had not occurred to either of them he might be called up for active service. She had fallen pregnant around the turn of the new year, though she had told him nothing until Easter had come and gone. Out of fear, he presumed, that she would lose this one too. His joy had been tempered by fear but Diana had bloomed. He had thought of requesting time off around the birth—the ministry had, at that time, been in a constant and escalating state of panic, every ministry was, but he felt sure they would agree. Then Dunkirk had happened and suddenly he had found himself attached to a tank regiment doing basic training and it had seemed the cruellest joke of all, that their child was to come just as he was to be posted overseas.

The baby was born at eight o'clock on a bright autumn morning exactly a year into the war and he had gazed upon this tiny thing they had produced together and had been unable to speak. And he had gazed at his wife and saw, perhaps properly for the first time, the grief she had endured that was, now, in this moment, gone. His indifference to all those childless years seemed to be that of another man, a misguided man who had been unable to imagine such a joyous thing as his own child, in a cot, red-faced and wrinkled and helpless, and a wife exhausted but so proud, so complete. And his imminent departure to fight in a war that Britain was losing on every front had hung heavily over it all, heightening every sense, lengthening and telescoping each moment. He had sworn to return safely to them but his awareness of the utter lack of control he now had over his own destiny had made his words hollow and meaningless.

But I am alive, he said to himself now, on a Cairo evening more than three years later, and the river lapped at his feet, the dock rats scurried along the waterfront and through the night air he could hear, distantly, the girls outside the brothels calling desultorily to passers-by. He had seen his child just that once when she had been a single day old. She was now three years and four months and he had missed one thousand two hundred and fifteen days of her young life. The fact of his absence dismayed him but her existence made every day and every battle worth the price. He thought of the last photograph that Diana had sent him, of three-year-old Abigail, seated stiffly in a chair in a pretty dress, her stubby little legs dangling high above the floor, a hairband pulling her fine dark hair back from her forehead. He had three photographs of her now, and he had peered into his child's eyes searching for some sign of himself, for some sense of her awareness of him, some comprehension in her eyes that he was the reason she went annually through this ritual. But he saw nothing. Her fingers curled around a ball that the photographer had placed in her lap.

Ashby had had a child too, a little boy called Marcus, and the fact of Marcus was like a pain striking his heart and he felt ashamed at his own feelings of helplessness and loss.

He returned to the barracks, passing through roadblocks and checkpoints, showing his pass to bored MPs who, like everyone, clearly wished they were somewhere else. A pretty young WAC from Cathcart's staff, in full uniform and smoking a quiet cigarette, was waiting for him with a message to report to Cathcart at once. He smartened himself up, in a perfunctory way, and presented himself at Cathcart's door to be given the news that he was going home in the morning.

∽

The call to prayer from a dozen minarets sounded distantly across the city's fading darkness. Not long after, dawn began to glow softly in the eastern sky like the embers of a dying fire, seeping between the slats of the blackout blind, and if Gerald had been asleep it would have woken him. He had not slept. His kitbag was packed, repacked, a dozen times. He heaved it over his shoulder and left, without a backward glance, out to the waiting car, his shirt already soaked through with sweat though the sun had hardly risen.

He travelled in an open staff car with three other officers, the sun now blazing, and the road ahead shimmered and rippled with the heat. A second car followed behind and they drove through the silently deserted streets north-west out of the city and along the Desert Road the hundred or so miles to Alexandria where the airstrip was, for they were going home not by troopship but in an RAF aircraft. With stops for refuelling, they would be home within a day.

They drew up at the airstrip where an aircraft was being readied for take-off, a twin-engine de Havilland Flamingo, a civilian plane originally, battered and worn, and for a moment Gerald's bewildered joy was tempered at the thought of flying anywhere in that thing. Aircraft in far better condition than this got shot down every day and being a transport carrier was no protection, quite the opposite: they would be a sitting target. Cathcart had said Gerald had only got a seat on the plane because someone else had dropped out at the last moment.

He stowed his kit and climbed wordlessly aboard, still numb from the early start, from the unexpected summons to Cathcart's office last night, and found a seat. He thought about the navy troopships in the harbour that were still avoiding the U-boats in the Med, still sailing via the Red Sea and the Cape. Going by plane was the difference between many weeks' voyage and a single day's journey. He pushed his fear down and out of sight. He strapped himself into his seat and the chap next to him told him that the man whose spot he had taken was an adjutant from the Royal Rifles who had shot himself at the barracks the previous night. The man had not died, he said, but was lying, critical and insensible, in the military hospital in Cairo.

The pilot and the co-pilot were already in the cockpit checking their instruments, a radio operator tucked in behind them. There were nine other passengers on the flight: a couple of doctors from a medical corps, two junior officers and a major all from the Durham Light Infantry, two NCOs from a New Zealand regiment, a captain from Reconnaissance and a South African sapper. One of the lieutenants from the DLI wore a bandage around his head and seemed not to be quite all there. His fellow officer stayed by his side the whole time, explaining everything, though the man seemed not to hear him. His major smoked foul-smelling cigars and ignored them both. The Kiwis and the South African began smoking and playing cards at once. The captain and the two doctors just smoked and looked out of the window or tried to sleep. No one spoke. As the aircraft lurched upwards Gerald felt his stomach tighten sickeningly. The aircraft banked steeply and he grabbed the seat in front of him, seeing the horizon at a crazy angle through the tiny porthole, sea one moment, desert the next. He relaxed his grip and folded his arms before him. He would think of nothing.

They flew west along the coast, covering in a matter of hours the mile after mile of rugged, mine-pocked desert that two armies had fought over for three years and where Ashby had died, coming down briefly in the afternoon to refuel in Tunis, where sandwiches were handed around, and again in Gibraltar, where blankets were distributed. After this they turned north, flying through the night over neutral Portugal and the Bay of Biscay, meeting no enemy aircraft but buffeted mercilessly by a fierce headwind, landing at RAF Exeter with ice on their wings in the frozen pre-dawn.

Someone on the ground yanked the door open and pulled down the steps and they climbed stiffly down from the aircraft and stood, like dazed animals, in the cold air, too stunned even to flap their arms or blow on their numbed fingers. Their bodies, which for years had sweated and laboured beneath a desert sun, went into shock—all except the captain from Recon, who had remained silent and sullen throughout the journey, and now fell to his knees and wept. No one said anything or even appeared particularly surprised but Gerald swallowed a lump in his throat and the de Havilland, the airstrip, the huts at the edge of the airstrip, blurred before his eyes. He looked upwards into a sky that was thick with impenetrable grey cloud, an English sky, and his eyes filled with tears.

They shuffled in a ragged, bewildered group towards the huts, where a red-faced woman with a streaming cold in a headscarf and a dirty apron with a cigarette in the corner of her mouth was ill-naturedly serving weak, undrinkable coffee, and they gazed at her and her undrinkable coffee with grateful and mute joy, even when she tried to charge them a shilling and demanded ration books they did not possess. The major from the Durhams had a car and driver waiting for him and was whisked away. The rest of them hitched a lift into the town in the back of an army truck. The cold sliced through their thin desert fatigues like a thousand unceasing pinpricks, numbing and painful at the same time, and they shivered, hugging themselves, teeth chattering uncontrollably as the open truck lurched through country lanes and onto a main road. It hurt to open one's eyes to the wind and the frozen air.

As they reached the outskirts of the town Gerald saw bombed buildings, whole rows of houses gone, in street after street, deep craters everywhere. The people were pale and gaunt, jumping over puddles and bomb debris, huddled in layer upon layer and hurrying as though they feared being caught outside. They seemed like a crowd in a wilderness.

The truck dropped them at the railway station and, seeing a public telephone, Gerald had the wild idea of telephoning Diana. It was dark but the day had begun, Diana would be at home. The telephone on the table in the hallway would ring. She would come to the phone, pulling on a dressing-gown, perhaps with Abigail in her arms, and pick up the receiver expecting—

Here his imagination stalled. For what would he say? *Hello, old girl, it's me. I'm back.* Dear God. It was dreadful. He baulked at the stilted blandness of his words but no others presented themselves. And in the end it did not matter, for the girl at the exchange laughed humourlessly and said there were no lines available and didn't he know there was a war on? and promptly disconnected him.

They boarded the next London train, finding space where they could in the corridor or standing. Fields and villages and lanes rushed past the window. England, it appeared, had changed out of all recognition and at the same time had not changed at all, and Gerald felt himself take pleasure in the tumble-down farm buildings, the canals, the frost on the ground, the bare branches of the trees.

*Now I am on my way!*

The train stopped and started again and was shunted into sidings to allow other trains to pass, it was rerouted and diverted and finally terminated altogether at Clapham Junction, which was not even on the Exeter to London line, but the line ahead was closed due to a bomb and they all disembarked.

It was late afternoon, around four. The day, such as it had been, had gone, and as Gerald stood on the platform with his kitbag the darkening evening air came at him through his ears and his mouth and his nose and even his eyes and he could not think.

There would be no more trains that day. They would have to continue their journey by bus or Underground. People drifted away, uncomplaining, numbed to discomfort, to unfulfilled expectations. Gerald could see none of his fellow Cairo travellers; they had melted away like the day itself, and any camaraderie that may have built up over the long and fraught journey had melted away with it. He left the station and found, outside, another public telephone and this one had a directory in it. He went into the box and closed the door behind him, enjoying the relative warmth that the enclosed space momentarily afforded him, and repelled by the long-forgotten smell of phone-box stale cigarettes and piss. He fingers went to the 'A's and he found Ashby's wife at 38 Commongate Road, Clapham. For Ashby had lived here, in Clapham, and of all the places he might have been stranded, fate had seen fit to dump him here, in Ashby's backyard. It was a penance for his survival, for his being spared while Ashby was taken. It must be done; why not now? God knew when he might find himself down here again.

He did not bother to try to telephone—the humourless laughter of the girl at the exchange in Exeter still sounded in his ear—but set off south and east towards the Common in the direction provided by a helpful clerk in the booking office.

There were Americans everywhere. He had not expected that. It seemed as though every uniform was that of a GI, every voice he heard an American one. They were fresh-faced and handsome, tall and lean and strong and smiling. He resented that. And so many civilians, hurrying home. Not one of them cast him a second glance, or if they did it was his deeply suntanned face that they saw, a visible sign that he had just returned from foreign parts, that he had just gone through a war in the desert.

Or did they think he had been on a long holiday on the Riviera?

No, they thought nothing, they turned away at once if they saw him at all. There was a barrier around him that they could not see and that Gerald was only dimly becoming aware of but it was swelling around him, intensifying, with each step he took among them. He very soon began to hate the civilians even more than he resented the Americans. He wished only to be among other military men.

His eyes had adjusted quickly to the blackout so that he found the road easily enough. Pale moonlight showed him elegant late-Victorian villas on the north side of the road and the south side bordered the Common, a void that stretched away into the night, impenetrable and uninviting, and Gerald felt a longing for the desert so strong it took his breath away.

This was not how he'd imagined his homecoming.

Number 38 was a double-fronted four-storey establishment with bay windows and a small paved area at the front from which white-painted steps led up to a raised entranceway and a lead-lighted front door. A decorative lantern hanging above the door was unlit. The windows were black, as were all the windows the entire length of the street, and he only knew it was the right house because he had counted and now shone a tiny torch at the brass numbers on the gatepost. He had not given a thought to what he was going to say but little could be achieved by his remaining on the doorstep, so he rang the bell and waited. It seemed a vain and rather shameful hope that no one would be in, he knew Mrs Ashby *would* be in, and when he heard footsteps in the hallway he was not even surprised. Just for a second Ashby appeared, startlingly clear, before him and Gerald uttered a few silent words to him, part in prayer, part in apology.

The front door was cautiously opened and light from a distant room seeped out so that the blackout was compromised. Gerald saw a woman silhouetted in the doorway, a matronly figure with hair tied up in a bun and a girth that filled the doorway; he saw a tight-fitting functional dress and swollen ankles above feet wedged into too-tight formal shoes. This could not be Ashby's wife. He had come to the wrong house.

The woman peered at him, and he could tell from the jerk of her head, her silence, that she took in his uniform, his kitbag. It was too dark for her to see his face.

'I'm so sorry to bother you,' said Gerald, and his voice sounded absurd, somehow. 'I'm looking for—is this the house of Mrs Ashby?' It was. He knew it by the way she lifted her chin, suspicion replaced by surprise, curiosity. 'My name is Meadows. I was a friend of Captain Ashby. I just wanted to—'

He stopped. He wanted very much for this woman to interrupt him, to announce that, unfortunately, Mrs Ashby was out. That Mrs Ashby no longer lived here. That Mrs Ashby had taken her child and gone to live with relatives in Bristol for the duration. But instead she said, 'Please wait here,' and went back inside, closing the door but reopening it almost at once and saying, 'Won't you please come in, Mr Meadows?'

He followed her down a short, ill-lit but graceful hallway with a parquetry floor that smelled of wax furniture polish and potpourri and something indistinguishable but distinctively comforting and familiar, the smell of English houses filled with old furniture and thick carpets and flocked William Morris wallpaper and burning coal fires. And disconcertingly the hallway banked suddenly so that he reached out a hand to steady himself. It had happened periodically throughout the day as his body readjusted itself to the solid ground after the day spent in the aircraft, but he wished that the woman, who had paused outside a doorway, had not witnessed this. Her face gave nothing away and she stood aside to let him pass.

He found himself in a large and comfortable living room carpeted in dark green pile and wallpapered with some kind of roses design, heavy velvet curtains at the window and mid-Victorian Pre-Raphaelite reproductions on the wall. Crowded bookshelves, glass-fronted cabinets of chinaware and a chintz settee with two matching armchairs made up the bulk of the furniture. A beautiful original marble fireplace filled one wall with coals glowing hotly, a coal scuttle and tongs on the hearth before it. It was all so very, very English and Gerald smiled help-lessly to see it.

Mrs Ashby was seated on the settee, perched on its edge, her legs crossed at the ankles, hands placed, one over the other, on her knee. It was her feet he saw first, black shoes, slender ankles, dark stockings, a charcoal grey skirt, a pinkish or mauve blouse with a bow at the collar and a black collarless woollen jacket of some sort, fitted and well cut. She sat very upright, and in the soft light of the lampshade and the flickering light from the coals one side of her neck was bathed red, the other side was in shadow. Even so, Gerald knew her, had seen her photograph and would have recognised her at once. The photograph Ashby had had was a studio shot, carefully staged, a woman swathed in furs, artfully made up and glancing at the camera with a still, serene face devoid of expression. Quite, quite beautiful yet utterly devoid of expression—and that was how she appeared to him now. She observed him as though she was that photograph brought to life, her face perfectly symmetrical, her mouth and eyes unmoving so that he had no sense of her at all, could not tell even if she wore make-up or not. A woman made of porcelain, perfect and flawless—and utterly breakable. For now he saw it, a flush of colour on both cheeks that might have been heat from the fire but he knew was not. She rose in one fluid movement, uncrossing her legs, standing up, holding out one hand, the other hand falling to her side, her eyes never leaving his face.

'Captain Meadows,' she said in a deep, clear voice, taking his hand as though she had been expecting him. 'Please sit down. Mrs Woodcock, would you be a dear and bring tea and cake?'

The utter conventionality of her words struck him mute and Gerald sat, at a loss where to put his kitbag, handing it finally to the waiting Mrs Woodcock. Mrs Ashby sat down again, exactly as she had been sitting before, and without realising it he mimicked her, sitting on the edge of the sofa, turned slightly towards her, hands on his knees. And all the while her face did not move. There was an intensity about her, held rigidly in check, and at the same time a languidness that defied—and denied—all feeling. Or did he imagine that intensity? Either way, he could not take his eyes from it, for the only women he had seen in three years had been the Syrian, Moroccan, Egyptian girls outside the brothels or the occasional WAC, twenty years his junior, gauche and giggling, swapping lipsticks like schoolgirls. Mrs Ashby was another thing altogether: a woman in her later thirties with all the poise and sophistication, the serenity and elegance that her age conferred on her but none of the petty anxiety and faded beauty of a woman past her prime.

'So kind of you to visit us,' she said. 'Christopher mentioned you often in his letters.'

For a moment Gerald had no idea to whom she was referring. Ashby, of course, whom he had never, in all that time, called by his first name.

'I wanted to pay my respects, Mrs Ashby. Your husband and I were in the same unit for a couple of years,' he heard himself saying. 'We went through it all. Together. We—' He stopped. It was not what he wanted to say, but what *did* he want to say? Something momentous, something fitting. Something worthy of Ashby, of Ashby's death. Ashby's tank had been hit by a shell and Ashby had been incinerated at the start of the battle in the Western Desert. He hoped she already knew this or did not wish to know these details, for he doubted he could relate them to her in this room, seated on the chintz settee with the Pre-Raphaelites on the wall.

But she did not ask. Instead she smiled, though her face did not move. Her eyes told him nothing. Where was she? It was as though he was making conversation with a stranger on a train. His presence seemed to make no impression on her.

The woman, Mrs Woodcock, came in pushing a trolley and they both watched her as she served tea in two bone china teacups and two very small slices of some indeterminate cake on little plates.

'Thank you, Mrs Woodcock,' Mrs Ashby said. 'Would you ask Marcus to come down?'

And when the woman had gone Gerald said, 'I hope you don't think me rude, turning up unannounced like this?' He searched her face to find some indication that she was put out or grateful— or something.

'Not at all. It's so very kind of you to bother about us.'

Her words cut him painfully because they were so horribly bland and meaningless and because, truth be told, he had not wanted to come here at all—as surely she must know—and now that he was here, he felt lost, somehow, in her presence. Did she see that?

A little boy appeared in the doorway. He was about four, dressed in too-large pink-and-white striped pyjamas and a dressing-gown that was tied around his middle. He had Ashby's hair, dark and wavy, and Ashby's ears, neat and small and flat against his head, but his mother's nose and eyes and mouth— watchful eyes, a delicate nose, slightly aristocratic, a wide mouth with narrow lips. The boy took in the tall, strange-smelling uniformed stranger and ran to his mother, wrapping his arms around her knees, burying his head in her lap.

And she gave the boy the same unsmiling smile, not moving other than to fold her arms around his small shoulders. She seemed to look over her little boy's head at the opposite wall, at something the rest of them could not see. 'Marcus, come along,' she murmured, stroking his head. 'Don't be shy. Say hello to Captain Meadows. He has travelled a long way to visit us.'

He *had* travelled a long way, but if his train had not terminated at Clapham he would not have come. Gerald watched them both wretchedly. The boy lifted his head and peered shyly, twisting his body as though he did not want the stranger to see him, or did not quite know what to do with it. 'Hullo, there, old man,' said Gerald and hated himself.

Mrs Ashby had not touched her tiny slice of cake and now she pushed it towards her little boy and he gobbled it up and Gerald thought, *There is rationing here, I had forgotten*, and he passed his own slice to the boy too, though he was aching with hunger. He drank the tea, which was almost black, a few flakes of dried milk floating on its surface.

'How long is your leave, Captain Meadows?' she said.

'No idea,' he said truthfully, as no one had told him. 'Not long, I expect. Once the paperwork catches up to me no doubt they'll ship me off again.'

'And have you a family of your own?'

'A wife and a little girl. In Buckinghamshire. I am on my way there now.'

She smiled but made no reply and Ashby filled the space between them with his absence.

The little boy stared at Gerald, picking at the crumbs on his plate and staring and staring.

'You're just like him, old man,' said Gerald, because the boy's stare was unnerving him and because, at that moment, Marcus was just like his dead father. Horribly, Gerald felt his own eyes fill with tears.

Of course they both saw it, the little boy and her, Mrs Ashby, and Gerald saw the muscles go rigid beneath the skin on her face as her mask slipped for one dreadful moment then it was back and she smiled at him and said, 'More tea, Captain Meadows?'

He did not want more tea but accepted with a nod and he knew the child saw through his politeness and despised him. But it allowed them both a minute of silence as she, his mother, carefully stirred the teapot, poured a small amount into Gerald's cup and offered him a spoonful of the dreadful dried milk, and her calmness, her poise, was devastating and magnificent now that he had seen the mask slip for that one vital moment. He wanted to reach over and fold her in his arms as she had enfolded the boy, to take her hand and hold it in his. He felt this need filling him up and filling the room as, a short while ago, Ashby had filled it.

'Ashby—Christopher—spoke of you often,' he said desperately.

Ashby had spoken of her hardly at all. It was not what one did on the eve of battle, in the mess, under a tarpaulin in the desert, on the terrace of a hotel in Cairo. One talked about tanks and munitions and the other officers and the CO and the mosquitos and the flies and the dysentery.

'Did he?' she replied, almost wistfully, and he saw that she knew he was lying. Why had he even said such a thing? But he had needed to bring Ashby back into the room. 'May I get you another slice of cake?' she said. 'Not that we have any, but it's conventional to offer, isn't it?' And before he could think of a reply, 'It's this damned war,' she said, uttering the usual cliché but dully, as though it had ceased to hold any meaning. Gerald wondered if she was referring to the lack of cake or the death of her husband.

After half an hour he got up to go; any sooner would have looked improper. She stood up at once the way someone does when they have been waiting for you to leave, but when she stood by the door and held his hand she exclaimed, 'Oh, you poor man! How cold your hands are!' and disappeared into a cupboard. When she reappeared she was holding two big thick sheepskin gloves and she took each of his hands and placed the gloves on him one by one, the way a wife might do for her husband. Gerald realised they were Ashby's gloves.

'We won't need them,' she said simply, as though he had spoken out loud.

He escaped with Ashby's gloves on his hands, fleeing the house, fleeing the woman, who was Ashby's widow, and her son, who was Ashby's little boy, bumbling his way in the blackout, not knowing where he was going or in which direction. Her calmness and her poise followed him, no matter which way he turned.

It was raining. The coldness of the rain shocked him into stopping and lifting his face to the rain till it was wet. He must get home. The delay seemed suddenly intolerable.

He found himself on a main road with a bus stop, where he waited, without hope, for a bus. When one came, he got on and an hour later was disgorged into the busy, choking melee around Victoria Station. It was a test, the visit to Mrs Ashby, some complicated test that he had somehow failed, though he could not put his finger on how, but now that he was away from the woman and her son, as every step put time and miles between him and them, the fact of his failure receded.

He walked north from Victoria, a part of, yet separate from, the melee, colliding with lampposts and other people, stumbling into craters and over bomb debris, making his way doggedly across the city that was his home and was as alien as the surface of the moon. And when he reached Baker Street Underground station it was closed due to the bombing, and when he went, instead, to Marylebone that was closed too and he was forced to give up and find a hotel—a wretched place off Dorset Square frequented by callgirls and Polish and Czech officers—where he put up for the night.

My first night back on English soil, he thought later, as he sat on the bed in shirt sleeves and listened to the pipes knocking behind the walls and the couple in the next room copulating. It was tawdry. Bleak, rundown, mean-spirited, inhospitable, unwelcoming. They had had it bad in London, of course he knew that, but the reality of it was . . . shocking. He pictured his home, so tantalisingly close now, but somehow as distant as victory had seemed in 1940. He pictured Diana in her Sunday coat and gloves after church, arranging flowers on the dining room table, turning to look at him, the secateurs in her hand, a look of calm contentment on her face; but he could not quite see her face, could only see Mrs Ashby's face, unsmiling and smiling at the same time.

He didn't want to lie down on the greasy pillow or beneath the sheets and the thin blanket, but in the end exhaustion overcame him and he wrapped himself in the blanket and pulled his cap low over his ears and slept.

He awoke with a start before dawn and for a disorientating moment was utterly lost. It was cold, numbingly cold, and when he struck a match in the grey light he saw his breath hanging in the air, he saw the ice on the inside of the hotel window. Gathering his things, he left at once, hurrying through the fading darkness to the station, catching the first Metropolitan Line train north, having a compartment to himself, and reaching Amersham an hour later. There he hitched a lift on a milk cart. Dawn had come, sluggishly and reluctantly, during his train journey, and when the milk cart dropped him on the Amersham Road his footsteps crunched in the frost.

*Why had they chosen to live somewhere so damnably difficult to get to?* he wondered as he walked briskly down the hill in the chilly early morning air. But it had seemed charming, he remembered, motoring up from Middlesex one late summer afternoon in 1930 and seeing a village barely touched by the modern world with straw on the ground and horse-drawn carts in the street.

They had found a village green lined with gabled red-brick houses overlooked by a medieval church tower, the church at the end of an ancient bricked lane, entered via a crazy Tudor archway. They had found a bridge over a stream and a pond bordered by willows and filled with ducks. They had found happiness here, even if they had failed to find a railway anywhere nearby.

Gerald crossed the bridge over the stream and saw that the pond had been drained. A large mallard waddled over in search of food. He saw that all the ducks were watching him, standing stock-still, as though waiting to see what he would do. He walked past them. People were about now—no cars, of course, due to the petrol ration, but on foot or horseback, men and women in working clothes making their way silently in the cold morning to the bus stop, the shop, the farm. Horse-drawn traps and carts, long abandoned, had been unearthed and put to work so that one could almost imagine the village had slipped back into the previous century were it not for the sandbags and stirrup pumps at every front door, the blackout curtains and the tape on every window. One or two people looked at him, frowning, wondering who he was perhaps, but no one passed close enough to recognise him and he was glad of that, for he had a sudden dread of being impeded, now, this close to home.

He left the main street and turned south into Milton Crescent, just as he had done every day for ten years on his return from his office, but he had never returned home in such turmoil, with his heart thudding in his chest and his head booming with some inner pulse that made it feel like he was in battle. He found he was staring at his boots as he walked, afraid to look up. He made himself look up. Yes, see! It had not changed, not much—despite the sandbags and stirrup pumps, the blackout curtains, the taped windows—and his sense of a previous century faded, for Milton Crescent was a between-the-wars development. Two rows of sprawling, mock-Tudor houses led up the hill away from the high street and into the fields that surrounded the village. The road veered sharply to the left two-thirds of the way along, almost curving back on itself. Their house, The Larches, was on the west side of the street, right on the apex of the curve, which provided a wonderful view from the front rooms looking back down the entire length of the street to the medieval tower of the parish church, with the rear of the house surrounded by fields. It was this double vista that had prompted them to take this house and they had enjoyed almost ten glorious years until the fields behind the house had been slated for development. Then the war had come. He could see the fields now and they stood fallow and untouched, exactly as they had been on the morning he had left.

His footsteps crunched on the gravel but fallen autumn leaves that had never been swept away and had turned to mulch soon dulled the sound. The clematis by the front door had grown monstrously, all but obscuring the door. The blackout curtains were drawn. Even now, this close, he hesitated. He wanted Diana to see him but the blackout prevented that. He wanted the front door to be flung open and her to run out, blindly, into his arms.

The front door did not open. So he walked up and knocked, like a stranger might, not using his key. He waited. He knocked a second time, louder.

'Mr Meadows! It *is*, isn't it? I saw you come up the hill but I couldn't be sure.'

It was Mrs Probart who lived next door and who was standing now at the entrance to her driveway. They had been neighbours for ten years yet he had utterly forgotten her existence. She stood now in a pair of outsized men's wellingtons and a big winter coat, blinking at the weak winter sunlight and he summoned a smile. 'It is. Hullo, Mrs Probart. How are you?' he said, feeling a sort of pounding impatience overcome him. He did not want Mrs Probart to be the first person he met, to be the woman to welcome him home.

But she was peering at him curiously now. Coming up the drive and peering at him. 'But surely you know Mrs Meadows isn't here?' she said, and for a moment he did not understand her. He remembered that Mrs Probart's husband had died many years ago, in a farming accident, that she had a number of grand-children somewhere. Leamington Spa, was it?

'I'm sorry, what do you mean?' he said.

'Mrs Meadows dropped in to say goodbye about a week ago. It was quite out of the blue—well, to me, anyway. She said she was taking Abigail away. She felt it wasn't safe here. Not with the bombs. Though I must say we've not had it at all out here. But she was anxious. She'd had a bad time of it in London, got caught in a raid, and that decided it for her, I suppose. Anyway, she left that morning—but surely you knew?'

# CHAPTER NINETEEN

Ely Levin, the man whose name Joe bore, though there was little else to connect them, had once walked these streets. Perhaps his ghost walked them now. It was even conceivable he was still alive, though he would be—

But Joe had no idea what age the old man would be.

Ely had lived his earliest years in Dukes Place at Aldgate, beneath the walls of the Great Synagogue where his ancestors had, for five generations, conducted their business, worshipped and raised their families. In his thirtieth year he had fled the confines of an Orthodox life and an early marriage to a suitable girl who had borne him five fine strong boys and two handsome and dutiful little girls but whose manner he had never become accustomed to and whose features he had never quite become reconciled to. He had fled a mile east to Whitechapel, just a week or two before the Ripper began his year-long reign of terror, and here he had met the fourteen-year-old Mary Pendergast, who knew the streets of Whitechapel well and who might herself have become a Ripper victim had Ely not taken her into his new home—two rented rooms in a tenement building in Yalta Street, in the shadow of the London Hospital—and made her his wife. An indifferent disregard for gentile law meant that Ely had not so much as changed his name before embarking on this, his second marriage. And in that district of London the name 'Ely Levin' was as common as 'John Smith' might be in other parts of the city.

There had followed a succession of children, all of whom died before their second birthday until Samuel had been born in the last weeks of the old century and had thrived. Harry had come along six years later and that had appeared to be that until the exhausted Mary, in her forty-fourth year and believing that such things were now, thankfully, beyond her, gave birth to her last child, Joseph.

During this period of uninterrupted pregnancies, births and deaths, Ely had worked for many years, though with little material gain, in the rag trade. Abandoning this vocation, he had dabbled in second-hand bookselling and the wholesaling of paper and parchment before becoming, in turn, a purveyor of spirits, of candles, of men's walking canes and of pins for ladies' hats and, finally, a supplier of hair—used in the manufacture of ladies' wigs—which he had procured, in bulk and on the sly, from a man at the London's mortuary.

He disappeared for good one bleak and windswept dawn in late October in the first year of the Great War, leaving his two sons to speculate that he had been seized by the Kaiser's spies and was languishing, forgotten, in some Prussian dungeon. It seemed more likely Ely had simply used the opportunity of a new war in

Europe to up sticks and move on to pastures new and, perhaps, to start his third family, leaving Mary to cope as best she could.

Mary's last child, Joe, had been born while the ink was still wet on the Armistice, which was to say some four years after Ely's disappearance, so the mathematical possibility of him being Ely's son seemed to be approximately nil, a conclusion that his two older brothers had reached far earlier than Joe himself and with which they had squandered no opportunity to baffle and later humiliate him as he was growing up.

∽

Joe opened his eyes to a Sunday morning in Whitechapel just as he had as a small boy. In those days he had woken to the bells of St Dunstan's at Stepney and St Mary Matfelon in Adler Street but today the dawn was still, eerie. The bells at St Dunstan's had long been melted down for the war effort and St Mary's had been destroyed by enemy fire in December 1940, so Whitechapel was silent this Sunday in wartime—more silent than in peacetime, at any rate.

At first Joe had thought himself back at the naval hospital in Liverpool with the brine encrusted on his skin and the taste of saltwater still on his lips and the memory of his rescue still raw enough to seem like a miracle. But this was not the naval hospital in Liverpool. He was in the London Hospital and a nurse, on whose ghostly face he could not quite focus, told him he had lain insensible for eight days with a concussion from a piece of shrapnel. Eight days had passed since he had parted from Nancy and fled the tube station during an air raid. Joe threw back the sheets and staggered to his feet only to fall back down again in a wave of faintness and nausea. The nurse reprimanded him, and when he finally made her understand he needed water she left and did not return.

He lay in an agony of thirst, enclosed in a vague and misty waking dream in which voices and people and smells and sounds wafted in and were swept away. Daybreak came and he only realised it had been night-time because someone opened the blackout shades and a shaft of light spilled into the ward, making him wince. He had a concussion, though he could remember nothing of it. He had a bandage around his head and when his fingers probed his temple he gasped and felt the nausea return. He decided to lie very still.

When he awoke a second time, he remembered where he was. He moved very slowly, turning his head to one side and seeing that he was in an overcrowded ward, beds crammed one after another and some people on makeshift camp beds. He found that he was still in his clothes—or still in the clothes he had stolen when he had ditched his uniform. He found he was so weak he felt ill.

'You have a concussion from a piece of shrapnel,' said a nurse, holding a cup to his lips, and he drank greedily, feeling his lips swollen and cracked, an ugly taste in his mouth, and he tried to reach the cup with his shaking fingers to keep her from taking it away. He had already known that about the concussion and the shrapnel and he wondered if the nurse had come here before and told him. The order of things was confused and slippery in his head. He fell back against the pillow, content to lie and not think any more. But he did think—about the great bells that would never ring again. About the little girl with the red hairband and the white face who was downstairs in the mortuary, dead. And about the house he had grown up in right here in Whitechapel in the shadow of this very hospital and how, until now, he had never even set foot in this, the building within whose shadow he had grown up.

It was a homecoming, of sorts.

༄

The man in the next bed had died. No one noticed. Joe had listened to the man's increasingly shallow, laboured breaths until a gurgle somewhere in the back of his throat followed by a prolonged silence, a settling of his form beneath the sheets, suggested he had gone. No one came. There was no one at his bedside. There was no way to tell if the man was old or young, married or widowed, brave or a coward. The dead man's hand slipped from the covers and hung down, a yellowish lifeless thing, the nails blackened, the fingertips nicotine-stained. Eventually a nurse came over and called out, 'Mr Trent?'

After that there was a flurry of activity. But no, not a flurry; merely a succession of persons coming and performing some necessary task and leaving, saying nothing. The body was removed, the sheets changed, the name on the chalk slate at the end of the bed rubbed out. No one spoke.

A dead man in wartime.

What name is written at the end of my bed? Joe wondered. For the first time he remembered to feel afraid. When, sometime later, a hospital administrator came to his bed with forms to be completed and questions for him to answer, a pencil poised to take down his replies, he feigned insensibility until she got up and left. This was a mistake, he realised, for he saw her a little while later talking to a policeman. No way to tell what they talked about. He ought to have given the woman a false name. A man with no identity is more interesting to the police than a man who has a name. But perhaps the administrator and the policeman were talking about Mr Trent or the weather or the raid (for there had been another raid the previous night and most of the people in the ward were here as a result of that). The administrator was the kind of middle-aged woman who before the war would have knitted baby clothing for other people's babies and grown prize-winning petunias but who now had a position that allowed her to stalk the hospital corridors with a clipboard and a pencil and talk with authority to policemen. She turned and pointed through the door of the ward at Joe and the policeman looked to where she was pointing.

Joe saw that his stay in the hospital was over. He waited for the dayshift to go off and the nightshift to come on and for the ward to settle down for the night, but it didn't settle down for a man at the end of the ward became delirious and then distressed and finally aggressive so that a stream of nurses and a doctor and two burly porters came and went one after another and no one got a moment's peace until the man was finally sedated an hour or so before dawn. When a quiet, of sorts, had at last descended and the people on the ward fell into a restless and exhausted sleep, Joe slipped from his bed and left.

He did not have far to go. He walked along a corridor into a larger corridor and out through the front door and no one stopped him or questioned him. He went down the front steps and slipped away into the darkness just as the moon shrunk away below the horizon and a faint greyish tinge coloured the eastern sky.

Monday morning.

He came, in a remarkably short time, to Yalta Street, where he hesitated, waiting across the street, silently observing the house he had grown up in.

Harry had said, *Even if things go bad, don't come here.*

But Joe had come, and in the greyish dawn it wasn't much to look at, was it, the house he had grown up in? None of the houses in Yalta Street were much to look at. It was a mid-Victorian slum built by the benevolent board of the hospital for the poor of the district and adequate for a normal-sized mid-Victorian family of eight to ten to live, if not in comfort, then at least with some modicum of dignity. But the houses had been subdivided by profiteering landlords so that each family-sized house soon housed three, four, sometimes five families, and what had once been a tight squeeze had, within a few short years, deteriorated into squalor.

Joe looked up, studying the sky. He could hear the rumble of the furnaces in the hospital's boiler rooms. If you gazed upwards from any point on Yalta Street the hospital filled your view, blocking out the sky and dwarfing the row of houses on the north side of the street, a constant and benevolent presence—and the place he had just run from. The distant rumble of the hospital furnaces was as familiar as the street itself, a street whose every cracked paving stone and overflowing drain, whose boarded-up windows and cheaply constructed and crumbing walls he knew without having to see them or touch them or smell them.

In the old days you risked cholera and typhoid and worse just setting foot outside your front door, or so the elderly Mrs Levin maintained in her more lucid moments, her recollections of the street half a century earlier always colourful if not particularly accurate. But who was to say the old woman was not right? Her first summer here the Ripper had stalked the dark passages and alleyways, and if Mary Pendergast was still alive all these years later, who was to say the Ripper himself was not?

Joe shivered. The hospital had been damaged badly in the first months of the bombing, and in the intervening years one street after another had been flattened yet Yalta Street had remained untouched, dodging every one of Hitler's bombs; not a single building so much as had its windows blown out.

Harry had said, *Even if things go bad, don't come here.* But it seemed to Joe he had little alternative, and if a man could not turn to his family in a time of crisis then what was his life—was any life—worth? Joe thought it would be worth very little. And with this thought he crossed the street, his collar turned up and his head down low, slipping through the departing darkness like a memory.

# CHAPTER TWENTY

The village of Kirk Deighton was situated a mile or two north-west of Wetherby. Gerald Meadows had reached it after an arduous journey by train as far as Leeds then via an infrequent and meandering branch line train to Wetherby and finally a local bus the short distance to the village. From here he had slogged on foot and without the aid of signposts, all of which had been removed for the duration, along a country lane and a dirt track in the sleet of a northern Yorkshire winter to Spofforth Cottage. For this was the address Mrs Probart had supplied. This was the place to which his wife had fled, taking their child with her.

'Mrs Meadows left that morning,' Mrs Probart had announced. 'But surely you knew?'

No, Gerald had not known. There would be a letter from Diana making its way to Cairo where he had, until five days ago, been stationed. Or a letter had gone astray; letters did go astray in wartime.

Spofforth Cottage turned out to be a snug, single-storey stone affair built into the hillside, its walls thick, its windows tiny, its doorways low, its stonework weathered so that it had a timeless quality to it, as if it had witnessed ancient wars, kings and queens come and go, dynasties rise and fall. It clung to a blustery hillside, the tussocky hills dotted with clusters of windswept, hardy sheep. A scattering of distant buildings suggested the cottage had once been part of a farm. Stone walls meandered in faltering, unrepaired lines up and down the hills and tumbled-down stonework was all that remained of some ancient outbuilding. The whole place had an abandoned feel to it. Yet the track from the lane was recently used, deeply rutted and muddy. The main part of the track continued on over the hill but a spur led across the tussocky grass past a collapsed stone wall and the remains of a gate to the door of the cottage.

Gerald stopped at the gatepost. Snow had fallen a few days earlier and still lay, white and untouched, on the north-facing hillsides, yet despite the cold he was perspiring. It had taken him another day of his leave to get here and already the sun, which this far north was fleeting at best, was slipping away.

Why had Diana come here, of all places? If she really was here—for he had begun to think of his family as a fairy tale that he had invented to get him through the war. But why *here*? She had no family nearby. She had never spoken of holidaying here as a child. They had never once come to Yorkshire during the ten years of their marriage. And yet this was where she had brought her daughter. Their daughter.

'Don't move! I've got you covered!'

A double-barrelled shotgun was aimed squarely at him. Holding the shotgun was a squat, stocky, red-faced and pugnacious farmer in soiled boots, tattered overalls and a worn hat, eyes narrowed against the sleet. The man's clothes, his face, the hands that gripped the shotgun had the same weather-beaten aspect as the sheep, as the ancient buildings, as the hillside itself, as though he had withstood endless winters out in the open with little or no shelter.

'I'm looking for my wife,' replied Gerald mildly, though he felt a blinding rage surge inside him at this fresh delay. 'Perhaps you know her? Mrs Meadows? She has a small child with her. And, I say, perhaps you wouldn't mind pointing that shotgun elsewhere?'

The shotgun wavered and after a moment was partially lowered. 'Aye, I know the lass,' the man admitted. 'Rented my cottage to her last week.' And he nodded towards the squat stone building. 'She never said nowt to me about no husband, though.'

'That's because she believed me to be abroad with my regiment. But as you see, I am returned and anxious to be reunited.'

'Show us yer papers then,' the man demanded, waving the shotgun's barrel towards the place on Gerald's person where he clearly imagined such papers to be.

'If you were a sentry or a policeman I would certainly show you my papers, but as you are neither I shall do no such thing.'

Gerald picked up his case and set off towards the cottage. He had just noticed a thin stream of black smoke coming from its chimney.

'How do I know you're not a Fifth Columnist, then?' the man called out after him, his voice louder but at the same time becoming doubtful.

'How do I know *you're* not?' Gerald countered.

At this the man blustered, 'Because I'm Inghamthorpe of Inghamthorpe's Farm, that's why! Been farming this land since George the Third were on't throne.'

'Really? You hardly look old enough,' Gerald replied. 'Now may we please get out of this filthy weather? I, for one, am heartily sick of it.' And he turned once more towards the house. The fellow could shoot him; it was the only way he was going to be prevented from knocking on that door.

But the man, Inghamthorpe, was not to be outdone: 'AHOY THERE, MRS MEADOWS!' he called out in a voice loud enough to send the nearest sheep scattering in panic, and Gerald saw a movement at the window, the twitch of a curtain.

A moment later a bolt was drawn back and the rough-hewn timber front door creaked open.

Diana stood in the doorway.

No one spoke. She did not run and throw her arms around him. She did not exclaim. She did none of the things a wife might be expected to do in such circumstances, merely stood there dumbly and into the silence a crow, very high up in the sky, cawed loudly over and over.

She was thinner and worn, her face wan with an odd, almost corpse-like pallor. She was wrapped inside a large winter coat, the collar pulled up and her arms hugging herself, and from within the folds of her coat her eyes searched his face, eyes he barely recognised. They were black, startled. But it was more than that; it was shock, the kind of shock he had seen many times etched on the faces of men trapped for hours under enemy fire. Now she moved, her mouth falling open. Her head went back, her eyes blinking. She shook her head as though disbelieving his presence here in the doorway and Gerald wondered, bizarrely, if his wife had thought him dead, if there had been some awful ministry cock-up and he had been reported missing, a casualty, for only that, surely, could account for her reaction.

'Ahoy, Mrs Meadows! This fella claims to be your husband. That right? Can you vouch for him? Else I'll be off t'police station this minute and have him delivered t'authorities!'

Diana turned, gazing at the farmer with his shotgun standing insistently and proprietarily a little way up the track, and it seemed to take her an extraordinarily long time to understand who he was and what he wanted.

'Yes, it's quite alright, Mr Inghamthorpe. This is Mr Meadows. This is my husband.'

Her voice was strained, the words forced, unnatural. But it was a long time since she had last said, 'This is my husband.' Years, in fact.

'Right you are, then,' called the man, who even now seemed reluctant to depart. 'I'll leave you to it then, Mrs Meadows. You know where I am should you be wanting assistance.'

They watched the man lumber away.

And now, at last, it was just the two of them.

'Gerald!' she said, stepping outside to place her hands in his and squeezing them. 'How marvellous! I cannot quite believe you are here.' Her eyes had a sort of wild intensity, her words a frantic cheerfulness.

*How marvellous*? *I cannot quite believe you are here*? They were like lines uttered by a second-rate actor in a third-rate play. Had he been away so long that she no longer knew him, no longer knew how to talk to him?

'Diana.' And he offered the same frantic smile but inside him something cried out in protest.

'Well, come in, come in, out of this perishing cold!' she said, pulling him into the cottage and closing the door.

She led him along a short passage into a surprisingly large room at the rear of the house, part kitchen, part sitting room, where a wood fire roared in a massive stone hearth and an equally massive range gently smoked. Rough, handmade furniture, worn smooth from years of usage, filled the space, the stone-flagged floor covered haphazardly with homemade rugs. A rickety wooden staircase in the corner of the room led to a loft that he had not seen from the outside. It was warm, almost too warm, yet Diana stood, hugging her winter coat about her, the collar turned up. Her fingers when she had squeezed his hands a moment earlier had been frozen. If he touched her face that would be frozen too. She looked at him with that same bright, brittle smile, then turned about in a circle like a tour guide, offering him the house, the contents of the rooms.

'This is us. It's quite cosy, as you see. But you must be cold. Here, sit by the fire. There's water boiling. I shall make us a nice cup of tea.' And she went to the range and began to make the tea.

Gerald stood in the middle of the room. The crackle of the fire, the warmth of the room, the comforting sound of the firewood splitting and falling and crackling was like a dreamed-of image of England, of home, but he was cold to his bones.

'Where's Abigail?'

She did not reply and the sudden hiss of the kettle rattling on the hob rising rapidly to a shrill shriek took up all her concentration and perhaps she had not heard him. He watched as she busied herself with the teapot and the cups and saucers, retrieving from the scullery a milk jug covered with a muslin cloth—real milk, he noticed, here in the country.

He placed his kitbag on the floor and slowly pulled out one of the wooden chairs at the kitchen table, sat down on it, aware as he did so that his movements were measured, almost deliberate. He felt as though he was watching himself from far away.

'Here we are!' she said, coming over with a tray with the tea things on. 'Real milk!' she said, sitting down. 'No sugar, of course. I haven't had time yet to register with any of the local shops. I brought the tea with me. I didn't know what they would have up here in the north.' As though they were in some wild and uncharted land and not twelve miles from Leeds.

She lifted the lid of the teapot and peered inside. He had forgotten that, how she always lifted the lid and peered at the tea before pouring it. Satisfied, she poured some into his cup and handed it to him, and that was something else she always did, handed the cup and saucer rather than slide it across the table, and he had always imagined that someone must once have told her that it was vulgar to slide it. It wasn't vulgar so far as he was aware but she apparently firmly believed it.

There were signs of her recent arrival: an empty packing case on the floor, books piled on the dresser as there appeared to be no bookcase, a pair of shoes still wrapped in tissue paper over by the steps. But how had she got here and got all her things here? Who had helped her? The farmer, Inghamthorpe? Or had she managed somehow on her own? And how had she found this cottage? And *why*? Why was she here?

And where was Abigail?

'When did you get back?' Diana enquired, as though she had gone out to the shops and come home to find him returned early from a day at the office.

'A day or so ago. They flew us back in a de Havilland, over Portugal.' He supposed that that was not careless talk, that he could hardly be censured for telling her that. 'I only got the news I was coming home the night before. There was no time to write. I tried to ring from Exeter but there were no lines.'

He felt as though he were explaining himself, as though he needed to explain his presence to her, when surely it should be the other way around?

'No, the telephone is somewhat hit and miss. How did you track me down? Did Mrs Probart tell you where I was?'

'Yes and—I was a little confused. To get home and find you not there...'

He heard himself say that but it sounded absurd, even to his own ears. *I was a little confused*! They were like strangers. He thought about the men in his unit, many of whom went home on leave and met and married some utterly unsuitable girl about whom they knew absolutely nothing and when they returned home a year, two years later, found they had nothing in common with the girl and the marriage had all been a ghastly mistake. But that hardly applied here—he and Diana had been married ten years before he had left for the war. And yet she was nervous, making small talk, avoiding meeting his eyes, fiddling with the teapot, starting at every sound. For the first time he wondered if there had been another man. The thought crept in, skirting just out of reach, and the air around him dropped a degree or two.

'But why have you come up here, Diana?' He saw her start as though he had banged the table. 'And why didn't you tell me?'

'But I did. I wrote to you as soon as I arranged it—though I see now that you didn't get the letter before you set off. And I left my details with Mrs Probart, just in case. But really, I had no reason to expect you back, you gave no indication . . .'

As I said 'I only found out I was going the night before. Someone got sick and there was a spot on the aircraft. You sound almost as if you wish I hadn't come home.' And he laughed, though the laugh was like a heavy object falling.

'Darling, that's absurd! How silly you are.' She reached across and touched his arm.

The touch made him recoil. He did not believe her.

'You still haven't told me why you've come all the way up here.'

'I'd have thought it was obvious, darling. It's safe here. There are no bombs. No air raids.'

'But there were no air raids at home! In London, yes, but not in Bucks, surely?'

She stood up, cradling her cup in her hand though she had not touched the tea. 'I was in London and I got caught in a raid. It was all rather beastly. I'm afraid I rather lost my nerve a bit after that.' She sat down again, made herself look at him. 'Darling, it's awful to have to admit it after what you must have endured, and I know other people have to put up with it night after night, but I couldn't do it. I just—the truth is, after that I no longer felt safe. Even in our home. It felt too close to London. And so I looked in the newspaper and I saw an advertisement and I wrote to Mr Inghamthorpe and here we are. I know it is cowardly of me, but surely you can understand?'

And this, finally, did sound like the truth, for Gerald could see how very frightened she was, had been in fact since she had opened the door to him. She had been caught in a raid. Well, tougher soldiers than her had lost their nerve after a night of shelling; Lord knows he had lost it himself, on occasion, though he had got adept at hiding the fact. She did not need to hide it, not from him. Of course he understood! And he felt an enormous relief overcome him and he leaned over the table and grasped both her hands in his.

'Diana, I do understand, of course I do. And there is no shame in it, none whatsoever. A lot of people have left London, I do realise that. Your safety is the most important thing, and if you feel safer up here then so be it.'

This ought to have reassured her and yet the smile she gave him was the smile he had seen on the faces of young men the night before battle, the smile on the faces of the young sappers stepping into a minefield with only a bayonet and some marker flags. So he got up and came around the table and kneeled on the floor before her, still holding her hands and searching her face.

'It really is alright, Diana, I promise. The war won't go on too much longer, and in the meantime you and Abigail will stay up here where it's safe and I'll stay with you as long as I can, and when I go away I shall sleep sounder knowing you are both safe.'

He reached up and touched her cheek, seeing all over again the girl from Pinner, anxious and out of her depth, whom he had met at a tennis party in Ruislip so many years before. He had fallen for that girl, had wanted to shield her from the world so that she never needed to feel anxious or out of her depth again, but he had failed. Failed her by his absence, failed her by his inability to grasp her fears. Gently he pulled her to her feet and enfolded her in his arms. He had failed her but, if he could, he would make it up to her.

But she was quite rigid in his arms. Neither of them spoke and, after a long moment, and finding the embrace somehow awkward, he let her go.

'But where is Abigail? I want to see her.'

Diana spun away from him then, wrenching herself free and colliding with the edge of the table. She steadied herself and reached for the teapot. 'She's upstairs. But, darling, she's sleeping. Don't disturb her. We must have more tea. Can't waste it, can we?' And she waved the teapot at him with that same frantic smile.

'But I don't care if she's asleep! It's not every day her daddy comes home from the war, is it?'

He started towards the little stepladder up to the loft but Diana darted forward and snatched at him, pulling him back.

'Please, Gerald, don't let's disturb her. She was so tired, so dreadfully tired. Please let her sleep. You've no idea what an ordeal it's been—first the dreadful raid and then the journey up here.'

He stared at her. 'You had Abigail with you when you were caught in the raid?'

'Yes.' Her eyes slid away from him. 'I—we went up to London, just that once. For a pantomime. Just that one time. The raids seemed so infrequent. I took her with me. To a pantomime. And she enjoyed it so much! She laughed and laughed! Oh, you should have seen her!'

So that was it. She blamed herself for taking Abigail to London, for getting them both caught in the raid. Gerald took a slow breath. 'Then I am glad you took her with you,' he declared, taking both her hands again. 'She deserves to laugh and so do you. And there was no harm done, was there? I mean, here you both are.'

But she ignored this. 'We must have more tea!' she said, pulling his hand.

And now he was irritated. Why this damned obsession with the tea?

'Later. Diana, I want to see her, even if she is still sleeping.'

And before she could stop him he went to the stepladder, climbing nimbly, half expecting her to call out, to make a grab for him, but she did neither and he found himself on the upper floor. Really it was just the loft, a single open space with a tiny window at one end, the roof sloping away on either side and even at its apex too low for him to stand upright. There was a bed in the centre and a smaller child's bed, hardly bigger than a cot, over by the window where his child slept. He felt a profound relief come over him and some part of him that had been wound very tightly slowly released. He moved softly over to the sleeping figure and in the fading winter daylight he gazed down at her beautiful fair curls.

Her beautiful fair curls.

Something clenched inside him. A pulse beat in his head. He went to the bed. He stood over her. Her beautiful fair curls. His little girl had fine dark hair. His little girl had a snub nose and her mother's chin. He had three years of photographs to prove it.

He did not know what it meant.

'Abigail!' His voice sounded unnaturally loud, like a shout on a morning that has been made silent by snow.

'Gerald, *please!*' Diana called to him, and he heard her coming up the steps, could not mistake the breathless panic in her voice that had been present, he realised, since she had opened the front door to him.

The sleeping figure in the bed stirred, murmured, half turned, the hair fell away from her face. Gerald shook his head violently, trying to dispel this image, trying to make some order out of the confusion, but the image remained and his thoughts could find no order. He yanked the bedclothes back, grabbed the child's thin little arms and pulled her up. The child's face was very pale, its features were alien to him, a small mouth, a straight nose, full lips, a high forehead—there was nothing of himself, nothing of his wife here. As he held her, the child's head lolled like a rag doll's and her eyes flickered and rolled back in her head.

'What's wrong with her?'

'I gave her a bromide to help her sleep. Poor little mite, she was so tired and distressed. You've no idea what she's been like—'

'*But it's not her!*' Gerald turned and stared at his wife, wildly searching her face. 'Diana, *it's not Abigail!*'

But she stared dumbly at him.

Gerald let go of the child and lurched towards his wife, taking both her arms, staring into her face.

'*Diana! It's not her!*'

'Of course it is,' she said simply, and her words were so calm, so quiet, but the ground had become a shifting sand dune beneath his feet.

## CHAPTER TWENTY-ONE

It was Harry who opened the door to Joe's knock, his fingers curling around the doorframe, grey in the grey dawn, and something glinted in the meagre light: the blade of a knife. Anyone arriving at the house at this hour could not have good intentions and Harry was prepared. A hand shot out and grabbed Joe by his coat collar and pulled him inside. A glance up and down the street, the door hastily shut behind them. The knife was gone, stowed in some hidden pocket ready for the next person.

'*I told you not to come here.*'

Harry was a slight man, hair cut short like a squaddie's and sprinkled with flecks of grey, a chin permanently darkened by stubble and unblinking pale grey eyes that rarely twinkled with laughter, quick movements and a quicker mind always four or five steps ahead of the man he was dealing with. How different might things be if it was Sammy opening the door on this frozen January dawn, but their older brother was doing a five-year stretch at Wandsworth Prison so it was Harry who peered at Joe in the half-light, his face displaying that habitual expression of watchful wariness, and when he saw it was his younger brother at the door the expression did not change.

'I been on the run,' said Joe. 'The cops was waiting for me at the docks. It weren't just some random security check—they was waiting for me.'

These words sounded to Joe like words spoken by another man living another life, not his words, not his life. He needed to explain the last eight days, his flight, the line of ambulances outside the hospital. But Harry had taken over the whole of the tenement house in Yalta Street where his father and mother had once lived in two rooms, and he had taken over the two terraces on each side, and he had taken over Myra, too, who had once been Sammy's girl, installing her in one house and using the other as a place of work. Harry wouldn't care about the line of ambulances. He wouldn't care about the dead little girl.

'And you come *here*?'

Harry grabbed him by the collar in the darkened hallway and slammed him against the wall. He had done this often when they were younger and Joe, even now he was older, bigger, stronger, had never fought back. He did not fight back now.

'I had nowhere else to go.'

'There's always somewhere else to go. If you don't have some place set up where you can hide out then you're a bloody fool.'

'I ain't like you,' Joe said. 'I don't need places to hide out.'

He was not like Harry. Harry was the ten-year-old boy standing on a corner, hands thrust deep in pockets, watching everyone and everything as though there was money to be made by it, as though the thing he could pull from his pocket might make his fortune or bring down his enemies. When the war had come Harry was ready. As the first ration books had flown off the government printing presses, as they had made their way by armoured lorry to the new Food Offices around the country, Harry had found a printer in Limehouse and soon the presses were running through the night spitting out fake ration books, then forged identity cards, and later, when clothes became rationed, fake clothing coupons too. As the war had progressed and it was simpler to go straight to the source, robbing the ration books directly from the Food Offices, he bought the stolen books for two quid each and sold them on for three. Lately he had turned his attention to the American and Canadian airbases that had sprung up and were stuffed to bursting with cigars, oranges, peanut butter, chocolate, coffee, fruit juice—and silk too, if you had no qualms about taking some poor sod's parachute, which Harry did not. It was a profitable time, war. As his older brother sewed mailbags and his younger brother shovelled coal in a stinking ship's engine room, Harry Levin had done very nicely. But with the war into its fifth year, with the government bringing in new laws and ever more severe penalties, the risk-free undetectable crimes of three, four years ago were a thing of the past. Harry was jumpy—Joe could see it, feel it, but he couldn't share it.

'I ain't like you, Harry,' he said again. 'I'm a sailor. A husband. A dad.'

Harry snorted. 'You gave all that away when you agreed to work for me—and what the hell happened to your head?'

Joe put a hand up to his head, touching the bandage. He had forgotten. He suddenly felt unwell. 'I got hit by something.'

Harry made no reply, studying Joe as though seeking some family resemblance, some hint they were related. He let go of Joe's collar and stalked off into the kitchen.

For a moment Joe didn't move. He had come home on leave in October and gone to work at the docks. He had returned home with tins of peaches in syrup, with a can of Carnation milk, and they had fallen on him, his wife and kids. And Nancy had assumed that was the extent of it, one or two items pilfered when the Docks Police weren't looking, a couple of cans hidden in his lunchbox, no harm done, everyone was doing it. And it had suited him that she think this. She didn't need to know her brother-in-law was at the centre of a full-scale operation that involved bribes to dockyard guards and a corrupt superintendent, holes cut into the wire of the perimeter fence, guard dogs doped and drivers waiting in stolen vans to cart the stuff away to receivers spread all across London; an operation that involved whole crates of sugar, tea, tinned goods—anything, really, that had made it across in the convoys and could be shifted through a hole in a fence and in the back of a lorry. Harry had required a man on the inside, someone he could trust. Who better than his own brother? So Joe had gone to work at the dockyard, Joe had become Harry's man on the inside.

He had told Nancy if he got caught he would get fourteen years and she had not believed it. She had said, *What if you explained it to them? If you told them we was starving, that you took one or two things. Maybe it wouldn't be that bad. Maybe it would be only a short stretch.* He had told her fourteen years' penal servitude. He would be lucky to get fourteen years. Theft on this scale, and from the docks, was a capital offence. He was glad he had not told Nancy this.

He followed Harry into the kitchen where his brother's girl, Myra, was seated at the kitchen table wrapped in a lurid turquoise dressing-gown, her hair in a net, smoking an Embassy and knocking the ash into a saucer. Her lips were made-up and a perfect red bow coloured the end of the burning cigarette. She looked up at Joe's early-morning arrival, her green eyes narrowing as she blew out a slow stream of smoke. She said nothing and her expression registered nothing. Myra did not care for Joe. It seemed to Joe that Myra did not really care for anyone— except, presumably, Harry. It was Sammy who had first brought her home the summer before the war and she had been Madge Carter then, in a cheap uniform selling cigarettes and ice-creams at the Regal in Mare Street. Now Sammy was in the nick and Madge Carter was Myra Cartier and it was a long time since she had trudged the aisles at the Regal plying her Pall Malls and her choc ices.

Harry looked at her irritably. 'For God's sake, get some bloody clothes on.'

When she had gone, resentfully, pulling her gown about her with a flounce, Joe pulled out a chair and sank down. He felt light-headed. He needed rest, to sleep. He needed to drink something, to eat something. His head throbbed. He concentrated for a moment on just sitting.

After a time, his head settled, the kitchen came back into focus and he looked about him, confused, as anyone is confused when returning to their childhood home after a long time away, after thinking they might not see that home again. He thought of the kitchen as it had been when he was a kid. It had been a communal room then, four families sharing it as they had all shared the outside lav in the backyard. There had been a gas ring in each room in those days, where each family did their own cooking, and this area here had been the scullery, being the only room in the house with a sink and cold running water. When his mother had moved in the only water had come from a pump in the street. Now they had running water and a kitchen all to themselves and briefly, before the war, gas lighting in the street. It was confusing.

Upstairs a door slammed.

Joe lifted his head. He wondered if his brother and Myra had got up early with the dawn or if they were just turning in for the night. That seemed more likely. He couldn't imagine any other reason they'd both be up at this hour. Harry certainly had not been on fire-watch duty. He had been thirty-three at the outbreak of war, which put him well within the age range for active service, but a medical exemption certificate had kept him out of it. This certificate had been provided by a helpful and hard-up doctor in Stepney whom a lot of young men had visited in those first heady weeks of the war and who now resided in the same wing of Wandsworth Prison as Samuel Levin. During those same weeks of September and October '39, Joe had waited at home with his new bride for his call-up papers, which had come soon enough. The difference between himself and his half-brothers had, at that time, never seemed so clear to him.

And yet here he was, a little over four years later, and the difference between him and them was no longer clear.

Upstairs another door slammed and he watched a flicker of

irritation pass over Harry's face. Why did they stick together, Joe wondered, Harry and Myra? They only ever seemed to irritate each other. If Harry wanted to score some point over Sammy by stealing his girl he had surely made that point long ago.

'Tell me again what happened,' Harry demanded in a low voice, frowning. He had not sat down. He paced up and down the kitchen.

'It's what I said. They was expecting me. Docks Police, six or seven of them, and a copper. Plainclothes. Soon as they see me, it was all up. I'd be banged up on a charge—half a dozen charges—right now if I hadn't legged it.'

'Did you go back to your house?'

''Course I didn't.'

'They arrest anyone else?'

'I didn't see, I were too busy running. No, I don't think so.'

At some point the sun had risen and a sliver of daylight crept into the gloomy room. Harry went to the window and twitched the blackout aside, taking a quick glance up at the sky before replacing it.

'Why're you here, Joe? What d'you expect me to do?'

'I need papers,' Joe said, and, seeing his brother unmoved: 'Blimey, Harry, if you can't get me new papers who the hell can? You could fit out the entire German army with new identities if you wanted to, just from the stuff you've got lying about in the house.'

'Yeah, and if he handed over four quid I'd fit out Hitler himself—and chuck in some clothing coupons for good measure,' replied Harry with a piercing look. 'You got four quid, have you, Joe?'

'I've got what I'm standing up in.'

Harry turned away, shaking his head. 'I don't keep none of that stuff here any more. It ain't safe.'

'Then what am I supposed to do?'

He hated this feeling of dependency. Harry had come to him in the pub and offered him an opportunity; that was what he had called it. What Joe had seen was a way to stick it to the government, to the navy, to the men who had sent him off to sea and left him to drown alone in an ocean when they didn't even get their feet wet. He had taken control of his own destiny. But now his destiny was in the hands of his brother.

'You have to help me,' he said.

'If I do, it'll be the last time,' said Harry.

❧

A narrow and treacherously steep staircase in very poor repair led to the upper floors where, in Joe's youth, a family called the Brownsteins had lived, and above them a family called the Buchmans, who had disappeared one night never to be heard of again. The Buchmans had been replaced by the Lipinskis, who in turn had been succeeded by the Mollers. Mr Lipinksi had fallen down the upper flight one Saturday night and had landed on his head and lain insensible and unable to speak in his bed ever after. The Brownsteins eldest boy had died of scarlet fever in one of these rooms. And the Mollers' baby had fallen from the top-storey window and perished, and some had said it had been thrown by Mrs Moller herself in a fit of despair. Mrs Moller had died herself not long after and, though no one had said it, everyone had known it was by her own hand. The Brownsteins and the Buchmans and the Lipinskis and the Mollers were long gone but still it felt odd climbing the steep staircase to the upper floors. Joe still expected the elderly Mr Buchman to come out of his room and shout at him. But now his mother lived where the Moller children had slept, and she sat in a chair in the room where Mr Moller had impregnated his wife year after year.

Joe reached the top of the stairs and paused. This was where his mother—at seventy, her body stooped and broken by years of childbirth and poverty—now spent her days. She never came downstairs or received any visitors and no one could remember the last time she had set foot outside the house—it might have been his own wedding day. Her sole contact with the outside world was through Harry and Myra and what she spied in the street far below from her upstairs window. How much she knew of, or cared about, the various illegal goings-on in the rooms downstairs and in the houses on either side of her was unknown, for she said little and when she did speak it was often to enquire after the husband who had abandoned her thirty years earlier.

She was seated now in her chair by the window in the same black crepe dress and mob-cap, her fingers in the same woollen mittens, that she had been wearing on Joe's last visit three months ago. Whether she had moved in all that time he could not tell.

'Mum, it's Joe.'

She turned her head sharply at his greeting but her eyes remained on the window as though his presence was no more than a sound heard in a distant room. The blackout had been pinned up to let the day in and a starling was perched unsteadily on the sill outside, buffeted by the wind. Mrs Levin studied the starling and when Joe came into the room the starling froze, sensing movement, its black eyes flickering, its wings shivering in preparation for flight.

'Nasty vermin!' she shouted furiously. 'I hate them.'

Alarmed, the starling flew off.

Joe pulled up a chair beside her and sat down. 'You been alright, have you, Mum?' he said, watching her warily. Each time he saw her she seemed to have aged a little more, her cheeks a little more sunken, the skin on her face and neck and fingertips a little more transparent, her eyes a little more clouded over. But her voice was strong enough. 'Are you getting enough to eat?' he asked. He never saw her eat. It seemed possible she didn't eat at all.

But the starling—or a different starling—had returned to the sill and she was fully taken up with retrieving her stick and rapping it furiously against the pane.

He had come to see her in this room the day before he'd left to join his ship three years ago and she had been angry with him. Angry because he had not got himself out of it like Harry had, like Sammy had in his own inimitable way. He was a fool, she had said, and perhaps he had been, for which one of them—Harry or Sammy or himself—was about to flee the country forever? The war would end and Sammy would come back and Harry would take over every house in the street and Joe would be gone. She would be gone, too, he realised, looking sideways at the old woman seated beside him.

'I couldn't sleep,' she said. 'Last night there was so much noise I couldn't sleep.'

'There was an air raid. You ought to go down the shelter.' He knew she would never go down to any shelter.

'That weren't no air raid. That was some tart turning tricks with some soldier down 'neath my window. Went on for ages, it did, and then she knifed him and robbed him and buggered off, far as I can tell. There was blood on the street.'

There was no blood on the street. She had told him this story many times. It was some incident she had heard about years ago or had witnessed, perhaps, as a girl. Sometimes Joe wondered if the story was about herself. He had long ago decided he'd rather not know.

'Well, it's quiet now,' he said.

~

The daylight had come and gone and Harry had been absent the whole time. He returned at nightfall, slipping back into the house, shaking the raindrops from his coat and bringing a rush of cold air into the kitchen.

'Here,' he said, thrusting an envelope into Joe's hands.

Joe turned it over, strangely reluctant to open it. Inside the envelope was a set of papers with the words NATIONAL REGISTRA-TION IDENTITY CARD stamped in big official lettering on the front and on the back: MUST NOT PART WITH TO ANY OTHER PERSON. Well, this person had parted with it. Joe opened the cover and read: *Septimus John Vasey*. What sort of name was that? There was also a buff-coloured ration book made out in the same name. He wondered if Septimus John was dead. He stuffed the papers in his pocket. He did not feel like a Septimus. The name had a sinister ring to it that he could not quite explain.

'Anyone come?' said Harry to Myra, who was seated at the kitchen table, where she had passed most of the day, smoking and flipping through a magazine, ignoring Joe. She shook her head, not looking up. Nancy sat like that too, perhaps all women did: legs crossed, an elbow on the table, cigarette held between index and middle finger an inch from her mouth, staring through narrowed eyes at endless photographs of the Royal Family and American film stars. But Myra had a diamond ring on her finger, she had another on her other hand and the silk dressing-gown she wore really was silk, not imitation, and the coat hanging on the back of her chair was fur, and not rabbit either, perhaps not even fox. It paid then, this life they lived, even if it meant living like you were under siege, always expecting the worst. But we're all under siege, thought Joe, we're all expecting the worst. The only difference was Myra had diamonds and silk and fur.

The stolen identity papers pressed uncomfortably into his side.

Harry wanted him to leave first thing in the morning, had provided a change of clothes—an old man's hat and a suit that smelled like an old man had died in it—and a walking stick. 'Use the stick and walk with a limp anytime you see anyone in authority,' Harry had said. 'That way people might not question why you're not in uniform. And keep the bandage, it adds to your cover. And travel by day, it's less suspicious. You're bound to be stopped if you travel after dark.'

And Joe thought: It's not just that he's worried the whole operation's in jeopardy. It's more than that. Harry wants me to get away to safety.

The thought confounded him for a moment.

They passed the evening playing cards using fake clothing coupons as stake and Myra listened to a comedy program on the wireless with a frown on her face as though she was listening to a Ministry of War casualty list. When the news came on Harry got up and turned it off. He poured them both a Canadian scotch and Myra a crème de menthe. She was in her dressing-gown, her hair back in its net, but she still wore the diamonds. They would both be here after he had gone, Joe realised, after he had made it, with any luck, to America, and it occurred to him to ask his brother to keep an eye on Nancy and Emily. He would not have dreamed of it twenty-four hours earlier but now it seemed possible. He would ask Harry in the morning.

∽

He passed a restless night in the armchair, eventually giving up and silently smoking as the dawn crept over the hospital buildings. Tuesday morning.

They had not agreed on a time for Joe's departure but already Harry was up and dressed and bundling him towards the front door. 'Be careful if you get a train from any of the mainline stations,' he said, his usual taciturnity overcome for once. 'The entrances are all watched. Someone's bound to stop you. Enter through the Underground station or jump a train once it's pulled out the station. Avoid Victoria and Kings Cross. Use Euston.'

Joe listened and nodded, trying to remember, but it was hard to take it in. He reached out and laid his hand on his brother's shoulder. It occurred to him they would probably never meet again. He pushed down the panic that seemed, now, always to be just beneath the surface.

They had reached the door and Harry eased it open cautiously, letting in the wan yellowish daylight. He stood perfectly still as a cat would, scanning the street, tasting the air, then he nodded and stood aside. As Joe passed him in the narrow hallway Harry said again, 'Remember: Euston. And use the walking stick.'

Joe nodded.

Harry gave him a quick push through the door, and under his breath he murmured, 'Good luck,' or it sounded like good luck.

Joe stepped out into the cold dawn, realising he had not asked Harry to keep an eye on Nancy and Emily. He turned back but the door had already closed behind him.

# CHAPTER TWENTY-TWO

Despite the fading light of the dimly lit loft Gerald could see the whites of Diana's eyes, the controlled panic on her face. There was a wildness, a desperation about her that silenced him. She was playing some dreadful game, he saw, was caught in some ghastly delusion and she needed him to play along. It seemed to him that she teetered, they both teetered, on a brink.

'Gerald, you're being quite absurd.' She said this with a little laugh, as though he had suggested she go to church without her gloves and hat, that she drink her tea black. She had turned away from him as she spoke and now she climbed back down the little stepladder with slow measured steps.

Gerald followed her, watching as she went over to the range, was aware of her moving things about: pots, crockery, a storage jar. None of it was quite real.

'How could she be someone else?' she went on. 'I mean, Gerald, you've been away such a long time. When you saw her,

Abigail was only a day old. And now she is a three-year-old child. Quite grown. It's hardly a wonder you don't recognise her.'

He could not see her face as she said this, only her back, which was perfectly straight, and her shoulders, which were perfectly still even as her hands moved feverishly over the things on the range.

'You must be hungry,' she said, as though the matter were now settled. 'Do let me make you some supper. Mr Inghamthorpe gave me some eggs. Just think! I can do you an egg like I used to before the war. Would you like an egg?'

'Diana, *stop*! For God's sake, *stop this*!'

Gerald placed his hands very slowly on either side of his head, pressing his fingertips into his scalp. If she didn't stop talking he knew he would go mad; already his sense of himself was slipping. The sand beneath his feet was rushing away into a hole and he was rushing with it.

At his words she had flinched as though he had struck her, but she did not turn around. She must know that what she was saying was a lie or, if she did not, then it was *she* who was mad. One of them, he realised, must be mad.

'I have photographs of her. Photographs you sent me.'

Gerald went to his bag, unfastening it with fingers that were thick and clumsy. He got it open at last, fishing among his things until his fingers found his pocketbook. He pulled it out and shook it vigorously so that any number of scraps and notes and cards fell out, falling any which way onto the floor, and among them were the three photographs, taken one year apart each Christmas. Three dark-haired little girls with dark eyes and dark eyebrows, a wide forehead, largish ears, the same contrary, slightly sullen expression on her face each time, in the last one a little ball in her lap.

'See! Here! *This is her!*'

He stood up, stumbling and unsteady. Diana was standing a little distance away, looking not at the photographs that he held out to her, but at his face. He lurched over, thrusting the photographs at her, making her look, but she would not—or could not—see them. The frozen mask that had descended over her face prevented her.

'For God's *sake!* Look, *look!*' And when she did not, he grabbed her hand and forced the photographs into it, he took hold of her head and forced her to look. 'You took these! They are *your photographs*! What have you *done? Who is the girl upstairs? Who is the girl in these photographs?*'

'Gerald, please, you're frightening me!'

And she was shaking, her eyes wide, trying to break free. He was frightening her, but she was frightening him, could she not see that? He let go of her and stepped back, and the photographs fluttered to the floor.

'Then tell me, Diana. For God's sake, just tell me what is going on.'

But she dropped to her knees. Then she let out a dreadful sob, just one. The sound was worse than the whine of a shell overhead, worse than the whoosh of the fireball that had incinerated Ashby. Worse than the sound he had made when he had stood in his form master's room receiving the news of his parents' death. He stood looking down at her as the fear seeped up from the floor and through his bones. Slowly he kneeled down, not touching her, waiting for her to speak.

'She's dead. Abigail is dead.'

⌁

Gerald was no longer in the cottage. He was standing outside in the frozen night some distance away without his coat, the hillside veering away steeply on his left, the hard tussocky grass beneath his feet, the freezing night-time air biting at his face, his eyes, his hands.

She was dead, Abigail was dead.

He had known it the moment he had gone up to the loft. How long, then, had she been dead? All this time, perhaps, three years, and the photographs were—what? Some other child. A fake child. All the time he had been in the desert, battling his way inside his tank and outside of it, from one side of the desert to the other, back and forth, losing and winning, giving ground and making ground, seeing death and facing death and cheating death. All that time doing it not for England, not for his commanding officer, not even for his troops, but for them: his wife and child. Now one was dead and the other—the other had lied or had perpetrated some deception. Either way they were lost to him. His child, whom he had seen only that once, a tiny, red-faced, writhing and wrinkled thing in his arms.

He fell to his knees and cried.

Much later he got stiffly to his feet and returned to the cottage because he did not know where else to go. And because there were questions he must ask.

Diana was crouched on the floor where he had left her, silent now and no longer crying, her knees pulled up to her chin. She looked up at him but he couldn't look at her. He saw an ancient armchair over by the hearth and he made for that, moving like an old man, sinking down into it and stretching his numbed fingers to the flames, desperate for warmth, to feel the blood flow once more. How could numbed fingers matter? But it was no different, he supposed, to being irritated by a fly buzzing in your face in the desert as shells landed all around you.

'When did it happen?' he said after a time.

'I took her into London with me,' Diana replied, her voice low, barely filling the space between the crackling of the fire and the rattling of the windows. 'For a pantomime, and there was a raid. We were trapped. We took shelter in an Underground station.' In the hearth a log split and shifted, sending out a tiny cascade of embers. 'It ought to have been safe. I thought it would be safe, but it wasn't. A bomb dropped and the roof collapsed. Abigail was in my arms—I tried to protect her—I thought I had protected her. But—'

But. She did not say the words and Gerald was glad for that. He sat quite still as her words slowly penetrated. So it had only just happened, the death of their child, just a week, two weeks ago, and it was as raw for her as it was for him. He saw it with a frightening clarity in his imagination, his wife holding their little girl as the roof collapsed around them, shielding her as best she could, alone and terribly frightened. He imagined her dismay on realising that Abigail was dead, her grief and the terrible secret she had kept since then, unable to tell him. He saw that she blamed herself, though it was surely no one's fault, or if it was it was the war.

He felt strangely calm. He wondered why he did not get up and go to her, why he did not comfort her. But he did not move. The calmness wavered and something weighed heavily on him, a suffocating weight. He tugged at the tie around his neck, at his shirt collar, which was too tight. The ancient armchair pulled him in and closed over him. He felt as if he had stumbled unwittingly into a dwarf's house, where all the ceilings were four-foot high and, no matter which room he entered, he could never, ever stand up.

'Then who is the child upstairs?'

Diana did not reply and Gerald realised that he had, even at this late stage, expected some simple account, some reasonable explanation. But Diana did not reply and with her silence the possibility of a simple account, of a reasonable explanation faded.

'Diana?'

At this she made an odd, rather ghastly choking sound. Was she crying again? He couldn't tell as he was staring into the fire and the fear that had turned to grief and then to pity now returned in full.

'Tell me. Who is she?'

'I don't know.'

A silence followed these words. Gerald turned his head very slowly and in the softly flickering firelight they looked at each other.

'I don't understand,' he said eventually, keeping his words even, measured.

'It's quite simple really.' Diana uncurled her arms from around her knees and stood up, coming over to the other armchair and sitting down, her hands laid calmly in her lap.

'There was a woman sheltering near me in the Underground station. A young mother with a small child. When the roof collapsed she was killed but her child was not. And Abigail was dead too. The little girl had survived but her mother was dead. And so—I took her.'

Her words seemed to come from very far away, and curiously they appeared to flow harmlessly over him and slice straight through him both at the same time. The world had changed, irrevocably, as it had the day his parents had died and as it had the evening he saw Bunny Lambton come home at midnight in another man's arms. Moments that changed your life and set it on another path—Ashby's death, he saw now, had not done that. Ashby's death made no difference at all. His little girl had died but quite suddenly, at his wife's words, the fact of Abigail's death no longer seemed the worst possible thing that could happen. For this was worse.

'You stole her.'

He addressed the flickering flames in the hearth. If his fingers had been numb before, now his brain was numb. Now his entire body was numb.

'I took her,' Diana said, as though changing the verb some-how made it alright. 'She had no one. Her mother was dead. She was alone.'

So many objections crowded into Gerald's head that for a moment he could not grasp at a single one.

'But how do you know she was alone? You didn't know her. *How could you know that she doesn't have an entire family? A family who are looking for her!*' His even and measured tone had failed him and he had got to his feet as his voice rose.

'How could they be looking for her?' she replied. 'They believe she is dead.'

Gerald did not reply at once. The implication of her words were a slow, creeping horror.

'Why would they think that?'

'There was a dead mother and there was a dead child. One mother survived and one child survived. No one questioned which child belonged to which mother.'

Gerald clamped his hands tightly over his face, his finger-tips squeezing into his eyeball, into his ears. He pushed himself up from the armchair and paced the length of the cottage. 'But it's *indefensible*. What you have done, stealing a child, it is *indefensible*.'

If he had expected her to cringe, to beg forgiveness, he was disappointed. She seemed, if anything, to grow in strength, though she remained seated in the armchair before the fire, her hands resting in her lap, studying the flames.

'But what sort of a life would she have had with those people?' She looked up at him now, suddenly animated: 'You didn't see what they were like, Gerald. They were barbaric. Primitive. Barely civilised. What kind of life could she have, could any child have, there? It was a kindness to take her.'

He stopped pacing and stared at her. Could she really believe this? He could not, in his heart, believe that she did. It was her way of dealing with the horror of what she had done, surely.

'That does not make it right.'

'I believe it does.'

'And so what, exactly, are you proposing? That we raise this child, this unknown stranger's child, as our own? That we can simply replace Abigail with another child and it will all be alright? As though she was a—a pair of shoes in the wrong size or the wrong colour that you can take back to the shop and replace with another?'

'Of course I don't think that! I am not that heartless, Gerald! How can you think such a thing? Abigail was our child! When she died—'

But here she stopped, attempted to catch her breath.

'When she died, I died too. I wanted to die. But I survived . . . I survived, and if I am to live then I would rather have a child to raise than have no child. Can't you understand that?' Her voice fell to barely a whisper: 'I don't love this child, of course I don't. But I do pity her. And I hope that, given time, I will learn to love her, that she will learn to love us. That you will learn to love her—'

'*No*. What you are saying—what you have done—*is monstrous*. I will have no part in it.'

As he had done before, he left the cottage, but this time he was aware of his footsteps as he walked down the short passage, his hands as they pulled open the heavy front door, carefully latching it behind him. He found his way with difficulty onto the track and down into the laneway, retracing his steps.

The absolute darkness and the piercing frozen night air hit him like a barrage of gunfire and for a time his thoughts fled, leaving him senseless. He walked and his footsteps made a dull thud on the road. After a time he came upon the village, along whose main street he paced. No one passed him. No light showed. The cloudy, starless night and the blackout meant that the scattering of houses were entirely in darkness.

She had left their child in an Underground station and taken another woman's child in her place. The fact of it made him reel. Who was she, this woman he had married? He did not know.

What was he to do? No solution presented itself. But clarity came to him, in one sense anyway, for he understood now his wife's reason for coming north where no one knew them, where no one knew Abigail. If she had tried to present this other child as Abigail at home she could not have hoped to get away with it. He tried to imagine Diana planning their flight, finding the cottage, writing her letter to Inghamthorpe, saying her goodbyes and giving her explanations, arranging the journey. How had she managed it, he wondered, with a small, terrified, unwilling child and all their luggage, travelling by train all this way and with every expectation of remaining here until the war ended? A year, two years? Dreading, the whole time, his return.

For she must have dreaded it.

He had reached the edge of the village and, not knowing what else to do, he turned around and walked back. It must have been well after midnight when he arrived back at the cottage, having missed the turning three times in the darkness and stumbled a quarter-mile in the wrong direction. He had eaten nothing since a sandwich at Leeds and his weakness now was as much from hunger and exhaustion as anything else. He let himself in. On the table a candle burned very low in pool of wax, flickering wildly. We have returned to the Dark Ages, he thought, seeing the candle. We have reverted to savages.

There was no sign of Diana other than the remains of a scratch tea at the sink. She was upstairs in the loft, presumably, though he could not imagine that she slept. He found a loaf and carved a ragged slice and ate it ravenously without margarine or jam. *It's this damned war*, Mrs Ashby had said, and he understood now how she could say this as though it no longer had any meaning. He pulled the two armchairs together and lay full length and closed his eyes.

⁓

He awoke to the sound of a child screaming. The sound tore through him and he opened his eyes with a start, heart pounding. The hearth had been lit, the blackout removed so that the cottage, which had been all dark nooks and shadows the previous night, was now bright and exposed in the weak winter sunlight. A succession of chaotic and random images filled his head, all that had happened since he had woken in the London hotel a day ago, and he lay unable to move.

And the child screamed.

He turned his head a fraction, dreading but compelled to see it.

She was squatting on the floor, hugging her skinny little knees, furiously shaking her head, squeezing her eyes shut. She was a wispy, undernourished thing, incongruous in a dainty little fuchsia nightdress, all lace and frills, and tiny child's slippers (whose nightdress, he wondered, whose slippers?) and, as he watched, she pulled first one slipper off and then the other, hurling them, not randomly but with purpose, at Diana. He saw, in a corner, a teddy bear that, too, had presumably been hurled in fury and he looked away. And the sound the child made tore through him. She opened her eyes wide and he saw the eyes of a wild animal, terrified and caged. He felt himself recoil.

He wondered how Diana could bear it for she kneeled before the child, coaxing her with a slice of bread and margarine on a plate, still in her own nightdress and slippers, and she held her arm up in front of her face to ward off the flying slippers.

'Oh do stop, *please!*' she begged the child, and Gerald turned away so he wouldn't have to see it. He found he was holding his breath, dreading—

'Please stop, Abigail.'

That was it. That was what he had dreaded. She had called the child 'Abigail' and he lay quite still as the horror rolled over him, wave after wave, unrelenting. He covered his ears. He found himself remembering the voyage he had made three years ago on the troopship around the coast of Africa and into the Red Sea, a voyage full of terror and foreboding, the ship buffeted and tossed day after day so that he had wished a torpedo would strike them. He remembered the night-long flight in the de Havilland five days ago, dropping and climbing and banking through the darkness so that the only thing that had been real had been his prayers, whispered over and over and with increasing urgency to a God he did not believe in. He had prayed for dry land, he had prayed to feel his feet back on the ground. And here he was, on dry land, his feet were on the ground and the horror rolled over him.

The child continued to scream. It was the scream of a child who knew its name was not Abigail and who knew it had no control over what was happening to it. She thrust the plate of bread and margarine away so that it flew from Diana's hand and fell to the floor with a crash, scrambled to her feet and made a mad, frenzied dash for the door. The door was closed but the child hurled herself at it, flying at the old iron door handle, her fingers scrabbling for purchase, unable in her panic to open it, screaming in her frustration. And when Diana tried to snatch her up, the child squirmed and fought and kicked and punched like a mad thing. Eventually she freed herself and, abandoning the door, scampered instead to the furthest part of room, where she crammed herself into a corner and would not come out again, her screams subsiding into a terrified, desolate sobbing.

Gerald had watched, unable to move, as this horror unfolded before him.

'Dear God, Diana! It's no good. This must end, surely you see that?'

Diana started, perhaps not even realising he was awake, but he did not wait for her reply, getting up and striding over to the little girl—but Diana thrust herself between them.

'What are you doing?'

He pushed her aside, surprised at how flimsy she seemed, that he could brush her aside like a fly. He went to the child and crouched down. She had curled into a ball, her arms over her head, silent now, her silence somehow more dreadful than the screaming had been.

'It's alright,' he said very gently. 'We're not going to hurt you. I just want to know your name. Please, can you tell me your name?'

But the child would not speak or could not, and they had done this to her, or Diana had, though he felt himself complicit. He did not know how to help the little girl and his heart was wrung.

'Please,' he said again, reaching out to peel her tiny arms away from her face but hesitating even to touch the child, for she seemed so utterly bereft, so broken. 'Just tell me your name,' he pleaded, knowing it was hopeless, uncertain if the child heard his words or understood. Did the child even understand English? he wondered. She might come from any sort of family, speak any language. He sat back on his haunches, reaching for the abandoned teddy bear, which was a sorry-looking creature, one ear missing, as though it had gone through a bombing raid too, but when he offered it to her she thrust it away.

Eventually he gave up and got stiffly to his feet, turning to his wife, studying her.

'Diana, where does she come from? Tell me where you were sheltering that night. What station?'

Diana had not moved, her arms by her side, her face with its now permanently pinched, aghast expression. But there was something else: a dreadful and desperate determination that he had not seen in her before. It was pointless, he saw. She would tell him nothing and he felt no anger or frustration, merely a sort of calm purpose. He passed her without a glance, taking up his coat and hat, the gloves Mrs Ashby had given him and the three discarded photographs. He would leave his bag. He had no need of it.

Diana had stood quite still, observing him, but when it became clear he was leaving she darted forward, panicked. 'Gerald, please, stop! What are you doing? Where are you going?'

'Back to London. To find her family.'

And he left at once, not giving her a chance to stop him.

# CHAPTER TWENTY-THREE

Septimus John Vasey had made his painful way from London's East End to Euston Station by bus and on foot, no mean feat for a man with a walking stick and a pronounced limp. He had been made lame perhaps at Dunkirk, perhaps at Tobruk. He wore a soiled bandage around his head and when he rested on a bench outside the station a woman in a smart hat and a coat with a fur collar pressed a coin into his hand.

He looked tired. He looked hungry. But so did everyone. After a time, he pulled himself to his feet and limped towards the station entrance. He had no luggage, not even a gas mask. Perhaps he was meeting someone. Perhaps he had no possessions. He wore a suit that looked like someone had died in it.

∽

Joe paused in the entranceway to the station. It was the first day of February, a Tuesday morning at a little after nine o'clock, an overcast morning with the promise of rain. Pigeons roosted noisily high up in the roof struts, thin and wasted because in wartime there were less crumbs to fight over, and wary because sometimes the people far below got so hungry they ate pigeon pie for their tea. Joe lowered his gaze from the ceiling and observed the many servicemen and women crowded into the station. The only civilians were wives and girlfriends come to wave someone off and mothers come up to London with small children on shopping trips or excursions or dental appointments.

So far no one had asked to see his papers.

Harry had said to be careful of the mainline stations, the entrances were watched. He had said to enter through the Underground station or jump a train once it had pulled out of the station. He had said use Euston. Joe was at Euston but no one was watching the entrance. Everyone was hurrying from place to place or standing in the middle of the concourse staring up at the giant departure board on which a large number of the trains had the word CANCELLED beside them. It seemed to be a feature of wartime that you always got to see what you were missing, what you couldn't have, what was no longer available. But some trains were running. The boat train departed on the hour for Liverpool and Holyhead, connecting with the Dublin steam packet. Why shouldn't he just go straight up and buy a ticket and board a train? thought Joe. Why should anyone stop him?

Why should anyone stop Septimus John Vasey?

A young woman and her little boy hurried into the station, passing by so close the woman's sleeve brushed against Joe's arm. She did not pause, pulling at the hand of the reluctant child, a handbag and a basket and a parcel tied with string balanced in her other hand. 'Come *on*! We ain't got all day,' she said, tugging the boy's hand, and when her parcel slid from her fingers and fell to the ground Joe darted forward to pick it up. 'Thank you,' she said, and when he offered to carry it for her, 'You're very kind,' putting a hand to her hair, adjusting her scarf as though she was not used to talking to strange men. And so they crossed the station concourse together, looking for all the world like an ordinary family, and no one gave them a second glance. At the ticket office signs in large hectoring black letters demanded, *Is your journey really necessary?* but despite this there was a long line of people queuing for tickets. Everyone's journey, it seemed, was necessary.

'Oi, mister. Why you got a walking stick when you ain't limping?' piped up the little boy, regarding Joe suspiciously. 'Why ain't you in uniform?'

'Ssshh! Archie, none of your cheek,' hissed his mother, clipping the child around the head. She smiled wanly at Joe. She wore a cheap coat that had seen many winters with a scarf tied around her head and knotted beneath her chin. Her shoes were soaked through and her legs were spotted with mud. She looked exhausted, but even as Joe thought this he caught her looking at him, at his walking stick, at the bandage, at the decrepit old suit, and wonder. He shifted the parcel to his other arm. He needed to say something to dispel her curiosity but he could think of nothing. So they did not speak. The line inched forward.

A man at the front of the queue wanted to travel to Sheffield and was insistent he change trains at Stoke-on-Trent. The ticket clerk was equally insistent he change at Manchester and a stand-off now ensued with the man—the retired colonel type in worn tweeds with a clipped voice and a waxed moustache—threatening to send for the station manager. Joe watched and a cold sweat broke out all over his body. His fingers curled tightly around the papers in his pocket. A man in front of him opened a newspaper and began to read, clearly expecting to be waiting a while. Behind him the mother of the little boy was pointedly not looking at him now, perhaps regretting accepting his offer of help, and now she did glance at him, showing him that same wan smile, but the muscles at the corner of her mouth were hard. She could sense his discomfort. He needed to say something light-hearted, something grumbling, the sort of thing people said to each other when they were stuck in a queue. He could think of nothing.

He stared at the back page of the man's newspaper. A man had been stabbed to death in an Underground station. Police were appealing for witnesses but so far none had come forward.

As suddenly as it had sprung up the stand-off ended, the retired colonel departing in fury, promising to write a letter to someone about something. In another moment Joe was at the front of the queue. He asked for a one-way ticket to Liverpool by the ten o'clock train. The clerk asked for no identification, did not so much as glance up as he punched buttons on his machine and printed the ticket. He took more notice of the coins he counted out than he did of his customer.

It was done and Joe walked away clutching his ticket and the woman's parcel, following them to the ticket barrier. The mother and her little boy were going to Chester, a different train to himself but from the neighbouring platform.

'I can take this now,' said the woman, holding out her hands for her parcel, offering another quick unsmiling glance. Joe gave it to her, happy to be rid of it. The parcel, the mother and child, had done their job. He no longer needed their cover.

As he thought this he saw two MPs at the ticket barrier checking papers and he went cold again. The two MPs worked as a pair, silently and thoroughly unfolding each person's identity card, their travel warrants, their train ticket, scrutinising each face implacably and handing back each item without a word. And perhaps there were MPs at each platform checking each passenger's papers, though it was hard not to feel that it was simply this platform they had targeted and he had blundered haplessly into them.

But he had papers. And they were genuine, if stolen. He was perfectly safe.

But *were* they genuine? The coldness spread through his body, making it difficult to think. He had only glanced at the papers for a second or two in the darkened hallway in the brief moments after Harry had given them to him. Just enough time to read a name and no more. If they were a poor forgery—or even a bloody good forgery—he hadn't noticed. Harry had given him no time to notice. He fought the urge to pull the papers out of his coat pocket right now and peer at them. They might be perfectly fine.

But they might not.

He was almost at the front of the queue and beside him the young mother made an impatient noise and attempted to undo the clasp of her handbag, letting go of the boy's hand to free up her other hand. The boy stood perfectly still, ignoring his mother, watching Joe.

His papers were genuine. He just had to bluff it out.

'Are you a coward, mister?' said the little boy, putting his head on one side and regarding Joe in his civilian clothes through unblinking, probing eyes.

His mother had dropped her handbag. The little boy, the two implacable MPs looked on, making no move to assist her as she bent down, flustered and exclaiming, to retrieve all the spilled items. By the time she had gathered her things together and straightened up, the man in the civilian clothes behind her in the queue had gone, was already walking across the concourse into the crowd and was lost from sight, and the little boy was right, it was odd that he had a walking stick but no limp.

∽

The ten o'clock boat train to Liverpool that connected with the afternoon ferry to Dublin had gone. By the time it passed through London's northernmost suburbs and crossed into Hertfordshire, Joe was already many miles away. He had abandoned the walking stick but the bandage on his head was genuine enough and he began to feel a little sick. There was a longish period immediately after he had fled the station of which he had no recollection. In the panic and confusion that he himself had created he had found himself somehow in Aldgate, and how much time had passed and how he found his way there he had no idea. The rain had come down, suddenly and in great sheets, pounding on the pavements and splashing up beneath the brims of hats. He had taken shelter and come to himself crouched in a bomb site, a crater so vast and so wide he had wondered what great building it was that had once stood here. When it had occurred to him that this was all that remained of the Great

Synagogue, destroyed in May of '41, and where generations of Levins had clasped their Talmuds and recited their prayers, the realisation that this, of all places, was where he had stumbled in his panic, had struck him deeply—until he had remembered that Ely Levin was not his father and that, as likely as not, he had no more connection to this place than to any other place, and he had got up and moved on.

The rain had stopped as suddenly as heavy rain does stop, the sun bursting through so that everything shone wetly and the despair that a sudden winter downpour could instil was mingled confusingly with a sense of hope.

The train ticket burned a hole in Joe's coat pocket. He had thrown his money away buying it and then he had bolted before he had even boarded the train. The stupidity of his actions hung over him as heavily as the sudden downpour had. Why had he thought he could just walk into a station and buy a ticket and board a train? The papers were good; he had just lost his nerve.

But when he pulled the identity card out and studied it in the daylight he saw that the man's date of birth was 1875. The holder of this card must be sixty-nine years old. Anyone looking at it would know at once it was stolen.

∽

In Yalta Street a stranger was standing in the doorway of his brother's house. The front door was open a crack, and a man stood on the doorstep conducting some furtive conversation. For you didn't stand like that in the doorway with the door almost closed and your collar turned up unless your business was furtive. Joe watched from across the street and after a short time the man slid away, walking quickly, head down. He passed right by Joe and Joe saw a long raincoat and a grey hat pulled low over an unshaven chin. He saw one arm of the raincoat hanging limp and empty and the arm inside the coat cradled in a sling.

He saw that it was the plainclothes policeman who had been waiting for him at the docks a week ago.

He stood and stared, unable to make sense of it. Could he have mistaken the man? He knew he had not.

When the man was gone Joe went up to the house and knocked softly. It was opened immediately by Harry, who must have been standing right there, behind the door. Harry's face did not change when he saw it was Joe returned, he simply reached out and hauled him into the house as he had done before, and slammed him against the hallway wall.

'I told you not to come back!'

'Them papers you give me are no bloody good!'

Harry shook him a second time then abruptly let him go and walked away. Joe followed.

'Don't you get it? I'm saying I almost got caught! I got as far as the station but they was checking everyone's papers—'

'I told you not to go there!' Harry turned back, his fists clenched, the veins standing out rigid in his neck. 'I said jump a train or catch it from a smaller station. You're a bloody fool. You deserve to get caught.'

'You never said that! You said Euston was safe.'

But Harry shook his head, denying all the advice he had given. Denying any responsibility. Joe thrust out a hand to stop him walking away again.

'You have to help me. You got me into this situation.'

Harry shoved a finger under his nose. 'You take responsibility for your own actions. That's the way it works. You knew what you was getting into.'

'But I'm the one taking all the risk! I don't see you out there risking your arse.'

'No, you don't. That's because I ain't the fool you are. Or Sammy. He's just as much of a fool.'

Harry stalked into the kitchen and yanked out a chair from the kitchen table, sweeping aside overflowing ashtrays, yesterday's newspaper, a ration book, half-drunk mugs of tea, dirty plates. Joe followed.

'Listen, Harry—'

'No, *you* listen! You know nothing, Joe. We all take risks. All of us.' He snatched up a packet of Pall Malls and began to light one. 'You think an operation like this runs itself? You think there ain't a dozen, two dozen blokes out there waiting to stab me in the back to take over my patch? Ready to sell me out for a packet of fags? People inside my own operation?'

He took a long drag and blew out a cloud of smoke.

The newspaper had reported a man stabbed to death in an Underground station. Was that Harry's fate? Joe wondered.

'There was a copper here when I arrived,' he said slowly, still standing in the kitchen doorway. 'A detective. Same one I see outside the docks a week ago.'

Harry took a second pull on the cigarette, his eyes narrowing as he aimed a stream of smoke at the brown-stained ceiling. He made no reply.

'I don't get it, Harry. What's he doing here?'

'Course you don't get it,' said Harry quietly. 'He's bent. That copper's bent. They all are. I slide him a few notes and he turns a blind eye.' He looked up at his younger brother. 'That's how it works. You don't run an operation like this without some copper knows about it and wants his cut.'

Joe pulled out a chair and sank down into it. He realised he felt relieved. The policeman's presence had rocked him; it had not made sense. Now it did make perfect sense. Now it was obvious.

'How much d'you give him?'

'A few notes. What's it matter?' Harry stood up. 'Joe, you can't stay here.'

And so they were back where they had started.

'Well, I ain't going yet,' said Joe. 'Not till I get some grub and a wash and a kip. This is my home too.'

He put his elbows on the kitchen table. It *had* been his home, once. Just because he no longer lived here and rarely came to visit didn't mean it wasn't still, wouldn't always be, his home. He remembered that there had been no table here in the old days, just the sink and a mangle and rows of washing, grey and steaming and always damp. Harry had found this table on a bomb site the morning after a raid. It had been unscratched. Three years in the Levin household and it was scarred, chipped and stained like a butcher's block.

'Mum would want me to be safe,' he said.

At this Harry laughed. 'Mum don't know what century it is. She don't care if you're here or if you're bobbing about in the sea or banged up in Wandsworth nick. You think she's given two thoughts about our Sammy these last four years?'

Joe said nothing. When he had left to join his ship early in 1940 his mother had refused to see him. When he'd come back in October her world had shrunk to the tiny upstairs room, the chair, the window and the starlings. And if she had any sense at all of time passing, it was time passing in another century before cars and telephones and wireless sets and aeroplanes and bombs dropping from the sky.

'Family should mean something,' Joe said, though what it should mean he did not know.

'You wouldn't be here otherwise. You'd be out on the street on your arse. And you wouldn't have got them papers for free when everyone else pays four quid for them and don't you forget it.'

'I won't forget them papers was no good and almost got me arrested!'

'I ain't got any more here! I told you that before. We been shut down. We've had to diversify, go offshore.'

'Then what you paying the bent copper for?'

At this Harry said nothing, just shook his head and smoked. He went to the window, pulled back the blackout as he had done the previous morning, but this time he pinned it up and let the grey light into the kitchen. Through the window a robin could be seen, perched on the slanting, falling-down roof of the outside lav, watching them. Harry finished the Pall Mall and stubbed it out, grinding the remains into a pulp.

'Myra's having a baby,' he said. 'And I can't be banged up inside when it's born. I can't.'

☙

Joe slept. One or two of the upstairs rooms still had beds in, still had the stained mattresses left behind by previous occupants who had departed in a hurry.

269

When he came downstairs it was late afternoon and there was no sign of Harry, but Myra was seated at the kitchen table in a mustard-yellow dress and stockings, flipping through a magazine. A cigarette burned in her left hand. She glanced up at Joe's arrival then down again. A heavy odour of frying fat and a pan still on the hob was evidence of a recent meal.

'Harry gone out?' Joe said.

For a moment Myra did not reply. Then she looked up. 'He told you to leave,' she said. 'Why you even here? This ain't your home.' She pulled on the cigarette and blew out a stream of smoke. 'We don't want you here. You're in the way.'

'Too bloody bad.'

He pushed past her to search for something to eat. But her words had stung him. Was that how Harry felt too? He found the end of a loaf of bread in a bread bin. No marg. He tore a hunk off and began to chew. If Harry had told him to leave it was simply because his being here put everyone in danger.

'I hear congratulations are in order,' he said, leaning against the sink.

Myra's eyes narrowed and she blew out another thin stream of smoke. She did not look pleased. And it was hard to imagine Myra as a mother. He thought of his own mother as she had been when he was a child, middle-aged and already broken by the mean existence that was life in Yalta Street in two rooms with three growing boys and no husband to speak of. But what did it mean for any woman to be a mother? She had done their washing and patched their clothes and there had been food on the table most days. She had never worn silk stockings, though, or a mustard-coloured dress or had a net for her hair or smoked Pall

270

Malls or sat around reading magazines. If she had, they would have gone without. But times were different now, he supposed. All the same, it was hard to imagine Myra as a mother.

'When's it due, then?'

'What's it matter?' She sighed and for a moment the bland coldness slipped and he saw Myra as she had once been, a little girl frightened and alone. In a second it was gone. 'You won't be around to see it.'

And that was true enough. When this child came into the world he would be far away—Dublin, New York. He would not hear of its arrival for many weeks. Perhaps never. He would never meet this child—his own niece or nephew—nor have any part in its life. Indeed, there was every chance it would never know of his existence. He would be as remote to this child as Ely Levin seemed to him. More remote, in fact, for at least Ely lived on in the stubborn memories of his wife, in the presence of his two sons. He would be as remote, then, as Joe's own father, who did not exist at all and was not even a name on a baptismal register.

'I'm sure you'll make a wonderful mother,' he said to hurt her. And for once she made no reply.

༄

'I need you to keep an eye on Nancy and my kid,' said Joe to his brother.

The afternoon was nearing its end and Harry had returned from wherever he had been all day, tired and thirsty and clearly in no mood for conversation, certainly not this kind of conversation.

'They're your wife and kid, not mine,' he replied, not looking up. 'If a man can't take care of his own family what kind of man is he?'

Joe was across the room in an instant, clenching his brother's collar in his fists and hauling him to his feet, his words tumbling out as though they had been there a long time, waiting: 'The kind of man who spends four years of his life in a leaky tin boat being shot at for his country while his older brothers sit it out on their arses!'

Afterwards there was a silence filled only by the sound of his own breath, coming quick and heavily, a pulse beating in his ears.

Harry shook him off angrily. 'Your wife and kids should come first. If you're dumb enough to end up in the navy that's your bloody lookout.' He sat back down again, straightening his collar, running a hand over his chin. 'But fine, if it means that much to you I'll look in on them. Not that that wife of yours will thank me for it.'

Joe took a deep breath. Whatever it was that had flooded his body and roared in his ears drained away, leaving him breathless, shaken.

'I ain't asking you to go round there and help Nancy hang new curtains or fix a leaky tap or play the kindly uncle. I'm just saying keep an eye. Make sure nothing bad happens to them. That's all.'

'I said I would, didn't I?'

Joe took another breath. He stood quite still, calming himself. He had never done that before, not to Harry, and the realisation of it shocked him a little. As a kid he had been frightened of Harry and with good reason, for Harry had had his own way of doing things and if you got in his way you felt it. It was hard to move beyond that, even now they were both adults, hard to believe Harry wouldn't make him pay in some way for what had just happened.

But Harry was reading the evening paper.

A soft tap at the front door cut through the silence as effectively as an air-raid siren. Harry looked up from his paper. Joe glanced over at him. And Myra, who must have been lurking and presumably listening just outside the kitchen, now appeared in the doorway, a suggestion of controlled alarm in her eyes as she tried to exchange a look with Harry. But Harry had already got up, casting aside the paper and pushing past her without a look.

They waited, Joe and Myra. Until Joe could wait no longer.

'Who is it?'

'What am I, a bloody mind-reader?'

But Myra knew, he could feel it. The suggestion of controlled alarm was not because she didn't know who it was, it was because she did know. Joe got up. He followed his brother out of the room and for a moment it seemed that Myra would try to stop him, then she shrugged and stepped aside to let him pass. The front door was slightly ajar. Harry was standing outside on the street. The low murmur of voices could just be heard. Joe took a step closer. The voices were speaking in angry whispers, there was no mistaking it. The room at the front of the house—the room where Joe had been born—was mostly unused now, except for storage. Joe tried the door and it was unlocked. He went in, stepping cautiously in the darkness, and made his way to the window and wiped his sleeve over years of grime so that he could see out to the street beyond. After a short time, he heard the front door click shut and a moment later a man in a long overcoat with his hat pulled down low, his arm in a sling, stalked past. After he had gone Joe remained where he was, at the window, watching the late-afternoon street. Then he left, closing the door behind him, and returned to the kitchen. Harry was back in his chair reading the same page of the paper. Myra was in the other chair. She looked up at him but Harry kept on reading the paper.

'It was him, the same copper,' Joe said. 'Why'd he come back?'

'They always come back,' said Harry, still not looking up.

Joe thought about this. 'Did you give him more money?'

'Leave it,' said Harry, a frown appearing. Myra shifted, uncrossing her legs and recrossing them, hitching up her stockings.

But something didn't add up. 'If you're paying this copper off then why was he waiting for me at the docks that day? Like he knew, like he was expecting me?'

He felt the chill of his words. The way they hung in the air, turning the air around them cold.

Myra let out a horrid little laugh and Harry shot her a warning glance. 'You, shut it,' he warned her.

'I don't understand,' said Joe.

And Myra, who couldn't shut it, got up and laughed again. 'Because you're a fool,' she said.

Harry shot up and in a second his hand was around her neck, his eyes blazing. 'I said *shut it*!'

She stumbled, and when, after a moment, he let her go, she shook herself, lifted her chin a little and strode out, wobbling slightly and putting out a steadying hand as she passed the table. Once she had gone, Harry sat back down, but he had closed the newspaper.

'Harry?'

'You *are* a fool,' said Harry, very softly, barely above a whisper.

The whole room had turned cold now.

'You set the copper onto me?'

'So what if I did?' Harry shrugged. 'I ain't paying him off. That copper ain't bent, and believe me I tried. He knows everything, the whole operation, but he thinks someone else is the brains behind it. He wanted names, dates, places, details. I gave him that, everything I had, in exchange for—'

'In exchange for me?'

'In exchange for my freedom, mine and Myra's. He needed someone, needed to make an arrest. It was a straight swap. Us or you.'

Joe thought of the man who had been stabbed to death in the Underground station. He saw now that this was not Harry's fate; that it was Harry with his hand on the knife, it was Harry ordering the hit. Joe felt his fingertips, his toes go numb.

'But what about family, Harry?'

'You ain't family, Joe. You never was.'

Ice had formed on the inside of the windows, on the walls, the very air turned to ice.

Joe found himself in the hallway of the house he had grown up in, though he had no memory of leaving the kitchen. He turned one way and then the other, trying to clear his head. Now he was walking back into the kitchen and the ice had gone, replaced by a red mist. He pulled Harry to his feet and landed a fist in his stomach, and Harry folded in half, then sank to his knees, gasping, and he did not get up.

Joe left then, going into one or two rooms, finding his coat, finding some money, taking what food he could find, and by the time he was ready to leave—just a very few minutes it had taken him—Myra was waiting for him and she flew at his face and he had to beat her away, making it to the front door, yanking it open and stumbling out and away with Myra's foul words following him.

# CHAPTER TWENTY-FOUR

Gerald went to see Yelland at the ministry. It was the only place, the only person, he could think of to go to.

He moved like a man in a dream, haunted by the ghost of the man who had made this same journey in reverse the day before, so full of hope then, so blissfully ignorant. On the train south he squatted in a few inches of space in the corridor, smoking cigarette after cigarette until they ran out.

His early start meant he arrived at Kings Cross by mid-afternoon and was outside his old building at the Ministry of Supply in the Strand at a little after three. It had hardly changed in the intervening three years—the same silver barrage balloons tethered high above the rooftop, the same stack of sandbags by the entrance, the same uniformed civil servants hurrying in and out with their leather portfolios and their attaché cases, the same babble of secretaries in their smart clipping heels and bright lipstick. But the hats and coats of the secretaries were a little more worn, a little shabbier after four years of war, their faces a little more gaunt. Opposite, the Elizabethan tavern and the little row of shops that had withstood plague and fire and civil war were gone, reduced to a large waterlogged crater, and the officers who passed by the crater, trying not to get their regulation boots wet, were all American. People no longer carried their gas masks—they were becoming careless or they were simply inured, by now, to war.

Or perhaps, for the first time, they had begun to sense victory.

He went up the front steps and presented himself at the porter's desk, having no appointment and trusting that Yelland still worked there and had not been seconded to Civil Defence or the Home Office or the Admiralty or the War Office or anywhere else.

After a short wait Yelland himself appeared, unexpectedly and somewhat sheepishly, in the uniform of a captain of the Household Cavalry. Otherwise he appeared unchanged—same self-conscious dipping movement as he approached, same unkempt prematurely grey thatch, same affable grin and innocently blinking blue eyes. A schoolboy who had never quite grown up and who, by a quirk of fate, found himself fighting a war, albeit from behind a desk.

'Meadows!' he exclaimed, with what seemed genuine pleasure, coming forward and extending both arms to him. 'Where the devil did you spring from? The Riviera, by the look of you!'

'Definitely not the Riviera! Yelland, it's bloody good to see you,' Gerald replied, pumping his former colleague's arm up and down and clapping him on the shoulder. And then, horribly, feeling tears prick his eyes.

'Well, come on in,' said Yelland, turning away, and whether he was being decent about it or had not noticed Gerald couldn't tell. 'All sorts of jolly forms to fill in, of course, before they'll let you inside,' Yelland went on, leading him back to the reception desk, where for the next five minutes he was occupied with said forms. Eventually a pass was produced and clipped on and Yelland led the way towards the lift. 'We're up on six now,' he said chattily, as the lift filled up and they waited for it to grind into action. 'Kemp and his lot got moved to seven and Meriwether—you remember Meriwether?—was relocated down to two, so of course that meant we got sent upstairs. Bit of a relief, between you and me. That basement was like the boiler room of a transatlantic liner during summer and like a gulag in the winter.'

'Yes, I remember,' said Gerald. He *did* remember: Kemp and his polka-dot bowties and his manner of barking every order as though he were on the parade ground, and Meriwether, who had a mirror in his office and paused in the middle of a meeting to reapply pomade and dab pungent cologne behind his ears and on each wrist. He remembered the indescribable heat of the basement in summer and the insufferable cold in the winter, he remembered how the lift creaked and the names of each of the girls in the typing pool—Miss Poulter, Miss O'Flaherty, Miss Hale, Miss Kovacs, Miss Lambert. He remembered it all with a kind of shock because he had not thought of it in three years. It seemed as distant as childhood.

'Yelland, you're a captain in the Household Cavalry!'

Yelland did his dipping movement. 'Yes, but I can assure you it's just an honorary title. They gave all of us a rank a while back. I think I only got this one because they happened to have the uniform spare in my size. I don't know one end of a horse from another, really.

This is us.' And he led the way out of the lift and along a shabby corridor towards a large, very cluttered, very crowded anteroom and from there into a smaller office, little more than a storeroom really, containing a desk and a number of telephones, a couple of chairs and a bulging filing cabinet with a wilting aspidistra on top. 'This is me,' said Yelland, squeezing into the chair behind the desk and indicating Gerald should take the other. 'I think tea, don't you? Miss Linklater! Tea for two, if you please.'

A young woman, very tall, very slender and smartly dressed in a chocolate brown suit, could be seen in the room beyond.

'Miss Linklater's recently joined us from five,' said Yelland. 'She's really jolly good.' He leaned forward. 'Between you and me, I don't think she really wanted to join us—bit dull after five—but it's wartime, isn't it? We all have to make sacrifices.'

Gerald turned around in his chair and saw Miss Linklater, who had made sacrifices, disappearing into a kitchenette armed with a teapot.

'Now, where have you just come from, Meadows? Can't divulge, I suppose?'

Gerald turned back to face Yelland. 'I travelled down from Wetherby this morning, as a matter of fact. I can't see there's any danger in my telling you that.'

'Wetherby, eh? I doubt that's where you picked up that tan.'

'No.'

'And Diana? She's well?'

'Yes. Yes. Quite well.'

Yelland leaned forward again. 'And is this a social visit or business?'

Gerald waited a moment before replying. 'Unofficial business,' he said, and he looked directly at Yelland as he said this, gauging his response. Appealing to him, he realised belatedly, as a friend and former colleague, in a way that did not involve words.

Yelland nodded slowly. 'Go on.'

'I'm trying to locate a missing child. She—the child—was possibly reported killed in a bombing raid a week ago, maybe longer, somewhere in London. That's about all I know. It's on behalf a friend. Rather urgent, I'm afraid . . .'

He had rehearsed this. Decided carefully how he would present it to Yelland in a way that might be plausible and was suggestive of urgency but gave absolutely nothing away about the actual situation.

Yelland listened, nodded again, his eyes sliding off to the right as he digested the words and they went skidding off in the myriad directions of Yelland's mind. He had been emeritus professor of analytical philosophy at Cambridge before the war—or something along those lines—and the affable schoolboy thing, while not exactly an act, certainly did a good job of disguising a very keen brain.

'Child's name? Location? Parents' names?' he said, cutting directly to the problem and not bothered by the whys and wherefores.

Gerald shook his head. 'It's a girl, aged around three years. Possibly from one of the poorer districts. That's really all I have.'

'Anyone else likely to be looking for it?' It was a shrewd question.

'I'm afraid I don't know that either.'

The chocolate-brown-suited Miss Linklater came in at that moment, giving a cursory rap on the open door and striding in to place a tray of tea things on the desk. Her wrists and fingers were very slender; like a pianist, Gerald thought. She left without a word but somehow a definite air of resentment followed her.

Yelland smiled apologetically at her retreating form then he got up and closed the door to his office with his foot. 'Shall I be mother?' He poured out two cups and he measured out a quantity of the dreadful dried milk with a beautifully engraved silver teaspoon as though he was a duchess in her drawing room. 'Here we are. I say, are you quite alright, Meadows?'

Gerald was not all right; his hands were shaking and his skin felt clammy. He couldn't feel his feet. There was a pounding in his head and it took all his concentration to focus.

'Touch of malaria.' He had never had malaria in his life but Yelland couldn't know that. He had a feeling that what he was experiencing was delayed shock, or exhaustion, or both. He took a grateful gulp of the tea and felt its comforting warmth spread through him.

'Yes, the malaria's particularly bad in Wetherby at this time of year, I understand,' said Yelland with a lift of his eyebrows.

'Quite.'

Yelland drank his tea for a moment or two in silence, and it was clear he was already working on the matter at hand. At last he looked up, having apparently come to a decision.

'Alright, Meadows, going back to your . . . request. There were raids on the twenty-first and the twenty-second, Friday and Saturday nights. I remember the dates because they were the first raids we'd had in London for months. Took us a bit by surprise, I don't mind telling you. If you want specifics about recent bombs and casualties and so forth, that kind of information's not collected here. It will be Civil Defence and they're under the Home Office, so that's the first place we must go. I have a contact there, Radnor—know him?'

Gerald shook his head.

'I'll telephone him. Ask a few questions. Find out what I can and report back to you . . . let's see, tomorrow morning? How's that sound?'

It sounded exactly what he had hoped for. Gerald nodded his thanks, unable to speak.

Yelland watched him silently for a moment then he reached over and patted Gerald's arm. 'Rough, was it, out there? Of course it was. Stupid thing to say. Ignore me. Now, how are you fixed for tonight? I'm probably staying at my post till late, then I'm on fire-watch duty, so why don't you take my key and stay at my bolthole in Bayswater? No hot water, I'm afraid. Come to think of it, no cold water either—but hey ho! All four walls and the roof are intact, or at least they were last time I was there. Help yourself to anything you find.'

So Gerald stayed in Yelland's Bayswater bolthole and helped himself to brandy, and pickles from a jar, and some biscuits that he found in a cupboard in the kitchen. It was tempting to finish off the brandy but he made himself stop. That was no way to repay Yelland's kindness. But it was seductive, the feel of the brandy burning the back of his throat, the fire hitting his guts, the gradual unfocusing of his eyes, the sense of the world receding. He made himself go to Yelland's bed and sleep, barely undressing in the unheated flat. Life had become transitory, thanks to the war and being back home seemed to have made no difference at all, had made it worse, if anything.

He pulled his coat around himself and slept.

∽

'Got hold of Radnor last night,' said Yelland at his desk the following morning. His unruly grey hair was more unkempt than usual and his uniform appeared to have been slept in, but no one in the office commented on it or seemed to notice—but, then, most of them looked like this, Gerald realised. The only smart people he saw were the Americans and Miss Linklater.

'Yes, Radnor was surprisingly forthcoming. Came back with all sorts of things. I wrote it down myself . . . sorry it's impossible to read. Here let me . . . Now, the raid on the nights of the twenty-first and the twenty-second were mostly in the Westminster area, Embankment, Pimlico, Clapham, Surry Docks, Poplar, Stepney, Bethnal Green, Rotherhithe. One or two further out, Home Counties, but you said just London? Alright, forty-eight houses destroyed or badly damaged, mains out in six locations, two warehouses burned down, a number of other commercial and civil buildings and utilities damaged. There are twenty-three UXBs still waiting to be dealt with. As for casualties. . . twenty-nine dead, another sixty or so injured or missing—that's everything from gravest not-likely-to-survive through to minor abrasions and concussions and the like.' He paused and looked up. 'Anything there sound like what you're after?'

'The buildings that were hit or damaged—any of them Underground stations or shelters?'

Yelland perused his notes. 'Railway lines hit at Clapham

Junction, no casualties . . . Roof collapse at Bethnal Green tube—that what you want?'

Was it? He could not imagine Diana travelling into the East End. She had taken Abigail to a pantomime, which surely would be in the West End somewhere.

'I'm not sure. The dead—do you have any details?'

'Family of six in Poplar, direct hit—grandparents, mother, three children. Elderly couple in their home. Three young women walking home in Stepney. One policeman. Four firemen. One warden. Man in his forties stabbed in an Underground station—though that was a murder, so probably not what you want.'

'Good God!' said Gerald, appalled. 'Do you mean to say someone was murdered in a shelter during a raid?'

''Fraid so. Not so unusual as you might think, sadly. But this appears to be a gang-related incident. Black market. All sorts of shady things go on, unfortunately, under cover of the blackout.'

'My God, we risk our lives while others line their pockets. It's unforgivable!'

'Quite so. Here we are: another family killed—four children and one baby. And an airman home on leave (unlucky) and two members of another family—brother and sister. Mother and child . . . and another mother and child.' He looked up.

'Where were the two mothers and children? Do you have that?'

'Rotherhithe: twenty-seven-year-old mother and ten-year-old boy. And . . . Bethnal Green: mother and female child—age not shown.'

Yelland looked up and their eyes met over the desk.

∽

Afterwards Gerald walked, in a sudden and heavy downpour up Kingsway to Holborn and caught the number 8 bus going east, which was a mistake. So many of the streets on the number 8's route were blocked off and impassable that his journey of perhaps two miles took him the best part of an hour.

The downpour ended as suddenly as it had begun. Seated, dripping wet, on the upper deck, Gerald looked out of the window at row after row of bombed buildings, at craters filled with water and choked with bomb weed that gave everything an abandoned, semi-permanent feel, as though the very landscape of London had been changed forever, as though an angry deity had torn the city up by its roots and tossed it about a bit then hurled it back down to Earth. He saw a city that had fallen from the sky.

It got worse the further east the bus went. As it rounded Liverpool Street and Bishopsgate, as it passed through Shoreditch into Bethnal Green Road, the rows of gutted, destroyed houses became whole streets, one after another after another. Why would Diana come here? he wondered. Why would she bring Abigail here? He made himself look away, watching instead a sailor and his girl across the aisle eating chips from a greasy newspaper, a little boy sitting with his mother idly drawing shapes on the misty window with his finger while his mother totted up her ration-book points with a pencil and a scrap of paper. He was the only one looking out of the window and seeing the devastation. He was the only one shocked by it.

The bus met an ambulance coming the other way and came to a juddering stop. In the street below he saw teams of workers— decontamination squads, Auxiliary Fire Service, rescue teams standing around a bombed-out building. Someone handed around mugs of tea. No one seemed in much of a hurry—a salvage operation rather than a rescue. The bus jerked forward and they made their way in slow stops and starts along the road. He saw a street market, a kosher butcher, a synagogue, a tailor, another tailor, shops advertising lockshen, borsht, salami, beigels. Most of the shop signs were in Yiddish. But what was there to buy? None of the shops he had seen so far had any food to sell.

The bus passed beneath a railway bridge and he jumped off. He had never been anywhere east of Liverpool Street in his life but here was the station, right on the corner beside a large Georgian public house, the London Underground roundel clearly visible, a flight of steps leading downwards. The station was clearly closed—temporary wooden barriers marked off an area on all sides, blocking off the pub and half the road. There would be nothing to see; indeed, he could not be certain that this was even the right station. He crossed the road and as he came nearer he saw that someone had laid a posy of daisies, dandelions and rose bay willow herb at the top of the flight of steps.

Quite suddenly his legs were encased in glue so that he could not feel the road beneath his feet. He groped for somewhere to place his hand, finding the solid and reassuring brickwork of the pub. Two people had died here—a mother and a little girl. People swirled around him, hurrying past with no more than a cursory glance, intent only on finding food to fill their empty baskets, on getting out of this cold winter morning. But the sun had burst through, unlikely as that had seemed just a short time earlier, and the fragments of broken glass in the gutters glinted brightly. After a while, Gerald stepped forward and climbed over the wooden barrier and made his way over. The posy had been laid against the steps and he crouched down and picked it up. It was bedraggled and rather pitiful after more than a week. There was no note, no card, no identification of any kind to indicate who had placed it there or for whom. A family member, or just a sympathetic neighbour? He sat back on his haunches and lifted his face to the sky, blinking in the unexpected sunlight. He closed his eyes and when he opened them again the sad little bunch of dead weeds was still clenched in his fist. He gently replaced it.

'Lose someone, did you, luv?'

He turned to see an elderly woman in a decrepit and sodden black coat and matching hat, leaning on an umbrella and peering short-sightedly at him. Wisps of long yellow-white hair escaped from the hat over a face that might have been beautiful half a century ago but was now puckered and wrinkled and mottled with age. She seemed to be about four foot tall.

'Yes, I have,' he replied, getting stiffly to his feet. 'I think they might be dead. Do you happen to know the names of the mother and child who died here?'

'Sorry, luv.' She gave a sad little smile. 'But you take yourself off to the Warden's Station. They'll be able to help you. It's just round the corner, you can't miss it.' She began to shuffle off, placing the umbrella on the pavement before she attempted a first step. 'I hopes you find 'em.'

Gerald watched her go, inching her way painfully along the path, returning home—what kind of home? he wondered—with her basket empty. But she had pitied him, he realised.

He found the Warden's Station easily enough. It was little more than an Anderson shelter dug deep into the ground with a wall of sandbags at the entrance. A short flight of crudely made steps had been cut into the ground and led to a door which, presently, was closed. He went down the steps and rapped loudly and a moment later the door was opened by a young lad with slicked-back hair and distrustful dark eyes in a crumpled and unbuttoned APR uniform. He viewed Gerald, his uniform, his stripes and insignia, with alarm, stepping out and hurriedly pulling the door shut behind him.

'Meadows,' Gerald said, giving the boy a brief nod. 'I'm from the ministry. I'd like to ask you some questions about the raids on the twenty-first and the twenty-second. Details of casualties, that sort of thing. Shall we go inside?'

The boy gaped at him, but Gerald pushed past him. Inside was an urn, a wireless, a field telephone, the hut lit by a single light bulb strung from the shelter's ceiling. A trestle table took up most of the space, though all that was on it was a pile of creased papers. Tacked to the walls were spotters' guides to enemy aircraft and diagrams of detonators and fuses. Logbooks were stacked against the wall and a collection of warden helmets hung from nails.

There was also a girl, a slight thing with tiny, flashing eyes and a small rather pointed nose, cheaply peroxided hair and smudged lipstick. She was pulling on a dress, snapping on suspenders with clumsy, hurried fingers, and she stared in dull horror at Gerald's arrival.

'Good morning,' he said, and waited as the girl pulled down the hem of her dress in a failed attempt at dignity, rammed her feet into her shoes and snatched up coat and hat and swept passed him.

The boy stood, wretched and uncertain, in the doorway, a schoolboy outside the headmaster's office.

'What's your name, boy?'

'Prentice. Arthur Prentice.' A chin thrust out in defiance.

'Well, Mr Prentice, are you the senior warden here, or do I need to speak to someone else?'

'Mr Regis's District Warden, but he ain't here. What is it you need to know?' The boy had regained his composure now and stood with eyes narrowed unsure whether to be helpful or belligerent, to be in awe of the man from the ministry who was seated at his table, or resentful.

'Alright. You'll have to do. I need the names of the two casualties from the raid ten days ago. It was a mother and a daughter, I believe. Do you hold that kind of information here?'

Prentice pushed himself up from the wall and nodded towards the logbooks. ''Course we do, that's what the logbooks are for, innit? Not that I need 'em cause I can tell you straight off. It was Levin. Nancy Levin. That were the mother's name.'

'And the little girl?'

At this the boy's knowledge apparently failed him, for he slid over to the nearest logbook and opened it, making a show of moving his finger down a list of names. 'Emily,' he said at last, reading from the page. 'Approximately three years of age. Killed when the roof collapsed at the station. Early hours of Sunday morning.'

'Who identified the bodies? Were there surviving family members?'

'Can't tell you that, can I?' replied Prentice, as though these questions were absurd. 'We don't keep that kind of information.'

'Well, then, where did they live? Do you have other family members in your list of shelterers? That *is* how it works, isn't it?

You have a list of the names and addresses of the people in your district, and where each person shelters?'

Clearly annoyed at being told his job, Prentice reached for another book and flipped through it with bad grace. 'Odessa Street. Number forty-two. No other family members listed.' He snapped the book shut with a bang.

Gerald stood up. 'Alright, one last question. Where are they now? Their . . . bodies, I mean. Where would they have been taken?'

Prentice shrugged. 'Mortuary, o' course.'

'Which is where?'

'Down the London Hospital, most likely. Or the temporary mortuary. They set one up in an old warehouse down Roman Road. You can't miss it. Smell'll take you there.'

༈

Gerald found Roman Road by crossing over Cambridge Heath Road and walking in an easterly direction. The only warehouse he could see had an ambulance stationed outside it and two women drivers standing beside the cab smoking.

'Is this the temporary mortuary?' he called out and they nodded wordlessly and looked away as he passed them.

He walked to a small doorway cut into the brickwork, hesitant to go in. When he did, the place was deserted and he thought he had made a mistake until he saw, laid out against the front wall, three lifeless forms on stretchers covered by black tarpaulins. One had a blackened toe poking out to which a label had been attached. A short distance away a little group stood in solitary communion, an elderly woman weeping, a younger woman, her daughter perhaps, patting her arm, and two men in overalls standing nearby but clearly separate, observing in silence. One of them saw Gerald and came over. The man was in his forties and had the unmistakable exhausted demeanour of a doctor in wartime who had worked a thirty-six-hour shift and had no real expectation of ever seeing his bed again. His face was very pale, as were his eyebrows and lashes, as though he had never got quite enough exposure to sunlight. He wore a dirt-stained apron over his overalls and was carrying a pair of bloodied gloves.

'Do you need help?' His manner suggested he had helped a lot of people recently and none of it with a good outcome.

Gerald gave the man a brief nod but did not introduce himself and the man did not look as if he expected it.

'I'm looking for two bodies from the raid on the twenty-first and twenty-second—a mother and child. Name of Levin?'

The man nodded. 'Yes, I remember. Long gone I'm afraid. This is very much a temporary facility. Not sanitary to keep the bodies here longer than a day or two. These poor devils—' he indicated the three covered forms '—were dug up last night. Been buried since Friday night. Now they've been identified they'll be moved.'

'Were they identified? The Levins? Were their remains claimed by the family?'

'Identified, yes. By the warden I think. But not claimed, no. There was no family, far as I recall. Or none that turned up here. They were only here an hour or two before they got taken off to the London. May I ask what your interest is, Captain?'

'It's possible there was a misidentification,' Gerald replied carefully. 'What happened, to the bodies if they went unclaimed?'

'They would have been cremated. But look here, I don't think you can be right about a misidentification, not if the warden made the identification himself. They know their patch.'

'Not the woman. The child. Easier to mistake a child, I think.'

The man looked away, thinking or just tired, and if he was surprised by this line of questioning he did not show it. 'Well, of course it's possible,' he conceded, turning back. 'But pretty unlikely. In '40 and '41, yes, I can well believe all sorts of errors occurred—frankly, it was nothing short of pandemonium—but now, well, I'd be surprised. Unless someone wanted to perpetrate some sort of fraud.'

He shrugged in a way that suggested it was beyond his juris-diction and, frankly, beyond his concern.

Gerald thanked him and left. It was, quite literally, a dead end.

The women ambulance drivers were still smoking, quite possibly the same cigarettes; he had been inside the warehouse so short a time. Despite Prentice's warning, the mortuary had not smelled. Perhaps that was because the bodies were frozen solid, or perhaps it meant he had got used to the smell of decay in the desert, where a man began to rot almost before he had taken his final breath.

They had already been cremated.

⤔

Afterwards, things became confused. He had been standing in the doorway of the warehouse watching the two women drivers, thinking about what he had just learned, but now, somehow, he was crouching on the ground with his hands over his ears as though in the middle of an enemy barrage. The world spun over and over itself like a film on a projector that has come off the spool. When it finally settled down one of the women was crouching before him, her hand on his shoulder, peering into his face. His eyes focused and he saw green eyes frowning a little, with concern and curiosity, the girl's skin mottled red by the cold, thin lips chapped from the wind. An ordinary face, an ordinary girl who should have been serving in a shop or raising a family but who, thanks to a quirk of fate, was driving an ambulance in a war. She offered him a cigarette, and he saw that she had seen many, many frantic and desperate people enter this place and the same people leave a few moments later, their hopes destroyed.

Gerald accepted her cigarette and got unsteadily to his feet. He had trouble lighting the cigarette and, when he had, smoked it quickly, feeling the nicotine blur his senses just enough to take the edge off them. The two women said nothing and he was grateful for this. When the cigarette had been smoked he left, pausing at the final moment to ask for directions to Odessa Street, which they gave him, promptly and without hesitation, and if you drove an ambulance in an air raid you probably did know your district pretty thoroughly.

He returned to Bethnal Green Road and fought his way through the market stalls, and there was food to be had, for he saw a woman deftly slice and gut a live eel and his faintness returned. Elderly Jewish women selling hot beigels called out to him but otherwise no one bothered him, though many people looked at him, at his officer's stripes. Sailors arm in arm with their girls met his gaze openly, while squaddies larking about fell silent as he passed, and he thought, for the first time in about a week, about Enderby and Crouch. It all seemed a very long time ago.

He left the market behind and turned off the main road, passing a pawnbroker, garment manufacturers and cabinet-makers, French polishers and upholsterers, all with European names—Jewish names—an entire cottage industry going on much as it had for a hundred years, untouched by war.

But nothing was untouched by the war. It was a delusion to think so.

He found Odessa Street and it was, for the most part, intact. It was a short street parallel to the main road, easy to miss in the unfamiliar warren of streets that looked, to the untrained eye, identical. Two rows of Victorian terraces faced each other barely more than ten yards apart, two-storey buildings with front doors that opened directly onto the street A pub on the corner was boarded up and abandoned, and a number of the houses appeared similarly vacated. One house at the far end of the street had been hit and was no more than a hole in the ground, the houses either side untouched. Large cracks, a gaping crater and piles of debris littered the street. You'd have a hard time driving so much as a bicycle along this street, but then it seemed entirely possible no one here owned a bicycle. Washing lines crisscrossed the street from which one or two greyish sheets limply fluttered. A cluster of children, inadequately dressed for the winter, were playing a noisy game in the gutter. A couple of prams were positioned outside front doors—abandoned or containing babies it was impossible to know—and a woman stood in a doorway smoking, observing him.

He could make out no house numbers. Indeed, most of the front doors did not even have letterboxes. Perhaps these people did not receive post. Perhaps they could not read. He didn't know, and he felt, for a brief moment, ashamed of his ignorance.

Gerald began to walk towards the woman in the doorway but she turned abruptly and went inside, the door slamming shut. The children stopped their game and stood up, gathering into a group, facing him expressionlessly.

'Hullo,' he called, expecting them to scatter as soon as he opened his mouth, but they did not move. It was unnerving. 'Can you tell me which is number forty-two? The Levins?'

None of them spoke or so much as gave an indication they had understood the question. He wondered if they only understood Yiddish. One of the children, a boy of perhaps eight or nine, in shorts and a pair of man's shoes that were far too big for him and with which he wore no socks, stooped down, feeling with his hand on the ground and not for a second taking his eyes off the stranger. His fingers found what they were looking for—a stone or piece of rubble—and curled around it. Slowly he straightened up. There no malice in the child's face, or fear. There was nothing.

'I've a shilling here for the first one of you who tells me which is the Levin's house.'

That did it. They broke ranks as quickly as a platoon after parade, rushing forward. A stick-thin girl with a dirt-streaked face, no more than five or six, got there first. 'That one! That one!' she screamed, pointing to a house on the other side of the street and three down. Gerald tossed her the coin. She snatched it but at once the others piled on top of her and a ruckus ensued. Gerald left them to it, but as he approached the property a stone whizzed past his ear. He ducked instinctively even as the stone hit the wall of the house and rolled harmlessly away. He felt irritated, his irritation fuelled by the brief moment of fear. He wanted to bang their stupid, ignorant, lice-infested heads together and tell them that he had fought a bloody war for them, damn it!

Number 42 had very little to distinguish it from numbers 44 and 40 on either side. The front door showed residue of paint so ancient its colour was impossible to guess; it might have been the original paint from the 1890s. Rubbish filled the gutter outside the house, dumped there or simply blown by the wind. Weeds grew in the cracks between the bricks but the doorstep was scrubbed clean, or had been scrubbed sometime recently. He caught a glimpse of a wisp of cloth hanging at the downstairs window. He knocked on the door twice, loudly, his heart beating fast.

# CHAPTER TWENTY-FIVE

Joe arrived back in Odessa Street in the late afternoon, approaching from the west by way of Silkweavers Row and Frenchmans Lane and so avoiding the main roads. He stopped in the shadow of the boarded-up Hero of Trafalgar pub, aware that any number of people might recognise him.

But no one stirred.

The street was silent, deserted, and its silence disturbed him. It was almost as though the people could sense there was going to be a raid. He had heard somewhere that birds and animals knew an earthquake was coming before it happened, that they flew off or slunk away into the undergrowth long before the first tremors could be felt. That was how it seemed to him, standing in the shadow of the Hero of Trafalgar pub.

He thought: Nancy will believe I am in Liverpool by now, perhaps even in Dublin. She will expect me to have sent her a postcard and here I am, hiding in the shadows not twenty yards from home.

Thinking this made his head throb. It made something surge up inside him that was part despair, part joy. He thought about the three days and three nights he had spent in a lifeboat adrift in the ocean wearing a dead man's clothes and how he had expected to die but he had not died, and in light of that miracle he attempted to make sense of his current situation but he could not. It did not make sense. He wanted to see his wife and child. It could not hurt to see that all was well before attempting his escape a second time.

As he waited a rabble of small children tumbled out of a doorway and began a noisy game. Mrs Bantry at number 4 came out onto her doorstep, her coat wrapped tightly around her, watching the children and smoking a Craven A. She was close enough that he could see the wisps of blue smoke from her cigarette whipped away on the breeze, he could see the dullness in her eyes that precluded either hope or fear. He remembered that Jack Bantry had knocked out all his wife's teeth one drunken Saturday night. Jack Bantry was a prisoner in Burma now, Nancy had said. It seemed likely that Mrs Bantry, silently smoking her Craven A, wasn't praying for the end of the war.

It was a clear sky above and Joe was no longer sure what he waited for. He felt as though he had spent all his life waiting. What did it matter if Mrs Bantry saw him, if the small children noticed him or not? He thrust his hands deeper in his pockets and set off towards the children, passing Mrs Bantry, and making for his own house. He would see Nancy, he would talk to her, just for a minute. It flashed into his mind that he could persuade her to come with him, that the three of them, he, Nancy and Emily, could journey to Dublin together—why not? She might be persuaded, though it was a crazy idea, impractical at best, suicidal at worst. Still, the thought flashed across his mind—how could it not?

His footsteps quickened as he neared the house and he remembered the trepidation with which he had approached the house three months ago at the start of his leave, uncertain of so much. Now he moved swiftly, reaching the door and letting himself in. Once inside he leaned against the door, catching his breath and listening, realising how tightly his nerves were wound. Upstairs he could hear the Rosenthal children, one of the boys left in charge barking out orders, suggesting that Mrs Rosenthal was out. But downstairs all was silent.

'Nancy?'

His voice was hushed, though it was daft to imagine that someone might be listening, that someone might be hiding in one of the rooms. He pushed open the bedroom door with his foot and looked inside, but it was clearly deserted, Nancy's things, and Emily's too, strewn about much as they had been that morning when he had left. He went into the kitchen and saw no sign of recent activity there either. Indeed, things were put away and cleaned up.

They had had nothing when they had moved into the house, he and Nancy. They had gone to the pawnbroker on Hackney Road and dug out mismatching cups and saucers and plates, knives and forks and some funny little teaspoons that had ivory handles and would have been expensive once, but the handles came off as soon as you picked anything up and that had made them laugh, each mealtime, without fail. But today everything was put away.

He pulled out a chair and sat down at the table because his legs were shaking and weak. His emotion, his love, had made him weak. Had made him fearful. He had got this table for Nancy not long after he had come home on leave, when he discovered she had burned the old table for firewood the winter before. He had following Harry's lead and scoured the bombsites and found this one, a card table, from a posh house up near Vic Park hidden in a back room beneath a half-crumbling wall and he had dug it out with his bare hands and carried it home over his head at midnight. And since then it had been constantly covered in newspapers and ashtrays and empty cigarette packets and the leftovers of their meal. For Nancy was unconcerned by housework. But now everything was neat.

He looked around the room, feeling her presence all about him. He smiled, a warmth spreading through him as he imagined her coming home and finding him here in their home, seated at the table. Then all he had to do was persuade her to come with him, now, right this minute. It would be easy enough to leave it all behind if they left together. And in his mind he had already left it behind and knowing this brought a sort of calmness.

But it was odd that everything was neat and tidy and put away.

'We had chips!'

He spun around to see one of the Rosenthal girls standing in the doorway in a long grubby dress, clutching a bedraggled doll in her arms. It was Pamela. Or Barbara. He had trouble distinguishing the younger ones.

'Did you, luv? That sounds very fine. Your mum in?'

The little girl thought about this then she shook her head very firmly.

'Who's in charge? Is it Billy?'

Again she shook her head and stuck her thumb in her mouth and the other one, Barbara or perhaps Pamela, appeared silently beside her in an equally grubby dress. 'We had chips for breakfast!' said the second child, echoing her sister. 'It was waiting for us when we come home from the shelter. Mum said it was the fairies what made it and left it for our breakfast.'

This seemed unlikely but Joe didn't argue. Whatever had happened had clearly made quite an impression. The kitchen didn't smell like chips had been fried recently and he wondered when this marvellous event had happened. But it hardly mattered, did it, in the scheme of things?

'Do you kids know where Aunty Nancy is, and Emily?'

But they both just looked at him.

The knock on the door made him jump. It shattered the peace.

# CHAPTER TWENTY-SIX

Gerald knocked a second time, louder, then he went to the down-stairs window, cupping his hand against the glass, and peered in. It was a bedroom, tiny, cluttered and cramped. He made out an old-fashioned iron bedstead, a thin mattress, blankets. Against the back wall was a narrow Victorian wardrobe, its door hanging open, but it was impossible to see what, if anything, was inside it. On the floor were items of clothing, shoes strewn about, a suitcase standing opened and empty.

He stepped back. It could be any room, belonging to anyone, recently vacated by the occupants who had just popped out to do their shopping or who had left in a hurry at the sound of the air-raid siren and never returned. It told him nothing. If there were no living relatives what became of a person's things, of their house? What became of the rooms they rented? The local authorities would sort it out, he presumed; indeed, there was probably a department that dealt solely with the possessions of dead people.

He stepped back and studied the upstairs window and at once saw a shadow pulling back out of sight. Gerald waited, standing there, gazing up, and sure enough, after a time, there it was again, a shadow at the window.

As he tried to decide what to do, he saw a woman making her way breathlessly along the street towards him, a shopping basket banging at her knees and two small children at her side. She paused at the sight of him. Even from a distance of twenty yards or more he could see a dozen frightened possibilities flit across the woman's face and she seemed poised to flee. Gerald had no clue how to reassure her so he just stood there and said nothing and after a while she started forward again, moving quickly like a bird hopping across a lawn, her eyes turned away from him, her hands grasping both the children—two little boys—tightly. They were coming to this house. He stepped aside, trying not to stare at her but still taking in a tiny shrunken figure bundled up in a headscarf and a man's overcoat but with bare legs and light summer shoes. He thought at first it was an old woman though, as she neared, he saw she was quite young but terribly worn down. Something about her pallor, her eyes, her posture spoke of complete and utter exhaustion. The children, by contrast, eyed him boldly; the eldest, who was all of nine or ten, shivering in a decrepit old pullover and a pair of men's trousers held up with string, pulled himself up sharply in a manner that suggested there was no father around.

They had reached their door, number 42.

'Mrs Levin?' said Gerald, knowing it was not her but saying it anyway. At his words the women's eyes widened for a moment then she turned away. The boy's expression turned mocking.

'She's dead,' he said. This earned him a clip around the ear from his mother. Clearly the boy had not yet learned that you do not speak to strangers, or not this kind of stranger.

'Then I wonder if you can tell me—'

But they were gone, the door opened, the mother bundling her children in, the door firmly closed.

He went after her and knocked loudly and repeatedly, and when he stopped the silence was no longer the silence of an abandoned house, it was the silence of people holding their breath, hiding and waiting, not daring to move. He backed away. He had the same feeling from each of the windows in each of the houses, shadows watching him, darting away when he looked at them. The cluster of children across the street had fallen silent and they too were watching him, and for a moment he felt the same unease he had felt walking through the streets of Cairo at night, waiting to get his throat cut and his body thrown into the Nile.

For God's sake, would no one help him?

He thought of the decrepit old woman at the station who had pitied him, the woman ambulance driver who had offered him a cigarette. He clung to these two oases of kindness in this desert of indifference.

He left, turning and walking rapidly away, wanting to put as much distance as he could between himself and that house, this street. The day had faded, seeping away in a slow and protracted death, and the night lay ahead of him, unrelenting and endless. He shivered. He had not felt warm since he had climbed aboard the de Havilland three—no, four days ago. He wanted to be back there, in the desert, in the dusty, fly-blown, teeming streets of Cairo. He wanted to wind the clock back four days.

Emerging again onto Bethnal Green Road at the start of the blackout he was lost for a time, trying to determine his location, trying to decide where he should go. He began walking in a westerly direction, hoping to find a bus. Instead he found a black hackney cab, pulling up at the kerb and disgorging a group of drunken sailors. He darted forward and climbed in before anyone else could

'Where to, guv?' said the cabbie, and behind them Gerald heard the first wails of the air-raid siren.

'Clapham,' said Gerald. 'Take me to Clapham.'

# CHAPTER TWENTY-SEVEN

Joe froze. A knock on a door in Odessa Street meant a stranger, not a good stranger, never someone you wanted to see.

He jumped up from the table. The two Rosenthal girls didn't jump; they remained in the kitchen doorway watching him. At the second knock, louder this time, more insistent, he went to the back door ready to run, then he turned back and stood, undecided. And the two little girls watched. He put his finger to his lips, not that they had made a sound, and crept past them and went soundlessly up the stairs and they followed a step behind. Upstairs, he found Archie, who was third oldest, and Norman who was next after Archie and who was holding the baby. They were standing at the window staring down at the street below, and when they saw Joe the two boys shuffled wordlessly up to make room so that he, too, could see.

Joe looked down and all he could see was the top of a hat and two khaki shoulders. It was an officer's hat. The head looked up at that moment and they all stepped back out of sight. Then the knocking started again and they leaned forward and looked down again. The man was an army officer, there was no mistaking it. And now he pressed his face to the downstairs window. Then he looked up.

'He's seen us!' squealed Norman.

The thrill of it seemed to electrify the squalid little room and its occupants and for a long moment no one spoke. Joe looked at the four little faces of the Rosenthal children—five if you counted the baby, who gaped at him, wide-eyed and toothless. They waited to see what he would do. But he couldn't think. He didn't know what he would do. A panic had gripped him at the sight of that hat, those khaki shoulders. What could it mean that they would send the army to pick him up? The police, yes, the navy—but an army officer? Was the man from the ministry? From military intelligence? Had he been watching and seen Joe come into the house?

His foolishness at coming here became horribly apparent.

And having now seen them the man was not going to give up and there followed another knock, loud, insistent.

Joe left then, sprinting back down the stairs, out of the back door and into the yard, across the fence and into the narrow laneway that ran along the back of the houses. A voice called out to him, he thought he heard his name called, and it might have been Mrs Rosenthal, though he could not be sure and he did not stop. There was a collapsed wall halfway along the lane that led into the backyard of a bombed-out house. He made for that, feeling his way, clambering through the rubble and popping out into another laneway. It was dark now, pitch dark, but out of nowhere someone shone a torch directly in his face.

Before he could throw up his hands to shield his eyes he was wrestled to the ground, where he lay for a moment, bewildered and winded.

'What's your game then?' sneered a breathless but triumphant voice right in his ear, so that it became clear that the person holding the torch was a police constable, massive in the blackout in his cape and domed helmet, the smell of cooked onions on his breath. Before Joe could think, before he could move, he was hauled to his feet.

And the air-raid siren began to wail.

Joe felt the siren filling his head, filling the laneway. He felt that he had never in his life been less afraid of its awful urgent sound.

'Show us your papers!' the policeman demanded over the noise.

'There's a bloody raid on!' Joe shouted back.

'Then you better hope no one drops a bomb on you.' And the constable roughly patted Joe down, finding his papers and angling his torch to read them, peering closer in the darkness. 'You're having a laugh. This says you're born in 1876.'

But Joe wasn't laughing. He could see a police van. He could see other men like himself, but not like himself, being lined up and loaded into the back of the van. They were doing a sweep then, picking up anyone who was out after dark and who looked suspicious. He had dodged the navy and the army and the detective who had pursued him for a week, only to be picked up in a routine sweep. He saw the faces of the men who had been picked up. They would be deserters, men who had been on the run and living in the shadows for months, years, and he saw the exhausted relief in their eyes. Their war was over. A year or two in prison, the war would end and they would be released. It would not end for him. If he stepped into that van he would never be free again. His life would be over.

He tried to run. Threw every ounce of strength into this last-ditch attempt, almost broke free, but the constable lunged after him and brought him down so that for a moment they wrestled, struggled, and a second policeman joined in and together they pulled Joe to his feet, holding his arms in a tight lock behind his back. They marched him towards the van, ducking at the roar of an aircraft engine overhead. It was followed almost at once by the whoosh of an incendiary then an explosion that could not have been more than a street away. Close by, a bomb-damaged shell of a house on which someone had tacked sheets of corrugated metal as a temporary roof shook and rumbled as some inner wall collapsed in a cloud of dust.

The raid had begun but it did not seem to matter.

'Move it!' shouted the first constable, a note of panic now noticeable in his voice. And suddenly the whole area was lit up by another incendiary and Joe saw that the constable was an old man, a special, not a regular at all, sporting a drooping old-fashioned moustache like the men had worn in the last war but white with age, the flesh on his face mottled and flushed almost purple by his exertions. A man who had done his forty years' service and hung up his policeman's helmet and his whistle and had no doubt looked forward to a quiet time in front of a fire with his pipe and his missus. Now he was back in uniform chasing looters in an air raid.

This was Joe's thought as his final few seconds of freedom

passed, one by one, stretched out and squeezed together both at the same time, an eternity and no time at all. He noticed how the old man raised his head to the sky, his eyes wide and fearful, and this was the last thing Joe saw before an incendiary exploded very close by.

∽

When he came to he was lying face down on the pavement and his ears were roaring as though he was underwater. The roaring would not stop but he lifted his head then cautiously pulled himself to his feet. He was unhurt and perhaps the incendiary had exploded further away than he had imagined for the police van was untouched, so too all the men lined up inside the van gaping wordlessly at him. A sheet of corrugated metal, blown from the roof of the nearby house, lay on the ground not far away, dark splatters all along one edge. And standing before him was the elderly special constable—or, rather, there was his body.

His head was nowhere to be seen.

His torso ended at the collar of his uniform and his cape. As Joe watched the headless body wavered for a dreadful second, then tipped forward and crashed to the ground with a thud. Joe looked down and at his feet was the man's head, the helmet still on, the eyes looking sightlessly up at him.

For a moment everything went black again, and when Joe came to a second time, he was some yards away, coughing up bile onto the pavement. He flung out both hands as the pavement reeled up before him and he tipped forward in a gross mimicry of the torso of the dead constable, his legs buckling beneath him.

But he pulled himself up almost at once, made his legs move. A moment later he was running, faster than he had ever run before and with less idea of where he was going than at any other time in his life.

# CHAPTER TWENTY-EIGHT

'Clapham,' Gerald had said. 'Take me to Clapham.'

He remembered little about the journey and could not be certain whether it had taken an age or an instant nor what route the cabbie had taken, but here they were pulling up in Commongate Road. And now he was standing in the doorway and he must have rung the bell for the front door was opening and Mrs Ashby herself was leading him inside. He found himself on the settee in the beautiful drawing room that he had visited, briefly, a few days before. There was no one else here, not the housekeeper—he had forgotten her name—nor the little boy, Marcus, just the two of them, seated side by side on the settee. He smelled again the furniture polish and the potpourri but it was mingled now with the slightly acrid smell of the coal burning slowly in the grate and with something enticingly like blossoms or tropical fruit or clean laundry or spice or all four. What *was* it? He could not place it.

She was handing him a drink, whisky and soda, which she placed in his hands and curled his fingers around, closing her own hands around his to make sure he was holding the tumbler, and he realised the smell was her, Mrs Ashby. The woman made of porcelain, perfect and flawless and utterly breakable. She had put on some scent, then, in anticipation of his arrival. But she had not known of his arrival until he had arrived. He had an idea he had simply turned up at her door, rather late at night, rather dishevelled and distressed. And now he was telling her about Ashby, who had died, horribly, in a tank that had been hit by an enemy shell so that nothing was left of him but a name. Not that he told her that. He told her about Ashby standing at the dockside in his khaki shirt and shorts throwing Gerald's gas mask into the Nile.

Some time had passed for he no longer had the whisky in his hands, though he could feel its warmth seeping through him, and he was telling her that his little girl was dead, killed in an air raid, and when he began to cry and seemed quite unable to stop, she held him. She kissed him, slowly, tenderly, in the same way she had said that thing about the damned war: dully, as though it had ceased to mean anything. He felt the effects of the whisky muddying his head in a pleasant way; he felt her kisses having the same effect. He sensed something in her that was dead but that still needed to be stirred up like ashes in the grate in the morning, and his arrival, his tears, allowed her to give in to it. He wondered how he knew all this from just a kiss, her arms urgently around him. Perhaps he did not know it, was inventing a world for her to inhabit. She led him upstairs to the room she had once shared with Ashby.

∽

314

Time had passed. It was still dark outside and he was glad of that. He had slept for a little while, he thought, but he no longer felt tired. It might be midnight, it might be eight o'clock in the morning and the little boy, Marcus, downstairs with the house-keeper whose name he could not remember, having breakfast.

'I'm afraid I don't know your name,' he said, ashamed of this.

'Marian.'

'Marian,' he repeated, tasting the word. 'I used to know a girl called Marian. I went to a tennis party at her house in Ruislip. Do you know her, perhaps?'

Their voices were soft, not subdued, just hushed, like the morning after a snowfall.

No, she said, she did not know her, and he could tell she was smiling.

'I'm Gerald.'

'I know. You told me.'

Had he told her? He couldn't remember doing so.

⌒

It was morning when he awoke again. A chink in the blackout cut a thin corridor of light across the bed, across her side of the bed, where she no longer lay. Gerald struggled to sit up, resting on his elbows, seeing her not far away, snapping her stockings onto her suspenders. He watched her, enjoying the intimacy that her movements implied. She looked up and gave him a gentle smile.

'Sleep,' she said, 'if you like.'

But he was no longer tired. Instead, he watched her. She neither hurried her dressing nor slowed it down at his gaze, just continued with what she had been doing. As he watched he was aware of many things crowding around the edges of his memory, but for the moment they did not matter. He felt as though he were sitting in a large, airy room from which many rooms led off, and each of those rooms was full of a great many people all wishing to speak to him but, for the moment, all the doors were closed and no one disturbed him.

'I'll see about some breakfast,' she said. 'Come down when you're ready.'

Once she had gone he sat up, placing his feet on the thick bedroom carpet, looking around her room—was it just her room now, or was there some trace of Ashby? He saw nothing but for a single wedding photograph on the dressing table. Was she the sort of woman who kept all her dead husband's things, his clothes and shoes? He didn't know. There was no wardrobe and, even if there had been, he felt no compunction to look. And then he saw a pipe, Ashby's pipe, or one just like it, on the bedside table, right at his elbow where, in his drunkenness, in his pre-occupation, he had missed it last night and had almost missed it this morning, and for a moment he could not move. He heard Ashby's wry laughter.

He got dressed and went downstairs, finding her in the kitchen.

The child was there, Marcus, and Gerald paused in the door-way as the child lifted a toy train into the air with a whoosh on an imaginary track, caught up in his game. Then he saw Gerald and stopped to stare at him with Ashby's eyes, reproachful, accusing—or just surprised, just shy?—before pushing past him into another room without a second glance. The boy's mother said nothing about the child, attempted no explanation, simply poured him coffee and cut some bread.

'No jam or marg; I have my toast plain,' he said, remembering the rationing. She sat at the kitchen table and watched him eat his breakfast as any wife did in the morning before her husband left for the office, and for a moment Gerald imagined himself staying here all day, staying here forever.

He stood up. 'Well, I should go,' he said, and she smiled that same smile and nodded, and he had a feeling she would have done the same if he had said, I'd like to stay the rest of the day, I'd like to stay forever.

She got his coat for him. Ashby's gloves were still in the pocket and she helped him on with them for the second time. At the door, she kissed him and said, 'This war. It gives us situations, moments, we wouldn't normally have. If we grasp them we shouldn't regret it. There'll be plenty of time for regrets and recriminations later, when peace comes. Till then, we must live, mustn't we?'

This was her creed. And there was no question it made things easier. There were no regrets, no recriminations yet. They may come later.

He squeezed her hand and left her, slipping out into the frozen winter morning, just as Ashby must have done that last time.

Gerald's train had been rerouted. They had trundled through Rugby and then Coventry so that Birmingham had seemed an inevitability, but at the final moment they had careered off onto a branch line and ground to a halt just outside Nuneaton. He was already tired of this journey, having made it now three times in four days, though admittedly it was never quite the same journey twice. The railway company always managed to surprise with its choice of routes. He found himself regarding each detour, each new station or branch line, with the incurious acceptance that every soldier cultivated in the army.

In any case, he was in no particular hurry, this time, to reach his destination.

It was a Wednesday, he saw, reading the date on the newspaper of the airman seated opposite. It had been a surprise to find a seat. When a very flustered young woman with a battered suitcase whose hat had come off had breathlessly boarded at Rugby there had been a moment of shifty-eyed and silent negotiation inside the compartment until the naval officer seated beside Gerald had gallantly given up his seat and the rest of them—two other naval officers, two junior lieutenants from the Yorkshire Dragoons and a captain in the Fusiliers—had breathed a sigh of collective relief and settled back into their journey. For the most part no one spoke, aside from an occasional exchange of cigarettes between the three naval officers, and no one seemed in the least surprised at the unlikely itinerary of places their train travelled through, and when the flustered young woman enquired if anyone knew what time they were due to arrive in Portsmouth no one seemed surprised by that either.

Gerald stared out of the window. Cathcart, his CO in Cairo, had told him to contact the divisional CO when he got back—not at once, but after a week or two. This morning he had telephoned the divisional HQ and been connected, after a lengthy delay, not to the divisional CO but to a Miss Littlejohn, whose exact position and location he had not quite been able to grasp but who had appeared to have been expecting his call.

'Good news, Captain Meadows,' she had announced in a plummy voice, as though she was studying his test results after a tricky exam or a medical. 'You're to report to the War Office, quartermaster-general's office, on the sixteenth.'

He had been given a desk job. In Whitehall. Doing what, exactly, he had not the least idea. Something to with movements, supply, ordnance, logistics. The disembodied Miss Littlejohn had clearly expected him to be pleased and had sounded disappointed when he had merely thanked her and rung off. No more active service. He had done his bit. His reward, a desk job at the QMG's office. He was forty-four. Soldiering was a young man's game and when he looked about him at the faces of the other officers in the train compartment he saw boys a year or two out of school or university; not one of them had seen his twenty-fifth birthday.

He turned back to the window. The train had just started up again with a jolt. The problem was, he was unable to see himself seated at a desk in the QMG, could not visualise a Captain Meadows of the Royal Tank Regiment presenting himself at the office in Whitehall on the sixteenth. He could picture the office, oh yes, he could picture it very clearly—the buff folders in filing cabinets, the classified documents tied with red ribbons, the petty office hierarchy, the puttering tea urn that was always breaking down, the frantic search for the critical document that had inexplicably got lost somewhere between the office and the typing pool—he could see it all, could hear it, smell it even, but his own place there, the desk at which he was to sit, he could not see.

The train was now passing through Coventry once more. The airman sitting opposite lowered his newspaper briefly to peer out of the window. With the slightest raising of his eyebrows and a tiny, almost inaudible sigh, the man shook out his paper and resumed reading. With any luck, Gerald thought, the fellow would finish his paper soon and offer it around. It had been foolish embarking on such a journey without anything to read, not even a fresh packet of cigarettes. He hadn't been thinking.

He had made himself not think. The telephone call to the divisional HQ had been made with a curious sense of unreality. He would not have been surprised whatever orders he had been given. It did not touch him. Any order or posting seemed to him inconsequential.

So far he had not thought at all about yesterday's frantic and futile search. It had already passed into that same place of unreality. He saw himself, a tiny uniformed ant, scurrying from one location to the next, randomly and with no purpose, vainly seeking answers, fruitlessly following each new lead and running into one dead end after another. He was no closer to the truth, though now he knew that two people had died and had been cremated. And he knew, he had caught the briefest glimpse, of the kind of place the little girl had come from. Diana had said, *What kind of life could she have, could any child have, there? It was a kindness to take her.* And that was all the justification she had required.

He was no closer to understanding how his wife could have swapped one child for another. His mind recoiled from it. It was like trying to pick up something with buttery fingers; he was simply unable to grasp it. How could she do this thing? Discard her own child and take up another. It beggared belief. He would never have thought her capable of such a thing. When he thought of his wife he no longer saw the anxious girl at the tennis party, the exhausted but triumphant woman in a maternity ward bed who had just given birth to their child. He wasn't certain what he saw.

He thought about Marian Ashby, viewing her and their night together with the cool dispassion that his wife had displayed when she had perpetrated her terrible crime. Had he done that, slept with Mrs Ashby, to punish Diana? He didn't think so, but he was unsure. How extraordinary it now seemed! He would not have thought of himself as a man who would sleep with another woman. But there you are, he thought now as the outer suburbs of some large city rushed past the window: sometimes you surprised yourself. His wife had surprised him. Mrs Ashby had surprised him. Why shouldn't he surprise himself?

Ah, here they were at Birmingham, and he felt a sort of grim satisfaction at the crushing, unavoidable inevitability of their arrival into Birmingham New Street. The flustered young woman seated opposite stood up in dismay, grabbed her suitcase and departed, and the gallant naval officer closed the door behind her and reclaimed the seat she had vacated with a little sigh.

In the end they reached Leeds from the north, going through Huddersfield and Bradford then on to Otley before swinging south and east and approaching the city from Headingley. If it was a route designed to confound the enemy, it surely succeeded.

Gerald had barely a quarter of an hour's wait for the Wetherby connection, which was enough time to purchase cigarettes, a newspaper, some sandwiches. But he found he could not concentrate on the paper and gave it up almost at once. The sandwiches he similarly abandoned. He had begun to rehearse what he was going to say.

Another brief winter's day was drawing to its conclusion as the train drew into Wetherby's Linton Road Station, but there was enough time. There was no reason to delay the thing until tomorrow. He left the station, paused, lit a cigarette and smoked it slowly, realising that he was merely putting it off. He tossed the end of the cigarette into the gutter and set off on foot, armed with the station clerk's directions, and after a mile or so located the police station. It was almost dark as he walked up the steps and presented himself to the desk sergeant.

'I wish to report a crime,' he said, the words sounding odd and unnatural.

'Oh aye?' said the sergeant, an ageing and complacent man with a cynical tone who made a show of placing his mug of tea down on his desk and sliding over a form and a pen with a bored sigh. 'What kind of crime is it, then, sir?'

'A child has been unlawfully taken.'

The police station had an interview room and this was where the sergeant took him and then he left, closing the door behind him. Whether the man was gone in search of a senior officer or merely to return to his half-finished mug of tea he did not say.

Gerald pulled out a chair and sat down. Now he wished he had retained the sandwiches and the paper. Anything to take his mind off the next few minutes, the next few hours. The next few days. He closed his eyes. He had said the part of his speech that was rehearsed. From now on everything he said would be impromptu, unprepared.

He wondered if he ought to have warned Diana. She would be terrified—a police car driving up to the cottage, a constable rapping loudly on the door. He pictured her shocked, frightened face, her fumbled gathering together of one or two belongings, scooping up the child—or would the constable take command of the child? Diana would be terrified. But he had not even considered going to her to warn her of his intention.

Was this another way to punish her then? No, it was worse than that. If he had gone to her and told her his plan she would have talked him out of it. He lifted his face to the ceiling but saw nothing. She would have condemned him—condemned them both—to a lifetime of deception and lies. A life lived in perpetual fear of discovery, of public exposure, of shame and criminal charges.

And what of the damage to the little girl?

No, this way was better. Even Diana would see that eventually. He wondered if he would be there to help her see it.

The walls of the interview room were brick covered by a cheap enamel paint, half cream, half green. There was no window, no other furniture save this table and the two chairs. The table was bolted to the floor. Not just an interview room, then. He wondered where they would put Diana. They wouldn't charge her; he was certain of that. Any doctor could see how the death of her own child had affected her. Grief, the trauma of the air raid, the sudden loss of a child, any part of it could turn a normal person temporarily mad, could make them do things they would not normally do. They would see that.

He began to count the rows of bricks.

The door opened abruptly on a youngish man in a dark blue double-breasted prewar suit that looked like it had never been fashionable even when it was new. The man who wore the suit looked like he didn't really care. He was powerfully built, with prematurely grey hair cut military-short and fierce blue eyes that seemed to do a recce of the room and the man seated at the table before he would deign to come in. Why isn't the fellow in uniform? was the first thing Gerald thought, but as the man, who was grasping the door handle in a vice-like grip in one hand and the frame of the door in the other now launched himself in an unwieldy and lopsided gait across the floor and towards the table, his reason for being in civvies was clear enough. Wounded in action or a condition that predated the war? Impossible to tell. It didn't really matter, in the circumstances.

'Brighouse,' stated the man, sitting down heavily and slapping a file on the table, and it sounded like this must be the name of some top-secret mission or an enemy combatant he was intent on tracking down. It was a full second before Gerald realised the fellow was introducing himself.

'Meadows. Captain, Gerald. Royal Tank Regiment.'

'Oh aye?' Brighouse eyed him thoughtfully, as though he suspected some trickery, or perhaps to make it clear that he wasn't impressed. He waited, seeming in no hurry to proceed. At last he spoke: 'A child unlawfully tekken, y'say, Captain Meadows? Your child, is it?'

'No. That is . . .' Gerald paused. 'My child is dead. She died during a raid in London on the twenty-first or the twenty-second of last month. My wife was with her but my wife survived.

A woman was also killed in the raid. A Mrs Nancy Levin of Odessa Street, Bethnal Green, but her child, whom I believe was called Emily, survived.' He took a deep breath. 'After the raid was over, with our child dead and the surviving child's mother also dead, my wife . . .' He searched for the right word, couldn't find it, and decided to be blunt. 'My wife switched our dead child for Mrs Levin's living child.' He stopped. 'Is it alright if I smoke?'

Brighouse shrugged. 'Be my guest.' He shifted then, from one buttock to the other, a pained expression on his face as though his injury was bothering him. Or Gerald's story was bothering him. Or perhaps he merely had wind. 'Now then, let me get this straight. Your wife's tekken some other woman's child home with her?'

'Yes. That's about the sum of it. Or no, not home. That wouldn't work you see, because the neighbours would see her and realise it's not the same child. She brought the child up here where no one knows us. She's renting a cottage from a farmer named Inghamthorpe at Kirk Deighton.'

'What you're saying is she's trying to pass this other woman's child off as her own?'

'Yes. That is precisely what I am saying.' Gerald felt something release inside him. It was out now and it could not be taken back. The secret was no longer his alone. Some part of him was relieved.

The policeman regarded him and a minute, two minutes passed.

'And why, Captain Meadows, would she do such a thing?'

For a moment, Gerald didn't know how to reply. He shook his head, spread both hands. 'Because she lost her child. She's not . . . thinking straight.'

'Are you trying to tell me a mother simply hands over her own child and teks another in its place, like—like, I don't know, choosing a new pair o' shoes when t'old ones have worn out?'

'Yes! Or rather, no, not like shoes, of course. But essentially, yes, that is what she has done.'

Brighouse sat back in his chair, put his head on one side and considered his response. 'Alright then, why not tek it back? This child your wife took, why have y'not just tekken it back?'

'Because until yesterday I didn't know who the child was; indeed, I cannot say for certain that I am right now. I simply didn't know where to take the child back to.'

'But now you do know?'

'I think so. But I haven't been able to trace any relatives. I hit a dead end.' Gerald leaned forward too, now. He still hadn't made up his mind about this man, and he could see Brighouse still hadn't made his mind up about him. 'Look, Inspector, Sergeant, Chief Inspector—I don't know what you are . . .'

'Inspector'll do.'

'Look, Inspector, my wife needs help. All I want is for the child to be safely returned to its family and for my wife and me to—to grieve for our little girl.'

'Do you now?' Brighouse's expression gave absolutely nothing away. Then he got up, picked up the file into which he had not written a thing and from which he had taken nothing, and made his awkward way over to the door and went out without saying another word.

Gerald sank back into his chair and found he had broken out in a sweat. Had the man noticed? It was chilly enough in here to freeze water. Brighouse would have noticed a man sweating.

Christ! And now it begins. How long would it take them to drive out to the cottage? He had walked there in twenty-five minutes in the blackout not knowing the way. In a police car it would take all of ten minutes. To conduct their business, another five or ten. And then the journey back. All up, say half an hour. Call it forty minutes, allowing for delays.

He stood up and went to the door, wondered whether to open it but thought better of it and instead paced up and down the room. The scene where two policemen—it would be two, they always did things in pairs—came to the door of the cottage kept playing itself out in his head. Sometimes he saw Diana submitting meekly to their instructions, understanding that the game was up; sometimes he saw her run from them in terror, clutching the child. And other times he saw her invite them in and offer them a cup of tea as though she were still keeping house in pleasant suburban Buckinghamshire, so wrapped up in her illusion as to be utterly oblivious to the implications of their visit.

He sat down and began again from the bottom, counting the rows of bricks in the wall.

The half-hour that they would require to go to the cottage and bring her back came and went, so too did the forty minutes. After an hour and with the tension too much to bear he got up and went to the door and opened it and was presented with a deserted and anonymous corridor that told him nothing. He went back inside and resumed his seat. Was it conceivable Diana was no longer at the cottage? That she had somehow got wind of his intention and fled? But where? Where could she go? He saw his wife fleeing across snow-flecked hills in the dead of night, dragging the wretched child with her, the entire

327

Yorkshire constabulary after her with whistles and dogs and torches.

The door flew open and Brighouse thrust himself inside, crashing down onto the chair, slapping the same file onto the desk before him and leaning forward as far as it was possible to lean, an intent expression on his large, fleshy face.

'Y'see, Captain Meadows, there's summat I'm struggling with,' he began, as though their previous conversation had never ended. 'If this child has indeed been tekken then why is no one looking for it? Why is there not a bloody great hue and cry at this child's disappearance?'

'I have already explained that, Inspector! There *is* no one to raise a "hue and cry", as you call it. No family member claimed the bodies. I could locate no living relative.'

'Ah yes,' said the inspector, nodding, pleased with himself, as though Gerald had just walked into a trap he had carefully set. 'The identification of the bodies. A couple of telephone calls to our colleagues in the Met . . .' He paused, clearly pleased with himself again. 'Oh yes, Captain, we've not been sitting on our hands, we're not the simple country folk you might tek us for op here. A couple of telephone calls is all it took to ascertain that the bodies you mention were identified by the local warden.'

Gerald gaped at the man, speechless. 'Yes—*I* told *you* that!'

'And that furthermore—*furthermore*—no foul play was suspected. Now, what do you have to say to that, Captain?'

'I'd say you're a fool.'

'There's no call for that,' replied Brighouse mildly, and no doubt he had been called worse things in his time. He studied

Gerald for a moment, seemed to reach a conclusion. 'You were in the desert, I tek it? No, don't answer—careless lives and all that. But still, you had it rough, you tank fellows. Don't think I don't know that because I *do* know it. Three years of it and now you're back. Teks a bit o' getting used to, don't it? Picking up yer old life? Being a husband and father after so long away?'

'What are you driving at, Inspector?'

'What I'm *driving* at is that we have Mrs Meadows outside with the little 'un and she tells a different story. The way she tells it, you come back a week or so ago and it were difficult for the two of you, and with the little child who'd only been a wee bairn when you'd left. The baby had grown up, you and yer wife hadn't seen each other in all that time. Bound to be tricky. We see it up here all the time. No shame in it. And she says the three of you come up here for a change, to get away, like. Some fresh air. And then, she says, you got into yer head that the child was not the right child, that she had swapped it for some other child. She said it became a sort of mania with you and, try as she might, she couldn't dissuade you of it.' He paused, seeing the expression on Gerald's face. 'Is that it, Captain? Is that what's really happened here?'

'Look at this! *Here!* Right *here!*' And Gerald thrust his hand into his inside coat pocket and pulled out the three photographs of his child. He slammed them down on the table and pointed a shaking finger, not trusting himself to speak.

The inspector did not so much as glance at the three photographs and he did not pick them up. Instead, he carefully placed his hands on the table before him, interlocking his fingers, and his thumbs began to beat an impatient tattoo.

'Aye, Mrs Meadows said you'd got hold of some photographs of a little girl and that you'd got it into yer head that they were photographs of your own little girl.'

Gerald sat back in his chair. That Diana could be so cool-headed in her deceit stunned him.

'This is wrong, Inspector. What my wife has told you is a lie.'

The inspector made no reply. It was clear he believed Diana completely.

'*Why?* Why do you believe *her* story rather than *mine*?'

Brighouse sighed. 'Ask yourself, Captain: how likely is it that a woman would swap her own child for another woman's child? Women—mothers—they form an attachment to their child, you see. A bond. They're not like us. What you're describing, well, it don't sound right. It in't natural. And I've met your lady wife and I can tell you now she in't capable of such a thing. And that's about the long and the short of it.'

Gerald laughed. Then he stopped, mid-laugh.

'And the child? Have you seen the child? Have you met it? Do you truly believe that child is ours? That she isn't a poor, lost, very frightened little girl who has been forcibly taken from her mother by a complete stranger?'

But even this did not shake the man's complacency, his utter belief in this version of the truth. 'I have met the child, yes,' he said. 'And what you're describing, well, it's not what I saw. Not a bit of it.'

'I don't believe you!'

'See for yourself.' Brighouse stood up.

Uncertain if he was calling the man's bluff, or if he or the inspector or both of them were part of some elaborate hoax,

Gerald stood up and together they left the interview room, went along the corridor to the front reception desk, where the desk sergeant watched him expressionlessly, then down another corridor, at the end of which a door stood half open. Gerald could hear the murmur of voices, a woman's voice. He felt the muscles of his stomach tighten. This is intolerable, he thought.

Brighouse went first, pushing the door open and standing aside. He did not look at the occupants of the room, he looked at Gerald. Gerald stood in the doorway.

It was an office, Brighouse's own office according to the name plate on the door, with a desk and a low table with chairs ranged around it. Diana was seated on one of the low chairs in her winter coat, her handbag at her feet, her hat and gloves on her lap as though she was having tea with the vicar. She was smiling and offering encouragement to the child, who was sitting cross-legged on the floor absorbed with crayons and paper. The little girl's hair was brushed and swept back off her head by a pale blue hairband that suited her fair hair. She was bundled up in a winter coat that was a miniature of her mother's but with the addition of a hood. Knitted red mittens hung from a cord at each cuff and her feet were encased in sturdy brown lace-up shoes and little white socks.

'How lovely!' Diana said. 'What a lovely picture, Abigail.'

It was quite clear to Gerald that his wife knew they were standing there, the inspector and himself, that this little charade was entirely for their benefit, and it made a pulse begin to throb in his head, it made the little scene shimmer nauseatingly before his eyes.

But the child! How had she done that?

Diana feigned noticing them, looking up, and surprise and concern showed in her face. 'Gerald,' she said gently, and, yes, she reached out a tremulous hand to touch his arm.

All men had a snapping point. You didn't fight in a war for three years and not know that, not see it, over and over again. A man, calm and rational and laughing one minute, a crazed madman the next, screaming to be let out of a moving tank, running across a minefield, picking up a machine gun and firing indiscriminately, walking into an enemy emplacement and shooting at men who had surrendered. Gerald had seen all of those things. He had wondered what went on in a man's head the split second before and during the long seconds afterwards.

Now he knew: nothing.

One minute he was standing in the inspector's office observing his wife, seeing her fingers reach out to touch his arm, seeing the child playing and absorbed like any other child with its mother. The next moment he found himself pushing open the swing door of the police station—though he had no recollection of leaving the inspector's office—running down the steps.

And the child was in his arms.

It was hard to run with a three-year-old in your arms but his pace did not slow. He was outside now and he saw that it had snowed during the time that he had been sequestered inside the police station, was still snowing. He was running on snow, his footsteps crunching, the snowflakes swirling in flurries in his face, settling on his nose. He felt the wonder of it, even in his madness, after three years in the desert.

The darkness had come, too, and with it the blackout. He was making for the railway station, he was going to take the child back to her home, but already he was uncertain of his way. He slipped, pulled himself up and stumbled on, uncertain if he was on the lane at all or if he had lost his way completely. A bicycle reared out of the darkness, silent and with no lights, seeing him and swerving violently at the last moment so that Gerald felt it brush against his shoulder and a man cried out angrily, his cry lost in the flurry of snow.

He was going to take the child back to her home. He closed his mind to all else. It was easy to lose your way in war, to lose a sense of right and wrong, of morality. He had lost his way, he realised, as all the men had in the desert, or they would have gone mad, but now his belief in what was right was unquestioned and losing one's sanity seemed a small price to pay.

Behind him, distant and distorted, someone cried out, a man's voice, then a woman's. They were on to him and he had only the smallest of head starts. And probably they knew the ground and had men and torches and perhaps dogs. It hardly mattered—he pressed on. The ground banked steeply downwards and he found himself at the water's edge and he remembered he had crossed a river to reach the police station. He paused, fighting for breath, hearing the rush of the water. Otherwise it was perfectly still and silent. The darkness and the covering of snow deadened all sound. Even the shouts of his pursuers had ceased.

In his arms the child squirmed and fought but he pressed her face hard into his coat, steeling himself against his own brutality. He was doing this for her. It was the right thing to do. He would not let the child thwart her own rescue!

But how was he to cross the river? He turned to the left and made his way, slipping and sliding in mud, along the river's edge. If there was a riverside path he could not locate it. If he was not careful he would have them both in the water. But there was the bridge, a dark shape dead ahead, the sound of the water muffled as it rushed beneath the arches. He scrambled up the bank, finding the road he had somehow missed before, and was up and on the bridge. But almost at once he lost his footing and fell to his knees and, weighed down by the squirming, terrified child, found it impossible to get up. She let out a scream, pounding furious fists against any part of him she could find.

It was almost a relief when they caught up to him. A constable and the sergeant came out of the darkness and onto him, one grasping the child, tearing it from his arms, the other pulling his arms back almost out of their sockets. He did not fight them. He had nothing left.

'*Let go of him!* LET HIM GO!'

It was Diana.

'Take the child to safety, please!' She was still some way off but she spoke in such a way that the policemen released him; their hands were full anyway with the screaming, kicking child. They had pulled him up to his feet in order to tear the child from him but now he sank to his knees once more in the snow.

And Diana appeared and kneeled before him. How oddly ghostlike she looked. He was uncertain if it was the darkness and swirling snow that gave her this ghostly look or if she was, in fact, a ghost.

'I'm so sorry,' she whispered. She lifted him by his shoulders, searching his face. 'I'm so very, very sorry.' She brushed the snowflakes from his lashes and nose.

He put his hands on her shoulders, gripping her, returning her gaze. 'Diana, it's not real.'

And she sat back on her heels.

'I know, Gerald, I know it's not real. I know she is not our child. I lied to the police but I won't lie to you. I've already told you what happened. But perhaps I didn't explain it well enough.'

He shook his head uncomprehendingly. 'What does that mean?'

But she looked away, at the panicked child, the two cursing policemen, the inspector a long way behind still making his awkward way towards them. She closed her eyes. When she opened them again she spoke calmly and steadily: 'I need a child. I'm thirty-nine. I won't have another baby. Gerald, nothing can replace Abigail, our child. But I *need* this. I need her. And I believe she needs us. Can you not see that?'

Someone had put a blanket around him and sat him on a chair. So far as Gerald could tell no one had been left to guard him. The constable had placed a mug of hot cocoa in his hands. They had left him in a room—not the inspector's office, not the interview room—and he could hear distant voices on the other side of the door and he presumed they were discussing him. It was curious how little it seemed to matter to him what they said. The cocoa steamed quietly, a few lumps of the cocoa powder and flakes of dried milk floated on its surface. Gerald blew on it, instinctively, because that was what one did with a hot drink. When they had first placed the mug in his hands he had not been able to feel its heat; now the warmth was slowing penetrating his fingers.

Diana had said, *I need her. And I believe she needs us. Can you not see that?*

And now, oddly, he could see that. He could see that his wife needed this child. That she was not mad or delusional or deceitful. She was desperate. And perhaps the child needed them. He wondered why he had not seen it this clearly before. Perhaps he had just needed her to say the words, *Nothing can replace Abigail, our child.*

It all seemed surprisingly simple and straightforward. He sipped the cocoa and waited for them to remember him and come and get him.

After a time, the door opened and Diana came in. He looked up at her gratefully. He could see the inspector behind her, frowning, still making up his mind, unhappy at the sudden and unpleasant turn that events had taken earlier in the evening. Diana kneeled before him and took both his hands.

'Darling, the inspector is concerned that you might be a threat to—to Abigail or to myself. Or to yourself. He needs to know that you're quite alright now. Then he'll let us go . . . won't you, Inspector?' She glanced over her shoulder.

Brighouse muttered noncommittally under his breath.

'Darling?'

Gerald nodded vigorously. 'Yes, quite alright now.' He summoned a smile for his wife, another for the inspector. 'So sorry to have been such a nuisance. Don't quite know what came over me. I think what I need is rest.'

He stopped, and Diana looked pleased with this. She turned again to the inspector.

'Aye well,' said Brighouse with another of his frowns. 'I'll give you the benefit of the doubt, Mrs Meadows; you know yer husband better than I do. But you mek sure you tek my advice and contact that doctor I told you about first thing. I've seen a lot of this kind o' thing up here. I'm no stranger to it. You tek my advice.'

'Oh, I most certainly will, Inspector. Thank you. You have been so very kind.'

A car was found and the constable dropped them back at the cottage. It was approaching midnight, or long after midnight, and the child clung to Diana and eventually she lay on the back seat and slept, the teddy bear with the missing ear clutched in her arms. The constable lifted her up and carried her inside and Diana led Gerald to the armchair by the hearth. There had been a fire in the grate earlier and he gazed at the half-burnt logs in anticipation of a new fire. He could hear Diana dealing with the constable, thanking him when he promised to look in on them in the morning, he was too kind, they had all been too kind. He heard the door shut.

Diana got the fire restarted, found a blanket and laid it over him, placed another one over the child. She poured him a tiny whisky and one for herself, and arranged herself at his feet. The child lay curled up in the other armchair.

For a while neither spoke.

'How did you do it?' said Gerald eventually, nodding at the sleeping child who two days before had been kicking and screaming and uncontrollable in the corner of the room.

'I bribed her with a bar of chocolate,' said Diana, as though it were the simplest thing in the world. 'She's rather fond of chocolate. Tomorrow we'll need to see if we can get hold of some more. I've used up my current supplies.'

Gerald gazed at the burning logs and thought about his wife bribing the child with a bar of chocolate.

At his feet Diana shifted, moving her legs to a more comfortable position.

'You found them, didn't you? Her people—you found out who they were?' she said, her voice very low, almost disembodied in the darkness.

'Yes I did. Almost certainly.'

'And there was no one, no other family?'

'None that I could locate, no.'

She gave a small sigh. 'Poor little thing.' And then, 'Don't tell me their names, Gerald. Do you mind? I think I'd rather not know.'

'Of course not.' A log collapsed with a soft crack, sending out a tiny shower of embers. 'Would you mind if I asked you a question?' he said. 'Just one, and then the subject will be closed.'

'Of course.'

'The child's mother. What was she like?'

Diana thought for a moment before answering. 'Fearless. She was fearless.'

Gerald nodded, pleased with this. Pleased with his wife.

# AFTERWORD

Joe Levin tasted seawater on his lips and, oddly, it made him smile. The B&I steampacket bucked and rolled as it headed into a squall and the seagulls swooped excitedly, trying to keep pace.

The Irish Sea was gunmetal grey, as welcoming as a day out at the seaside in winter. But Joe smiled. He sat on the deck and pulled his coat tighter around his shoulders and concentrated, a pencil wedged between his teeth, a postcard on his knee. The postcard showed a view of Liverpool's Royal Liver Building on one side. He had bought it just before he had boarded the steamer and he studied it now. It had been strange to be back in Liverpool, however briefly. The week he had spent in the naval hospital after being torpedoed now seemed like another world, seemed like it had happened to another person.

He sucked on the end of the pencil, thinking. After a time, he began to write to his wife and child.

# AUTHOR NOTE

London experienced a 'little Blitz' between January and April of 1944, which began with the raids on Friday 21 and Saturday 22 January. This raid did not hit the Bethnal Green area and the events I describe in Bethnal Green are entirely fictional. Bethnal Green Station was still under construction at the start of the war and was used extensively as a shelter during this period though it escaped any direct hits. The '*horrible death by suffocation*' to which Nancy Levin briefly alludes at the end of Chapter One refers to the 173 civilians killed in a crush entering Bethnal Green Station during a raid on 3 March 1943, an incident that falls outside the scope of this novel but which is well-documented, as are the fates of the *Polyanthus*, the *St. Croix* and the *Itchen*.

# ACKNOWLEDGEMENTS

Thanks are due—as ever—to my agent, Clare Forster, and my publisher, Annette Barlow, for your invaluable and continuing support, guidance and belief in me; to my editor-extraordinaire, Ali Lavau; to my dearest friend and supporter, Tricia Dearborn; to my dear friends Liz Brigden and Sharon Mathews who will appreciate the underground/overground reference; to my mother Sheila Joel who made the arduous journey with me by public transport to Chalfont St Giles, and my aunt, Anne Benson who was on the train that got stuck outside Neasden; to Peter Brigden for allowing me to use the story of the midwife; to Brian Christie who supplied invaluable information on Chalfont St Giles; to all the wonderful people at Curtis Brown and Allen & Unwin for your assistance, support, expertise and encouragement during the writing and publication of this book; and to the fine people at the Australia Council for the Arts who continue to provide me with encouragement and inspiration and who allow me the space to write, in particular Carolyn Watts and Michelle Brown.

# SOURCES

The following publications, histories and memoirs proved invaluable in the writing of this book.

*A Bethnal Green Memoir: Recollections of Life in the 1930s–1950s* by Derek Houghton, The History Press, Gloucestershire, UK, 2009.

*A Short Guide to the Parish Church of Chalfont St Giles: An Outline of the History of the Church* by Anon.

*An Underworld at War: Spivs, Deserters, Racketeers and Civilians in the Second World War* by Donald Thomas, John Murray, London, 2003.

*Bombers and Mash: the Domestic Front 1939–45* by Raynes Minns, Virago, London, 1980.

*Cairo, Biography of a City* by James Aldridge, edited by Jimmy Dunn, Little Brown and Company, Boston and Toronto, 1969.

*Carry on London* by Ritchie Calder, English Universities Press, London, 1941.

*Desert Rats: The Desert War 1940–3 in the Words of Those Who Fought There* by John Sadler, Amberley Publishing, Gloucestershire, UK, 2012.

*Going Green—The Story of the District Line* by Piers Connor, published by Capital Transport Publishing, London, 1993.

*London's East End—Life and Traditions* by Jane Cox, Seven Dials, 1994.

*Many Histories Deep: The Personal Landscape—Poets in Egypt, 1940–45* by Roger Bowen, Associated University Presses, Cranbury, NJ, USA, 1995.

*Our Street: East End Life in the Second World War* by Gilda O'Neill, Viking, London, 2003.

*Social History of the Jews in England 1850–1950* by V.D. Lipman, Watts & Co., London, 1954.

*The Bull's Eye* by Reginald Bell, Cassell, London, 1943.

*The Jewish East End, 1840–1939* edited by Aubrey Newman, The Jewish Historical Society of England, London, 1981.

*The Story of the London Underground* (Unapix Entertainment Inc., 1999)

*Wartime Women: Sex Roles, Family Relations and the Status of Women During World War Two* by Karen Anderson, Greenwood Press, Connecticut, USA, 1981.

*Whistling in the Dark: Memory and Culture in Wartime London* by Jean Friedman, University of Kentucky Press, USA, 1999.

*Women in Wartime—The Role of Women's Magazines 1939–1945* by Jane Waller, Macdonald Optima, London, 1987.

And the following history websites:
http://www.desertwar.net/british-7th-armoured-division.html
http://www.desertrats.org.uk/history.htm

http://ww2history.com/testimony/Western/desert_rat

http://www.flamesofwar.com/hobby.aspx?art_id=700

http://en.wikipedia.org/wiki/Light_Tank_Mk_VI

http://en.wikipedia.org/wiki/Panzer_III

http://www.griffonmerlin.com/2011/02/11/
    recreating-wartime-cairo/

http://en.wikipedia.org/wiki/HMS_Polyanthus_(K47)

http://uboat.net/allies/merchants/crews/ship3075.html

http://www.leithshipyards.com/ships-built-in-leith/1939-
    to-1945/114-hms-polyanthus-yard-no-309-flower-class-
    corvette-royal-navy-built-1940.html

http://ianchadwick.com/blog/the-sinking-of-the-st-croix-
    september-1943/